THERE WERE BOYS . . .
AND THERE WERE MEN

RICO — The Italian deckhand who took Robbie's innocence for his own macho gratification.

THEO — The Greek Adonis who gave himself wholly to Robbie, and shared him with his brothers.

YANNI — The lean, darkly brooding biker who never did it with men, until he met Robbie.

CARL — The golden German playboy who couldn't resist Robbie's young desires—or Robbie's mother.

JEFF — The suave American tourist who befriended Robbie's parents, in order to have their son.

TONI — The French actor who adored women as much as they adored him, but who found a special love with Robbie.

Other Avon Books by
Gordon Merrick

THE GREAT URGE DOWNWARD
NOW LET'S TALK ABOUT MUSIC
ONE FOR THE GODS

GORDON MERRICK
PERFECT FREEDOM

AVON
PUBLISHERS OF BARD, CAMELOT, DISCUS AND FLARE BOOKS

PERFECT FREEDOM is an original publication of Avon Books. This
work has never before appeared in book form.

AVON BOOKS
A division of
The Hearst Corporation
105 Madison Avenue
New York, New York 10016

First Avon Printing: June 1982

AVON TRADEMARK REG. U.S. PAT. OFF. AND IN OTHER COUNTRIES, MARCA
REGISTRADA, HECHO EN U.S.A.

Printed in the U.S.A.

K-R 10 9 8 7 6 5

For C and G who deserve it.

THE HOUSE

"They say they're going to rebuild it exactly as it was before. Good luck to them." The French officer stood amid the rubble of the ruined port. For a brief vivid moment, his memory put it back together again the way it had looked when he'd last seen it—the sagging pastel façades of the waterfront aglow in the same westering August sun, the uneven orange-tiled roofline, the crowd beginning to gather for the *apéritif* hour as a prelude to the licentious night, probably including a visit to his dance act. His eyes roamed over tumbled rocks and shattered masonry and settled on a squat tower at the edge of the sea. "There. You see that thing that looks like part of an old fortress? That was a nightclub. That's where I got my first big break."

"Yeah? You worked in nightclubs?"

"Just that once. I got signed for a picture and the rest is history." The Frenchman flashed his famous smile. "It seems like a lifetime ago but it was only just before the war. Only about six years ago." His smile faded as he gazed at the surrounding devastation. "The bastards. If we'd had to bomb the place to prepare for our landing, okay, but this is so senseless. The bloody Bosches did it out of pure spite. What difference does St. Tropez make to winning or losing the war? It's a wonder they didn't blow up Notre Dame."

"They probably would've if we'd given them time. Let's get going, Anthony. We're supposed to invade Cannes this evening."

"Toni. With an *i*. That's the way I was billed when I was dancing here. Just plain Toni. It took you Americans to turn me into Anthony Beaupré. Okay. Let's go, but I want to make one more quick detour before we get on with the war."

He drove the Jeep along the familiar road that led out to the end of the peninsula, thinking of the first time he had seen the house, hoping that what he'd heard wasn't true, begin-

1

ning to feel a little hollow of dread in the pit of his stomach as he neared his destination. He had felt a tremor of dread the first time, too, with Stuart in the Rolls, half expecting the older man to make a pass at him. Stuart had already mentioned his wife and son and everybody spoke of the fabulous Coslings as a model family, but you never knew.

"I almost fell in love with a beautiful boy the last time I was here," he said.

The American uttered a snort of laughter. "You're kidding. You?"

"It would come as a shock to my various wives and assorted lady friends, but it was a very close call. If you're going to put it in one of your intelligence reports, be sure to say it was six years ago and that nothing like it has ever happened since." He slowed and turned into the narrow road that ran through vineyards and a stand of cork oaks to the sea. He passed between the stone gateposts at the entrance to the property and noticed with a thickening of dread that the gates were missing. He rounded the final curve of the drive and experienced an odd sense of disorientation and then slammed on the brakes and came to a jolting halt.

Not long ago, he had seen a friend with his head blown off; for endless seconds his mind had simply refused to accept the evidence of his eyes while he tried to find the missing part. He went through similar mental gymnastics now. He wondered if he could have taken a wrong turn although he knew that the drive led nowhere but here, to this abandoned litter of stone and tile and broken beams that looked as if a giant fist had slammed into it. Even the ground looked bruised. He could barely force himself to turn toward the terraced citrus grove where Robbie's little house had stood. Only a scar on the hillside was visible amid the foliage.

"Jesus," he murmured, again looking straight ahead of him across the scattered ruins to the steps that descended to the sheltered cove. "I can't believe it. This was the most beautiful house I've ever seen. You can't imagine what it was like. It wasn't just a house. It was a whole world. Who would dream of destroying it? The Germans, naturally. I heard a vague story this morning. It seems they found the body of one of their big shots hidden somewhere on the property. They couldn't figure out what he'd been doing here. I wonder. I have a hunch it might have been a crime of passion rather than anything to do with war." Carl and Helene. Carl and Robbie. Stuart, the avenging husband and father? Pure melodrama, but it might have happened that way. The Frenchman closed his eyes to let his imagination restore the material world to its vanished beauty. It was all there, the olive grove, the hanging gardens, the statue standing against the eternal sky. He opened his eyes to reality. "Well, that's the end of that," he said. He sat back with a sigh and heard Robbie's voice calling to him from the cove. "I wonder if Stuart knows," he mused, addressing himself, since the man at his side didn't know who he was talking about. Strange to be in St. Tropez with somebody who had never heard of the fabulous Coslings.

THE COSLINGS

When Stuart came out of the station at Monte Carlo, he was almost run over by Greta Garbo. At least, Greta Garbo was sitting beside the man at the wheel of the Daimler that swerved around Stuart as he scrambled for the safety of the sidewalk. For an instant, the divine eyes met his from under a big hat. It was a good omen, he decided, simply because he was in the mood for good omens. He wanted the day to shine with a special radiance, although nothing very important was likely to happen. The impending meeting with his uncle was only a formality. The old boy wouldn't say no to a perfectly natural eagerness to snap up a real-estate bargain. A good case could probably be made for it as a sound investment, but that wasn't Stuart's line; to him it offered an escape to freedom—freedom from the confining artificiality and financial hysteria of New York. The country he had so recently left was still reeling from the blows of the great stock-market crash. Why not choose the natural life of the land, in which values were rooted in something more durable than figures on a ticker tape?

Thinking about money, he decided to splurge on a horse-drawn taxi although the long uncomfortable train trip he'd just completed had been undertaken as an economy; driving over in the Rolls at barely eight miles to the gallon had seemed an unjustified extravagance.

He climbed into the first carriage in the line in front of the station and gave the name of his uncle's hotel. It was unseasonably hot for September, the movement of the carriage was soothing; in an instant, Stuart was asleep. He was awakened by a uniformed attendant bending over him.

"You wish to descend here, sir?" Stuart pulled himself together with a start and, all arms and legs, fell out of the carriage. As he fumbled in his pocket to pay the driver, he

5

glanced over the hotel gardens that adjoined the Casino and realized how inappropriately he was dressed. After these months in an obscure fishing village, where nobody cared what you put on, he had forgotten that on this part of the coast men wore hats and jackets and ties.

"Sir Bennett Cosling," he murmured apologetically to the attendant who was hovering beside him. He hitched up his linen trousers and tucked in his white open-necked shirt. "That is—I'm Mr. *Stuart* Cosling. I have an appointment with Sir Bennett." His height and the distinction of his features could always be counted on to allay the suspicions of hotel employees. The attendant turned and gestured grandly to a boy in uniform.

"A gentleman to see Sir Bennett Cosling," he said with a bow. Stuart followed the youth into the hotel garden and then, catching sight of his uncle at a table in the corner, thanked the boy and hurried forward. Sir Bennett was reading a paper, a straw boater tipped forward over his eyes, a red rose in the buttonhole of his beautifully cut beige jacket. He looked up as Stuart stopped before him and his eyes narrowed in twinkling appraisal.

"Well, my boy, France seems to agree with you. You look about twenty—not what one expects of a man of your years, you know. Somebody steal your cravat?" The older man rose and offered Stuart a warm handclasp. As the two stood together, the resemblance was startling—the same long lean frame, the same shaped head with the same thick just-off-blond hair, the same wide forehead, long nose, prominent blue eyes. The similarity of the mouths was striking, the slight fullness of the upper lip suggesting a childlike innocence. Time and custom, however, had frozen Sir Bennett's face into immobility, whereas Stuart's expression was intensely revealing. One could read clearly his sensitivity, his optimism, his stubbornness and, now, a sort of explosive satisfaction with life. Although he was thirty-two he might have been taken for a college boy. His uncle waved him to a chair.

"What'll you drink, my boy? A whisky? My own taste runs to champagne when it's as warm as this. Never been here before at this time of year. I hope you appreciate my stopping over specially for you." The older man had adjusted his hat square on his head and he sat erect, trim and elegant in his stiff collar and his beautiful suit. He signaled a waiter and they both ordered champagne. Stuart looked at his uncle and smiled.

"How do you stand it, Ben? I'd drop dead if I had to wear all those clothes."

"My dear boy, not even the fear of death would impel me to appear in public looking like you. The latest thing from the States, no doubt." Sir Bennett's eyes twinkled. "And how is Helene? She couldn't make it?"

"Too much of a trip with Robbie."

"How is the boy?"

"Growing like a weed. He's going to take after the Coslings." Stuart spoke of his son as if he had just discovered him. It was only during the last few months that Stuart had begun to recognize that the boy was a being in his own right, a wonder of his creation.

"We'll take lunch out here," Sir Bennett said to the waiter who brought the champagne. He turned back to Stuart. "Shall we settle your business before we eat?"

"There's not much to settle." Stuart leaned back with a grin. "I told you just about everything in my letter. Think of it. Somewhere between three and four hundred acres—there's some sort of confusion about the boundaries—and the whole thing for five hundred pounds, less than three thousand dollars." For an instant, it occurred to Stuart that his uncertainty about the acreage might make the whole project sound rather dubious and he hurried on to other details. He spoke with enthusiasm of how the land was situated along the sea, on a peninsula that commanded a view of the Esterels and the lower Alps; of its rich vegetation, olive groves, forests of cork oak, and dilapidated vineyards; of its abundant water and its miles of beaches, the best in the whole area.

He had no experience in making purchases of such importance, although his father, Bennett's younger brother, was probably one of the richest men in the world. He knew his father only slightly. As a young man, Barry Cosling had run off to Canada and quickly amassed a fortune. One of the first things he had done to celebrate his success was to get rid of Stuart's mother, an American.

Stuart had been brought up in Canada, in the States, on the Continent by his Cosling connections, aged maiden ladies, nondescript families in the suburbs of London or New York, widows in gloomy flats in Paris or Florence, all of whom were glad to take in Stuart for the sake of gaining the favor of his illustrious father.

Then, barely a year earlier, one of his numerous foster parents (he hardly remembered Aunt Ada) had died and left

7

him her sole heir. The great stock-market crash occurred almost simultaneously and Stuart was obliged to watch helplessly while his dream of unexpected riches dwindled to a reality of very modest proportions. When everything had been settled, he found that what was left would provide him an income of a bit more than five thousand dollars a year, very nice as a supplement to his editor's salary in a publishing house but hardly enough to alter his life radically. Recognizing this, he found that he had developed a strong urge for radical alterations. The carefree twenties had been brought to a shattering halt, as if a curtain had been dropped on a chaotic and misbegotten play that could have no other ending. What was going to happen now?

Stuart knew that his background made him something of a misfit wherever he was. Why not make the most of it and create a life tailored to satisfy his individual needs? He wasn't quite sure what they were but he knew that New York and his job didn't weigh heavily in the balance. He discussed it with Helene all through that grim winter of '29 and into the dawning months of the thirties, and as summer approached and Robbie's school finished, he quit his job and they set sail, third class, for the unknown. It was a small reversal of the expatriate trend; everybody was hurrying home that year.

Their goal was modest—look around, see if they could find a place where they could make a good life on their limited income, take a year or two to work things out. If nothing came of it, they could always go back. The discovery of the property brought everything suddenly into focus. Stuart's capital was unencumbered but Sir Bennett had been given a controlling voice should Stuart wish to liquidate any part of it. Hence this meeting.

"It sounds jolly good," Sir Bennett said when Stuart had completed his glowing description of the place he hoped to buy. "But what are you going to do with it?"

"Live on it," Stuart said. "Settle down. Develop the land. Have a good life. I'd have asked you to take care of the money weeks ago, but the bloke who owns the place has disappeared. An old bachelor called Giraudon. He's quite batty but he's bound to come back eventually. Of course, I can't do a thing till he does."

"What does Helene think of it?"

"She's crazy about it. Think how wonderful it'll be for Robbie."

"Hmm. Still doing nothing about getting married?"

Stuart flushed and took a sip of his champagne. There was no way of making his uncle understand his and Helene's indifference to the legal forms of marriage. Their relationship had been necessarily illicit at the beginning, for her husband had been insane and she couldn't divorce him. By the time he died, Robbie had arrived and Stuart had adopted an attitude toward their irregular situation that made marriage superfluous. What had started as a youthful extramarital fling had become a completely satisfying union. What could a legal technicality change or add?

They had discussed the possibility of getting married to facilitate travel, but Helene's French passport was issued to Mrs. René de Chassart, her legal name, and it hadn't seemed worthwhile to take the time to have it changed. Although she hadn't lived in France for years and had Americanized her Christian name by dropping the accents, she was simply going home.

Stuart put his glass down carefully. "When we get settled, there'll be plenty of time to think about marriage," he said quickly.

"Well, my boy, there's no question about your having the money but I can't say I'm mad about the idea."

"Why not?" Stuart asked cheerfully.

"These are uncertain times. You can't afford to start eating into capital," the older man said.

"Sure, but good Lord, Ben, with all that land, I'll be practically self-supporting. Besides, the dollar goes a long way here, God bless it."

"What will you be doing? Something in the literary line?"

"God forbid. I'm going to be a beachcomber." Stuart laughed. He knew that his uncle regarded him as "artistic" because of his job in publishing and that the move he was contemplating would be much more acceptable to the old man if it were given a gloss of creative or intellectual justification. Stuart refused to indulge in the pretense.

"What I mean to say, old boy, is what are you going to *do*?" Sir Bennett asked with gentle insistence.

"You're a great one to ask that, Ben," he said.

"That's where you're wrong, my boy. I follow a very rigorous schedule. I'm in London for the season, I go to the villa on Como for the summer, I'm at Barstlow for the shooting, and I come to Monte for the winter season. Not now, heaven forbid. Dreadful sort of people here now. Don't know the place." He made a gesture with his glass.

"You're a fraud, Ben. You just try to create the illusion of having something to do."

"Illusion?" Sir Bennett cleared his throat and fixed Stuart with his pale blue eyes. "There's a good deal to be said for illusions if it comes to that. What would we do without them? Whole world's gone to jolly-oh since the war. No more illusions. No respect for the old values. It's all very well for a peasant to talk about living on the land. That's what he's made for, but you're not."

"Okay, Ben, I promise not to live off the land," Stuart said with a chuckle. People like Ben clung with innocent tenacity to the "old values." As far as Stuart was concerned, the old values were permanently discredited. They cost too much money and injustice. He wanted to find new values. As a friend in New York had said, "You haven't any real roots. The usual rules don't apply to you."

No roots. No compelling ties with any class or locality. No rules. Total freedom. Stuart went on playfully, "You don't mind a bit of animal husbandry and perhaps a touch of viniculture in a gentlemanly sort of way, do you? I just want to live on my own land and not bother anybody. Fish, grow things, give Robbie a good life. I'd have a thousand kids if Helene could have more. That's my religion—let nature take its course."

"So be it. But I've learned one thing in my life. There's nothing more unnatural for a man than the so-called natural life. A man's mind won't let well enough alone. A fellow wants to feel part of something bigger than he is. Nothing duller than life if you don't believe you've been put on earth for some purpose."

"That's because you don't live right, Ben." Stuart enjoyed baiting his uncle. Why did people want to complicate matters so? Put on earth for some purpose? Why not accept life as a matter of satisfying one's natural appetites and let it go at that? "You wait and see," Stuart said. "I'm going to have such a good life I won't have to pretend that God has selected me for some inscrutable mission. I won't even insist on a hereafter."

"I'm not a religious fellow, my boy, but I'd hesitate before I provoked the Almighty. And now that I've performed my avuncular duty, let's concentrate on lunch. We're having sole."

Waiters began to fuss over them with cloths and cutlery, they chatted, they ate their carefully selected meal. Sir

Bennett was still lingering over some admirable brandy when it was time for Stuart to catch the train back. The two men rose for farewells.

"I'll expect to see you when I come in January," Sir Bennett said. "Perhaps I'll be invited to—what's the name of your place?"

"St. Tropez."

"Never heard of it. Beyond St. Raphael, you say?"

"A bit, but the trains are terrible. You'd better hire a car."

"Odd part of the coast to choose. House all ready to move into, you say?"

Stuart grinned. "I forgot to tell you—there isn't any house worth mentioning. That's one of the things I like best about it. We'll just build what we need as we go along. I've seen what happens to people who get stuck with houses. I hope I never have a house I'd mind leaving. Freedom—that's what I'm after. What more could I buy with Aunt Ada's money?"

Sir Bennett waved his hand dismissively. "You must be quite mad. I say, I do hope you can afford to buy some clothes before I see you next."

Stuart lolled on the hard bench of the empty third-class car as the train carried him back past Nice and Juan-les-Pins and Cannes, and thought of the immediate future. The die was cast, if only the owner, mad M. Giraudon, would come back to sign the papers. Regardless of M. Giraudon, he was committed now to the challenge he had chosen. Talking about it with Ben had made him see it a little more clearly. He and Helene would be embarking on a life that neither of them, let alone little Robbie, knew anything about, but he had yet to feel a twinge of apprehension. In New York, the word that had been bandied about when he talked about his vague plans was "escapism." People said, "You're trying to turn your back on your times"—but was he? He hadn't turned his back on the twenties and had the memory of a thousand hangovers to prove it. If he hadn't known rich people, the twenties would have turned their back on him. What were "his times"? He was alive and the world was all around him. Why not use his unearned freedom to take what he wanted from it?

He was fairly sure that what he wanted made sense for Helene too, although he couldn't quite see her drawing water from a well or tending chickens. They had come to each other slowly—the best way, he eventually came to believe. He had been inclined in his youth to fall in love blindly and extravagantly, ready, with any encouragement, to indulge in all the

11

fireworks of a grand passion. When it happened with Helene, she reacted like a sleepwalker, shuttered and withdrawn. He learned that she was terrified of passion; she felt responsible for her husband because she had been unable to match what proved to be his insane love for her.

Slowly, he had learned balance, he had learned to curb the demands he was accustomed to make of love. He discovered that he could breathe freely in the space Helene created around them. She was passionate in bed but otherwise they treated each other like loving friends, with delicate consideration and reticence. Her husband's death was the removal of a nuisance; by then, they were too firmly established together for it to amount to more. Stuart couldn't imagine anything changing between them now, no matter what they did.

At St. Raphael, he changed to a tiny, antique train for the second leg of the journey to his remote peninsula. Slowly the seats filled up. He thought of himself just a few months ago, riding the subway with hordes of hard-faced men studying the disasters recounted in the financial columns. How good to be away from it all! How good to strip off the harness of city life, the ties and garters and heavy shoes, and let in the sun and air. How good to be with people who couldn't even imagine the world he had left behind. He was grateful for the discomforts of the journey. If his land were easy to get at, it wouldn't be going for a song.

The last months in New York had been more distressing than he had realized until he was well out of it. He had been appalled by the fear-dazed eyes of his friends, intelligent cultivated people stricken by the loss not of anything real, but of an illusion of guaranteed ever-increasing material prosperity. Few of them lost their jobs. None of them was hungry. Watching his own unexpected and superfluous fortune dwindle to a shadow of its former self threatened to infect him with the same virus of terror. He clung to sanity by reminding himself that his self-made father's dedication to accumulating possessions had never inspired him with envy or respect. Better to find something worthwhile to do with the money that was left than to be sickened by greed for more. Olives and grapes growing on his own land. That was real. He hoped he would never again live in a world where money for its own sake could get such a grip on people's minds. A narrow escape. He would buy freedom.

A muffled rumbling filled the air. The whole train started to shake. The passengers fell silent and sat tensely, looking

12

straight ahead of them. Suddenly the engine uttered a piercing scream. There was an enormous hissing and the train lurched forward. Stuart closed his eyes as the first cloud of smoke enveloped the passengers.

An hour or so later they reached the peninsula and the crossroads where Stuart changed to still another little train to make the final run out to St. Tropez. He was covered with grit but he had a pleasant memory of pretty little stations covered with bougainvillea and surrounded by zinnias and daisies, of rocky coves overhung by wind-twisted pines, of sea and sky and the explosive good humor of his fellow passengers. None of them had heard of General Motors Preferred.

Crossing from one train to the other in a grove of venerable parasol pines, he caught sight of Maître Barbetin, the notary handling the property transaction, and he hurried forward.

"Any news of M. Giraudon?" he asked as he had every time he had encountered the old gentleman in the last three weeks. The notary was a little bearded old man tightly buttoned into a rusty frock coat. He wore no tie but on his head was a hard squarish black hat with a hard curly brim.

"None, my dear sir. None at all." His chin whiskers bobbed up and down as he began a rambling account of his progress in straightening out the boundary dispute. Since it involved an adjoining property whose owners had died twenty years earlier, leaving no heirs, Stuart suspected the old man made much of it only to enhance his own importance.

"In any case," Stuart put in as soon as Maître Barbetin paused for breath, "I'll have the money in two weeks. You'll have time to get everything in order." He let himself get separated from the notary and settled down to wait for the first glimpse of what he was beginning to think of as home.

Located halfway out on a peninsula that thrust a ridged and wooded finger into the Mediterranean, St. Tropez seemed destined to escape forever the tourist invasion that had overrun the rest of the coast. We'll damn well keep it that way, Stuart thought. The train offered a succession of vistas as it chugged nearer. His first view of the town, as they rounded a bend, made him catch his breath. The sun, dropping toward the horizon, had turned it to gold. Sea and sky flowed around it; it was a golden citadel set in azure, rectangular patterns piled up in a jagged pyramid against a low hill. In the foreground, the slanting bough of a pine tree served as an oddly oriental frame and the town seemed cut off from the mainland, floating between sea and sky, lighted from within by a golden fire. Yes, Stuart thought as he looked at it with a touch of awe, this will do. Unexpectedly, his eyes filled with happy tears.

As the train clattered into the station, Stuart caught sight of the enormous Rolls-Royce, part of his legacy that had been waiting for him in London, and a second later, Helene, standing a little apart from the villagers who had come to watch the train's arrival. He jumped off and ran over to her, tempted to throw his arms around her, but curbing his exuberance to kiss her decorously.

As they looked at each other, the pleasure they felt in each other's company spread and enclosed them. Helene thought as usual of how distinguished he looked in the midst of this noisy jostling crowd. Even in his rumpled casual clothes, he had great style. He saw the admiration in her eyes and took her hand.

She was grandly beautiful. The fashion of the day didn't suit her. She suggested trailing Edwardian elegance, ropes of pearls, great plumed hats to add shadowed mystery to her enormous dark eyes. She had recently had her hair chopped off and Stuart still regretted it. He thought again of the primitive life he was planning for them and he smiled at the incongruous picture of Helene as a farm woman. He looked around and saw that Robbie wasn't with her.

"Where's our young man?" he asked, taking her arm and turning her toward the car. As he did so he caught sight of a dark, cheerfully pretty girl across the heads of an intervening group and for a moment their eyes met. Stuart lifted his hand in a perfunctory gesture that bore no relationship to the glance they had exchanged.

"Who did you wave to?" Helene asked.

"Oh, uh, Maître Barbetin," Stuart said as the notary passed ahead of them. Helene saw his scurrying figure and then, turning slightly, she, too, caught sight of the girl. Following the direction of her eyes, Stuart said, "Oh, there's Odette," feeling like an idiot. Did he think she was blind?

"Don't let's stop," Helene said. "I left Robbie with that little monster at the inn."

Stuart shrugged. It was true that Michel, Boldoni's little boy, was not very clean and used foul language, but it was good for Robbie to grow up with all kinds, especially since his difficult birth had made it impossible for him to have any brothers or sisters.

He helped Helene into the car and climbed in beside her and set the enormous thing into motion, all the while telling her about Uncle Ben and Greta Garbo and his brief conversation with the notary.

"We've done everything we can do," he said as he edged the car around the corner into the narrow main street. "You do think we'll get it, don't you?"

"If you want anything as much as you want this, you usually get it," Helene said with a little laugh.

"As much as *we* want it," he corrected.

"Of course," she said, settling back against the cushions. Of course. Yet all the changes that had taken place in the last few months had left her rather bewildered. The inheritance, Stuart's decision to give up his job, their haphazard arrival in St. Tropez, the weird little man who was ready to practically give away a vast estate, their uncertainty now that he had disappeared—it was a lot to assimilate after the familiar routine of existence in New York. There, their numerous interests, their wide circle of friends combined to give her the illusion of being a normally wedded woman.

It was rather thrilling to be reminded that she wasn't, that they were adventurers, that they were once more embarked on the unknown. Only Robbie provided the drag of domesticity. Already, she had begun to realize that the child who fitted so unobtrusively into their New York life could easily become a source of resentment. As on other occasions, she could have gone with Stuart today if it hadn't been for Robbie. If they were going to isolate themselves, she sometimes wished it could be an isolation shared only with Stuart even though she had always been frightened of becoming obsessively dependent on him. The memory of her husband's mad eyes would always haunt her. Carried to its highest pitch, passion brushed insanity.

The view of the port opening out ahead of her looked as remote from the world she knew as anything she could imagine. It was enclosed on two sides by buildings set well back from the wide quais. They were plastered with a local ochre clay that, in the rays of the setting sun, turned to gold, and they leaned against each other exhaustedly, some of them rising as high as five stories. Painted shutters hung crookedly on their faces, pale blue, pink, orange, faded by the wind and the sea air. Halfway along one quai a sheer wall rose mightily and stopped in a jagged clutter of ruined masonry, the remains of a fortified château. Next to it was a dingy bar, the

Café de la Mer. At the end were additional fortifications and a squat medieval tower.

In the port, a dozen or so wide clumsy-looking *tartanes*, the coastal traders, creaked lazily on the still water, their painted hulls glowing deep red, black, dark green in the late sun. Two of them were being loaded with bundles of cork. An ox drew a heavy cart laboriously along the quai. Otherwise the port was quiet. St. Tropez in the autumn of 1930.

Stuart brought the big Rolls to a halt near the Café de la Mer. "Let's get Robbie and go out to the place," he said. "I want some measurements. I wouldn't mind a swim, either. I'm filthy."

"That ghastly train," Helene murmured sympathetically.

"It's sort of fun," he said.

They penetrated the village on foot through a high, thick, arched portal and mounted a narrow stepped street, across which high pointed arches were flung at irregular intervals. Little groups of old women, bundles of black rags, sat in the street in straight-backed chairs, gossiping, some of them working over long dark coils of fishnet. Children went careening by. Men were scarce. Helene and Stuart nodded occasionally to people they passed. Because they had been living at the inn, they had had little opportunity to know many of the tradespeople but those they'd met had struck them with the agreeable eccentricity of their business methods.

"I don't know the price. I will have to look it up. You can pay next time." Who could bother to look up a price for the sake of a few centimes?

After a steep climb, they came out at the top of the village in front of Boldoni's inn, which commanded a view of the whole bay and of St. Tropez's orange-tiled roofs.

Robbie must have been watching for them because he came hurtling out of the inn to greet them. He collided with Stuart's legs and hugged him. "You're back, Daddy," he shouted. He looked up at Stuart adoringly. "Did you buy our house? What's an *emmerdeur*?"

"I'll explain if you really want to know. It's not a pretty word."

"Is it something you can't say in front of ladies?" Robbie asked hopefully. He was big for his nine years and both Helene and Stuart had contributed to his features. His mouth was his father's, with the slight fullness of the upper lip; his

16

eyes were enormous like Helene's and his hair was dark like hers.

"Most definitely not for ladies," Stuart said with a wink at the handsome little boy. "Want to come with us? We're going for a ride."

"Sure. There's nothing to do around here. Michel is an awful boy." He moved in close against his mother and they started down through the town again. Stuart experienced a twinge of jealousy as he watched the child put his arm around Helene's waist and he promptly mocked himself. Look at me. Pay attention to me. It was downright sordid. He stayed a little behind them on purpose to see if Robbie would turn to include him. When he didn't, he told himself that it served him right for thinking of such a silly little test.

"What *is* an *emmerdeur*, Daddy?" Robbie asked again as they were driving out of town. He looked tiny bobbing about in the extensive reaches of the back seat.

"Well, you know what *merde* means, don't you?" Stuart asked, stealing a glance at Helene. She didn't always approve of his frankness with the boy.

"Yes," Robbie admitted with a trace of hesitation, the enormity of the word beginning to dawn on him. By the time Stuart had completed his explanation, the child had subsided into self-conscious silence. He wanted to be the good boy they expected him to be, but it wasn't always easy to get it right. They praised him for his sweet nature, his nice instincts, his good manners and truthfulness, and he hoped they were right about these things but he wondered sometimes. They of course were perfect, like God, but he couldn't help noticing that they often took opposite sides, without actually putting it into words. His father enjoyed talking to him about all the interesting naughty things that kept catching his attention; his mother obviously felt that a good boy shouldn't find them interesting. He did his best to satisfy them both.

They followed the road that led out to the end of the peninsula, passing vineyards, scattered farmhouses, an occasional terrace of olive trees. Eventually they turned off to the left toward a wooded rise. The road grew increasingly difficult, twisting through uncultivated land sparsely broken with pines and high cane. As they reached the top of the rise at the edge of the wood, the road narrowed still more and Stuart stopped the car. They dismounted and continued on foot along the cart track. This was the beginning of the domain that Stuart hoped would soon be his.

17

The trail descended gently through cork oaks and pines, offering occasional glimpses of the sea. They walked in silence. Under the trees, crumbling retaining walls indicated that this whole tract had once been terraced.

The trail took a final turn and came out into a wide glade just above the sea. Seven thick twisted olive trees had survived the encroaching forest here, and just beyond them was the ruin of the one-room stone house. Below, red rocks jutted into the water, enclosing a short sandy cove.

Stuart stopped and looked toward the house. The day had had a special importance after all; the meeting with his uncle made him feel that the place finally belonged to him. He even hoped for some sign of M. Giraudon's return, but all was silent. He shrugged and put his arm around Helene and hugged her to him.

"I'm going to plunge stark naked into our sea," he exclaimed. "It shall possess me as utterly as I intend to possess it." She laughed and pushed him from her. He peeled off his clothes and stood carelessly naked, his body lean and finely muscled. Helene caught her eyes wandering admiringly over him and, remembering Robbie, turned hastily away. She was intensely jealous of his body and the casual way he exposed it made her feel it more acutely; she couldn't help thinking of him in the full splendor of his erect masculinity. If Robbie weren't here, he could easily coax her out of her clothes.

"How about you, infant?" Stuart demanded of the boy. "Coming in with the old man?"

"I'll stay with Mummy," Robbie said, avoiding looking at his father's nakedness, too. "I've been in dozens of times today."

"Okay. You can start building the house." Stuart ran down the rocks and plunged into the water.

He emerged sleek and glistening and quickly clambered up to where his family was waiting for him.

"What a pair of loafers," he said, panting. "Come on. Get to work." He splashed them both with his dripping hands and snatched up his clothes and the meter stick he'd brought from the car and ran off down the clearing. Helene and Robbie rose obediently and followed him.

"Why does Daddy go without his clothes?" Robbie inquired.

"He thinks it's healthier—more natural," Helene said hesitantly.

"What's natural?" he asked.

18

"Why, darling, you know what natural means. Like nature. After all, we aren't born with clothes on."

"Why do you wear them then?"

"It's a matter of habit. Perhaps if I live here long enough I'll get used to going without them, too."

Robbie had never seen a naked woman and recently he had had reason to grow curious. It was obvious that they had much fuller chests than men but a little girl he had seen under circumstances he was not soon to forget had seemed to be made differently from boys in another significant way.

"I've never seen a lady without any clothes," he said as if disclosing a gap in his education that somebody should do something about. Helene managed a hoot of nervous laughter and rumpled his hair to cover her embarrassment. No, this really wouldn't do. She would have to tackle the question with Stuart once more. Robbie was too young to be subjected to Stuart's "naturalism." She was relieved to see him putting on his trousers as they approached.

Robbie, quick to sense withdrawal in his parents, wondered what secret was being hidden from him. Were women deformed in some way so that they couldn't take their clothes off? An impulse to talk it over with his father, who was always ready to talk about anything, came and went. After what had happened this summer, he had begun to feel that there were some things he didn't want to know about, for his mother's sake. He hoped they were going to live here. He wouldn't have to go back to school; he had found it awfully easy to get into trouble at school, although he hadn't been caught at anything very bad. Once here, away from the inn and Michel's influence, he doubted if he'd find anything to do that he need be ashamed of.

"Here, youngster, take hold of the other end of the meter," Stuart said. "I want to see how big our house is." Robbie hastened to assist. They measured the foundations of the ruin while Helene watched with fondness touched by envy as she thought that father and son seemed almost the same age. Stuart straightened and calculated the height of the roof. As he did so, he peered in through the one small window. There was a hole in the roof, a litter of filth around a rusted iron cot.

"Now that the money's on the way, I want to get estimates for stones and cement and tiles for the roof," he explained to Helene. He turned back to Robbie. "We've got to build an addition for you. How big do you want your room?"

19

"Well, I'm not very big yet but I'm growing," Robbie said judiciously.

"All right." Stuart drew lines on the ground with the meter. "There. How's that? Measure it." He handed the meter to Robbie, who measured with infinite care. Stuart hooked his arm through Helene's and started wandering about with her, talking animatedly of his plans. "We'll have to get that well cleared. And here we could build an outdoor kitchen. Down there." He led her away from the house past the row of olive trees to the sharp drop down to the cove. "I thought it'd be good to have some sort of shack so when it's really hot we can sleep by the water."

"Marvelous," Helene said, trying to believe in it.

"Of course, next year if we've saved enough by living here, I'd like to build a proper house. How about over here? We could use the other for guests or give it to Robbie. What do you say, my lad?" He turned back to the boy, who was trailing after them. "Would you like to have that house all to yourself?"

"Perhaps when I'm bigger, it'd be nice."

"We'll have steps coming up from the beach to a terrace," Stuart went on, scratching at the ground with a stick. "And we'll put the house here."

Helene laughed suddenly with the peaceful joy that only he could offer her. "Oh, darling, you're absolutely incredible. It's such a dream. I just can't believe it." Stuart looked about him with surprise, trying to see it as she saw it, but his imagination carried him beyond his modest plans. He saw it as it might be if one were rich and had a taste for that sort of thing—enormous arched openings, perhaps a few classic touches, fountains, a colonnade, a few statues, exotic flowers. But that was not what he was after. He wanted no elaborate screen to stand between them and nature. They would live under the sky, bathe in the sea, nourish themselves from their own labor on the land.

"Just wait and see," he said confidently.

"And what are we going to call it?" she asked teasingly. "Something clever like 'Eden'?" When she smiled it was with elegance, lowering her head slightly and looking up with glowing eyes. Her lovely mouth was incapable of being stretched out of shape. They laughed together.

"I don't intend to be turned out. And we'll have no Cains and Abels, either," he added with a small pang of regret. Not that he was sure Robbie might not have at least a half-brother

20

somewhere. He seized the boy by the scruff of the neck and shook him playfully. "Come on. It's time to get back. Old Boldoni will throw us out if we're late for another meal."

The inn where they were staying had no name. It was known simply as Boldoni's. For a few dollars a day, Boldoni produced meals of stupefying proportions. Lobsters, mussels, sea urchins, fish stews, slabs of ham, spiced sausages, partridges, quail, roasted baby boar, jugged hare, mushroom pies, dark stews of tomatoes and hearts of artichoke and eggplant, mountains of fruit, and whole cheeses were regular fare and the one thing Boldoni couldn't stand was a finicky appetite.

Of the rooms, nothing could be said except that there were four and they were clean. If they could live this well in a hotel, Stuart figured that they could get by easily for three hundred dollars a month in a house of their own, leaving some leeway within the limits of his income.

He couldn't wait to tell Boldoni about his successful mission to Monte Carlo and share his new sense of proprietorship. It was the innkeeper who had found the Giraudon place for them in the first place. "Well, the money's on the way," Stuart announced when he found the big shapeless man slumped at a table near the kitchen door, a bottle of *pastis* in front of him. Helene had taken Robbie up to get ready for dinner. Boldoni grunted and reached for a glass and poured a drink for Stuart. "You don't think old Giraudon will change his mind, do you?"

Hair sprouted from Boldoni's nose and mingled with a small moustache. His carelessly shaven beard grew close to his eyes and above them were generous brows. He peered out from a good deal of hair and shrugged. "His mind? He can't change what he hasn't got."

Stuart laughed. Although Boldoni didn't appear to make friends with his clients or concern himself with what they did when they weren't eating or drinking, Stuart had the feeling that the Frenchman had taken him under his wing, perhaps because he ate a lot. He counted on his encouragement. "You said I could trust his word."

"He won't sell to anyone else even if they offer twice what you've agreed on. He's refused to sell to any of his neighbors. He's fought with all of them. He'll sell to a foreigner to spite them."

"Then why doesn't he get it over with?"

"He's mad. He hears voices. Maybe they've told him the

21

money hasn't come yet. Doesn't Maître Barbetin know anything?"

"No. I saw him at the train. He just goes on talking about the boundaries."

"You mustn't pay money if the title isn't clear. When you first spoke about looking for property, I almost didn't mention the Giraudon place. The family used to own the whole peninsula. They've been selling off pieces for generations. There might be complications."

"Nothing of great importance. There's some old dispute about a small part of it. It doesn't matter to me. I just want the part I know is clear."

Boldoni shrugged again and refilled their glasses. "I don't know about such things. What does a man need in life? Plenty to eat. Plenty to drink. A sensible woman who keeps out of his way. Why does he want to break his back over a lot of land?"

Stuart smiled. Simple-minded but it corresponded more closely to what he was after than his uncle's ornate view of life. "The land is supposed to provide all that food and drink," he said.

"Ah, there is that." Boldoni's eyes twinkled through the hirsute maze. "What are your plans if M. Giraudon is never seen again?"

"Don't even talk about it," Stuart protested. The memory of his brief dealings with M. Giraudon a month ago was bright and clear in his mind. A tiny old man in a tattered frock coat, a dirty handkerchief knotted around his throat, black trousers stuffed into high boots. His eyes had glittered with maniac gleeful guile but Stuart hadn't had a moment's doubt that he knew exactly what he wanted and was delighted to get it. They had made a quick tour of the property together. They had made a formal call on the notary. The deal had been set in motion. M. Giraudon had disappeared but it had taken Stuart until today to consider the possibility that the transaction might be imperiled. "I've got to get the place," he said with a new note of urgency. "Until now, I haven't quite been able to believe in it. But it's got to be mine now. I feel it. I'll never find anything else that makes such complete sense. Don't you have any idea how I can find the old fool?"

"I'll inquire but he has no family. No friends, I shouldn't think. What can you expect? He lives on boiled roots and wild berries."

He said it as if there were nothing to hope for from such a

miserable creature, but Stuart's sense of possession was undiminished, and sharpened his enjoyment of the Saturday night festivities a few days later.

On Saturday night Boldoni's turned into a dance hall. Boldoni had a mechanical piano and at one end of his trellised terrace he had laid a patch of cement. Every week, dock-workers, fishermen, sailors—the "rough" element of St. Tropez—spent a share of their earnings here. Boldoni's wife and his boy, Michel, spent the evening carrying up wine from the *cave* while Boldoni kept the piano cranked up. A warning painted on the wall of the inn testified to the explosive nature of these evenings: *Les rixes doivent se poursuivre à l'exterieur.* All brawls will be settled outside. There was a shortage of women, for St. Tropez's three prostitutes could only be split so many ways, and while the sailors were used to dancing with each other, this shortage led to violence.

What Boldoni's Saturday evenings lacked in finesse, they made up for in a sort of animal honesty. Stuart saw in them a microcosm of the way he would like the world to be and he had soon started talking to Helene about staying on. Here was life, simple needs being simply satisfied, the conflict of needs being met with the rough respect of man for man and, when the conflict broke social bounds, getting settled simply and with no major bloodshed by the matching of wits and muscle.

He found poetry in those evenings, too. When you stepped out from under Boldoni's vine-covered trellis, the clanking music of the mechanical piano become oddly haunting under the stars and the moon. The moon cast a ghostly sheen on the sea and glistened on the roofs of St. Tropez, and in the shadows you could see couples locked in each other's arms. Sometimes when Boldoni would forget to crank up the piano, the men would break into song, sweet songs of their child-hood or bawdy songs of the barracks. It was tenderizing, Stuart thought once to himself wryly, searching for the equivalent of the French word, *attendrissant.* One could say "Wall Street" to oneself, and feel that if such a place existed it was only a momentary aberration of the race. The same was true of Greenwich Village. Stuart tried it with "speakeasy," too. The effect, sitting under the southern moon in the soft night, was in each case mind-boggling.

Thinking of himself as a resident after his meeting with his uncle, Stuart found that the Saturday dance suddenly became a family event, the gathering of a community to which he belonged. As soon as he saw Odette, he felt the tensions that had been accumulating between them ease. There was no need to feel furtive about their playfully flirtatious friendship. After the last few weeks of provocative glances, the sexual undercurrents would run their course and give them something to laugh about in the future. They might be seeing each other for the rest of their lives. When they had danced together the first time over a month ago, she had unabashedly offered herself to him in the way she folded her body against his but she seemed to grasp his message of restraint and thereafter behaved more decorously. Still, the looks they'd continued to exchange were frequently inflammatory. Tonight, Stuart's curiously tranquil yet euphoric conviction that he was home seemed to match her mood. They danced but drew over to the sidelines several times while she talked more about herself than she had earlier. She had been here only since the beginning of the summer, little longer than Stuart, and had come to join a girl friend who was working at the local brothel. She assumed that she would end up in the same establishment but so far had managed to scrape by and was still holding out.

"It's funny," she said valiantly. "The pay's good and my friend says it's not so bad, but there's something about it I don't like."

Stuart was delighted with this estimate of prostitution. Odette was a round jolly girl with a pretty dimpled smile who had reminded him from the beginning of Marguerite, his first love. Like Odette, Marguerite had been undisguisedly captivated by him. That had been just before the Great War during one of the rare periods when his mother had been occupying herself with him, though by that time he was quite able to take care of himself.

Stuart had long since forgotten the circumstances of that distant summer in France. How had they happened to go to that lost little village on the Brittany coast? What were they doing in Europe in 1914 within weeks of the outbreak of war? Why had his mother left him there? He remembered her coming and going all summer long.

He was always glad to see her go, for he had met Marguerite Sémillon. She was the daughter of shopkeepers. He had met her when he had gone into her family's establishment for some ink and she had smiled her radiant dimpled smile. She was little more than a child, scrubbed, plump, her pale-golden hair in plaits coiled around her head, but she became his mistress a few nights later on the beach. He was sixteen, a grown-up. He had wanted to marry her and told her so often and she would giggle delightedly and tell him to make love to her some more. Her enthusiasm matched his own. He was careful not to mention her to his mother until, when the summer was well advanced and the war was suddenly practically upon them, Marguerite told him she was pregnant. She was frightfully pleased with herself and they talked more about getting married. The next time his mother arrived on one of her brief visits, he told her all about it.

"But, my poor Stuart," she said, poking at her brittle-looking tinted hair, "you're even more of a baby than I thought."

"There's no point making a fuss about it, Mother," Stuart said coolly, feeling very adult in the face of paternity. "I've made up my mind."

"And what are you going to live on, pray? You have a summer affair with a village girl and she tells you she's with child. And you believe her! There's barely been time for her to know. No, no, no, my baby boy, be thankful you have me to look after you."

"Yes, Mother, except that even if she isn't with child, as you put it, I'm going to marry her."

"Fortunately you're not of age, so we won't have to argue about it," Mrs. Cosling said brightly. "Really, Stuart, think of your position."

"What position?"

"Why, you're a Cosling, my dear. You're my son." Stuart was tempted to make a rude reply but the occasion seemed too grave for flippancy.

"We'll see," he said darkly.

"Indeed we shall, my dear, indeed we shall."

That was at lunchtime. Later in the day, Mrs. Cosling came bustling into their modest hotel to join Stuart for tea.

"Well, we're off," she announced. "It's all arranged. We're going back to Paris tonight."

"I'm not. We have another week here."

"A change of plans," Mrs. Cosling cried, her eyes every-where except on Stuart. "Everybody says a war is about to start."

"But, Mother, you're out of your mind. What about Marguerite? What about—"

"Oh, I have news for you. It's just as I suspected. The whole thing's trumped up. She confessed everything."

"You mean you've seen her?" Stuart gasped.

"Of course, my dear. Her and the parents. She broke down finally and made a clean breast of it. Naturally, you seemed a wonderful catch to her. And she *is* quite pretty. But really, darling, the parents!"

Stuart rushed from the hotel and ran in search of his love. He found M. Sémillon behind his counter and demanded his daughter. M. Sémillon told him that she had just left to visit some relatives in the country. Stuart was confused by the man's manner.

"Come, monsieur," he said soothingly. "There has been a youthful folly. It is over. We live and learn."

"But Marguerite and I are going to be married," Stuart cried stubbornly.

"Now, now, monsieur, you are both too young to think of such a thing."

"This is my mother's doing. What's she said? What's she been up to?"

"Madame was most understanding. You are fortunate to have such a mother."

That was all Stuart was able to get out of the man and although he never believed his mother and suspected, as was the case, that money had changed hands, he allowed himself to be carried off to Paris and then back to the States to finish his last year of prep school. He intended to come back and find out the truth for himself but war intervened and when, four years later (his mother was dead by then), he was again in a position to investigate, he had acquired sufficient experience to know that it was too late. He wondered sometimes, though, whether he had a child, some six years older than Robbie, growing up somewhere on the coast of Brittany, and he thought occasionally that it would be interesting, should he find himself some day in the region, to make discreet inquiries.

Thoughts of his lost love made him feel a tender responsibility for Odette. When she told him that she had left home because her father had tried to seduce her, he decided he had to try to save her from the fate she had so far avoided; it was as if one of his family needed help.

"*Ah, qu'il est beau,*" she proclaimed of him to the world at large as he led her from the floor. It was time to rejoin Helene. "It's a shame you're not as rich as you are handsome." Her mockery was playfully impudent.

"That's not possible, is it?"

"Me, I'm so poor. Isn't it terrible to be so poo-oor?" She made poverty sound absurd. Fun bubbled close to her surface. So like Marguerite, dark and older, but giving him the treacherous feeling of being a kid again. He reminded himself to act his age and spotted Helene surrounded by men. Tables were pushed together helter-skelter and everybody sat wherever they found themselves. He and Odette squeezed in beside her and Helene greeted the girl kindly. She was amused by her ingenuous infatuation with Stuart and was pleased with herself for not feeling the slightest twinge of jealousy. Everything about these Saturday evening gatherings was too remote from her experience to seem quite real. Despite the infectious *joie de vivre* that was generated, she couldn't overlook the fact that the men were rough and coarse and were inclined to put their hands where they shouldn't if she didn't remain on her guard. Once upon a time, Stuart might have made a scene about the way they pulled her up for a dance without a word. Now he made her feel as if she were on her own. Too much so? No, they had achieved what she had always wanted. Balance. An even keel. They wouldn't have been able to handle so much that was new and unfamiliar a few years ago. Even though she couldn't think of anything to say to Odette, she understood Stuart's interest in the cheerful little waif. She was another ticket of admission to the alien environment that he was so enthusiastically adopting as his own. With a shiver of delight, she watched him dazzle the girl. She loved his feeling free to show off in front of her.

When Odette was unceremoniously lifted out of her chair, Helene laughed and pressed herself briefly against Stuart. "You haven't lost your touch," she said into his ear to make herself heard above the din of laughter and music.

Stuart shifted uncomfortably in his chair. He had a hard on. Odette had deftly stroked his cock and given it a squeeze just before she was dragged away. It made nonsense of his placid thoughts of assigning her an uncomplicated place in his life. He liked her playing with his cock and now couldn't help wanting more. It was obviously out of the question. If circumstances were absolutely right (a chance encounter on neutral territory with no chance of their seeing each other again) he might succumb to her appeal, but nothing was right about getting involved here. To demonstrate that he wasn't launched on a secret life, he gave Helene a fragmentary account of Odette's story against the sounds of revelry

27

around them. "I feel as if I ought to save her from a fate worse than death," he concluded.

"Think of something."

"It's just a question of money. Don't you think an offer of money might be misinterpreted?"

"We'll do it together. That should make it clear that your intentions are honorable. Would a hundred francs do any good?"

"She could probably live on it for a month."

"Good. I have it with me."

When Odette returned she squeezed in beside Stuart and moved her thigh against his. Helene leaned forward with her elbows on the table to make contact with the girl, although conversation was more a matter of smiles and gestures than words. He felt Odette's hand slip over his thigh and settle once more on his erection. She stroked and explored it and seemed to be gauging its dimensions. He was tempted to slip a hand under her skirt but there was no room to maneuver and he submitted helplessly but not unwillingly to the exquisite torment. He made an effort to keep his expression from relaxing into sensual lethargy. Her hand grew bolder. Buttons gave way. He felt her fingers on his tautly stretched naked skin. He took a quick breath and suppressed a gasp. Her hand grasped all of him and moved up and down slowly and purposefully. A passing sailor seized Helene unceremoniously and carried her off. Stuart turned to his tormentor. She sparkled with mischievous glee and squeezed the swelling flesh.

"*C'est trop beau,*" she exclaimed. "*Vous êtes magnifique.*"

"You're very naughty."

"*Vous êtes extra-orrrdinaire.*" She rolled the *r* extravagantly and giggled. "What girl could resist? We're a little bit lovers now. I know how big I can make you."

"Girls have that effect on me. You'd better let go or we might have an unfortunate accident."

She withdrew her hand hastily. "Oh no. Not like that."

He buttoned himself up. "You notice I didn't do much to stop you, but don't expect this to go any further. You can tell from the way I look at you how tempted I am."

"You look at me and make me very daring. It's very wonderful that you're going to live here."

"I think so. If my wife gives you a present, will you take it without making a fuss?"

28

"Your wife? Why?" She looked shocked, almost frightened.

"It's just an idea. She likes you. Will you take it?"

Her eyes yielded as she looked at him. "If you wish me to."

He touched her hand, which was now on the table. Helene was returned to them and he shifted so that this time she was seated between him and Odette. He had indulged himself sufficiently. He had made a declaration of sorts and the girl knew that he liked her. It was time to rally his forces. He danced with both of them and the crowd began to thin. The Saturday night gatherings were never very late but the Coslings were always the last to turn in because sleep was out of the question while the fun was going on. Conversation became more possible and Stuart emptied the bottle of wine into their glasses and settled back contentedly. Helene slipped something into Odette's hand. He saw the girl's expression cloud. She looked both bewildered and indignant and with a glance at him accepted grudgingly, as if she had been compromised in some way.

"It's been such fun having you with us," Helene said. "We must make a regular thing of it. Everybody has hard times. It's so lovely to be able to help." She was pleased with herself. She had lived up to Stuart's expectations of her by demonstrating that she sympathized with his impulse to help the child. She felt the gesture, as she was sure Stuart did too, as another small commitment to the place. She was beginning to wonder what they would do if their dotty landowner didn't reappear soon. Summer was almost over. Even Stuart couldn't be planning to stay here indefinitely, although he wouldn't talk about alternatives. They had to find something more comfortable, with a bathroom of their own and heating and hot water. They had to settle something about school for Robbie. Stuart didn't think it was urgent because the boy was a year ahead of his age group, but she wanted to re-establish the routine of New York so that they could have some privacy. She could accept his self-proclaimed liking for "plain, ordinary people," although they had never known any, and try to enter into the spirit of an occasion like tonight, but she was soon going to have to force him to face practical realities.

They finished their wine while the crowd dwindled rapidly. Odette stood and said goodnight with French formality and they all agreed that they'd be looking out for each other next

Saturday. The Coslings went upstairs arm in arm and Stuart made love with unusually thrilling inventiveness. There had never been anything he could do that she didn't want.

Stuart's sense of responsibility for the girl survived the night. He was confident that sex had very little to do with it. He had felt a strength of character struggling to emerge in her and his creative urge, which had found earlier expression through the writers he had worked with, was aroused. He wanted to help her find an honorable place in the community. He and Helene had turned the offer of money into a family philanthropy but there was something private and personal (he thought of her hand and laughed to himself) that he might be able to offer her, more important than money. He wished he had an opportunity to talk to her under more favorable circumstances so that he could find out if she thought she could make something of her life or if it would be only meddling to impose his aversion to prostitution on her.

He ran into her in the street one afternoon only a few days later. He had just had his hair cut and was going back to the inn where Helene and Robbie would be waiting for him after an afternoon on the beach. He got the impression that Odette had tried to slip past him without speaking.

"*Ça, alors.* Have you forgotten me?" he demanded.

"Oh. *Pardon. Bonjour, monsieur.* I didn't see you. How do you do?" She was prim and polite but she suddenly smiled her winning smile and added, "In fact, you look different."

"I've just come from the barber."

"It makes you look—I don't know. Different." She giggled and became more like the girl he had been flirting with for weeks.

"How goes it? Still saying no to your girl friend?"

"Thanks to you, for a little longer, but perhaps I'm making a mistake. It's a good opportunity." It seemed to cost her a slight effort to strike the tough realistic note.

"You may yet find something else," Stuart said, aware of the emptiness of the words.

"What work is there for a girl? In Paris, perhaps. But here?" She shrugged again and her habitually cheery expression faded. Stuart thought he recognized her little summer dress from the other night. The sleazy material looked as if it would smell cheap and musty but he remembered she smelled of good things, soap on fresh skin and an indefinable odor he associated with the sun. Her broad face was turned up to him, wide mouth, tilted little nose, dark eyes capable of melancholy. His glance wandered down over her generous breasts, her sturdy but well-shaped legs. She looked as if she would be good at the job she was trying to avoid.

"Let's talk about it. Come have a drink."

She hesitated and then looked at him candidly. "You're sure it's all right? People know why I've come here."

"Then they must know you haven't started yet," he said. They were standing in one of the narrow streets in the interior of the village and there was not a soul in sight. It was intensely hot and the still air smelled of open sewers.

"I was thinking of your wife," Odette said.

"My wife liked you. She'll be interested to hear that we've had a talk." In spite of her forthright manner, the girl was sensitive. He had been aware of it at Boldoni's. "Let's go over to the fishermen's port," he suggested. She acquiesced and they walked side by side without speaking until they were there. It was much smaller than the principal port—a small jetty covered with a web of drying nets, a small square above it out of which grew an enormous plane tree, a café with a few rickety chairs and tables set out before it.

They sat and ordered *pastis*. When they were served, he sipped his in silence, organizing his thoughts. He was feeling her attraction and thinking of Marguerite again. Perhaps wanting to help her was after all only wanting to get her into bed. He preferred to think otherwise. Infidelity hadn't been a problem for so long that he'd forgotten the arguments against it; he knew only that all his instincts were trained to resist it. In New York, sex seemed as mechanical as all the mechanized artificiality of the city so that it was easy to keep it in its place. Here, it drifted in the air like dust. The sun made him want to cast off inhibitions just as it made him want to throw off his clothes. It would be fun to throw off his clothes with Odette, reveling in the approbation of the new world he was discovering.

"Well, what about it?" he asked finally. He looked at her and caught a puzzled expression in her eyes. "Can we work something out together?" He wanted to establish the difference between helping her and buying her but it was a difficult point to make with a girl who had held his cock. He thought of his finances. The summer had been much cheaper than he'd expected. He could afford a small offering to the gods. Odette was watching him expectantly. "What if somebody gave you fifty francs a week?" he asked. "Could you get by until some other work turns up?" He leaned back, holding his

31

glass up between them, and their eyes met. The desire in hers was unmistakable; he supposed that his were revealing, too. They burst out laughing together.

"Why would anybody give me fifty francs a week?" she asked.

"Just like that. Because they like you. Why did we give you that little present the other night?"

"I've wondered. I wondered if it was right to take it. I think not. You can't take money from people just like that."

"But it's all right if you do something for it—like going to bed with them?" This was the tricky part, this was where he risked hurting her feelings.

"That's natural," she said as if it went without saying.

"Even if you go to bed with people you don't want, just for money?"

"Want, want," she burst out. "Rich people do what they want. The rest of us do what we have to do."

He smiled at her placatingly. "Not necessarily. You didn't have to do anything for that present. Would you've preferred it if you had?"

"I wouldn't have wondered then," she said.

"You make it difficult for me," he said, his smile becoming mischievous. "I can't do anything for you without asking something in return."

"Of course if you put it like that—" She took a thirsty swallow of her drink and looked at him with unabashed desire. "I find you odd. You make everything seem different from the way it usually is."

"You haven't answered my question. Can you get along on fifty francs a week?"

"I could manage for the moment, as long as my friend lets me stay with her."

"Well, I can spare it for the moment. I don't know for how long. For the next few weeks anyway."

"Just like that?" she asked.

He avoided meeting her eyes directly so that whatever she might see in his wouldn't give her the impression that there were strings attached. "Just like that."

A small frown creased her brow. "I don't understand you. When you look at me, you make me feel that I please you."

"You do, very much." He wished she were holding his cock again to prove it. "I just want you to know the money has nothing to do with it—"

"I don't understand but I believe you. You're nicer than

most men. You know what I want more than money. You've warned me not to expect it." As she spoke, she became merry and playful once more.

Stuart was pleased. He had managed it without offending her. He chuckled as she leaned her breasts against the table and tilted her head flirtatiously at him. "Then it's all settled. I don't have much money with me. I'll give it to you at Boldoni's on Saturday."

"You're very good. Maybe some day I can pay you back. Anyway, I would do everything I could to stay out of that house—because you want me to."

He touched her hand and let himself enjoy the titillating sexual currents that swirled around them. A man could want every girl in sight without doing anything about it. He shifted in his chair and put a hand in his pocket to make adjustments for comfort. Her hair was bobbed and combed out around her head in a windblown effect. He wanted to run his hands through it. He thought of the fun he'd had with Marguerite and felt sixteen again. It would be ridiculous to start acting sixteen. "I really must stop thinking how much you please me," he said, letting her hand go. "After all, I'm a married man."

"Oh, married men." She gave a saucy shrug of her shoulders. "We'd all be virgins if it weren't for married men. I'm sure your wife would agree."

"I doubt it. I haven't been unfaithful for years."

"No? If you make love I'm sure it must be in style—candlelight, champagne, silk sheets. That would make infidelity difficult." She was teasing him but it summed up the impression he made on her. He seemed made of some finer substance than any man she had ever known. The texture of his skin looked smoother, his coloring finer and more delicate, his whole being godlike. She could see the hard line of his chest muscles under his light shirt and the thought of being taken by him made her head reel. In spite of his exquisite perfection, he was a real man where it mattered but even there he was different, hard but smooth, like iron sheathed in satin.

"Specially the silk sheets," he said, laughing with her. "I can't take them with me wherever I go. What about you? Can you be seduced without candlelight and champagne?"

"Me, I'm French. Wherever we find ourselves, that's the place to make love." Her laughter sounded rich and creamy in her throat.

"Well, here we are. Is this a good place?" he said, taunting her. He couldn't see how she could take him up on it.

She met his eyes boldly. "We wouldn't have far to go."

"You mean it?"

"But of course. We want each other. I found that out the other night." She dropped a hand onto his lap and ran it over him, exerting pressure. He remembered the arguments against infidelity. They had to do with lies and deception, with mutual consideration and not cheapening the relationship he valued most in life. They were useful in circumstances that offered time for thought but lacked force when a pretty girl was caressing his cock. He began to ache for release. Their eyes explored each other and little bubbles of mirth escaped her.

"Nobody will know?" he asked. He wasn't going to a room with her or anywhere that Helene might find out about. The possibilities were safely limited although he wished she could go on playing with his cock to her heart's content.

"Don't worry."

"I don't have anything with me, let alone silk sheets. Is that all right?"

"Everything is all right." Her last abortion had taken care of that problem.

"I'm fascinated. What do we do now?"

She gave him a marvelously frank and lustful look. "Come with me."

The price of *pastis* was marked on a blackboard beside the door. Stuart put a few coins on the table and they rose together. He kept a hand in his pocket for decency's sake and checked their surroundings as they started along the uneven cobbles of the little quai. There were a few fishermen in sight puttering about with their boats. One of them lifted his eyes to them as they passed. Would village gossip travel as far as Boldoni's? She wasn't holding his cock now; perhaps this was the moment for thought.

The buildings facing the tiny port petered out at a big ramshackle structure near the jetty that thrust a short arm into the sea. It looked as if it had been a boat-building works—wide doors on rollers like barn doors, rusty tracks running out from them. They skirted it and were immediately cut off from the little port. Rocks tumbled into the sea in front of them and beyond was a stretch of beach curving around in front of low farm land. It looked awfully exposed for what she had in mind. He didn't know whether he was glad or sorry.

"What a wonderful spot," he said. "Somebody should do something with this place."

"It's convenient for us." She followed the back of the building until she came to an open door sagging on its hinges. She stepped through it, reaching back for his hand to lead him in. He was definitely glad to get out of sight.

They were in a vast dim cathedral of a room that rose two stories around them. It was cool and smelled of mildew and the sea. Light entered from windows high above. Some old crates lay about, and an overturned boat. He saw at the farther end a sort of loft with a ladder leading up to it and sails hanging over a railing. She started for it as if it were their destination. Had she brought other men here? He was thinking hard now, wondering if he could withdraw gracefully.

"You've certainly learned your way around town," he said, remaining near the door. The loft looked like a trap he didn't want to get caught in. Anybody could walk in; she was pushing spontaneity to extremes.

"My friend warned me about certain places," she explained. "They call this *la batellerie*. It's used for lovers' meetings. She warned me not to come here with a man unless I wanted it to happen. I never have." She took a few steps back to him and faced him, looking playful and alight with anticipation.

"If it's so well known, I'm not sure I should be here." He lifted his hands tentatively toward her, preparatory to suggesting that they postpone their pleasure for a more favorable time and place. She moved quickly to forestall his reluctance. Buttons no longer confined him. His cock sprang out rigid in her hands. He gasped with the thrill of the release.

"*Ah, quel bel animal,*" she exclaimed, staring at it and sliding her hands along it. She made quick adjustments to her clothes and directed it into her. It was happening before he had time to take any initiative. He was being raped. "*Va-s-y. Fonce. Oh, que c'est bon. Fonce jusqu'au bout. Quelle bitte incroyable,*" she cried.

He was suddenly gripped by basic urges, exulting in the excitement he was arousing in her and in his mastery of her. He planted his hands on her buttocks and tilted her to him and drove hard into her. She locked her legs around him and

35

they grappled with each other to discover the possibilities of this impromptu position. She rode him avidly, crying out and moaning, her eyes rolling ecstatically in her head. Her body opened to him and he felt himself asserting his possession deep within her. There was no question of prolonging or embellishing the act. They were copulating as simply as animals in a field. He cried out with his orgasm and slowly released her and they leaned against each other for support, her head against his chest. When he'd caught his breath, he wondered what the excitement had been about. It was over as quickly as it had started.

"Je vous adore, mon beau," she murmured. She lifted her head, looking tousled and radiantly pleased with herself. "Am I very wicked? I couldn't let you go. I've never seen anyone like you—your man-part is superb. I hope I'll see it often. I must find a better place for us."

He detected a calculating note in her voice but dismissed the thought. There wasn't a calculating bone in her body. He stroked her hair and smiled down at her. "Well, we managed without silk sheets."

She laughed and they broke apart and shook their clothes into order. "I'll go first. Wait a moment. If you go to the right, you'll find a path that goes up to Boldoni's. You don't have to go back through the port."

"Good. I guess we better not push our luck. I'll see you Saturday if not before." They kissed lightly and she was gone. Alone, he almost convinced himself that it hadn't happened. It had been like pausing to light a cigarette. It didn't count as an infidelity. Yet a connection had been made, a connection with the girl, a connection with the life here. It could have happened only in a place where he felt at home. He glanced up at the high loft. One of the locality's secrets. Definitely not for tourists.

He found his family sitting out under the trellis with books. He greeted them from the door. "I'm sorry if I'm a bit late. I've got to run up and change my shirt. I'm covered with hairs." He had a quick wash under the primitive shower and checked his discarded clothes. There were no telltale traces. He changed and joined Helene and Robbie under the trellis, feeling recharged with energy and high spirits. He ruffled Robbie's hair as he sat and felt Odette's against his fingers. "Did you have a good afternoon, youngster?" he demanded.

Robbie lifted his startling eyes from his book, Helene's

eyes, full of adoration. "Oh yes, Daddy. We swam and swam. I made a picture of Mummy. Do you want to see it?"

"Of course." The boy jumped up and ran inside.

"That's a very good haircut," Helene told him.

"I had to wait long enough for it. I didn't get away until about half an hour ago. I ran into Odette. She didn't recognize me with my new coiffure. I took her around to the little fishing port for a drink."

"That was kind of you, dearest. I was beginning to worry about you."

"The perils of St. Tropez. Did you think I'd got run over by a bullock cart?" They laughed comfortably together. "I talked to her some more about finding other work. She—"

Robbie came scooting back to his father's side. He held out a sketchbook open to a pencil-and-crayon drawing. Stuart recognized Helene instantly. The boy had caught her elegant line and the set of her head as she sat in a deck chair wearing her bathing suit.

"Excellent. You're getting very good, young fellow. Maybe we have an artist in the family. Should we get you some watercolors? Have you tried them?"

"They're quite difficult," Robbie admitted, basking in his father's interest. "Maybe if I practice with them, I could learn to use them."

"Good. I'll look around for some in town." Stuart called out in the direction of the kitchen. Boldoni's boy, Michel, appeared, a sullen loutish lad, two years older than Robbie but not much bigger. Stuart ordered *pastis* for Helene and himself and a lemonade for Robbie. The boy punched Robbie's arm as he passed. Robbie leaped up and landed a punch on his retreating back.

"Tu me fais chier," he cried.

"Hey. That's enough of that," Stuart reprimanded him.

"But he hit me. You saw him," Robbie protested, dropping back into his chair.

"I'm not talking about what you did. I'm talking about your language."

Robbie's great eyes widened. "Oh. That's another bad word, isn't it?"

"Of course it is."

"He uses those words all the time."

"Well, it may be all right between boys, but not in front of ladies—remember?"

Helene didn't think it was all right at all. Finding suitable playmates for the boy would be a problem if they stayed. She doubted if there was much to hope for from the local school but Stuart seemed to think he offered all the companionship a nine-year-old needed. She had to admit that he was a wonderful father, almost too devoted for her comfort. "You were telling me about Odette," she interjected, feeling as if she were intruding. She gave herself a little mental shake. Only an unnatural mother could be jealous of her son. Michel provided a further distraction as he brought the drinks. Hostilities hung in the air but weren't resumed.

"About Odette?" Stuart said, returning his attention to her. "Let's see. Oh yes, I gathered that she could—" He glanced at his son. "Well, that she could remain an honest woman if she had fifty francs a week. I thought maybe we could let her have it for a few weeks to give her a little time."

"It's very good of you, darling, if you don't think we'll get too involved."

"There's no involvement. She seems quite sensible and independent. It's rather frightening to think how little it takes to alter a life. It can't be for long. We might not even be here in a month."

"Why say that?" It was the first doubt he had expressed about the property and the thought of his being deprived of his dream brought reassurances rushing to her lips. "Boldoni says there's nothing to worry about. You said yourself you had a feeling it's ours."

"I do but I can't expect you to rough it indefinitely. Not that there'll be much luxury if we *do* get the house. Our seaside hut. Are we crazy?"

"Probably, but you seem happy."

"I am if you are." He had safely diverted attention from Odette but his thoughts of her were unexpectedly affectionate. In retrospect, the little adventure seemed slightly comic in a way that sex rarely was. It was something they could giggle about and repeat under more favorable circumstances, a highly enjoyable joke they could share. In this more natural world, there was probably a lot about sex to laugh at. Despite the arguments he'd remembered against infidelity, he couldn't see that it touched Helene in any way.

Another drink did nothing to lower his spirits. He made a point of speaking seriously to Robbie about what he'd been reading (Dumas in French) but joked with him like an equal about everything else. He drew Helene into the fun and they laughed a lot during their usual enormous dinner under the stars although she could see that Robbie was getting overexcited. He was a robust-looking boy, but troublingly highstrung. In absentminded moments, she sometimes got confused about his paternity and was touched by panic as an image of her husband screaming at her filled her mind. She tried to apply brakes with soothing words to Robbie and warning glances at Stuart. She wished she could send the boy to bed but that would be gross abuse of parental authority; his bedtime was fixed by solemn treaty. Instead of being able to enjoy Stuart's odd reckless gaiety she found herself resisting it for the child's sake. What had started it in the first place? There had been nothing notable about the day. A swim? A few hours in the sun? A haircut? At the risk of a childish tantrum she called a halt shortly after they had finished eating.

"All right, darling," she said to Robbie. "You've had a long day. Run along up. You can read for a little while to put yourself to sleep."

"But I'm not sleepy yet," he protested, cut off in the middle of a rambling story he was trying to tell his father.

"Obedience above all, youngster, if you want to go to Heaven," Stuart put in. "Don't argue. We'll have the rest of the story tomorrow." He gave the back of the boy's hair a little yank and watched him shuffle off, reluctance in every step. Stuart laughed rather heartlessly, Helene thought. She was glad he could still be tough with his offspring.

"Thank you for not encouraging him," she said.

"Oh, he's a good boy. We don't have to worry about him."

"I still think you should be more careful about the things you say to him. He's growing up. Is it usual, your being so casual about being naked in front of him?"

"Why not? I like being naked. Men can be naked together, dearest."

"But he's not a man yet and you're his father."

"That's all right. Fathers are supposed to be models for sons. It's good for him to feel there's no great mystery about my parts, if you'll pardon the expression."

"They're rather conspicuous," she said with a fleeting little smile. "He'll be finding out about things. It's all so new for him here. He'd never seen you naked before, had he? I think it might embarrass him."

"You mean the dread fact that his mother has been known to pleasure herself with his father's conspicuous parts?"

She blushed. She supposed that was part of it. She didn't like the idea of Robbie being aware of his parents' sex life. "It's a question of civilized reticence," she said, looking her grandest. It made Stuart chafe against civilization's restrictions. He laughed and gave her shoulder a little shake.

"I don't remember being embarrassed by anybody's parts, conspicuous or otherwise. I always knew what they were for. I just assumed that's the way things were."

"You had a rather special background, dearest."

"I want Robbie's to be special, too. Living in the sun—it gives you a healthy attitude toward life. He won't be all tied up about sex. It'll be wonderful for all of us. He won't be embarrassed by my parts. He'll be much too preoccupied with his own."

"All in good time, perhaps, but we have a duty to protect him during these formative years. Children know much too much about everything these days."

"Children always do. In only six or seven years, Robbie will be the same age I was when I first thought I was going to be a father. Maybe I was. At least, the girl said I was going to be. I wish I knew." He sprang up restlessly. Thoughts of Marguerite ran headlong into thoughts of Odette, both bright with simple careless pleasure. He wished Helene wouldn't be quite so tight-lipped about the facts of life; it made him think of the fun he'd denied himself this afternoon. Self-denial was life-denying. That's what they were trying to escape. *Had* escaped. His high spirits were bursting his seams. He had done his duty by Robbie for the evening. His real fun was always with Helene, the deep rewarding fun that could be shared only by two people completely known and attuned to each other. He circled around behind her and touched her hair. "Come on, old love. Let's take a stroll down to the port. A little wild night life. They're going to invent the Charleston any day now."

"I don't know." She congratulated herself for not leaping to her feet at his summons. If they were going to cut themselves off from the world, she felt obliged to test herself to make sure she wouldn't become slavishly dependent on him. She had resisted his earlier exuberance. This was a good time to prove that they had achieved self-sufficiency within their close-knit devotion to each other. "You go ahead. I'll be fine here."

"Come on. The exercise'll be good for you."

"Are you telling me I'm getting fat?" she asked, between laughter and reproach.

"Fat? What a word to use about you. It's a wonder we're both not as big as houses, but you *can't* get fat. Grow more opulent, maybe, in a very grand sort of way. Come on. Let's parade you around the port. There might still be a couple of cats out." Odette? Who else did he expect to see? It was too much to hope that they'd run into M. Giraudon at this hour.

"I don't think I want to." Had she carried independence far enough? It would be a great triumph if he changed his mind and decided to stay with her.

Because thoughts of Odette had something to do with his restlessness, his conscience compelled him to make a particular effort to take her with him. He moved behind her and ran his hands along her shoulders. "We can't go to bed yet. We haven't had time to digest that meal. It's such a lovely night."

"I'm sure it is, dearest, but I've told you. I don't want to go anywhere."

He had practically begged her. His conscience was clear. "Suit yourself. I'm just going for a wander. God knows, I won't be late."

"I'm sure you won't in this godforsaken little place," she burst out, feeling her triumph slipping away from her.

He chuckled as he took a few tentative steps toward departure. "What do you want me to do? Knock you down and drag you off with me?"

Yes, she thought avidly. Something violent and unpardonable. The memory of a maniac shouting her name was always close to the surface of her mind, terrifying but striking some obscure response in her. "Never fear." There was an unexpected edge of bitterness in her voice. "I don't expect extravagant gestures. We're much too sensible for that." Her breath caught. Had she gone too far? Would he turn on his heel and go?

Her voice brought him to a halt. What was she driving at? Had some careless residue from this afternoon's frolic affected his behavior so that she felt left out in some way? The bitterness in her voice echoed painfully in his ears. He had never loved her more or felt so protective toward her. He took a few steps back to her and lifted a hand to her neck and stroked it where the heavy knot of hair had been. "I don't know what you're talking about but I'm sure you didn't mean it the way it sounded," he said gently.

41

She breathed again. Her triumph was once more within her grasp. The odd keyed-up exhilaration in him had been replaced by his irresistible tenderness. He was with her again. "Forgive me, darling. I'm sorry for the way I sounded. I didn't mean anything. I don't know what was the matter with me."

"Adjustment," he said, giving her neck a squeeze. "Too much sin and gin. We got out in the nick of time." He felt her yielding to him. He wanted her. Perhaps some day the world would accept the fact that there was enough love in people to offer it freely, not measure it out according to convention. He and Odette had exchanged a small gift of desire but it hadn't diminished the great reservoir of love in him that belonged to Helene. He sat beside her and took her hand. "I don't give a damn about taking a walk. Let's have a final glass of wine and go to bed."

"Yes, darling. That would be lovely." Her triumph was complete.

He filled their glasses and took a thoughtful sip from his. Not for the first time, he was aware that by dispensing with the legal formality of marriage he had denied himself the liberties that ordinary married men could permit themselves, safe in the knowledge that the bond wasn't to be lightly dissolved. Odette had been a liberty he had taken too casually. He thought of their haphazard copulation, stumbling about for balance while he drove into her eager body. He had been putting down roots, he thought with private amusement, but he wouldn't like it if Helene felt the need for similar roots.

"I've been thinking," he said, breaking a brief silence. "There's no reason we should leave ourselves completely at old Giraudon's mercy. We might be able to rent a comfortable house while we're waiting. If the old devil doesn't turn up in the next day or two, it'll be quite a scramble getting the hut ready before the bad weather anyway."

"Poor darling. Is it dreadful being burdened with a woman? I'm sure you'd be perfectly happy pitching a tent on your land."

"Who'd keep me warm?"

"I have my uses. It's sweet of you to worry about a house for me. I must admit that Boldoni's for the winter doesn't appeal to me."

"We'll go looking tomorrow. Maybe that'll break the Giraudon jinx."

"I'm sure it will."

"The perfect wife. Are we ready for bed?"

"Very much so." Their eyes met and she glanced hastily away so that he wouldn't see the craving that she was sure hers revealed. He could always melt her resistance when he set his mind to it. She wished she were smaller so that he could sweep her up in his arms and carry her off to their room.

The next day, a notice from the local bank arrived informing Stuart that the money had been credited to his account and the Coslings spent a good many fruitless hours asking every likely source for houses to rent. Renting was a concept that had apparently not yet reached St. Tropez. Every habitable house was inhabited by its owner. Others were falling to ruin because families had been disrupted or died or drifted away. They found a few more places for sale but nothing to compare to the property Stuart regarded as already his.

"That settles it," he said when they returned to Boldoni's for a drink before dinner. "We've got to find the old man. We have no choice. I'll give him two more weeks and then I'm going to the police. He might've dropped dead somewhere."

"Will you still have time to get the house ready before the bad weather?"

"With luck. Now that the money's here, I can start ordering materials. Boldoni's got that builder friend of his. We'll be ready to go before the ink's dry on the deed."

They continued to discuss the housing situation and didn't pay much attention to Robbie when he joined them, wearing a look of angelic innocence. Helene had excluded him from the house-hunting on the grounds that it would be tiring and boring. In fact, she hadn't wanted him to interfere. Stuart was inclined to invite his opinion of matters he knew nothing about, which was sweet and sometimes entertaining but often wasted a lot of time. She didn't want finding a house to turn into a game.

When Boldoni lumbered out of the kitchen to tell them that dinner was ready, Stuart questioned him further about M. Giraudon's habits, trying to think of some angle he'd overlooked.

"I wish you'd tell everybody we're leaving if we don't finish with this deal in two weeks," Stuart said. "Maybe word will get to him."

"He speaks to nobody. Perhaps you should be thankful

43

that he's disappeared. Has Maître Barbetin got the papers in order?"

"We saw him this afternoon. He's still fussing about the confusion in the title I told you about. I said I didn't care, for the hundredth time."

"You may be right. Nobody wants land here. It's not like farther along the coast. Giraudon won't let you get away."

Property remained the topic of the evening. Confident that nobody would take much interest in anything he said, Robbie was emboldened during dinner to ask the question that had been on his mind most of the afternoon. "Daddy, doesn't *baiser* mean 'to kiss'?" he inquired.

"Sure," Stuart answered with a smile.

"It doesn't mean anything else, does it?"

It did, but it seemed a bit soon to explain to Robbie about fucking. Perhaps Michel had already done so. On the chance that he had, Stuart elaborated to demonstrate that there was no need for embarrassment or mystery. "It can mean other things in slang, anything to do with making love. You've seen people making love in movies, all the kissing and hugging and all that—the part you always say bores you. The French say *'on baise'* even when it isn't actually kissing."

"I see." Robbie tried to keep his expression neutral as if he were digesting an ordinary bit of information. He saw his mother give his father an odd look as she cut in quickly with another remark about a house, leaving him to his thoughts. Michel had been right. There *was* something about the word he hadn't understood. He still didn't. He wasn't sure he wanted to. It sounded as if it were the sort of thing his mother didn't like him to be interested in. The afternoon had confused him thoroughly without being enjoyable.

It had all started with the word. *"Tu es trop jeune,"* Michel had taunted him when Robbie had won a game of *boules. "Tu ne sais pas baiser,"* he had added as if everybody didn't know how to kiss. Insults were exchanged. Action followed. Michel led the way around to the back of the hotel and summoned a plump little girl who was sitting on the steps of the house next door. She approached sullenly through a row of tomato plants. It was the same little girl who had let them watch her take a bath earlier in the summer. She had kept her legs pressed together so that she looked as if she had no pipi. He didn't want to do anything with her. Something furtive about his two companions made him nervous and after that everything became sort of blurred. He was sure they were doing

44

something bad. Bad things could be fun sometimes but he didn't expect to have any fun with the girl around.

They went to a room in a part of the hotel Robbie didn't know. It was musty and hot and strange things began to happen. The little girl lay on her back on a rusty iron bed. Her skirt was up around her waist and she had nothing on under it. She again kept her plump legs pressed together so that she looked as if she had no pipi. Robbie turned his back on her. Michel took all his clothes off. Something was wrong with his pipi. It was surprisingly big and stuck out straight in front of him. He jeered at Robbie for hesitating to take his clothes off and the word cropped up again. How did he expect to kiss the little girl if he didn't get undressed? Robbie had no intention of kissing anybody but he took his clothes off to prove that he knew what it was all about. Michel sneered at him because his pipi was *mou.* Having a soft pipi also seemed to have something to do with the word. Michel tugged at it and, to Robbie's astonishment, it got bigger than he'd known was possible and also stuck out. He was afraid that it would stay that way but it felt very pleasant. Michel ran his hand rapidly back and forth on both of them, producing an odd tingling sensation that ended in a sort of spasm. Robbie was relieved to see that his pipi was returning to normal as a jet of liquid burst from Michel's. It looked as if he were trying to pee into the air. It was the sort of dirty thing he would do. Michel bragged about it. It proved that he was old enough to kiss. His pipi stopped sticking out.

This seemed to displease him. He made Robbie run his hand back and forth on it until it grew amazingly hard and stood up again. Robbie was pleased to learn how to do it. For a moment, there seemed to be some point to what they were doing. At least he had accomplished something.

"Now I'll show you," Michel said. "Watch."

He turned to the bed. Robbie didn't want to watch. The way the little girl lay there, inert but somehow expectant, annoyed him. She was stuck up. Complacent. It was a word he'd learned recently. That was what she was. He didn't want to have anything to do with her.

Michel lay on top of her. Robbie thought maybe they were going to wrestle but Michel began to pump his bare bottom up and down over her. It was ridiculous-looking. He would never want to be so silly. He was aware that the odd thing was happening to him again down there. It was amazing how big it could get and stand up by itself. The tingling sensation was very pleasant. You were apparently supposed to rub it when it got like that. He did so and had the spasm and it shrank back to normal again. It was better when Michel did it. They could do it together without the girl. It was having the girl with them that made it so bad. Boys could do things together but girls weren't supposed to see them with no clothes on. She was a bad little girl.

When Michel stood, she was still lying with her legs pressed together and her air of complacent expectancy. Robbie felt a little shiver of revulsion at the thought of touching her—what would she want of him?—but Michel didn't insist on his lying on top of her.

"*Ça va,*" he said when Robbie told him he was too hot to stay in the dusty little room any longer. "*Maintenant tu sais baiser.*"

His father's explanation that the word was used in many ways should have cleared up his confusion but it hadn't. Making love was something grown-ups did before they got married. His parents may have made love long ago before he was born but he was sure they'd never done the things he'd seen this afternoon. He couldn't imagine either of them with their pipis sticking out. From now on he must try to avoid looking at his father when he was naked. His big body suggested mysteries he wasn't ready to face. He should probably stop asking him so many questions, too. He was safer with his mother; she would never say anything that would remind him of the things he should feel ashamed or guilty about. He wanted to be as good as she thought he was. She could be very sharp to him when he wasn't. But the image remained of plump legs pressed together and of a bare bottom pumping up and down above them. What had they been doing?

After dinner, he didn't mind being told that it was his bedtime. He wanted to go to his room and find out if he could make it big and hard by himself. . . .

Having the money in the bank turned the property and M. Giraudon into an obsession for Stuart. He asked everybody at the Saturday evening gathering if they'd seen the old lunatic. He had mentioned to Odette that they were planning to settle here but now he told her about the deal in detail, including the disputed boundary. It was supposed to be bad luck to talk about something you wanted until you had it, yet there was nothing to be secretive about and he couldn't resist describing the beauties of the place. Having it to talk about relieved some of the sexual tensions between them. It was difficult to suppress all trace of intimacy with a girl you'd had, but since Helene's little outburst he'd been especially determined that his transgression should have no repercussions. The girl was obviously eager for further developments. Whether there would be any depended on chance and circumstances.

She listened to him, enthralled. During the week she had gone to the Gypsy to have her fortune told and the old crone had seen a man in her future and a business transaction involving great property. Since Stuart was the only man she was ever likely to know who might have great property, she had asked if the man was her lover. The Gypsy had muttered and made strange signs over her palm and said that she saw a lover and a husband. She could tell her no more. Now Stuart was talking about vast property—two hundred hectares, even if some of it wouldn't be his. She was sure that she was destined to play an important part in his life. She thought of her friend at the brothel. She often learned things that nobody else knew.

"I think I might be able to find that man," she said. "Giraudon? I'll try."

Stuart almost threw his arms around her. It was the first positive reaction he had had. The sexual current surged up strong between them. He looked into invitingly dancing eyes. "I wish I could give you an enormous kiss. Finding him would be the best thing you could ever do for us."

"When you look at me like that, there are many things I would do for you." Her smile was a merry promise of future pleasure. "I've been waiting to tell you. I've found a widow who'll let me have a room for helping her around the house. I'll be able to move out of my friend's place. Will you come see me sometimes?"

"Perhaps when you're well established and you're sure the widow doesn't spy on you." Whatever happened, Stuart intended to let enough time pass before their next meeting so that she couldn't think they were having a regular affair. By then, their little physical hunger for each other might have worn itself out. He smiled at her, making it as winning as he knew how. "Everything's going to work out for you. I'm glad. Now you've got to get me fixed up. It's tricky not having any routine. When I do, I'll know what I can do with my time. I have to be careful."

As if to underline the point, Helene, who had been kissing

47

Robbie goodnight, rejoined them. Stuart told her that Odette was going to solve their problems and nudged the girl up for a dance.

On the floor, she pressed herself to him and felt his thrilling man-part stirring against her. He still wanted her. If she found his landowner, gratitude might overcome his caution. She would learn how to make him want her often.

He looked out at the star-filled night and knew there were lovers out there who were free to take their pleasure as it came. He was achieving freedom but he didn't want to do it at Helene's expense. He would be free for this merry girl when the time was right. The mechanical piano clanked to a temporary halt and he guided her back toward his wife.

Days passed while Stuart raged with frustration. He had visions of them years hence, still sitting at Boldoni's waiting for M. Giraudon. In order to soften the blow she felt might be coming, Helene spoke of the impossibility of trying to do business with a madman. It was perhaps a mistake to treat the question of the boundaries so casually. Maître Barbetin seemed genuinely worried about the question. Stuart knew she was trying to make it easier for him but he refused to try to reconcile himself to losing the place. He clung to the faint hope Odette had offered him. At least she was doing something to help. He was keyed up and watching for her the following Saturday night. Helene was dancing when he spotted her. He rushed to her through the crowd. Her face lighted up as it did whenever she saw him but he hardly bothered with greetings.

"Have you found out anything?" he demanded.

She looked briefly puzzled and then her expression cleared. "You mean about your M. Giraudon? A little something. My friend knows somebody who thinks he knows where he might be. My friend is waiting to find out more. I wasn't going to tell you until she did."

"But that's wonderful," he burst out. He gripped her arms in an exuberant little hug. "The first clue. You must come tell me the minute you hear more." He moved with her toward the dancing area.

"I'm with the widow now," she announced happily. "She says she'll pay me a little if she has any sewing for me. Isn't that wonderful? Perhaps soon I won't need your money. I can't believe I was actually planning to go to work in that house." She looked up at him, her eyes filled with an unsettling blend of gratitude and sexuality, and melted into his arms as they began to dance. *"Tu es trop beau, tu sais. Je te sens toujours dans moi. Ta grosse bitte.* I don't want to forget it."

"It was supposed to be unforgettable," he said, keeping it a joke. "You're going to find M. Giraudon. You're my only hope. I don't want to give up and go."

"You mustn't talk of leaving. We're both strangers here. Who will look after the other if one of us goes?"

He let her press herself to him. A girl who could speak of his *grosse bitte* with such enthusiastic admiration was difficult to resist. It hardened and stood up against her. She would probably love to suck it. He glanced out at the night. A few paces in the dark and it could be done. A few minutes' absence nobody would notice. No risks. Yet there were always risks, no matter how slight. An inconsequential pleasure loaded with potential disaster. He coaxed himself back into virtue while the troublesome part of him subsided.

M. Giraudon returned as unexpectedly as he had disappeared. The Coslings were finishing lunch in the mild late-September sun when he came scuttling out of the kitchen and stopped several yards from their table. He was dressed as he had been on their previous meeting. Stuart leaped up from his chair as he caught sight of him.

"At last," he cried. "Where in the world have you been?"

The old man edged away cautiously. "I fooled you, eh?" he cackled. "I put one over on you. That's the kind of man I am."

"Yes, that was very clever of you," Stuart agreed wildly, pumping the old man's hand. "Very clever. Just when I had the money and everything. I almost decided not to wait for you."

"Oh, I knew you'd wait. One knows you have a reason for staying." He said it with such a leer that Stuart thought immediately of Odette and glanced instinctively at Helene. Their eyes met for a split second and then Stuart turned quickly back to M. Giraudon.

"It's after two," Stuart said hastily. "Maître Barbetin will be in his office. He's got the money. You're here. Why don't we settle this thing right now?" He switched to English for a quick aside to Helene. "I'll get his signature. You can sign later. He may not like women." Stuart, still holding the old man's hand, began to urge him forward.

"Why put off till tomorrow what one can do today, eh?"

M. Giraudon cackled gleefully. "That's the way to do business. You deliver the goods, you pocket the money, and there's an end to it."

Helene watched them go with a sudden quickening of her heart. What had his look meant? There had been something furtive in his eyes. There was something she had missed. Robbie saw her eyes go empty and staring. It was frightening. She made him feel as if he didn't exist. He put his hand out to hers to make her recognize his presence.

Stuart sat with M. Giraudon in front of Maître Barbetin's desk while the notary droned endlessly through the act of sale. Stuart didn't attempt to follow it. Generations of Giraudons were named, dates reaching back into the eighteenth century cited. When he reached the end, the notary looked at the two men.

"That's as satisfactory as it can be in view of certain discrepancies," he said.

"Yes, of course," Stuart muttered hastily.

M. Giraudon leaned forward. "I shall have to read it myself," he said.

"But I've just read it to you," the notary snapped.

"How do I know what you read is what's in there, eh? I know my rights. I have the right to read it myself."

"No one questioned your right." The notary's voice was raised with indignation. "You're not going to bore us with your talk of rights now?"

"Bore you? You think I care whether I bore you?"

"*Crétin*. What good would it do for you to care?"

Stuart began to fear for the outcome of his business and was about to intervene when the notary picked up the document and held it out to M. Giraudon.

"Read it, if you know how to read," he said witheringly. The two old men glared at each other for a moment, then M. Giraudon snatched the papers and began to read. Stuart watched intently. Were there to be more complications? Was the absurd creature going to make some objection? At last M. Giraudon came to the end and handed the document back to the notary.

"Quite satisfactory," he said as if no words had passed between them.

The notary turned to Stuart. "You are sure you wish to sign before I terminate my inquiries about the boundaries?" he asked.

"Yes, indeed." Stuart didn't attempt to keep the urgency out of his voice.

"Very well." Maître Barbetin rose solemnly, picked up a quill pen, dipped it into a brass inkwell on his desk, and held it out to Stuart with a ceremonious bow. Stuart was reminded of the Great Powers at Versailles as he moved around the desk to put his signature on the document. M. Giraudon in his turn attacked the paper as if he were an artist confronted with a virgin canvas.

Stuart's fate was sealed.

He returned from the notary's office bursting with his victory. Helene was dazzled by the blaze of his enthusiasm. He herded his family into the car and they drove out to the place and sat in the sun beside the olive trees, looking over the sea, and drank to the future from a bottle of champagne provided by Boldoni. Robbie got quite drunk on one glass and went to sleep in the back seat of the car. His parents looked around them with new eyes. Everywhere they looked belonged to them. Every tree, every rock, every vista acquired a unique value by being theirs. The property seemed suddenly enormous.

"Well, what do you think?" Stuart asked with a touch of awe in his voice.

"It's totally unbelievable. We've talked about it so much, I suppose I began to think it couldn't happen."

"It's happened, all right. Wait till you see all the documents. When we go back, I'll take you to the office so you can sign and then everything'll be registered. We'll finally have a legal paper with both our names on it."

She laughed and reached for his hand and gripped it. "We hardly need that after all these years but it's rather marvelous to know that we own it together. It's ours. It'll be Robbie's. How extraordinary. Think of what people at home would say. It *is* unbelievable that we can buy so much beauty for so little."

"I don't suppose we can, really. We're going to have to work for it. I'm glad we can't afford to do anything elaborate with the house. You don't mind?"

"Good heavens, no, darling. I'm going to love our little house. You're right. It'll be so good for Robbie, growing up simply out of doors. Heaven knows what'll be left of the world when he's a man. They say the depression is only just beginning in Europe."

"Well, I'm not depressed. Incidentally, *this* is home."

"So it is, darling. I suppose we ought to be doing something about Robbie's school."

"There's no hurry. I want him to do his share getting settled in. He can start next term or however it's arranged here."

The next day work began. With two men recruited by Boldoni, they started with the road. Stuart had never chopped down a tree but he quickly learned to manage the smaller ones. It was an act of possession. Robbie and Helene were assigned to the brush and to stacking branches and although Helene broke most of her fingernails and scraped her knuckles, she didn't mind. It was such a joy to watch Stuart, stripped to the waist, his bronze skin gleaming with sweat, his muscles bunching up in his back as he swung his axe. The workmen obviously admired him, too. He was more devoted, more charming, more considerate than Helene had ever seen him, with his special capacity for making everything seem fun.

In less than a week, they had cleared a road down to the olive grove, in the process chopping enough wood, Stuart figured, to last them the winter, and filled in the badly rutted stretches. As an inauguration ceremony, the Coslings and the workmen climbed into the Rolls-Royce and drove grandly through the woods down to the sea. The place was taking on a new shape, their shape. It really belonged to them now.

Next it was the mason's turn to pull the house together, with Stuart quickly learning to be a useful assistant. They had a few days of gray weather and there was a new chill in the air and they were aware that the sun was beginning to set earlier. There was no longer any question of plunging naked into the sea.

After another few weeks, the work was terminated, including a shelter of cane reinforced with pine timbers for the outhouse and a garage of similar construction where the road ended some hundred yards from the house. They bought beds and a table and some straight-backed chairs and dishes and pots and pans. He had the feeling that all St. Tropez was smiling encouragingly on their homemaking efforts. Villagers whose faces were only vaguely familiar spoke to them like old friends.

One morning at the end of October, they moved in. It was an easy move for it took place piecemeal over a period of several days and when they said good-bye to Boldoni, none of them could quite believe that they wouldn't be back that evening.

"Are we ever going to eat at Boldoni's again?" Robbie asked rather wistfully as they carried their few light bags and bundles across the sunny glade to the house. Stuart laughed at the note of regret in his voice.

"You beginning to worry about the cuisine out here?"

"Well, Mum hasn't had much practice, has she?"

"It's going to be all right, darling," Helene reassured him. "After all, I *am* French. We're born cooks. Just remember that when you're thinking about getting married."

"You're going to have a hard time making us forget Boldoni, old girl," Stuart warned her. He unlocked the front door and threw it open. "Shouldn't I carry you over the threshold or something?"

"Thanks to Boldoni, I don't think you can," she said.

They spilled into the house, strewing their luggage about them. The whitewashed walls were bright with sunlight. In the big fireplace to the left a fire had been laid the day before. Next to it, in the corner, was Stuart and Helene's big double bed for which she had made a cover of black rep, piped in rose, so that it could be used as a sofa in the daytime. Curtains of a stout rose fabric hung at the big window looking out to the sea and the table at the other end of the room was painted white, as were the cane-bottomed chairs around it. Behind the table was the wood stove, a sink, a cupboard, shelves on which were ranged dishes and glasses. Copper pots hung in a row beneath them. The effect was gay and cozy, with a touch of the quaint that pleased Helene.

Robbie headed for the new door leading to the only major addition. "I want to get my room all arranged," he said importantly. They watched him fondly as he withdrew and then turned to each other. Stuart spread his arms with a smile.

"Well, here we are." She went to him and put her hands on his chest and he held her lightly. "Satisfied?" he asked.

"It's marvelous. I feel like a child playing house."

"I rather suspect that there's going to be more work than play."

"Well, I better get at it if we're to have any lunch." She laughed and turned to her cupboard.

Stuart was right. There always seemed to be something to do. There were the household chores, the water to haul, the wood to split for the stove. And there was the problem of

53

turning the land to some profit. In front of the house the rocky wooded ridge descended to the sea. A narrow path twisted around it and came out on several miles of beach, which also belonged to them. Behind the beach was a wide sweep of open land, an extremity of the central plain of the peninsula, broken by clumps of trees. It had once been farmed but all that was left were the few acres of vineyard that M. Giraudon had allowed to run almost wild.

As Stuart understood it, it was over this whole area, some eighty acres in all, that a controversy had raged at some time or other and about which Maître Barbetin had continued to be concerned until the papers had been signed. Stuart proposed to nurse the existing vines back to health and little by little to return the entire area to vines. With eighty acres of vines in production, he would be rich.

Aside from the site of the house, this was the part of his property that he liked best. The wide sweep of the beach bordered by clumps of tall cane offered a prospect that was peculiarly Mediterranean, both romantic and austere. A mile or two behind it, the land was a gently rolling panorama of neat cultivated rectangles, squat blank-faced farmhouses guarded by cypresses and great umbrella pines and, against the near low hills, the tracery of retaining walls. Beyond, the hills rose in receding bands of lavender and blue, and in the distance Cap Camarat was visible, topped by the white column of its lighthouse.

He particularly liked the lighthouse. It gave him the sense of being on an island although the sea wasn't visible on that side. A number of years passed before he learned how crucial this view of the lighthouse was to him.

They quickly established their routine. The heavy labor was of course reserved for Stuart, but Helene displayed an unexpected and gratifying readiness to help. Her mornings were given over to Robbie's lessons. The weather turned increasingly cold and it was disagreeable sometimes working out of doors, but Stuart was determined to make the best of it and Helene seemed positively to enjoy it. Robbie found that whining wouldn't get him anywhere with either parent and he was too pleased to have escaped school to draw attention to himself. In his spare time, Stuart paced his acres until he felt he knew every foot of them by heart. So much land. So damn much land. He didn't know where to begin.

For advice, he walked over to visit his nearest neighbor, whose name was Antonin Roquiètta. Stuart was aware that his purchase of property that had been coveted in the neighborhood might have created some hostility toward him, so he went with trepidation.

Roquiètta turned out to be a short wiry man with dull black hair. His dark ruddy skin and his slightly beaked nose made him look like an American Indian. He invited Stuart into the kitchen, where he was received by Madame Roquiètta, a good-looking woman with soft humorous eyes.

"Won't you sit down?" she said formally. Everything in the kitchen was clean and bright and ugly. Stuart sat at the table and Roquiètta sat beside him. The woman placed two glasses before them and an enormous jar of cherries floating in a pale amber liquid. She remained standing as they talked about the weather. When he told Roquiètta that he would like advice about his vineyard he was aware of a lightening of the atmosphere. Roquiètta was full of his agricultural exploits. He had a happy grin, childlike in spite of, or perhaps because of, the fact that he had no front teeth.

"The monsieur doesn't want to hear all your stories," his wife interrupted. "Give him something to drink." Roquiètta looked hurt but obeyed. They drank the cherry liquor and with a little encouragement from Stuart, he was off again.

Roquiètta had a habit of making disparaging statements that seemed like willful rudeness at first. When he came over to see Stuart's vines he shook his head. "They're not worth bothering about," he said. When Stuart protested, the other insisted until Stuart could say no more. "But maybe Antonin has an idea. We'll see about that," he finally agreed. He referred to himself frequently in the third person.

"That? That land's exhausted," he said when Stuart showed him where he planned to start his vegetable garden. There was another argument, which ended the same way. "We'll see. I think Antonin has an idea."

Stuart learned that once Antonin had convinced himself of the hopelessness of a project, he was ready to tackle it. He had a store of practical folklore. At his instigation, Stuart bought a rifle and a small rowboat for hunting and fishing. He sold the furniture stored in New York to have a little extra money to play with. Also at Antonin's suggestion, he bought a dozen chickens and half a dozen pairs of pigeons and some rabbits, after building suitable housing for them. The total investment was more than he had expected but he told himself they would quickly pay for themselves.

He put Robbie in charge of them and passed on what

Antonin had told him about their mating habits. The boy did not connect this information with the mystery that remained at the heart of adult life. Animals were different from humans. Animals didn't have to get married to have children.

Stuart thought Robbie too young to handle a rifle but he did take him fishing the first time he went out in the boat. Since they didn't catch anything and it was frightfully cold, Robbie couldn't see why they didn't buy fish at the market in St. Tropez, but his father seemed to think they were enjoying themselves so he played along with him.

Stuart's hunting expeditions were also largely fruitless. He was a good shot but he rarely saw anything to shoot at. Antonin frequently brought them gifts of fish and game, laughing when Stuart asked him where he found them. Antonin treated him with the tolerance of an adult for a child. Whatever he attempted, whether it was sowing seed, or killing a chicken, or turning up the earth, Antonin would take over, saying:

"Here. Let Antonin do it. You're not used to such things." He reminded Stuart of Uncle Ben.

"I don't suppose you play *boules*," Antonin said one day when he had brought his horse and plough over to work Stuart's ground.

"Sure I do. Not very well, though."

"Me, I'm a champion." Antonin grinned. "We often have a game on Sundays. Perhaps you'd like to come. Of course, we're not educated people." Antonin spoke as bluntly about himself as he did about everything else. Stuart accepted with pleasure and began to meet the farming community.

Helene was tolerant of his interest in the local people though they meant nothing to her. If it was friends they were after they would have done better to stay in New York. When Stuart asked the Roquièttas for dinner, she resented them for coming. They should have known as well as she that they had nothing in common. She was sure Stuart blamed her for the stiff formality of the evening. It was one of the few small clouds that had darkened the uneventful contentment of her days. She was as happy as she could remember ever being. She was working hand in hand with Stuart; she was essential to the realization of his dream of making a self-sufficient life. At times, she caught herself thinking that Robbie really *should* be at school. Perhaps next year, when they knew more about living costs, they could send him away to a good school and she and Stuart would have each other to themselves for months at a time.

The expenditures Antonin encouraged Stuart to make didn't always strike her as sound and when the chickens didn't lay, the pigeons produced unfertilized eggs, greens for the rabbits became increasingly difficult to find, she began to wonder if their neighbors weren't amusing themselves at Stuart's expense.

Of course, the unusual cold was to blame. Everybody agreed that it hadn't been so cold since . . . Various remote winters were cited. In an ordinary winter, Stuart would have had a reasonable chance of putting his modest projects on a paying basis. But tools, feed, fertilizer, countless unexpected expenses were all pure loss and instead of catching up, as he had planned, he found himself falling farther and farther behind. Debts accumulated imperceptibly until as Christmas was approaching he discovered that he had committed all of his next two months' income. He expected the first few months to be difficult and he could always draw ahead a bit, but spring suddenly seemed a long way off.

One of his first economies had been to stop Odette's allowance; he and the girl had reached the decision by mutual consent the afternoon they encountered each other for the first time after his move to the house. Nothing had changed. They had only to look at each other to know what they both wanted. He had spent weeks of dedicated labor creating a home for his family and the time had finally come. He had earned the right to a brief change of pace. He wanted to throw off his clothes with her and share the pleasures they had denied themselves. All work and no play was the order of the day but the lustful kid in him clamored to be let loose for half an hour. She immediately felt the renewed liveliness in his response to her and warmed to it with delight.

"Enfin, chéri," she exclaimed. "Will you let me show you where I live?"

"Nothing more?" Their eyes teased and taunted each other.

"You've made me wait so long. I should punish you but why should I punish myself?"

The village had two centers, one of which was the main port, the other this big plane-tree-crowded square away from the sea where the vegetable market was, and the notary's office and the cinema and numerous other little businesses.

Stuart found that as a householder this was where his errands usually took him and weeks often passed without his seeing the port. There was more human activity here and he felt less self-conscious about being seen with Odette than in the narrow empty little streets leading up to Boldoni's.

She hustled him across the square under plane trees that were losing their leaves. They exchanged odds and ends of news to keep from laying hands on each other, then looked at each other and burst out laughing.

They turned into a side street. He took the precaution of glancing about to see that nobody he knew was in sight before she led him through a doorway that gave on to a narrow stairway. They hurried up it, jostling each other, panting slightly. At the top of three flights of steps, she flung open a door and quickly closed it behind them and they lifted their arms to each other and exchanged their first real kiss. She drew back, giggling breathlessly while she pulled her dress over her head.

Stuart tossed his clothes aside and looked around him. They were in a large room with sloping ceilings, a bed against one wall, a fireplace with some pots beside it, a table with chairs around it in the middle. It was shabby but immaculately clean. A curtain masked a makeshift bathroom. He caught a glimpse of a tall enamel pitcher on the floor beside a portable bidet. He got his shoes off and freed his legs and straightened to feel her nakedness against him everywhere. He held her away from him and looked at her. She was roundly, prettily naked. He had known her for so many months, had imagined this happening so often that there was no danger of its altering life in any way. Their friendship would simply acquire a new dimension.

They moved against each other slowly, discovering the secrets of their bodies. He touched at last the firm gentle curves of her breasts. She lowered her hands to his erection and stroked it, her eyes on it.

"Oh *chéri. Ta grosse bite.* It looks even bigger when you having nothing on." It was a part of a man she had never particularly wanted to look at. It served its purpose but she didn't think it deserved any prize for design. His was different, long and straight, lifting superbly from his lean, muscular, mostly hairless body. His nakedness was marvelously naked. It made her feel that their bodies could perform miracles of union. They both uttered sounds of delight as they moved in close against each other and tumbled onto the bed. They played together, they kissed, they rolled about on her bumpy mattress. She wriggled out of his embrace so that she could look at him. His big body was more beautiful than she had known a body could be.

"*Chope et fume,*" she cried and illustrated her meaning by sliding down over him and drawing his erection into her mouth. He was reminded of Marguerite again. She looked as happy as a child with a lollipop.

She wanted to take outrageous liberties with him to convince herself that she had him. He was a god. She could have wept with happiness, but was careful not to let him feel the intensity of her worship. There was a carefree boy in him who wanted the girl she had once been. He somehow made it possible for her to recapture her old self. She led them easily from play to the ecstasy of his possession of her. She gave herself unstintingly to the magnificent demands of his body. She was wholly his and was beginning to make the boy in him hers. She had felt from the beginning that it could happen. By taking her, he ennobled her, lifted her out of what she thought of as her class. If she couldn't have him all to herself, at least she would never give herself to one of the crude uneducated men she had thought of until a few months ago as her lot in life.

Stuart reveled in her cheerful uncritical adoration of him; it was balm to his beleaguered spirit. Burdens and responsibilities dropped from him. Life could be fun. He felt nothing like it with Helene, nor did he want or expect to. Every moment with Helene was an experience, defining and shaping the future, tempered by the worries and problems that they shared. It was real. Taking Odette was a happy self-indulgence that couldn't form the basis for an everyday life.

When they had exhausted their lusty ingenuity, Stuart had a quick wash at the sink behind the curtain and dressed. Odette put on a plain little dressing gown. She looked up at him, sparkling with pride.

"That was worth waiting for. I've never known anything like it." She turned, taking in the room. "You see what you've done for me? I'm a respectable member of the community now. You don't have to be ashamed of your girl."

"I knew I wouldn't ever be."

"The Widow Muguette is pleased with my sewing. I'm going to be making enough to take care of myself now. I don't

59

need your money." It was the happiest moment of her life. She was no longer a charity case. She was his girl, his mistress, his equal.

"You're sure?" He took her hands with a quick smile of affectionate relief. "I can't pretend that I haven't wondered how much longer I could let you have it. Everything's costing more than I expected."

"Don't wonder. You've saved my life. I'll never be able to repay you."

"We have a beautiful time together, don't we? It's about time we let ourselves enjoy it."

A pattern evolved. He never went into town expressly to see her, but when he had half an hour to spare after he'd finished his errands, thoughts of being naked with her sent him to her room and he usually found her there. She was a warmly loving connection with town, his only recreation as life became more difficult, permissible because it cost nothing. Because desire for her never hit him except when he was within reach of satisfying it, she remained safely compartmentalized, outside the mainstream of his life. If it had been otherwise he wouldn't have let it happen; his goal was freedom, not the bonds of a demanding mistress.

Leaving her one afternoon, he ran into Antonin's wife and offered her a lift home. He nodded toward the bakery two doors away, which he'd known from the beginning might prove useful as an alibi. "I was just going to pick up a loaf of bread."

A few days later, the farmer's wife happened to say in reference to a story she was telling Helene, "Oh, but of course, you know *la Veuve Muguette.*"

"No," Helene said. The Widow Muguette? She had never heard the name.

"Then your husband does. I ran into him at her house the other day. No, no. I'm forgetting. He was going to the bakery next door." Mme. Antonin went on with her story while Helene made a mental note to ask Stuart who the woman was.

When Stuart was finishing his work in the vineyard that afternoon, the sky cleared after several dull days and a wind sprang up. He was aware of it as he started back to the house and saw, toward Italy, range upon range of mountains he had never noticed before. The weather was about to spring another surprise on them. Everything had become hard and brilliant in the late-afternoon light. When he got to the house he called Helene out to look.

"How superb," she exclaimed. "It must be the *mistral*."

"I suppose." Stuart had heard the local people speak with awe of the wind. There was a legend that it blew always in multiples of three, for three, six, or nine days. They stood for a moment, hand in hand, looking at the mountains and at the waves that were beginning to dash up on the rocks below them.

"It looks almost like a real ocean," Stuart said.

They knew they were in for trouble when Helene tried to light the stove to cook dinner. In a few minutes the room was filled with smoke and when Stuart opened the door to clear it out, he was almost knocked over by the force of the wind. It swept through the room, extinguishing all the lamps.

"What's the matter with that damned stove?" he demanded.

"I don't know," she replied with exasperation. "It just won't start. Why don't you light the lamps?"

"Easy does it. Don't get excited." He found a lamp and struck a match.

"How're we going to cook dinner?" Robbie inquired anxiously. Helene frowned at the boy, confident that Stuart would set things right. He relighted the lamps and went to the stove and jiggled the draft to make sure it was adjusted properly.

"Shall I try more paper?" she asked. "We don't want to go without dinner."

"Try a pine cone. If that doesn't burn, nothing will." She did as he suggested and together they peered at the stove as the wind forced the smoke out into the room once more. He looked at her and shrugged. "Experiment concluded. I'll have to ask Antonin if there's anything to be done about it." Unlikely, he thought. Even Antonin would be powerless against the elements.

"Let's think," Helene said. "Isn't there something we could do? We should have one of those kerosene stoves."

"We should have but we don't," he said, groaning inwardly at the thought of additional expense.

"What about Robbie? The child needs a hot meal at night."

"The child will survive." He cocked an eye at Robbie, who was sitting on the foot of the bed, watching them intently and wondering how he could draw some advantage from the situation.

"Come on, old love. Throw us a bone. Don't you have something we could roast over the fire?"

She laughed, ready to take her cue from him in a crisis. "No suckling pigs in the larder, but we'll manage." She put odds and ends and leftovers on the table. They ate in enforced speechlessness. The wind made a steady roar around the house. Before they had finished, the room began to fill with smoke again.

"Oh damn," Stuart shouted. "I suppose the fireplace's going to act up now." It was. He struggled with logs but stood back finally, his eyes closed to ease their smarting. "I'll have to get these logs out of here. Robbie, put the lamps over there in the corner." He posted Helene at the door, seized a log with the tongs, and rushed it out. Showers of sparks were caught by the wind and thrown into the air. "Quick. Get some water," he shouted. There were a few moments of chaos as the logs were removed one by one and extinguished. By the time the fire was out, the room was icy. Stuart pushed the door to, breathing heavily. "Well, I guess that puts an end to the evening. We all better go to bed."

The thought of going alone to his dark room with the wind howling around him frightened Robbie. "I'm so hungry I won't be able to sleep," he suggested piteously.

"Now, none of that nonsense." Stuart saw the boy looking to his mother for support and was pleased that she offered him no more than a dutiful kiss.

"You poor darling," she said with marked irony.

"All right. Run along. Skip," he said sharply. Robbie disentangled himself from her embrace, kissed his father, and departed with dragging feet.

"We can't have any of that," Stuart said when the boy was gone.

"Of what?"

"We mustn't baby the kid. I don't want him to be a softie."

She was aware that the wind had keyed them both up to the snapping point. Having to raise their voices to make themselves heard distorted everything they said. Stuart might not have meant to speak so harshly to the boy but Robbie probably deserved it. She suspected that he tried to cause trouble between them when it suited his purpose. The thought made her feel like an unnatural mother. How could

Stuart accuse her of being soft with the child? "Do you think I baby him?" she shouted.

"Not particularly." He approached so that they could speak in more normal tones. "It's something we're both apt to do with an only child."

"Speak for yourself," she burst out. His proximity made her skin crawl with desire. The wind dinned at her nerves. She wanted him to tear her clothes off and take her violently. "At times, I can't bear him. It's all very well for you. He worships you because you only see him when you're ready to give him your full attention. I have him underfoot all the time."

"Come on, my dearest. You sound as if you were jealous of him."

"Jealous? Maybe I am." The word reminded her of Mme. Antonin's reference to an unknown woman and fanned an ember of suspicion. "You see people when you go out. I'm always here. Who's the Widow Muguette?"

"The Widow Muguette? What an absurd name. I don't know her." He was prepared for it to come up sooner or later. He couldn't feel guilty about Odette. She was completely extraneous to their life. The only wrong was to be found out. "Wait a minute. *La Veuve Muguette.* Of course. That's the name of the woman Odette works for. It didn't sound right in English."

"She lives near a bakery?" Helene demanded while her suspicions died.

"Does she? Possibly. She lives somewhere around the square. That's where I always run into her. Odette, I mean. As far as I know, I've never laid eyes on *la Veuve Muguette.*"

The careless humor in his voice almost brought her to her knees before him to beg his forgiveness for something she couldn't define. She covered her eyes with a hand and tried to collect her thoughts.

"I don't know what this is all about," he said lightly. "I better take a look around outside before we turn in." He put on his leather jacket and picked up a flashlight without looking at her again. He needed air. It hadn't been a close call exactly but it had given him a slight jolt. Eventually Mme. Antonin or somebody else was bound to mention seeing him near the bakery. He would get Odette to introduce him to her widow so that he could tell Helene that she had shown him her room. Keep it as open and truthful as possible. He couldn't allow his harmless fun to assume any importance between them.

It was bitterly cold outside. It seemed as if a hole had been torn in the universe. Everything was in an uproar. The wind screamed in the trees and the sea crashed against the rocks and under the beam of his flashlight the world was pitching in violent motion around him. He discovered that one of the supports of the outhouse had given way. He tried to do something to secure it but found it was hopeless in the face of the gale.

He struggled against the wind up to the garage and was relieved to find it still standing, but as he played his light on the cane roof a strip flew up into the air and slapped down on top of the car. He leaped up onto the hood and pulled himself up onto the crossbeam, tearing his hands. He managed to pull it into place across its supports and lay on it. He yelled for Helene and the act of calling for her strengthened the bond between them like an embrace. The cane roof rattled beneath him. If he wanted to save it, he would have to wait here until she grew uneasy and came to look for him.

She sat with her head propped in her hand, her eyes closed, fighting a sudden inexplicable despair. She had driven him from her. It was so senseless. When he was with her, she was happy. It was simple but it didn't include Robbie. *At times, I can't bear him.* She couldn't believe she had said it but it was true. His constant presence inhibited her. Even when she and Stuart were making love, she felt Robbie near. She was appalled that she could think of her son as a barrier to her happiness. It was enough to plunge any mother into despair. What of the satisfactions of maternity?

She lifted her head and her emergence from the protection afforded her by her closed eyes made her feel as if she were coming out of a sort of madness. She forced herself to think of Robbie's difficult birth and how she had prayed for his survival. She had made him with Stuart. He was an extension of their love. If she thought of him as an intruder at times it was an aberration she would get over. She hadn't yet adjusted to their altered life.

She pushed her hair into place with her hands and held them pressed against her cheeks, absorbed in thoughts of welcoming Stuart in a way that would make him forget everything she had said. She rose and went to a chest and pulled out an extra blanket. Aware of how cold it was in the house, she wrapped it around her and sat on the end of the bed. What had he said? He was going to look around outside. Why was he taking so long? She stood up and threw aside the blanket and went out.

It took all her strength to close the door behind her and she clung to it for a moment, hunched against the wind. She could see nothing. She called and the wind almost choked her. She called again and then pushed herself out from the shelter of the door and stumbled up the glade.

He heard her call and bellowed in reply. He fumbled for his light. He had put it on the roof beside him and couldn't find it.

"Where are you?" she called.

"Up here, on the roof," he yelled. He could see her dim shape moving in front of the garage. "Up here. Up here," he shouted with all his strength. His hand found the light at last and he switched it on quickly. She stumbled in under the shelter of the garage and peered up at the light.

"What are you doing up there?" she asked. Out of relief, she burst into laughter, hysterically at first, but as he responded, it deepened and became real.

"For God's sake, get me the hammer and some nails and that wire in the bottom of the cupboard," he blurted out between her paroxysms.

"Oh, darling, you look so funny up there." She doubled up with renewed giggles and then pulled herself together and let herself be blown back to the house, happy again and at peace with being useful to him. Together they reinforced the roof, Stuart hammering and wiring while Helene held the light, perched on the hood of the car. They returned to the house, tingling with cold but closely joined by their shared effort. They undressed hastily and plunged into bed, moving close to each other for warmth.

He took her to him with a fierce abandon generated by the fury of the wind and his need to reaffirm the transcendent bond that joined them. She knew that only he could offer her the whole sensation of love and she listened to the wind beating at the house as if it were an exultant beating in her veins.

Robbie had trouble sleeping. He heard his mother's voice raised angrily although the roar of the wind was so great that he wasn't able to hear the words. He must have dozed but he woke again and there was no sound but the sound of the storm. He was terrified by its violence. He got out of bed and tiptoed to the door and peeked out for reassurance. The lights were on but the room was empty. His parents sometimes went for a stroll before bedtime but why would they go out tonight? He closed the door and hurried back to bed.

Everything seemed to be moving in the room. He closed his eyes and hid his head under the covers. He dozed again. He awoke a second time with a prayer that his parents had returned and he rose once more and opened the door cautiously. The room was in darkness. His parents must be there. He strained his eyes against the dark and then he saw movement on the bed in the corner. He looked hard for another moment and then the movement came so clear that it brought a dreadful image to his mind. Michel and the little girl. He stared with disbelief. The world seemed to crumble and fall to pieces around him and he stumbled blindly back to bed.

It couldn't be. It mustn't be. Not his mother. The plump little girl grew monstrous in his mind and he buried his head in his pillow to shut the image out. His heart pounded and his body was rigid with horror. He would kill his father. He would run away with his mother. She would protect him from everything nasty and hateful that threatened to overpower him. A great sob burst from his chest and his tears flowed with pity for himself in the face of the terrible unknown.

The wind blew. On the second day a branch crashed into the roof and from then on there was the clatter of tiles being hurled to the ground. The wind dropped suddenly on the fourth night and by next morning rain was falling steadily. The Coslings watched with dismay as a stain spread across the fresh white ceiling. At least their fires were working again.

They went to Boldoni's for several meals while the wind was blowing and it surprised Stuart how much he begrudged even such a small expenditure. It took him several days to tidy up the place, including the installation of caps for the chimneys. They cost money, as did new tiles for the roof and materials for consolidating the outhouse. They were all a bit nervy and Stuart and Helene paid little attention to Robbie's odd sullen hostility.

Christmas was spartan. Wind followed rain in dreary succession. With the coming of the new year, the money situation looked increasingly alarming. After a hard day's work, his will weakened by exhaustion, Stuart couldn't help wondering if he'd be able to hold out against continued adversity.

The news in the paper about the deepening depression was

some consolation. These were tough times for everybody; Hoover's attempts to create prosperity by proclamation had failed. When he steadfastly reminded himself of the value in the life he was making, his independence of others, the satisfaction of making things grow, of turning the land to productivity, the healthy contact with nature he was providing Robbie, the close intertwining of his and Helene's lives away from city distractions and city nerves, he could almost convince himself that anything that made so much sense was bound to work out.

A note arrived from Sir Bennett, who was in Monte Carlo, proposing a trip to see them. Helene refused to let him come and Stuart to his surprise found that he agreed with her. After his proud self-confidence of the late summer, he didn't want Uncle Ben to see them now. The house looked battered and shabby, with its stained ceiling and smoke-streaked fireplace, and he knew that they did, too. He wrote saying that Helene and Robbie were both under the weather and suggested that they put it off till a little later.

It was like inviting the judgment of God. The letter was barely dispatched before Robbie took sick. Within twenty-four hours they realized that it was a serious illness and they bundled him into the Rolls and rushed him to Cannes. It was scarlet fever.

The hospital, which looked like a rather grand villa, the faint slap and swish of rubber-soled nurses moving through linoleum halls, the medicinal smells, the depressing paraphernalia, the whispered conferences with self-important doctors, the terrible words mastoiditis and meningitis and others Stuart didn't know, above all Robbie, turning and twisting in his bed, crying out incoherently—it all became a dull repetitious nightmare.

Through it all, Helene thought, when she could think at all: I've been selfish. I haven't given him all my attention. I've thought too much of Stuart and myself. Oh, God, let him live. Let him live and I'll never think of anybody else again. He'll be all my life. I don't ask for anything else. Let him live.

And Stuart: It's going to be all right. It's got to be all right. He's tough, he'll be all right. We'll be closer than ever. These things are hell while they're going on but there's good in it, there's something to be learned. A deeper awareness of themselves as a family. Goddammit, Robbie, my boy, you've got to get well.

When the crisis had passed, Stuart was faced with the ruin

of all his plans. "I better go back tomorrow," he told Helene as they were having lunch in a modest restaurant next to the hospital the day after they had been assured there was no further cause for alarm. "It's just an extra expense my being here."

"I suppose so," Helene said listlessly. For the first time in their life together, she believed that she didn't care what he did. A mood of self-sacrifice was strong within her. If she allowed herself a second to think of Stuart, Robbie might still be snatched from her. Let him do what he pleased. She would be free to devote herself to Robbie during the long convalescence.

"Don't worry about anything. You have enough money for the moment. I'll arrange to get more for the doctors and the hospital." How? He hadn't the slightest idea. Uncle Ben had come over from Monte Carlo and had given him a check "to help out." It barely made a dent on the medical expenses. While he could accept a present from him, his relations with Uncle Ben had never been such that he could ask him for more help. The old man would definitely not consider it good form. Of course, he could draw on his capital but even considering it felt like failure. He had accepted a challenge. He had been able to afford the place only because it had been an incredible bargain. If he went on putting money into it, it would no longer be a bargain but a folly. As of now, he needed half its purchase price just to keep afloat, without anything left over for developing the land further. He appeared to be headed for the moment when his income would go below survival level and there would be no alternative but to go back to New York and get a job. While they still could, wouldn't it be more sensible to revert to their original plan of renting or buying a small house and living reasonably comfortably without struggling with the elements? It was too soon to discuss it with Helene.

Reluctantly he drove back to St. Tropez the next day. He would have preferred to stay. He would have liked to make sure that Helene had a good rest and he wanted, too, during the difficult period of convalescence, to counterbalance her growing tendency to pamper the boy. Money finally settles everything, he thought bitterly. The admission went against the grain but the fact remained that he was no longer his own master.

There had been more wind while he was gone. He found several fallen branches around the house. His vegetable plot showed no signs of producing anything. Antonin had taken care of the animals but three pigeons had met mysterious deaths. Stuart made the rounds of the place in growing gloom and drove back into town to seek comfort with Odette. The thought of selling the place had moved into the front of his mind and he couldn't face it alone.

Odette received him, as always, as if she had been expecting him although he hadn't seen her for several weeks. His response was reserved. His mind was full of Robbie and Helene, and Odette's happy reception made him conscious by contrast of Helene's willingness to have him go. Money settles everything, he repeated to himself gloomily. Money had determined Odette's future, too. Irrationally he resented her for it. A fire burned brightly in her fireplace. She looked as if she had found a good life for herself.

"So you're in great difficulties?" she asked after he had told her of the events of the last weeks. The bare bulb hanging over the table highlighted the roguishness of her features so that for a moment he thought she was laughing at him. He took a long drink of the wine she had put before him.

"I'm thinking of getting rid of the place," he said, trying it out for sound. Get rid of a dream, get rid of all the hopes and ambitions that its purchase had brought with it.

Odette lifted a hand and thoughtfully stroked her throat. It was a gesture full of poise and his resentment was superseded by astonished awareness of the change that had taken place in her since summer. She had become a woman. The breathless giggling girl had vanished. This discovery distracted his attention from his troubles.

"That would be dreadful," she said.

"It's something I've got to consider. If all this had happened a little later it would have been different. The place would be paying its way."

"How so?" she asked with a little frown. People who owned property managed to survive every crisis; when he was wearing his clothes, he possessed the godlike quality that placed him beyond the concerns of ordinary mortals.

"It's a matter of time. I was wrong to move when we did. I should have waited till spring. With a few months of good weather I could cut our living expenses to nothing."

"Then you must hold on," she said.

"It's not so easy with a wife and child. I can't subject them to real privation, especially now."

"Don't say more. It's bad to talk about serious matters on

an empty stomach. Mme. Muguette has given me some soup. It's good. I have bread and cheese. We'll have our first meal together." She left him with a full glass in front of him and moved deftly around the room, placing a pot that was on the hearth in among the embers, bringing out bowls and spoons and the bread and cheese from behind the curtain, making cheerful comments on her limited domestic facilities. "This isn't much as a first meal. If you're going to be alone for the next few weeks, I can do better. Let me think. I could do eggs on the fire. And roast potatoes. I could even grill a fish. I must get a few more things and open a restaurant. The soup will be hot in a moment. I must get candles, if not champagne, so you can seduce me. Will you let me cook for you often even if it's not very elegant?"

"It sounds wonderful," he said, trying to respond to her generous concern for him.

She pulled the pot out of the fire and brought it to the table and filled the bowls. She was coming to a decision. She had gone over the possibilities and knew what she could do. It was something that her nature rebelled against but she could do it for him. It was *why* you did things that counted. He had taught her that. She sat with him and they took a few spoonfuls of the substantial soup.

"Mmm. It *is* good," he said.

"Yes. Now we can talk seriously." She looked at him, her mind made up. "I can get you money. I can start by paying back all you've given me."

He wasn't surprised by the offer. It came naturally from this new assured Odette. "It's very good of you, but there's never been any question of paying back. Besides, it would only help out for a few weeks."

"I can get enough," she repeated firmly. Having said it, she was triumphant at finding their roles so unexpectedly reversed. It filled her with hope that this was the opportunity she had dreamed of. Perhaps he would be all hers. Being able to help him made anything seem possible.

"How?" he demanded.

"That's of no importance," she said quickly. "In another month or so the weather will be good. If what you say is true, it's only a matter of a few months. I can manage it."

"It's good of you but there's no point talking about it. I won't consider it." He couldn't tell her how much he needed. Fifteen hundred dollars would seem a fortune to her. He hated to nip her generous impulse in the bud by mentioning the figure.

She lifted a hand palm out, emphatically. "You can't stop me," she said. "It would be wicked for you to refuse to take the money if I go to the trouble to get it. You've said yourself that people aren't realistic about money."

He hesitated a moment, looking into her eyes. He was not only touched by her but impressed. Looking back at the summer evening when he had first met her, remembering the hesitation with which he had proposed the weekly allowance, he realized that accepting money from her wouldn't represent failure. This wasn't the rich man's standard expedient of falling back on capital but an opportunity to benefit gratefully from an evolution of circumstances that he had had a part in creating. "Before I tell you how much, how do you intend to get it?" he asked again.

"I've never asked where you get *your* money."

Fair enough, he thought, suppressing a smile. She would never have thought of such a reply six months ago. He held out his hand and she looked at it for a moment before she very deliberately put hers on top of it. It was like sealing an agreement; they had become partners as she had always wanted them to be.

"It's really not the same. I'm talking about quite a lot of money," he pointed out. False pride wasn't involved but he had to be sure it would involve no sacrifice on her part. He named an approximate equivalent in francs. Her eyes widened, but only briefly. She seemed undaunted. "You see? There shouldn't be any secrets about this," he added.

Her satisfaction at entrenching herself in his life enabled her to lie convincingly. "I've told you. I know people here now. Mme. Muguette has told me she'd lend me money if I need it. She's rich." He gripped her hand and looked into her eyes.

"There's no point my trying to tell you what I'm thinking," he said. "You must know. You're wonderful."

She pulled her hand away, forcing back sudden tears. "Don't let the soup get cold," she exclaimed, making an effort to keep her voice steady. A few spoonfuls restored her equilibrium. She improvised to divert any questions Stuart might have and almost began to believe herself. Mme. Muguette had come to regard her as a daughter. She wanted Odette to take care of her in her old age and would do anything to keep her here. As a final persuasive touch, she admitted that the old lady would have to be paid back but there would be no hurry about it.

Could he repay the money within a reasonable length of time? It was the only question that made Stuart hesitate but, as Odette pointed out, he could always sell the place later if worse came to worst. He had no intention of selling now or ever. He would make it pay. This reprieve was all he needed.

He was seized by a voracious appetite. He polished off the soup and the bread and the cheese, a robust Cantal, and drained the wine. They were soon in bed playing their favorite games. He slept more soundly than he had since Robbie had taken sick but was away at daybreak so as not to be observed by the neighborhood.

He had been reprieved and he didn't take it lightly; the crises of the past weeks added a down-to-earth note to his thoughts of the future. If he wasn't going to be knocked off his feet every time life dealt him a blow he must learn in the next few months what the local farmers had absorbed in a lifetime, work methodically and without sparing himself until he was sure the land could support him. No more romantic notions of a carefree Robinson Crusoe existence.

He was stimulated by the prospect. He felt as if he had already learned a lot. The struggle awaiting him was a clean one, between himself and the land and nature, not with people. That was what mattered. He had stumbled on one of the few corners left in the world where people could afford to be kind, where human warmth overbalanced human calculation, where competition was limited to a game or a girl, since there was nothing else to compete for.

He was glad that Robbie's convalescence would keep his family in Cannes for the next few weeks. By the time they came back the weather would have moderated and he would have things under control.

He spent many evenings with Odette. She produced the money within four days so that as a topic of discussion it quickly faded into the background. She was impressed by the magnitude of the sum she briefly had in her possession and she was affronted when he seemed to take it so for granted. Of course, he couldn't know what such an amount might mean in terms of humiliation.

She was very happy practically living with him but she soon sensed that nothing had really changed. Though always playful and loving, he still eluded her in his dedication to his land and preoccupation with thoughts of his family. She couldn't even count on his coming in the evening. Several times he didn't, always with a reasonable excuse the next day.

Her conviction that the money would guarantee a growth in their intimacy was so strong that she tried to ignore her disappointment. Still, in the back of her mind lingered a suspicion that she hadn't taken full advantage of the opportunity chance had provided. Perhaps if he had signed something . . .

As the almonds were bursting into bloom, casting a pale pink haze over the land, Helene brought Robbie home and Odette's evenings with Stuart ended. When she found herself once more eating lonely suppers in her bare room, his failure to make the most of his brief freedom became intolerable in retrospect. Did he think she'd picked the money up in the streets? No matter how much she loved him, she wasn't going to be made a fool of. There was always the chance that he might have trouble paying the money back when the time came . . .

Changes in the Coslings' life were imposed by Robbie's convalescence. There was no question for the time being of his doing any of the chores he had done earlier. Since he couldn't be left alone, it meant that Helene, too, ceased to help Stuart in important ways. They became the companions of his leisure. As the brief spring passed and summer moved in and Robbie was bronzed by the sun and regained his strength, this way of life somehow became firmly established.

Robbie was aware that he was being treated as if he had been changed in some way by his illness. He didn't think he had been particularly—in fact, he would have forgotten about it once he was up and about again except for his new status. He liked being pampered and petted by his mother. He liked having his whims indulged. He liked having his tenth birthday turned into a much greater occasion than his previous birthdays had ever been, like a delayed Christmas. Even his father took some time off to celebrate it; usually, he could think of nothing but the new vines he had planted or how well the tomatoes were doing. Robbie couldn't see anything special about things growing; the countryside was full of vineyards and the market full of tomatoes. Looking back, he realized that he hadn't really liked the things his father expected him to enjoy—fishing from the cold uncomfortable little boat, the long tiring tramps looking for a bird to shoot, struggling with the clumsy bucket in the well while his father tried to teach him the proper technique for bringing up water. He was acquiring skill with watercolors and loved to paint. His mother made schoolwork interesting, except for mathematics, which she had no more feel for than he did. They made a joke of it as they struggled dutifully through long division. They tended the animals who had finally settled down to do what they were supposed to do, multiply and provide eggs. They planted flowers around the house according to Robbie's design and were soon enjoying their fragrant blossoms. They played together on the beach.

Helene found the compensations of motherhood more than she had dared hope they would be. Robbie was a delight. He never made her feel insecure. She didn't have to wonder if he would leave her or get carried away by unexpected caprices. He freed her from the rack of passion. She had feared that living once more with Stuart would shake her determination to devote herself to her child, but Stuart's consuming efforts on behalf of the place reduced contact between them to a minimum. He was asleep almost before he stretched out in bed and at dawn he was up and out again.

Stuart remarked the change in her appearance. She was letting her hair grow back and she didn't bother now to arrange it modishly. She had stopped lacquering her nails and rarely used any makeup. The only additions to her wardrobe were a couple of printed cotton dresses of the sort worn by the local women. She lost the slightly flapperish look that had suited her so little and became timeless and more feminine. She consciously neglected herself and regarded it as an atonement for the self-absorption that she mystically linked with Robbie's nearly fatal illness.

The result was to make her more attractive to Stuart. She didn't need makeup and stylish clothes. Her fine features and coloring, her generous, finely modeled body made of her a civilized sort of earth goddess. To Stuart, it was a further indication of how completely she had accepted their new life. He had so organized his time before her return that he had had qualms about how she would be affected by his new routine. Would she get bored with the task he had set himself? Would she feel he was neglecting her?

At first he thought he detected a certain sharpness in her replies when he apologized for having to devote the day to this or that chore, but he soon realized that she had made a happy adjustment to necessity. The nervous intensity that had provoked the small crises in the past seemed to have vanished. She was more tranquil than Stuart had ever known her. She seemed happy with Robbie's companionship and apparently enjoyed whatever work there was for her to do, the cooking and preserving and taking care of the animals and flowers, with which Robbie helped her. Stuart felt no hesitation, therefore, in offering his services to Antonin for the grape harvest at the end of the summer although it meant being away all day while it was going on. Antonin had spent two days helping him gather his modest crop.

Antonin had a real working vineyard and Stuart loved the work, imagining how satisfying it would be when he was the master of such bounty. The men and women and children joked and called out festively as they worked their way through the rows of vines. It was good to handle the grapes, which were beautiful to look at and sweet and cool and sunny in the mouth. It was fine to be accepted by Antonin and his relatives as a friend, an established member of the community. Stuart enjoyed himself even though it added to his heavy schedule of work.

He shared vast boisterous midday meals with the grape-pickers for the ten days the *vendage* lasted and Helene was delighted to have Robbie even more to herself. They had the last of the tomatoes to put up. She watched him proudly as he carried a basket of the fruit around to the front of the house where she was installed with basins of water preparatory to washing them.

"This work isn't too hard for me?" he asked, as he set the basket down in front of her.

"Good heavens, no, darling." She smoothed his dark hair lovingly. "You're as strong as an ox."

"But you said I wasn't strong enough to help with the grapes."

"That's different," she said easily. "That's all day long in the hot sun, bending and lifting. Besides, you wouldn't want to leave me here all alone, would you?"

"Of course not." Actually, the grape harvest sounded sort of fun with lots to eat and other children to play with, but he knew she thought he was above that sort of thing. "I like being with you."

"I'm afraid you won't always think that," she said with a smile.

"Of course I will, always." He stood before her sturdily and spoke with passionate conviction. She wiped her hands on her apron and reached out and drew him close.

"Is that a promise?" she murmured, kissing his ear. She felt soft and comfortable and he liked the way she smelled. He let himself be caressed and was sorry when she let him go. "Will you look after me when I'm an old lady?" she said, running her finger over his cheek.

"You're never going to be old." He stood close to her with his hand on her shoulder. "Why does Daddy help with the grapes when he says he never has enough time to do everything here?"

It would have been easy to explain that Stuart felt heavily indebted to Antonin and was glad of the opportunity to repay him, but instead she said, "Stuart likes a lot of things we don't like. He likes to work with Antonin in the vines."

"I suppose so," he said. "I think he even enjoys chopping wood." It wasn't the first time that she had made him feel the gulf that separated them from his father and this awareness was translated into a unconscious explanation for certain things he didn't dare think of. The long-ago windy night before his illness had faded into a dim, carefully repressed nightmare. It simply seemed right that his mother should be engaged in a constant struggle to protect herself and him from Stuart and he gave free rein to his growing instinct to ally himself always closer with her.

"Everybody has different tastes," Helene went on. "You mustn't feel you have to like everything Daddy does. And there's no question of your chopping wood for a long time yet. Of course, we all have to do our share of chores but we don't all have to enjoy the same things."

They had many such moments together but Helene took care that he was always obedient and courteous to his father and she went out of her way to praise him to Stuart for the help he gave her around the house.

As Stuart had expected, the long summer months were a period of easy economy and when he sold his crop of grapes he was able to pay back half of his debt to Odette. The property had actually brought in some money—not much, but the psychological boost was enormous. With the coming of winter, he could see no risk in reducing his income slightly to embark on the second phase of his program, a major expansion of his vineyard. This involved a capital investment and when he wrote to Sir Bennett to explain his needs, he asked for enough extra to pay off Odette entirely.

Well under a year after he had borrowed it, he went one morning to take her the final payment.

"What do you expect me to do with it?" she demanded. As long as he owed her money, she had been able to go on hoping that maybe one day something would happen, something would change. Now she was filled with dismay at the thought that her chance was passing. She didn't even look at the money but left it on the table where he had put it and went on with her ironing.

"What do you mean, what'll you do with it? You'll give it back to the Widow Muguette, won't you?"

"Yes, of course," she said. She slapped the iron back onto its cradle and carried the finished linen over to her bed. She was indignant. She knew his time wasn't his own but his returning the money in the middle of the day underlined the fact that this wasn't to be an intimate occasion. The last time they had been to bed together was that late-summer afternoon when he had come into town to collect the first money he had earned from his grapes. He had been eager enough to celebrate with her then. Was he planning to dispose of her as easily as he was disposing of his debt? She wished she could think of some way to show him that she was to be taken seriously.

"You've saved my life, you know," he said in the tender way that completely unmanned her defenses. "I wish I could afford to give you something that's good enough for you. Is there anything you want?"

She straightened and turned to him and looked at him levelly. "You know what that is."

He smiled affectionately and went to her and took her hands. "I know I haven't been much of a lover recently. Do you realize it's been more than a year since the first time? That means we can count on each other. You know how tied up I am."

"Oh, I understand," she said, trying to hold out against him but unable to keep a tremor out of her voice. "Now that we've repaid each other, we have no more obligations. Is that what you mean "

"No more obligations about money. That's good, isn't it?" She obviously didn't think it was good. He knew he could dispel the odd reproach he felt in her by making love to her but he resisted the impulse. Calculation implied responsibility. He had carefully avoided that sort of tie with her. He added gently, "The important obligations don't change—obligations to the love and generosity and support you've given me. I'll never forget all that."

"I'll be interested to see how it affects your actions."

He heard the bitterness in her voice and immediately made allowances for it. She apparently saw the settlement of the debt as some sort of ending. He didn't see why it should be. "I'll be along as usual, next time I'm in town," he said. He lifted her chin and kissed her lightly on the lips and went. She remained motionless for a moment, tears swimming in her eyes. She shook her head angrily and returned to her ironing.

The winter was mild and by spring Stuart had fifteen acres planted in vines. The new ones wouldn't bear for several years but it was a big step toward making the place self-supporting. Multiply that acreage by five and he would be a prosperous viniculturist. He found time in the midst of his daily labors to make some improvements in line with his original conception of the place as a sort of semi-tropical paradise. He built an outdoor stove of fieldstone so that cooking would be pleasant for Helene during the summer and a palm-frond shelter down in the cove where they could camp out on hot nights.

Their first visitor from the world they'd left behind turned up that summer. Stanley Hilliard wrote that he expected to be driving through their part of the country and asked directions for finding them. Hilliard was no longer the unknown writer whom Stuart had nursed through his first book, but a successful novelist who was turning out things for the magazines as fast as they could print them. Thinking about his arrival, Stuart was very conscious of his own small success with the land. If Stanley had announced himself a year ago, he would've wanted to hide. Now he was ready to show off a bit. Stuart replied, welcoming him, and heard nothing more.

Stanley arrived without further warning in a flashy car on a summer evening when the Coslings were just sitting down to eat out of doors. The headlights of the car picked them out through the olive trees and Stuart advanced toward them, shielding his eyes.

"Yes? What is it?" he demanded as he neared the car. "My God! It's you, Stanley. You've found us."

Hilliard had had a good deal to drink. Helene cooked a few more eggs and he stayed for supper. He had been one of Stuart's editorial discoveries but he hadn't seen him since his success. It sat oddly on him. He had been a serious youth, and drunken attempts at cleverness seemed to suit him as little as his expensive sports clothes. It turned out that he had left a girl at Boldoni's to wait for him but seemed disinclined to hurry back to her. He wanted to talk about Franklin Roosevelt, whose presidential campaign he was going to join in the fall. Socialism was going to save the country. Stuart had met Roosevelt a few times and thought him an unlikely socialist. He talked about the local winegrowers' cooperatives, which were a form of socialism. Hilliard dismissed winegrowing as irrelevant to an industrial society. The disjointed discussion ended with his staying the night. Stuart and Helene led him down over the rocks to the shack on the beach.

"God, I feel like Gauguin or Willie Maugham or whoever it was," he declared as they left him perched on the edge of a bunk.

The next morning he wanted a drink with his coffee but Stuart had nothing but wine to offer and persuaded him to make a brief tour of the place instead. Having experienced the primitive sanitary arrangements and looked at the vegetables and the vines, the pigeons and the rabbits and the chickens, Hilliard collapsed in the shade of a tree.

"It's very pretty but, Jesus, you're nothing but a dirt farmer," he protested as Stuart squatted beside him.

"That's about the size of it," Stuart agreed with a chuckle. They were sitting on the edge of the area under cultivation, in back of the long beach and out of sight of the house.

"I thought you were coming over here to lead the good life."

"This is it." Stuart made a slight gesture around him.

"Do you travel? Do you get to Paris much?"

"Lord, no, I have to be here to make this place pay."

"And to think I've been envying you all this time. You're nothing but a slave."

"I'm my own master, I'm as free as air," Stuart said.

"Nonsense. You're stuck with your goddam vegetable plot, just like me. I've got to turn out three more fairy tales between now and the end of September if I want to keep up my insurance and pay the rent. Not to mention dear old Mother and the ancestral hut."

"Why do you do it? Why don't you take all the money you've made and write what you want to write?"

"And live on spinach? That *is* spinach I see before me, isn't it? No, thanks. We're all goddam slaves one way or another. That being the case, I shall slave in the greatest comfort I can possibly buy."

Stuart plucked at a clump of thyme and crumpled a sprig under his nose. He loved this land. He loved the vines spreading their tendrils across the field. This was his. He was creating it. Hilliard was such a cliché of success gone wrong that he was almost embarrassed to feel so much better off than he.

"People want different things. This is what I want," Stuart said, standing up. They started toward the house.

"I really must get back and see what's become of Peaches," Hilliard said.

"Good God, is your girl friend called Peaches?"

"I doubt it. She's French. I call her Peaches."

"I shouldn't think you'd be much in favor this morning."

"I'm afraid not. However, she likes the car so she'll probably forgive me." They talked a bit about his plans and Helene came up from the beach where she'd been with Robbie and together they saw him off.

"I'm glad he came," she said, "even if he was drunk most of the time. We mustn't let ourselves get too out of touch."

"If only to remind ourselves how good it is here? Old Stanley isn't going to be in touch much longer if he doesn't cut down on the booze. I want to get in touch with the sea." He took her hand in his. She let him hold it until they came within sight of Robbie lying on the sand below when she made an excuse of adjusting a sandal to free herself. . . .

Two more years flew by, vanished into the smooth stream of their well regulated lives. It was with a sense of wonder at where the time had gone that they found themselves celebrating Robbie's thirteenth birthday and a few months afterward the fourth anniversary of their purchase of the place. They had a son in his teens. Another five years would see him fully grown.

If these years had been uneventful for the Coslings, they hadn't been for all the inhabitants of St. Tropez. Because the Coslings went into the village only for shopping and never in the evening, it meant little to them that the Café de la Mer had changed hands and been transformed into a smart bar. When they heard that Boldoni's had been discovered by the fashionable world and that he had extended his Saturday night festivities into the whole week, that Mistinguett appeared there frequently surrounded by a bevy of boys and performed when the spirit seized her, they congratulated themselves that it hadn't been like that in their day.

Stuart got used to shopkeepers greeting him on his trips into town with, "Did you see Chevalier? He was here yesterday." Or: "You should have seen the Prince of Wales.

He was so drunk he had to be carried back to his yacht. He was with an American lady."

They heard that people had started buying up abandoned houses in the town and remodeling them, with plumbing and roof gardens, but it was slow to affect the appearance of the place.

It was the summer following Robbie's thirteenth birthday that forced Stuart's attention on the changes. He was struck by the bustle he encountered everywhere, the cars and people coming and going, scaffolding being erected on housefronts, trucks making deliveries in front of shops and cafés, yachts gliding into the harbor. More than once a shopkeeper murmured to him, "For you, monsieur, the price is still so-and-so." Two events pinpointed the shape of things to come. The first he learned about one day when he dropped in for a drink with Boldoni.

"Here's to you and here's to the end of Boldoni's," the big man said solemnly, lifting his glass. It was midafternoon and they sat alone under the trellis at one of the long scarred tables.

"I won't drink to that," Stuart said with a smile.

"You might as well, for Boldoni's is finished. I've decided to sell. What do you expect? These people don't want to eat. They want to drink and dance on empty stomachs. They behave like pigs. When people are well fed they are happy and cheerful, if sometimes a bit rough."

Boldoni's eyes wandered to the legend painted on the wall. In his mind, Stuart saw the tables crowded with laughing, shouting fishermen and their women, the soft air washed by moonlight, and he heard the gay tinkle of the mechanical piano. He found Boldoni's news unaccountably saddening. Was money taking charge even here? Thank God, it couldn't touch him. He was protected by his vast domain. He sighed and finished his drink and told Boldoni how sorry he was.

During an equally casual encounter with Odette, she told him she was going to get married to a man called Etienne Dunan, the proprietor of one of the new cafés on the port, La Bouillabaisse. Their desultory affair had trailed off some time earlier, not because of the canceled debt, which he would have hated, but because she was beginning to meet men who could offer her a future. He withdrew discreetly. Now, he bombarded her with the intimate questions the past gave him the right to ask. She looked proud and flustered and Stuart was glad that her life was taking such a satisfactory turn, for

Dunan was apparently a brilliant catch, young and on the way up. She deserved it. It made what was happening to the town less deplorable. Such good fortune could never have befallen her a few years back.

He and Helene went to the wedding. Etienne Dunan turned out to be a muscular young man with ordinary good looks but a controlled vitality that somehow suggested danger. Stuart felt that he wouldn't be a pleasant man to cross.

He thought a lot that summer about Robbie's schooling. It wasn't Robbie's education Stuart was concerned about, but his complete lack of contact with other children. If he had had any brothers or sisters the problem would have been less acute. Stuart couldn't help indulging in fancies about that other child, though he knew they were absurd. Reason told him that if he had really left Marguerite pregnant a speedy marriage would have been arranged and the child placed beyond any claims he might have made. He didn't take his imaginings seriously but he couldn't suppress them altogether when he thought about Robbie's solitude.

He wasn't displeased with the way the boy was turning out but thirteen was a difficult age and it was time for the toughening process that could come only from being thrown with his contemporaries. He had heard that the French-English school at Cannes was excellent but also expensive. He now had over forty acres of vines under cultivation and in a couple of years there would be no problem, but that was too long to wait. He decided that if that autumn's vintage turned out well he would enter the boy after Christmas, for the second term. The conspiracy was about to unfold, however, that was drastically to affect this decision and a number of others for several years to come.

His first intimation of it came from Antonin one sunny autumn afternoon. They had been hunting together, though it had turned out more like a stroll since they had shot only a few small birds.

"Have you heard they've found an heir to the Ladouceur place?" Antonin asked. The question was posed too casually for it not to seem significant.

"Is that so?" Stuart asked. "The place's been abandoned for twenty years or so, hasn't it?"

"Since the war. Fifi Ladouceur was killed and the widow died giving birth to their first child. The child was born dead."

"And now an heir has turned up?"

"A cousin, I think. For a long time there was a dispute between the Giraudons and the Ladouceurs about part of your property."

Stuart thought of Maître Barbetin's warnings and he felt resistance stiffening in him. "The Ladouceurs have no claim whatsoever. I went into it thoroughly. That is, Maître Barbetin did."

"So much the better, if you're satisfied," Antonin said. They emerged from the wood at the side of Stuart's vineyard. Antonin stopped and gestured. "Here's the place." He might have planned the conversation to coincide with their arrival at this spot.

"Yes, I know," Stuart said. "Something to do with the beach there and the strip that goes up by the onions."

"You can't see it so well since you've been planting more vines." The farmer moved forward, pointing out imaginary boundaries. "The Giraudons never had vines between here and the ridge there. Here. You can see. From the beach across to here and then on all the way over to that clump of cypresses—the far ones in line with the lighthouse. It cut the Giraudon place in half. At one time, the Ladouceurs tried to stop the Giraudons from crossing it to go from one part of their property to the other. Of course they couldn't. It's a nuisance, though, the way land is divided up sometimes."

"How many times must I tell you?" Stuart insisted. "There's nothing whatever to support any claim of the Ladouceurs."

"Yes, of course, that's what you believe." If Stuart hadn't such confidence in his neighbor, he would have suspected in his tone a trace of satisfaction at the prospect of trouble. But could this new Ladouceur heir make trouble? Of course not. Anybody who had waited twenty years to claim an inheritance wouldn't involve himself in an ancient undocumented feud.

At lunch, Helene noticed a break in Stuart's usual good temper. He seemed preoccupied and spoke sharply to Robbie several times. He had made a mental note to drop in on Maître Barbetin one day soon, just to reassure himself. Not that there was the faintest possibility . . . The next time he went to town, he stayed away from the notary's office. Inquiries seemed like an admission of some uncertainty about his position.

A few days later, he received a note from Odette. He read

it with his other mail at lunchtime and put it down where Helene could see it. "Funny," he said. "There's a note from Odette asking me to come see her."

Helene was working around the stove and paused to peer over his shoulder at the letter. "From Odette? How grand she's becoming. Could she be having trouble with her husband already?"

"I wonder. I better go in this afternoon. She says it's important."

He found Odette installed behind the cash desk of her empty bar, knitting. She greeted him cheerfully but her old spontaneity was smoothed over with professional cordiality. The way she rolled up her knitting, let herself down from her tall chair, and set about putting glasses and a bottle on a tray struck him as well ordered, possessive, every gesture somehow suggesting the careful handling of small sums of money.

"You got my letter? It's nice of you to come so quickly. I perhaps should have suggested coming to you but it's difficult without a car. Etienne hopes to get one next year." As she carried the tray down around the end of the bar, Stuart thought he detected the slight broadening of her body that he had expected. The decor was nautical and he had to stoop under a fishnet to join her.

"It's warmer back here away from the door," she said as she started to pour them drinks. Stuart took the chair opposite her and tried to fix her in his mind as the simple girl he had been so fond of.

"How is everything?" he asked with a smile.

"Oh, everything's wonderful. The season was a bigger success than ever." Her old manner suddenly shone through.

"I'm glad for you," he said. "You deserve it."

"*Tu es gentil, chéri.*" She blushed and clapped her hand to her mouth and giggled. "Oh, dear. I must remember not to call you that. I don't think Etienne would like it."

Stuart laughed at her slip and began to feel more at home. "Tell me all about it," he said. "Do you know this is the first time you've ever asked to see me?"

"I know, but this is important." She hesitated an instant and then went on, "I suppose you've heard about the Ladouceur place?" A pang of alarm made Stuart shift in his chair.

"The Ladouceur place? What about it?"

"We've heard they're going to try to get back part of the Giraudon place that belongs to them." She paused to let this

84

sink in and then with the pleasure of revealing an unsuspected silver lining, "Of course, I've told Etienne all about your place. I remembered there was this question about the Ladouceur claim when you bought. Well, Etienne has some friends who will buy the disputed area from you. Think of the money you'd make. If they go to court, it might drag on for years."

"Cheerful prospect," Stuart said. Well, he couldn't say Maître Barbetin hadn't warned him. But four years ago it had seemed to make so little difference whether there were a hundred acres more or less. Now it was his living, and four years of hope and effort. What if the land were worth millions? He didn't want money. "What do these friends of yours want with it anyway?" he asked.

"They want to build a luxury hotel on the beach, for one thing," Odette said, "and villas. The thing that's holding St. Tropez back as a resort is the lack of good beaches and land for building. Everything belongs to farmers who are too stupid to take advantage of their opportunities."

"I'm afraid I'm with the stupid farmers. St. Tropez has changed enough as it is." That settled it. He must see the notary immediately. It distressed him to hear Odette talking like a real-estate developer.

"But think of the progress that's been made," she said. "Everybody benefits. Do you remember what it was like when we first came here? There wasn't a shop where you could buy anything less than ten years old."

And you didn't have any money to buy anything anyway, he thought. And it was fun. "Yes, well, I'm very happy for everybody," he said wearily. "And it's nice of you and Etienne to think of me. But I'm just not interested in selling. Let the Ladouceurs do what they will."

"You're making a mistake," she said with sudden sharpness. He didn't like her tone as she went on, "I think you will change your mind. But don't wait too long. These friends of Etienne are naturally anxious to act as quickly as possible."

"Naturally," he agreed sardonically. And then because it seemed wrong to hold her responsible for some scheme cooked up by her husband, and because he didn't want misunderstanding to cloud the real gratitude he felt toward her, he put his hand on the table so that the tips of his fingers just touched her arm. "Don't get mixed up in this," he said, "and don't *you* change too much."

Her eyes softened for a moment and then she looked down

hastily. His fingers exerted a slight caressing pressure on her arm and her body tightened as if she were making an effort to control herself. You've learned your lesson, she was telling herself. It was all over but she could still teach him that she counted for something.

"You don't understand," she said in a strained voice. She seemed on the verge of saying more but managed only, "I'm trying to—" She broke off.

"Sure," he said. He gave her arm a final little caress and withdrew his hand. She watched it close around his glass. "Don't let's think about it any more. Here's to you. I must go. I'm a workingman."

He stopped after he had passed through the cluster of tables in the deserted playground of the port and looked around him, sorting out his thoughts. The clear October air was fresh off the sea. Hard blue wavelets slapped smartly against the hulls of three yachts with stripped spars laid up for the winter. Stuart looked vacantly at the empty tables set out on both sides of him. L'Ancre, La Tante Claude, La Bouillabaisse. Brightly painted signs proclaimed their identity. A pile of building bricks and a cement-mixing machine lay in front of an arched doorway.

Another café in preparation? The more the merrier. And hotels and villas until you wouldn't be able to tell the place from Monte Carlo. That was what Etienne and his friends were after. Well, so much the worse for St. Tropez. Stuart was dependent on the town for marketing but otherwise his life was tied to the land, which didn't change. He would see that it didn't change.

What was Etienne up to? Why handle it through Odette? He pulled his sweater down over his trousers and started off toward Maître Barbetin's office.

He reached it by instinct, like a horse going home, so it was rather a shock after he had entered the door to be confronted by a young woman behind a modern desk in an unrecognizably redecorated anteroom. For a second he thought he must have made a mistake and was on the point of leaving when he recognized the chandelier hanging over the young woman's head.

"Maître Barbetin?" Stuart said to the girl, who was looking up at him questioningly. At this, her mouth dropped open and she took a quick breath.

"But, monsieur, you don't know? Maître Barbetin is dead."

"Oh?" Stuart tried to remember when he had last encountered the notary. It might have been a year ago. "Is there a notary here who has taken his place?"

"Mais bien sûr, monsieur. Maître Payrout."

"Are Maître Barbetin's dossiers now in the hands of Maître Payrout?"

"Of course. Maître Payrout has taken over the succession of Maître Barbetin."

"Good," Stuart said. "Then I'll see Maître Payrout."

"Do you have an appointment, monsieur?"

"But, mademoiselle, how could I have an appointment?"

"Oh yes. Of course," the young woman agreed imperturbably. "Who shall I say?"

Stuart gave his name and she left him. He sat on a hard little modern chair and picked at the calluses on his palm. In a moment she returned and held open the door.

Stuart entered a freshly painted room filled with new filing cabinets and conventional office furniture. All of Maître Barbetin's dusty clutter had been swept away. A slim man of more than medium height stood behind the desk with his back turned to Stuart, looking through the drawer of a file.

"Bonjour, Monsieur le Maître," Stuart said with an affable smile. The notary turned and looked at him coolly and gestured to a chair. He watched while Stuart seated himself and then turned back to his files. Stuart's smile vanished. He felt suddenly big and awkward. He crossed his legs and saw the frayed cuff of his trousers and put down his feet squarely in front of him so that they would be hidden by the desk. Never before in his dealings with the people here had he been conscious of his clothes. Maître Payrout turned with a familiar folder in his hand and sat at his desk.

"What was it you wished to see me about?" he asked, resting his cheek against his hand with languid superiority. Stuart remained silent. I'll be damned if I'll be turned on and off like a spigot, he thought. I'll speak when you're ready to look at me. Maître Payrout lifted dark cool eyes toward him.

"I expected to find Maître Barbetin," Stuart said. "It has to do with the boundary between my place and the Ladouceur place."

"The Plain of the Saracens." The notary opened the folder. "The area lying between the sea and the Ladouceur place is known locally as the Plain of the Saracens. In the act of sale Maître Barbetin drew up for you he attributed it to the Giraudon holdings."

"That's right. It's part of the land I bought."

"Ah, about that I know nothing. I'm handling the affairs of M. Ladouceur also. In such cases a notary is not in a position to judge. The documents are here. It is for a court to interpret them."

"But who has taken over the Ladouceur place? Why was no claim made for twenty years?"

"M. René Ladouceur. Another branch of the family. He comes from a town about thirty kilometers from here. When M. Dunan came to me—"

"M. Dunan?"

"Yes, M. Etienne Dunan. When M. Dunan came to me about buying property, he was particularly interested in the Ladouceur place. I traced the succession to M. René Ladouceur. He had known of it, but as often happens when land has no value, he didn't want to pay the inheritance tax. Now, of course, everything has value here and he has taken possession. He has signed an agreement with M. Dunan. They intend to press the claim to the Plain of the Saracens."

Stuart looked at his dusty shoes. *I've told Etienne all about your place*, Odette had said. All about the fact that he controlled access to the beaches they were so eager to get their hands on? "On what would they base their action?" Stuart asked numbly.

"In the will of the Widow Ladouceur, Lucienne, dated 1884, there is specific mention of the Plain of the Saracens. That of course proves nothing. I could leave you the Eiffel Tower if it amused me. At the same time, in numerous acts of succession of the Giraudon property, including one dated 1896, boundaries are established which also include the Plain of the Saracens. I haven't the slightest idea what the explanation is."

Stuart squared his shoulders. "Well, it all sounds pretty vague. I think I'll just wait and see what happens." His manner was deliberately breezy. He hoped to draw some reaction from the notary that would clarify the situation. Maître Payrout stroked his nose with the tip of one finger.

"As I say, it's not for me to judge. However, you might be well advised to reach some compromise with M. Ladouceur."

"That's the one thing I'm not going to do." Stuart rose.

"I'm at your service, of course, if there's anything I can do," Maître Payrout said impassively. He got up with a compressed economy of movement and conducted Stuart to the door. Stuart found himself regretting the absence of old

Maître Barbetin. At least he would have known where he stood with him.

Documents. Proof. The ill-concealed maneuvers of Etienne Dunan. It didn't add up. If there were documents why should Dunan offer to buy? If there weren't any documents what did he hope to accomplish through Odette? Surely nothing would come of it.

Stuart couldn't shake off a sense of foreboding. He needed home, he needed his family. He drove the big car as fast as he dared on the narrow road. When he reached the house he didn't linger outside to do any of the things he might ordinarily have done, but went straight in. Robbie looked up from the sofabed where he was curled up reading as Stuart entered. He waved a greeting to the boy and crossed the room to the sink beside the stove where Helene was peeling chestnuts. He put his hands on her waist.

"It's good to be home," he said. Helene looked up at him with a smile.

"What was it all about?" she asked.

"I'll tell you but first I want a kiss." He was tired and a little frightened from the afternoon and he needed reassurance. Over his shoulder, Helene saw Robbie lift his head slowly from his book and regard them with wide dark eyes. She twisted her body away from Stuart and picked up another chestnut.

"Don't be silly, darling. Tell me what Odette wanted." The force with which she had torn herself from him was like a slap in the face and for an instant he was stunned. He touched her lightly on the shoulder and withdrew to a chair beside the table and started to tell her about the afternoon. There were times when Robbie's constant presence got on his nerves. In his present mood it would have been a comfort to make love to her. Always having to wait until the day was done and he was sleepy and Robbie had been sent to bed, it was no wonder their physical relationship should have been so drastically curtailed. It's school for you, my boy, he thought as he reported his conversation with the notary.

Her mind fixed on all the unfamiliar talk of the money Stuart might make. Money to send Robbie away? Money to restore Stuart's leisure? No, things were better as they were. She refused to acknowledge the constant effort she was obliged to make to resist him, to sublimate her passion in her devotion to Robbie, but she sensed danger in anything that might ease the burden of his work. She warmly endorsed his stand against the threatened invasion. It was all he wanted to hear from her. So long as they were in accord they would win in the end.

He talked himself into believing that he would hear no more about it, that Odette's offer had been made in good faith, but he couldn't recover his peace of mind. It was almost a relief when a second note arrived from her asking to see him.

His own nerves were partly responsible for the conversation getting off to an unpleasant start. The setting was the same; they were alone again in the bar. This time, she didn't prepare a tray of drinks but came out from behind the bar and locked the door.

"You won't get anywhere by taking me prisoner," he said with a playful smile.

"I don't want to be interrupted," she said without looking at him.

"Listen," he said, "I haven't much time. I suppose it's more about Ladouceur?"

"Yes, I—"

"In that case, I have even less time. It seems to me that Etienne is playing a dirty game."

"He's offered to buy your land at a fair price," she said. "There's nothing dirty about that. If you refuse to sell, why shouldn't he be interested in how M. Ladouceur's claim turns out? What's wrong in that?"

"I should think our friendship would mean enough so that you'd persuade him to keep out of it."

"Our friendship!" Odette cried. That was all it had meant to him. She had expected very little, only some small recognition of a girl's blind love, but he had always remained aloof, playing with her. If he had shared only one defenseless moment with her, she would be defeated now. "Our friendship?" she repeated. "I have a husband. How dare you think I would consider you before him? I will do everything for him that I would once have done for you."

Stuart's own anger was checked as he realized how much it must be costing her to be caught between two loyalties. "Yes, I understand," he said placatingly, "but what do you want of me now? I would never ask you to betray somebody you care for."

"You wouldn't? But you would take money and not be too concerned about where it came from."

"What's that supposed to mean?"

"It means just that—the Widow Muguette!" She laughed harshly. "A child wouldn't have believed such a story. Where do you think I got that money? I got it from a married man who made the mistake of writing me letters. I'm ready to do as much for Etienne. I warn you you'll be sorry if you refuse his offer."

So that was it. Stuart shook his head. "Is it possible you mean what I think you mean?" he asked quietly. "Is it blackmail you're suggesting?"

"I don't care what you call it."

"But I didn't make the mistake of writing any letters."

"Your wife will believe me. I can tell her enough in five minutes so she'll believe me."

Stuart was too shocked to protect himself. Afterward he realized he had only to tell her that Helene knew all about it to take all the wind out of her sails. "You're talking like this because you're angry," he said, "but I know you're not capable of doing such a thing." He reached out and gave her arm a little shake as if to coax her into being herself, but she shook him off.

"I'm capable of many things you know nothing about," she cried. "The man I went to had plenty of money. I did him no harm. And I made it possible for you to have what you wanted most in life. Now Etienne has his chance to make his fortune and he's willing to pay you well. There's nothing wicked about that."

Stuart turned away from her with a sigh. Had he completely misjudged her? Had she always been a tough little schemer? He was so hurt at her turning on him that he kept forgetting the threat she represented. Her voice recalled him to the business at hand.

"Shall we discuss the details?" she suggested.

"Do you really want me to believe you'd go to Helene?"

"You're making a great mistake if you don't believe it."

"And you think you're doing nothing wrong even though I tell you I don't want to sell? What if I sold the whole place and made my fortune, too? You know I don't care about being rich. I like the way I live now. You know how grateful I am to you. Don't you think it's wrong to try to destroy the good you've done?"

"Most people are happy enough to make money," she replied. "Maybe you'd better stop trying to be so different. It doesn't get you anywhere. I've found that out." Her tone was bitterly vindictive and he knew that there was nothing more he could say.

"I suppose eventually you'll make me angry, but for the moment I'm too surprised by you to feel anything else. Now I think you'd better unlock the door and let me go." She glanced up at him, as he lounged against the bar, and in spite of his shabby clothes his look of unattainable superiority made her courage falter.

"You might as well face it," she said defiantly. "Either you accept Etienne's offer or I go to your wife and you'll lose the place anyway. Do as you like."

"Let me out of here." His voice was filled with such violence that she fumbled with the key and it took her a second to get the door open. He didn't move until she had done so and then he strode past her without a word or a glance. He went to the car and started home with a pounding heart. How could he have been so wrong about her? A blackmailer! She had blackmailed to help him. Everything he had done with the money seemed tainted in the shock of the discovery.

He gripped the wheel and felt pain all through his body as if he'd been poisoned. He rolled through the familiar country without seeing it but aware that it was threatened, just as he was threatened by a danger to which he could no longer close his eyes.

All the while, there was the other aspect of the situation clamoring for his attention. What was he to do? Tell Helene? The alternative was to give in and let Etienne have his way, but Helene had made it clear that she thought he should hold out. The place was hers as much as his. He would have to take his medicine. They could face this together. The affair with Odette had had no real importance and had been over for years. He reminded himself how Helene had developed and he was able to hope she wouldn't take the matter as seriously as he did.

Dinner was difficult. Robbie really was a nuisance sometimes. Even after he had gone to bed and they were alone, they would have to whisper. Several times during the evening Helene asked if he was worried about anything and each time he had to lie. When Robbie finally kissed them both goodnight and left, Stuart stood in front of the dying fire and waited while Helene prepared for bed.

"There *is* something I have to tell you," he said in a low

voice when she approached. She glanced at him in surprise and began to gather up the cushions.

"Well, come to bed," she said. "It'll be warmer."

"No, I'd rather tell you now."

"What are you whispering for?" She joined him in front of the fire, holding the cushions in her arms. He nodded at Robbie's door.

"He mustn't hear." He looked at her gravely for a moment and then with head averted he told her of Odette's threat of blackmail and of the circumstances on which it was based. He spoke rapidly and it took only a minute to cover the facts, including the part Odette had played in helping them through the difficult period of Robbie's illness.

As Helene grasped the import of his story, a strange hollowness grew in the pit of her stomach. She felt her arms go tense and she wanted to lift her hands and strike out at the head bowed in front of her. The peace she had achieved was shattered in an instant. I don't care, she told herself. Let him sleep with anybody he likes. She saw his mouth moving, with the full upper lip that had once so touched her; she saw his powerful shoulders and arms and imagined them locked around another woman.

"It had no importance as far as you and I were concerned," he was saying in his hushed voice.

Of course it had no importance. Nothing he does has any importance. That's the meaning of these recent years. It's simply disgust I'm feeling, disgust at his man's body and its trivial needs. She found her fingers clamped into the pillows and she threw them down. He looked up, prepared for an outburst, ready to humble himself in any way. He was astonished to see so little emotion in her face. She looked rather seriously preoccupied, as if he had asked her opinion about some household problem.

"I suppose you should expect this sort of thing if you let yourself get involved with a cheap little creature like that," she said coldly. She had scarcely dared speak but the words came out quite easily. She wouldn't give him the satisfaction of knowing she despised him. Wasn't the fact that she could speak at all proof that she was cured of him? There was no further need of any communication between them. Her life was complete and whole with her child. She was glad they weren't married. It might make things simpler some day. There was no doubt in her mind about where Robbie's loyalties lay.

93

"It's been rather a blow," he said. "I didn't think of her as a cheap little thing." The equanimity with which Helene had listened to him was a letdown and he felt a perverse regret that such a revelation hadn't provoked her to throw things at him.

If only there were a little more money. He would like for them to be able to park Robbie somewhere and go off together, just the two of them, and recapture the old sense of excitement. She had picked up the pillows again and piled them on a chair. She started to turn from him but he caught her hand. "I'm glad to get this out and over with," he said. "It's good of you not to try to punish me." He thought she was very beautiful in the flickering firelight as she glanced at him composedly and then looked away.

"Why should I want to punish you?" She was determined to reveal nothing of the crisis she was passing through. She wanted to weep and she wanted to snatch her hand away and she wanted to strike him. Even while she was shaken by these conflicting emotions, she knew that it had nothing to do with now. The deception he was referring to had taken place during the happiest period of her life when she had lived for him and believed in him completely, to the point of denying Robbie the love she owed him. She had been a fool, a wicked fool. She would never trust him about anything again. "If you owe her so much don't you have an obligation to let her have what she wants?" she asked.

"Certainly not. I paid back everything she lent me." Because Helene was being so sensible he didn't feel he had the right to exact the absolution of an affectionate gesture so he let go of her hand.

"And you're not afraid they're apt to cause you trouble with their legal actions?"

"I don't think they have much of a case. Of course, I've got to find out what lawyers cost. I don't want to get involved in expenses that would make it even more difficult to send Robbie to school."

She started to take the cover off the bed. "I don't think legal costs are high here," she said.

"They may realize they haven't got enough to go on. I think they counted on blackmail to force my hand."

And it didn't work, she thought as she folded the cover briskly. It didn't work because you can't blackmail a man who's willing to tell his wife about his affairs. From now on, she would make the decisions concerning Robbie.

He watched her going through her familiar routine. These were surely the worst moments they had gone through since they'd started living together and she seemed to have taken them in her stride. Perhaps she hadn't yet taken it in. Perhaps there would be a delayed reaction. He squared his shoulders. He was prepared to atone for his transgressions.

Two days later a letter came addressed to Helene. She recognized Odette's handwriting and handed it to Stuart without opening it. He tore it up. Then, with the torn bits of paper in his hand, curiosity stirred in him. What had she written? He held the torn letter thoughtfully, wondering whether she might not have committed some indiscretion that he in his turn might use against her. Then he walked across the room and threw the crumpled paper into the fire. Descending to her level, doing battle with her would become a greater involvement with her than making love had ever been. He had always avoided any real entanglement.

In the next few weeks the attack being prepared by Etienne Dunan unfolded. Papers were served indicating that Ladouceur had instituted suit. In addition, somebody called Marville had taken action to have the sale of the whole Giraudon property declared illegal on the grounds of the old man's insanity. The two procedures were independent of each other and Dunan's name figured in neither.

To Stuart, seeing it all in writing was almost as much of a blow as if a judge had handed down an adverse decision. The unexpected attempt to dispossess him completely made it seem more likely that they might win at least part of their action. Had they prevailed on M. Giraudon to go along with them? He wanted to feel the support of the community and he went immediately to see Antonin.

"*Tenez*. Warm yourself with that." His neighbor handed him the inevitable glass of cherries. They were alone in the Roquièttas' clean ugly kitchen. The winter rains had started and it was cold and blustery out.

"Have you heard what they're trying to prove about M. Giraudon?" Stuart asked.

"Mmm," Antonin grunted, looking at the cherries in his glass.

"It's nonsense, of course. Everybody knows the old man was queer but he was quite able to take care of himself."

"I've heard things that make him sound pretty crazy." Antonin's sharp seamed face looked stubbornly secretive and Stuart found himself struggling against a sudden distrust.

95

"Well, the old man himself can prove he's not crazy."

"But surely you know," Antonin looked at him directly for the first time. "M. Giraudon is dead. He died over a year ago." Stuart's heart sank. Maître Barbetin. Now M. Giraudon. Thank God for Boldoni, he thought suddenly. Boldoni was his man. Boldoni had participated in the transaction.

"Well, you knew him," Stuart persisted. "You can tell them he was sane."

"Oh, moi, vous savez—" Antonin had to say no more to make it clear that he didn't consider it his affair. Stuart chose to ignore the remark and hurried on.

"It's good I'm holding out. You know what they want to do? A hotel and villas and God knows what."

"Yes, things are changing. Still I understand they want to bring water out and electricity. Even the telephone. That would be an improvement. I understand they offered you a good price."

"I never bothered to ask the price." Stuart stared at him gloomily. His neighbor wouldn't help him. If he wasn't actively against him now he would be eventually. Community solidarity and self-interest would be too much for him. Only Boldoni was left. He wasn't for "progress." He would testify to M. Giraudon's sanity. Stuart must look him up right away. He must find a good lawyer.

He finished off his drink and left with a feeling that he would never again be really welcome here. After deluding himself that he belonged, that the faces he saw around him were approving, that his affection for Odette was reciprocated, that Antonin was a loyal friend, what was left? Only Boldoni—and perhaps even he would fail when put to the test.

He had no trouble finding the house on the outskirts of town that Boldoni had retired to. Boldoni greeted him with shaggy cordiality at the glass-paned front door and led him back through a narrow corridor to the kitchen, which was littered with newspapers and magazines. The stove was making a gurgling noise and it was very hot. Boldoni's massive bulk seemed to crowd the room as he moved clumsily to fetch a bottle and glasses.

"You see what I'm reduced to," he said when he had seated himself, breathing heavily. "It isn't like the old days, eh?"

"It certainly isn't," Stuart agreed, "and they're just beginning to go to work on me." He told his story while Boldoni grunted in indignation.

"Well, you should have expected it," he said when Stuart had finished. "They can't do much without you. They need room to expand. After all, you have the best beach in the region."

"At least you're still here. You can tell them I didn't swindle a crazy man."

"Everybody knows old Giraudon was crazy," Boldoni exploded, throwing out his arms. "He ate nothing but roots. But he knew what he was doing. He told me his price and he got more from you. He wasn't crazy when it came to money." He hunched himself over the table studying his glass. Stuart felt considerably cheered.

"That's all I wanted to hear," he said. "Just don't let anything happen to you until the hearing comes up."

"Happen to me." Boldoni grunted. "I sit here all day long. What is there to do? If I go to town all I hear is money, money, money. I hear they have a jazz band at my place and little tables with candles on them. I do nothing but sit here and look at my wife. I'll live forever." He seemed profoundly depressed at the prospect. Having achieved the purpose of his visit, Stuart encouraged him to talk about himself and stayed longer than he had intended.

Through Boldoni he found a lawyer in Draguignan who had no local interests. The case had given the innkeeper a new interest in life. He admired Stuart's intransigence and Stuart appreciated his support. But it was Stuart who had to pay the lawyer's fees and the cost of his trips to Draguignan and the lawyer's expenses when he came to St. Tropez to search through the records at the town hall in a vain effort to throw some light on the Giraudon-Ladouceur controversy. The case wasn't scheduled to be heard before spring.

Going ahead with his plans for the place, he found himself wondering constantly what he would do if he lost. Boldoni served as a terrible example of a man who had been deprived of his life's work. "I just sit here all day long and look at my wife," he had said, and Stuart imagined himself saying the same thing in a year's time.

It irritated him even more to realize that all the hotels and villas in the world wouldn't impinge on the charm of the glade where the house was situated because of the ridge that protected it. His decision to fight would have been more generally understandable to others, he felt, if an obvious threat to his privacy had been involved.

Helene awaited developments without knowing whether

she wanted Stuart to win or lose. She refused to consider how it might affect him; her only interest was how it would affect Robbie and herself. She was particularly careful that no hint of conflict between her and Stuart should be apparent to the boy. She was determined to maintain her position as the one right, sure, devoted element in his life. As he approached fourteen, she began to speak to the boy about sex and love, of the relations between men and women, not openly but in casual asides about the books he was reading; if there were a villain who mistreated women, she would refer to the ugliness of man's animal nature and conversely to the life of the spirit. She spoke for herself as much as for Robbie, to reinforce the revulsion she felt toward Stuart and the importance she had once allowed him to have for her. She confirmed in Robbie his tendency to close his mind to certain things he had seen and done.

Everything she said fitted in with the memories he didn't allow to surface—that dirty Michel, the horrid little girl from next door. What could they know of the life of the spirit? Everything fitted except for that other memory, too appalling to be thought of at all but which he *had* thought of without being conscious of it, just enough to see his mother as wounded somehow, a sacrifice to— The awfulness of it added to his determination to be always worthy of her ideal, never to sin in that way. It was a bulwark against the guilt of his growing knowledge.

Robbie's interest in painting continued to develop and Stuart denied himself a new coat that winter in order to equip the boy with oils and expensive brushes. Helene encouraged him to think of it as a profession. Painting was just the career she would wish for him. There would be no need for education in distant universities nor the danger of jobs on the other side of the globe.

Whenever the weather was favorable, they took walks after lunch until he found a good spot to set up his canvas and work while she sat knitting nearby.

Robbie's creative ability was, to Stuart, an additional reason for him to pass his formative years with other youths. He had let this school year slip by, had let money slip away in legal expenses, and after his confession he was anxious to please Helene in every possible way, but this fall was the limit no matter how much of a wrench it would be to her to be deprived of the boy's company.

One morning a search for a mislaid tool led him around to

Robbie's end of the house where he rarely had occasion to go. He didn't find what he was looking for and started back around the house, glancing at Robbie's window as he did so. Part of the bed was visible and a second glance told Stuart what was taking place in it. He wasn't surprised; it was the most normal thing in the world. What Robbie was holding looked very well developed for his age. Stuart grinned to himself. The boy was going to take after his daddy. Memories crowded in upon him as he was confronted with the fact of Robbie's growing up.

After lunch Helene left the house to carry a light bundle of laundry up to the well. Robbie was finishing the dishes and Stuart lingered behind with him.

"I guess you'll be pretty glad not to have to do this any more when you're at school," Stuart said conversationally.

"Am I going to school?"

"Of course. In the fall. You'll be ready to start whatever they call it here. What we call high school. The lycée, I think."

"I don't see what good it'll do. I like being at home," he said.

"Well, I don't suppose you'll necessarily get a better education but there's lots besides books to learn at school. It'll be good for you to be with kids your own age."

"All the kids I've ever known have been silly."

"That's just it," Stuart said. "You haven't known very many. It's time you had friends your own age. This is an important period for you. There're so many things to learn. You know, it's not going to be long before you start getting interested in girls."

"I'm never going to be interested in girls," Robbie muttered. He had finished putting things away and now spread the dishtowel out to dry like a good little housewife. Yes, he needed roughing up. He turned, pushing the hair back from his forehead with the flat of his hand. Stuart was struck by his resemblance to Helene. His skin was dark, his lips curved like hers to reveal even white teeth. Going to be a hell of a good-looking guy, Stuart thought. He smiled and settled back against the table, preparing to take the plunge.

"Most boys your age think that," he said, "but they change their minds later. Sex can sometimes seem a big problem at your age. Things like masturbation, for instance—" Stuart got the word out with commendable ease and paused to congratulate himself.

99

"What's that?" Robbie inquired with the interest he always showed at a new word.

"Well, you know you can get a sexual thrill by yourself. Every boy does it at one time or another. Later on when you grow up, it just stops being interesting." A pinched look had come into Robbie's face but Stuart admired the steadiness with which the boy looked at him. He was straight. He wasn't all tied up in knots.

"I don't want to go to school," Robbie said flatly. He was thinking: So it isn't anything special after all.

"School can be more fun than you think. Anything new is apt to seem a little frightening. But I'm sure you'll like it once you're there. You're—"

"I don't want to go to school," Robbie cut in.

"Now wait a minute." Stuart stood and straightened the boy's collar. "What is all this?"

Robbie tore himself free and backed away, his eyes wide and fixed on his father. "I won't go. You can't make me. Mother won't let you. You wait and see. She wants me to stay with her."

Stuart stared at him. This behavior was so unprecedented that he couldn't think what to do. Should he give him a good spanking? At this moment of indecision Helene returned. She came in with a bantering word for Robbie on her lips and then stood stock still. Stuart turned toward her and her eyes traveled swiftly from him to Robbie.

"What's the matter?" she said sharply.

Stuart made a bewildered gesture. "I wish I knew," he said. "We were just talking about—"

"Don't you tell her," Robbie screamed. He flung himself savagely on his father. Stuart hadn't realized how big he had grown. He staggered under the attack.

"Why, you little fool," he cried. He seized the boy by the arms and shook him.

"If you tell her, I'll kill you. I'll kill you. Don't say it." Tears were beginning to choke his voice but he struggled viciously in Stuart's grip. His only thought was that this new word must not be spoken in front of his mother. He kicked out blindly at Stuart, who shook him so that his head wobbled giddily. Helene was beside them.

"Let him go, Do you hear me? Let him go. You devil, let him go." Stuart released him with a little shove and he fell to the floor, sobbing hysterically and beating the floor with his fists. Stuart looked at him with astonishment. In an instant a quiet, well-behaved intelligent child—not such a child anymore—had become this crazy little animal. Stuart pulled himself together and straightened his sweater.

"Get up this instant," he commanded before Helene had time to make a move toward the boy. "You ought to be ashamed of yourself." He leaned over and seized Robbie's arm and pulled him to his feet. "Get up like a man and go to your room. I'll deal with you later when you've had time to think things over." Robbie staggered toward his door and Helene started after him.

"Wait." Stuart gripped her arm firmly as Robbie's door closed after him. She drew her arm away from him.

"If you have something to say, say it," she said. "I don't want to leave him alone."

"I want him left alone until I decide what to do with him," Stuart said. Had she called him a devil? "I think we'd better talk this over." He went to the front door.

"Where are you going?" she asked.

"We can talk more freely outside."

"But I can't leave him like this," she announced. The sound of muffled sobbing came to them from the next room. Stuart held the front door open.

"I tell you I want him left alone for the moment."

She sighed and preceded him out the door. It was a clear cold sunny afternoon and the sea glittered as coldly as cut diamonds. He directed their steps up the glade past the olive trees.

"What is it he didn't want you to tell me?" she asked when they were out of earshot of the house.

"God knows. I was talking about his going to school next year when he suddenly started snarling at me like a panther. Then you came in. I must say you weren't much help." In retrospect the episode began to acquire comic overtones and Stuart laughed briefly.

"I wish you'd tell me the whole thing from the beginning," she said. The sight of him shaking Robbie and hurling him to the floor seemed to her no laughing matter.

"There's not much to tell. I was talking to him in a general sort of way about how being with boys his own age would be a good thing when life's little problems began to crop up, like girls and so forth." He had no intention of mentioning what he had seen that morning or uttering the dread word. Respect for Robbie's privacy? Male solidarity?

"I might have known it," she said, almost with a shudder of

loathing. It was one of the things she couldn't bear about Robbie's going to school. He would be corrupted, dragged off to bordellos, perhaps get seriously involved with some girl. "Do you have to force your preoccupation with sex on him? Can't you understand that he might have sensibilities that you know nothing about?"

"Oh God, I want him to be a man, not a plaster saint."

"All men don't feel they have to run around having sordid little affairs to prove their virility." The words were out before she could stop herself. They implied a reproach and it was by not reproaching him that she denied him the opportunity of making amends. She added more mildly, "I don't see why you need harp so on sex. It's nothing he's worried about."

They had reached a sunny spot on the rocks and they stood facing each other. He touched her arm and sat down but she remained standing in front of him, her hands plunged into the pockets of her short leather coat.

"Let's talk about it," he began. "Of course he's beginning to think about sex. Whether we like it or not, in another four or five years he'll be grown up. I think you've been wonderful with him up until now. I wish I'd had the same sort of home life he's had. It would have given me some roots. But I don't think we have any more to offer him. We can't let anything stand in the way of his school in the fall." Stuart paused, surprised at himself. He had always valued his rootlessness. The last months had tried him more severely than he had realized. He felt a new uncertainty, a wistful sense of homelessness, of being excluded.

"How can we afford it?"

"We'll have to, even if it means cutting down still more."

"Why do you make everything so difficult for us?" she burst out. She was ready to be poor if it meant keeping Robbie with her, but to go on struggling without him seemed more than she could bear. Stuart looked up. Standing above him in her worn leather jacket and her shabby tweed skirt, she looked like some peasant spirit of vengeance. "Why don't you sell that damn land everybody seems to want so much? We'd have a little money. We'd be able to stay somewhere in Cannes where we could look after him."

"But that's just the point," Stuart said reasonably. "He should be completely on his own."

"Oh, it's easy for you. You have your work, something to keep you busy all day long. But what about me? What kind of a life is it for me? Look at my hands." She wrenched her hands from her pockets and held them before him. Stuart was astonished to see that they were trembling. The nails were cut short, the skin over the knuckles was rough. They looked strong and capable. She thrust them back into her pockets. "This is what you've done to me. You love it. But what about me?"

His first reaction was embarrassment at having to see her like this. The way people said "me" when they were distraught was so lacking in dignity. He looked at the house beyond the olive trees. It looked as if it had been there forever, snug and solid, with smoke curling out of the two chimneys. He looked down at the cove below him, at the hut boarded over for the winter, and then out at the sparkling sea. He thought of all the good times they had had here. She didn't like it? She couldn't mean it. How could she even talk about selling it?

Here were the roots he had struck down into life. Sun, sea, this land and its reluctant abundance, freedom—what wouldn't most people give to possess it? And above all, love. He looked across the water. In the distance the blue coast thrust out to meet the sea. The farthest lavender ridge must look down into Italy. He loved Helene. He loved Robbie.

"What's the matter?" he asked. "We're here. Everything's the way it should be. Since when don't you like it?" He heard her sigh.

She was abashed at the appeal in his voice. It was an appeal to something that no longer existed between them, something that she could not permit to exist. Nevertheless, it put an end to her brief tirade. She couldn't change anything by direct conflict. She must wait. She must prepare herself. Robbie would be hers when the time came. "I don't know. I don't suppose I meant it," she said. She looked across at the house and thought of Robbie and of her being here next year without him. It was unimaginable. "I suppose everything will work out. As far as Robbie's concerned there's still lots of time between now and next autumn. I think the less we talk about it in front of him the better."

"That's all right so long as *we* know what we're doing," he agreed.

"Yes, of course. Shouldn't we go in now? I'm getting cold."

"You go ahead but please leave him alone. He's got to be punished."

He heard the scrape of her shoes against the rocks and she

was gone. He watched a little fishing boat crawling up the bay and he thought how pleasant it would be to go somewhere alone with her in a boat. It was all they needed. A complete change from the grueling work on the land, from the strain of legal complications, from the increasing demands of a growing boy. For the moment, there were simply too many conflicting preoccupations. They must win the suit. They must send Robbie to school. After that, they would be together again. What else was there to believe in?

The case, scheduled to be heard in April, was deferred until autumn. An additional problem was thus created, for the legal contest had made the disputed area a sort of no-man's-land. The vines it bore belonged to nobody until a settlement was made. An order was issued forbidding Stuart to touch the grapes; violation made him liable to criminal action for theft.

Stuart decided to ignore this order and to take his crop. On the second day the *huissier* came out from St. Tropez and witnessed what was taking place, refusing in the performance of his official function to speak to Stuart although they knew each other well. It was a frightening experience. He had to keep telling himself that even if worse came to worst no court could seriously regard him as a thief. Besides, he was a foreigner—he, who had been so proud to feel himself part of the community.

At least Robbie would soon be at school. When they received a list of books he would need, Stuart went with him to the new bookshop just off the port while he self-importantly made his purchases.

Stuart followed at a little distance, idly flipping through books until he came to one with a lurid sunset and a multicolored *tartane* tied to a quai on its cover and the title *St. Tropez: Port of Dreams*. He felt like tearing it up in protest. That was the St. Tropez Dunan and company were trying to sell, this synthetic sunset and picturesque quai. Port of dreams, indeed. Port of thieves was more like it. Robbie called him and Stuart slapped down the book and went back to pay the bill.

"I really ought to have one of those fountain pens," Robbie suggested, and Stuart bought it, too.

Even when they were driving him, all dressed up in his new school clothes, over to Cannes, Helene couldn't believe that she would be going home without him. As for Robbie, he was ready to believe that school might be all right, since his mother seemed resigned to his going. She had always protected him from things he didn't like. There was no denying his pleasure in having such a fuss made over him, in the new clothes, in the adult suitcase, in the feeling of acquiring a new identity. They left him at the school looking solemn and covering his bewilderment with a disdainful manner.

"Well, here we are," Stuart said as he turned the car back onto the road for home. "It's like starting out all over again." He reached over and touched her hand.

His words chilled her; he spoke as if Robbie had been banished permanently from their lives. She allowed him to replace his hand on the steering wheel. "It's really no distance at all," she said to comfort herself. "We can go over on Sunday every few weeks and have lunch with him."

Stuart, wanting to make the separation as easy as possible for her, agreed. He felt as if one of the knots in the tangle had been undone. In just a few weeks the case would be heard and he would be able to go back to work as his own master. He hated to have his land-development program delayed.

During the last weeks of waiting, a new figure entered the picture. His name was Bernard Godet and he was a real-estate agent from Toulon.

When he arrived unexpectedly one morning Helene directed him to the vegetable gardens where Stuart was working. Stuart looked up as he approached. Godet introduced himself. He was a big expansive man with a humorous air who reminded Stuart of an American Southerner. He looked around him, nodding at the long stretch of beach and the gentle rise of cultivated land behind it.

"*D'une beauté extraordinaire,*" he announced with orotund authority. He came quickly to the point. He wanted Stuart to let him handle the sale of a large part of the property in return for his cooperation in the legal battle, which he seemed to know about, hinting that he could provide decisive evidence. The prospect of acquiring an ally was agreeable but it was still the same old story—sell or get out. His affable manner didn't carry him to the point of revealing the nature of his evidence. Stuart reiterated his determination to hold on to everything he had.

As Godet fumbled in his pocket for a cigarette, Stuart saw that among several books he was carrying there was the gaudily covered one about St. Tropez that he had seen in the bookshop a few days earlier. It was a black mark against the newcomer. Port of dreams, indeed.

He accompanied the real-estate agent back to his car without considering that Bernard Godet might hold the key to his future. He paused to tell Helene about the interview and its outcome.

"Do you think that was wise?" she asked.

"Wise? What do you mean, wise? What else should I do?" As he spoke he was aware of the wonderful freedom Robbie's absence offered him and he snapped the last question at her, deliberately inviting an argument. They could say what they really meant at last. They could clear the air. He was ready for a fight, if only for the sake of the ultimate reconciliation, of re-establishing the old warm contact. She only looked at him with a faint smile.

"Oh, nothing, I suppose," she said. "I'm sure you're quite right. I just asked."

Finally, the day of the hearing in Draguignan was upon him. An early rising with a tight knot in his stomach. The questions: Have I done everything I could have done? Should I have made some concession to that real-estate agent? A silent drive with Boldoni. The crowded, stale-smelling courtroom. The waiting . . .

"You mustn't expect too much," the lawyer friend of Boldoni barked at him. "The others may have some evidence we don't know about. I can only hope that the judge will accept the fact that you bought and developed the land in good faith. That should establish your rights."

"I should hope so," Stuart exclaimed indignantly.

He kept looking around him at the press of litigants without being able to find one kindly or generous face. He wanted to dissociate himself from them. They were a single intent, fretful, covetous mass. More waiting. The sound of feet shuffling. A sudden incoherent outburst of an angry lawyer. A surge forward carried Stuart before a gray man seated at a raised desk who never lifted his eyes from the papers in front of him.

Everybody was suddenly talking at once. He caught a glimpse of the handsome features of Etienne Dunan twisted in a grimace and he heard Boldoni's voice above the others. Before Stuart knew what was happening, his lawyer was explaining to him that at least there would be no more talk of M. Giraudon's insanity: the Marville case had been dismissed.

Stuart nodded and tried to concentrate on the next step. He wished they'd all stop talking so that he could grasp the mechanics of the thing. The gray man behind the desk was devoting all his attention to his papers. When he asked a question, it seemed to have no bearing on the case as Stuart knew it and, as far as he could see, nobody answered. After a minute, the man behind the desk gathered up the papers, put them aside, and picked up another bundle. Stuart's lawyer turned with a shrug, spreading his arms wide and letting them slap down to his sides.

"This is what I was afraid of," he sighed. "I warned you to compromise."

"What do you mean?" Stuart demanded. "When are we going to be heard?"

"But, my dear sir, it's over, settled. The Ladouceur claim has been recognized."

"Salauds," Boldini rumbled behind Stuart, as he was being carried away from the desk in the advancing tide of litigants. Settled? How could it be settled? How could a man's whole life be settled without his being given a hearing?

"But you're not going to let them get away with it," he gasped at his squat swarthy lawyer.

"Come. There's nothing to be done. The dossiers are there. There was nothing I could say."

"It's all very well for you to say there's nothing to be done. I'm not satisfied. You've got to appeal."

"How can I?" the lawyer demanded.

"You've got to. They'll be having me up on that damn felony charge next."

"I told you that was a foolish thing to do. I can't appeal without fresh evidence."

"Tell them you *have* fresh evidence," Stuart ordered. "Tell them anything. Stall for time."

"And where will I get this evidence?" the lawyer pleaded.

Where, indeed? There was only one answer. Stuart had no reason to place much confidence in it but it was the only hope. And—yes, by God, he'd accept any terms. If he were going to lose, he might as well be paid for it. Money. Lots of it. He could drive a hard bargain along with the rest of them, or go down fighting. This was a moment of immense decision. He needed time to think. There wasn't a minute to lose.

"I'll get your evidence," he said curtly. "I don't know what it'll be worth but it'll be something. Start an appeal." He turned to Boldoni, who was staring at the crowd. "Come on. We've got to find that man called Godet."

ROBBIE

Not moderating his pace or shifting his course as he moved through the press of cars and people along the port, Stuart emanated the air of authority that a crowd will instinctively make way for. When he encountered local people, he turned and nodded coldly. He was too envied to be liked. Summer tourists noted his striking figure. The simplicity of his shirt and slacks suggested a man traveling without baggage; it was in striking contrast to the attire generally worn on the port.

The British favored multi-colored blazers and brilliant silk scarves; the French, the Americans, the Italians had adopted outlandish variations of local attire—fishermen's jerseys in silk, gilded sandals, stocking caps with tassels. The women for the most part wore shorts, exposing as much of themselves as was considered decent, but a few still clung to outmoded beach pajamas.

It was obviously going to be the biggest season ever. Every year it was the biggest season ever and now, thanks to Stuart, the lid was definitely off. The quai was an unbroken field of gay beach umbrellas sprouting from iron-topped tables. Yachts glittering with brass and chromium had finally crowded the easygoing commercial shipping from the harbor. Drawn up in front of them, a fleet of luxurious automobiles from every corner of the earth stood waiting to convey the late-luncheon crowd to the sun-scorched beach.

As he approached La Bouillabaisse, Stuart let himself be drawn into the milling throng. He knew that Odette would probably be greeting her customers at this hour and it still made him uncomfortable to stalk past her without speaking, even though the ultimate triumph had been his. He hid himself in the crowd and let it carry him past the danger point. Once his pace was slowed, it was unbearably hot. Smiling faces seemed to press close to his. One was that of a famous woman novelist, another an American film star. A car pushed its way through the throng, followed by a bear on a bicycle. Stuart supposed it was a man dressed up as a bear but it might really be a bear. One learned to accept anything on the quai at St. Tropez.

He disentangled himself from the crowd and turned up toward the center of town. As soon as he was in the shade of the narrow street, he stopped and unbuttoned his shirt down to the waist. He squinted up at the cloudless sky. It was going to be the best year for grapes he had ever seen. He had to remind himself that it didn't matter to him anymore.

He looked over his shoulder, craning his neck to see the clock in the church tower. Already five minutes late. Well, they would wait. He looked back at the port. The crowd was thinning. Groups were piling into cars; the procession to the beach had started. In another hour, the quai would be deserted until the cocktail hour. In this brief interval, one could almost believe that nothing had changed. You're getting old, he told himself. Approaching forty, a man should still be looking forward, not back. His eye followed the soaring thrust of a mast and then dropped to the sleek gleaming hull of a yacht on whose stern several youths were lolling. That would be the British admiral's boat. Very handsome, and yet none of these impeccable craft had the charm of the clumsy old *tartanes*. You're an enemy of progress, my boy, he told himself.

He ran his hand over his chest and wiped the sweat off on the side of his trousers. His hand felt rough against the fabric and he looked at it, pushing the calluses with a forefinger. All that he had to show for his productive labor. It had taken him seven years to acquire them and they were already softening up. He hitched up his trousers and rested his hands on his hips. He knew he must look odd standing here in the street. What am I waiting for? he wondered. Everything is settled. The others are waiting. I know what the port looks like by heart. Yet he felt that it should look different today. It should look bigger or more crowded or, if possible, richer. Richer . . . That word prodded him into movement and he went on into the town to collect a fortune.

He was glad he had planned it just this way. From the moment he had reached his decision a year and a half ago in that stinking courtroom, he had been following a schedule that went out of effect as of today.

110

Godet and his damn book. If Stuart hadn't been so determined to deny the existence of all that the book represented, he would have looked into it himself and saved himself a great deal of heartache. The author of *St. Tropez: Port of Dreams* had told a tale of a brief period when the countryside had been threatened by pirates and of the warning lights communicating with the lighthouse. The Plain of the Saracens had been an essential link between the lighthouse and the town and it had been bought by a nineteenth-century Giraudon who had been instrumental in setting up a defense.

It was this public-spirited Giraudon who had created all the confusion by not taking over the land for farming but making a loan of it to the community. He hadn't even bothered to make sure that his purchase was properly registered. It was a good enough story but it turned out that the author had it on hearsay from his grandfather. Once Godet had told him what they had to look for, it had taken six months to assemble documentary proof from fragmentary evidence in old records and to have it recognized in court. It had taken another year to sell off the land.

He had moved slowly, forcing up the price by skillful maneuvering and allowing the money to accumulate until the last of the almost three hundred acres he had agreed with Godet to part with had been sold. He didn't want the money in dribbles. The sum he had realized was greater than he had dreamed of—not millions, as he had been accustomed to measure riches in New York, but very nearly one million after Godet had taken his share. It had turned out that an acre was now worth more than the purchase price of the whole property.

He supposed that receiving so much money all at once must carry with it its own imperatives. He didn't know what kind of a life he wanted to lead as a rich man and he was waiting for the money itself to give him a clue. He was determined not to be submerged by it. He was not so foolish as to think that money would make no difference but he had seen nothing in the lives of the rich that offered the satisfaction he had found in his vineyard. He must learn what he could from it, alone, as if he were the first rich man on earth.

Robbie opened one eye as Stuart climbed down the rocks to the cove where the boy was stretched out almost naked, sunning himself. "Did you get the loot?" he called lazily. He had shot up in the last two years and was now as tall as his father with the beginning of a fine physique, although there was still a coltishness in his big-jointed limbs.

Stuart squatted beside him. "Yes, it's in the bank. Where's madame?"

"She's taking a siesta, I think. She went up about an hour ago. It must be almost time for tea." Robbie had acquired a wordly manner but underlying it was an undecided quality, tenebrous and provocative. It showed in his movements, in the way he rolled over now onto one elbow and studied the nail of his index finger. Everything he did seemed to sketch a loose eccentric line.

Stuart had a deep respect for the boy's talent, which had developed enormously in these last years. He had enjoyed planning with him the new house they were finally going to build and he had admired the taste and imagination that this project had revealed in the boy. Even so, he was never sure that he was really getting through to him. He might have put this down to an inadequacy in himself but the fact that Robbie had made no real friends at school suggested there was more to it than that. His scholastic record was admirable, he was apparently well liked, but he remained aloof from his fellows, aloof and a trifle melancholy.

"You know," Stuart suggested tentatively, "I think it's about time we had a taste of our own creation. I think we should have a real bang-up touristy night on the town. Cocktails, dinner, nightclubs, everything. Find out what the summer folk see in it."

"That'd be wonderful." Robbie laughed abruptly and inexplicably. The laughter ended as suddenly as it had begun. "It's funny. The kids at school know more about St. Tropez than I do."

"That's what comes of being one of the underprivileged. Now we're definitely *nouveaux riches*. Do you have an elegant shirt you can lend me for the occasion? I'm afraid mine are all rather threadbare."

"I guess so. But what'll we do about Mum? Her clothes look like something the cat dragged in."

"Do they? I'm afraid I hadn't noticed. She must have something put away for best."

"I'll go see what she's doing." Robbie stood up in one lithe movement and sand showered from him. He looked at Stuart sideways, his dark hair falling over his forehead. His eyes were beautiful like Helene's, but with a hard, penetrating look that revealed nothing. "You did mean tonight?" he asked.

"Oh yes, definitely tonight. Tell your mother it's to be a thoroughly trashy evening."

Robbie threw his head back with more laughter and went leaping off up the rocks. Stuart watched him reflectively until he was gone. He lay back on the warm sand and looked up at the sky. White puffs of clouds passed above him, giving him the uncomfortable sensation of feeling the earth turning, and he closed his eyes.

Robbie's laughter echoed in his ears, a reward. The boy needed to get out more, have fun, find his place in the world. Well, the money was there. A fuller life for Robbie. The new house. Some new clothes for himself and Helene. A new car or two so that they could get about a bit less sedately than in the Rolls. That was as far as he could see now. This was clearly a beginning, a starting all over again; it was also a farewell.

Farewell to the land and its creatures. Farewell to Antonin and the others and to the jolly vintage parties and shared toil. His riches and the grand new house would finally sever whatever link still existed between them. There would be no more Odettes. Farewell to her, too, to the sweet animal warmth she had offered at the beginning. Farewell to the world in which shopkeepers didn't want to be paid and Boldoni fed you like a king just for the fun of it. Farewell to all of it.

And Helene? he thought, wondering. Perhaps their farewell had taken place a long time ago. When his work had kept him in the fields for long hours he could tell himself that any withdrawal he felt in her was the result of his having so little energy left to devote to her. There had been the bad year after Robbie's illness when she had seemed to recoil from any physical intimacy. He had worked his way through that but he hadn't been able to recapture the old passion. When the appeal was pending and he had little will to work on land whose ownership lay in the balance, he had learned that whatever had happened between them had happened, that whatever had been lost was lost. He had counted on the past to bridge the gap of the years, but the past had given him no insight into the placid agreeable remote woman who looked out at him from Helene's once burning eyes.

He had learned that you can't start over again with people. The past is there and sometimes it's a barrier. No matter what

113

people say, you can't always build on it. He loved her, she loved him, but he knew they had missed something along the way. Perhaps it was only time taking its inexorable toll. Was he ready for a mistress? He wondered why he felt so little inclination to stray. He hoped that Odette had cured him of thinking that lighthearted liaisons could do no harm. He sat up suddenly and wiped the sand off his hands, squinting against the light on the sea.

Why? he thought. Why am I living? Given life, it was easy enough to fill it one way or another. But why had be been placed on earth? If one didn't see oneself as a function of some divine plan, what was the meaning, what was the purpose? He thought of how simple everything had seemed at the beginning when he believed that all he had to do was take his clothes off and get into the sun. This view seemed hopelessly inadequate now. People were fighting all over the place. Was that what you needed to give you a sense of purpose? Not even the Abyssinians seemed to expect anybody in his right mind to help them once the important powers had failed to take any concerted action, but should he volunteer to join the Loyalists in Spain? He had given it serious thought during the last year when he wasn't thinking about money. Somebody was going to have to stop Hitler and Mussolini from bullying the world, but the right moment always seemed to slip past. His generation had already lived through a war and he couldn't see that it had accomplished much. He doubted if there would be another one in his time simply because the people who devoted their lives to thinking about money, like his father, hadn't figured out how to make it pay. There was too much danger that the Reds might walk off with all the stakes. He should probably be grateful for the opportunity to find some answers in himself.

He stood up, shaking sand from his trousers, and followed Robbie slowly up the rocks.

The place was a shambles. There were piles of building materials everywhere; work on the first of their proposed houses, here on the edge of the cliff overlooking the small beach, was to begin day after tomorrow. Just in the last few weeks he had arranged for preliminaries to get underway. Plumbing was being installed in the old house, which was to be expanded into a guest house and the glade was crisscrossed with trenches.

Stuart paused when he reached the top of the rocks and looked around him in order to see it in his mind's eye, the landscaped terraces, the fountains, the great rooms opening wide to the sea. The final plans were settled on and drawn up. He couldn't wait to get started. He leaped a ditch and ran down the glade to the house. He found the door to Robbie's room closed and he heard them laughing behind it. Robbie's room was being turned into a modern bathroom. His bed and chest of drawers stood in the middle of the living room. He called out and Robbie answered.

"Don't come in. We're trying to repair the ravages of time." This was followed by an explosion of laughter and muffled exclamations. Stuart smiled at the door and then pulled off his shirt and went to the kitchen corner to wash.

He was rubbing his chest briskly with a towel when Robbie flung open the door and announced, *"La Reine de St. Tropez."* Helene followed, not liking to be in the position of asking for Stuart's approval but doing so because Robbie expected it of her. She stood beside Robbie and took his arm. She was wearing a white skirt and blouse she had had for years but Stuart was scarcely aware of her clothes. They had worked on her hair, arranging it softly around her face. Her eyes and mouth were subtly made up, her tanned skin glowed, her hair shone, her body looked rich and ripe and desirable. She bloomed. It seemed to Stuart that she must have been storing up her beauty for this moment. There was poise and maturity in it but none of the blurring or softening of age; she looked indestructible and eternal. Stuart stared in dumb amazement and Helene looked from him to Robbie with a slight shrug as if repudiating his admiration.

Stuart moved forward to her. "Give me a kiss. You're the loveliest in the land." She turned her cheek to him and laughed deprecatingly. Then she slipped away from him.

"Let's see what you have in the way of a shirt for the old man." Stuart followed Robbie into the embryonic bathroom.

They left the house when the setting sun was bathing the land in a rosy glow. Even the piled-up sacks of cement beside the garage had acquired a luster. The air felt new. Their voices as they walked to the car fell into the glade clear and liquid. The shared felicity of being washed and cool and looking their best drew them together and created the illusion of profound harmony.

"Let's tell everybody you're my sister," Robbie said excitedly to Helene. She blushed and looked up at him adoringly.

"My poor motherless children," Stuart said. Robbie laughed and took a couple of exuberant skips beside them.

Everything stood out separate and distinct as they drove up through the woods to the main road; every twig, every leaf seemed to make a shadow of its own. Our park, Stuart thought. "Woods" wasn't grand enough to go with the new house.

When they reached the town Stuart let the Rolls drift with the crowd along one side of the port and around the other, past the British admiral's yacht. He found a parking place at the end of the quai near the old tower. There was a perilous-looking gangplank leading across the rocks to it and a sign in lights over the door proclaimed it to be LA TOUR ENGLOUTIE.

"Well," Stuart said, "where shall we start? The Café de la Mer or whatever it's called now?" They climbed down from the car and paused, bracing themselves to face the crowd. Robbie was looking around, wide-eyed and solemn. "Yes. It has seniority—like us. Come on, into the fray." He took them both by the arm. The bear bicycled past them, wheeled sharply, and pedaled off down the quai. Stuart burst into laughter at the look of amazement on Robbie's face.

"This looks like fun," the youth exclaimed.

Stuart guided them across the quai to what had once been the Café de la Mer. He noticed that the men they passed cast speculative glances over Helene and he was proud of her. He caught the eyes of a few girls himself. He saw both males and females doing double takes at Robbie. The place had already acquired a reputation for sexual variety. They were a triple threat.

When they reached the edge of the plot of red and white tables enclosed by boxes brimming over with pink and mauve petunias, they stopped. Every table seemed to be taken. A plump dark man in a waiter's white jacket was in front of them, bowing and smiling.

"Ah, Monsieur Cosling. We are so glad to see you at last. How fortunate there is still a little room, though of course for you we would always find a place."

Stuart glanced from Helene to Robbie, feeling rather pleased with himself.

"Very kind of you," he murmured. They followed the waiter through a narrow aisle to a vacant table wedged in between the others. People looked up from their drinks with curious stares as they passed. When they had seated themselves the waiter rubbed his hands.

"Now what can I offer you? A nice champagne wine? The management would be proud to offer you a bottle."

"Why, yes," Stuart said, "that would be very nice, thank you." He waited until he was sure that the waiter was out of hearing and exploded with laughter. Helene and Robbie joined in.

"Well," he said when they had subsided, "it apparently pays to play hard to get." The sky was a pink dome shading down to reddish orange at the horizon, and the yachts rode motionless in a copper sea. Stuart was so intrigued by a woman who strolled by with a curious loose-jointed sway that it took him a moment to realize that it was Marlene Dietrich. He leaned forward to impart this information to Helene and Robbie. Music began to thump from the interior of the café. The waiter returned and presented the champagne with a flourish.

"I trust this will be the first of many visits, Monsieur Cosling."

"Thank you, I'm sure it will be." The Coslings caught each other's eyes and their mouths twitched with amusement. Stuart lifted his glass when the waiter had left them and bowed first to Helene and then to Robbie.

"To the first family of St. Tropez," he said solemnly, and they all drank.

The color faded from the sky as they drank their champagne and the blue-gray mist of twilight drifted over them. The sea turned to lead and the encircling hills became an inky black. The day was dying and the languor induced by the white heat of the sun was thrown off. People sat up in their chairs, voices grew sharper, eyes looked into eyes with a new intensity. Music erupted from the row of cafés in sudden blasts. There was laughter in the air, tense and anticipatory. Lights glared on all the way around the quai, limiting the world to the area they illuminated.

"Well, you must admit it's nicer than the way it used to be," Helene said to interpose herself between father and son. Stuart was treating Robbie like a contemporary, urging him to drink up and ragging the boy about his inability to keep pace with him. She was already aware enough of Robbie's increasing maturity.

"Come on. We'll share the dregs," Stuart teased.

"The bubbles tickle." Robbie giggled and almost upset his glass as he put it down.

"Remember how you got drunk the day we bought the place?"

"I did *not* get drunk." The fun drained out of his expression.

"Oh, yes you did. We had to put you to bed in the car." Helene and Stuart laughed at the recollection but Robbie couldn't join in. Any suggestion of grossness in front of his mother troubled him. He fixed a pale smile on his lips.

"Isn't it about time for dinner?" Helene suggested, watching him. They had settled on the restaurant on the fishermen's port that was reputed to be the best or certainly the most expensive in town. They emptied their glasses and rose and the round little waiter was once more at their side, assuring them of the joy of the management at being so honored. Stuart gave him a handsome tip.

The dingy little square of the old port had been transformed. The great tree was still there but under it the whole area was filled with tables that glittered with silver and crystal. Again, Stuart thought at first glance that every table was taken and again he was greeted by name.

"Ah, Monsieur Cosling, you should have called for a table," the maître d'hôtel cried with elaborate dismay as he hurried up to them. "Of course, we'll find room for you but it won't be the best." He snapped his fingers and issued orders to waiters who swarmed around him. Yes, this was definitely celebrity and definitely agreeable.

A table was squeezed in close to the sea wall for them. A full moon was just rising above the nearest roofs. Everything looked expensive and desirable. Stuart glanced out at *la batellerie*. It had been converted into a handsome private house.

The maître d'hôtel continued to devote his attention to them. When they were seated he handed them enormous cards bearing the bill of fare and left them. Robbie's eyes widened as they ran down the list of prices.

"Can we afford it?" he gasped.

Stuart encouraged him to order lavishly and to select his wines carefully. Aside from his boyish exclamation at the prices, Robbie remained rather haughtily indifferent.

"This sort of elaborate food doesn't mean much to him," Helene said approvingly. So long as Stuart didn't try to win Robbie away from her, she was delighted to be away from the stove, to be cool and perhaps not too dowdy-looking. It

118

would be pleasant to spend some money on herself again. She was aware that Robbie took an interest in her appearance. And Stuart would no longer have any excuse for neglecting himself. He really must buy himself some new clothes and do something about his hands. Not that she cared, but it would be nice for Robbie to have presentable parents.

After dinner, Stuart proposed a visit to Boldoni's old place as the first stop in their sampling of the local night life. As they climbed to the top of the town, the whole quarter, once so abandoned at this hour, was alive with activity. Under the streetlights one caught glimpses of pretty girls and smart women and well-dressed men. When they arrived in front of the old inn Stuart and Helene made an unconscious move toward each other, for here one could believe that nothing had changed. For a moment, Stuart was tempted to go no farther.

"Let's see what they've turned this into," Helene said, and they went on.

The only changes were those that Boldoni had described—a coat of paint, little tables with gay covers instead of the long bare ones, a low wooden platform covering the cement patch where a five-piece band was banging out jazz. Several couples were dancing. The Coslings sat in silence for a moment looking about them and remembering. Around the corner of the main building Robbie saw the shed and the clump of mimosas that screened the house next door and he looked away, feeling his skin prickling under his shirt. Helene looked up through the vines at their old bedroom window and saw that there was a light in it. Stuart was threatened with melancholy as a succession of memories crowded his mind.

"Well, what will it be now?" he asked. "More champagne?"

People were arriving in increasing numbers. As one group passed their table a gray-haired, square-faced woman detached herself from it and stopped before them with a cry of recognition.

"It's the Coslings! Stuart! Helene! How delightful. It's been years." Stuart rose, startled, and recognized Mrs. Rawls, a widow who had been among their acquaintances during the New York years. She entertained lavishly and had cultivated Stuart for his connection with the publishing world. She was the sort of person one would expect to meet at a newly fashionable resort. Before he could speak, she had taken Helene's hand and was concentrating on her the full force of her charm which, Stuart remembered, was overwhelming.

"My dear, you're absolutely breathtaking," she announced. "I've never seen anything so lovely. Where have you been? What have you been doing? You simply disappeared. I want to know all about everything." All this came out in a flat harsh voice but there were undertones in it. Her words trembled with delight. Stuart remembered this quality and her trick of tilting her head slightly and smiling with winsome girlishness. "And dear Stuart. It's so very nice to see you. You've both discovered the secret of eternal youth. Who is this enchanting creature? It can't be your son." Robbie had followed Stuart to his feet and it was now his turn to receive the benefit of the smile.

"I'm beginning to feel as if St. Tropez were the hub of the universe," Stuart said.

"You must've just arrived. But wait, you'll see everybody you've ever known. You must let me take you under my wing. You might say I discovered St. Tropez. Don't you think it's fascinating how rich everybody seems over here? Such a relief after the States. I couldn't stand the drabness another minute. Though I do think Roosevelt is doing wonders. So handsome. Of course, I've known the whole family for years. Why don't you come join us? I'm with some people you must meet." This last was addressed to Helene with the winning smile.

"It's very nice of you but do excuse us tonight," Helene said. She was suddenly overwhelmed at the prospect of social intercourse. She would have to recover her ease so as to be ready when the time came to make an effort for Robbie's friends. "We're having a sort of family celebration. Do come see us one day. We're in the midst of building so we can't make it a real invitation."

"Building? Here?" Mrs. Rawls asked vaguely.

"Yes, we've lived here for years," Stuart interposed. "Just ask for the place. Everybody can tell you how to find us."

Mrs. Rawls appeared not in the least discomfited. "How stupid of me. Can you be the mysterious Americans I've heard about who own all St. Tropez? How clever of you. And how fascinating. You must come to dinner with me. I know some charming girls who'd give a great deal to meet this delightful young man. I'm hoping for Cole and Linda. Marlene's here already. Oh yes, we're going to have a grand time. You're quite the most attractive family I've ever laid eyes on. A real addition. *A bientôt. A bientôt.*" She shook hands warmly with each of them and made her way buoyantly over to her table, nodding and waving to people as she went. Stuart and Robbie dropped back into their chairs.

"How can anyone be so ridiculous?" Helene wondered aloud. "She made me feel as if I were losing my mind."

"I thought she was quite nice," Robbie said judiciously.

"Flattery works," Stuart said. "You liked the idea of those girls."

"I did not." Robbie blushed deeply. "I don't want to meet any of her girls."

"Don't worry," Stuart said. "We're not going to get tied up with her fancy crowd."

"Heavens, all that seems far away," Helene murmured, and Stuart smiled in agreement. Yet who were they going to see? For whom were they building the guest house? When was Robbie going to make friends of his own?

The music stopped abruptly. There was a fanfare and as heads turned the band burst into a familiar tune. A small woman with a pert urchin's face walked briskly through the crowd to a table beside the dance floor, followed by a handful of good-looking young men. It was Mistinguett.

The evening was getting underway. The dance floor was suddenly crowded. Somewhere a woman screamed and a violent argument broke out behind the Coslings. Stuart turned to see a large dark man and a small red-headed woman snarling at each other in Italian. They were interrupted by a powerful man in a tight striped jersey and tight white pants. He seized the woman by the wrist and lifted her out of her chair.

"Viens, ma poule," he said rudely and led her off toward the dance floor while her abandoned companion half rose, spluttering, and then sank back into his chair. As he followed the oddly matched couple with his eyes, Stuart saw a younger man in sailor's uniform approach the Mistinguett table. He tapped one of the young men on the shoulder and said something to him. The party clapped and cheered as the young man rose and was led off in a dance by the newcomer. Stuart felt it was time to leave.

"Let's see what the other places are like," he shouted above the din.

On the way down toward the port they passed a lighted doorway from which issued the sound of music and laughter.

"Hold everything," Stuart said. "We might as well have a

look at this one." The door opened onto a stairway leading down to a cellar. They couldn't see what they were getting into until Stuart had reached the foot of the stairs and a fluty male voice cried, "A man! Divine!"

There was a burst of laughter and he saw they were in a low, vaulted cellar around three sides of which ran banquettes and tables. The only light seemed to come from a small bar in one corner. On the floor in the middle, men and women were dancing with partners of their own sex. Stuart's first impulse was to turn and run, but he thought immediately of Robbie. Stuart didn't want to give him the impression that they were flying from some terrible mystery. In his moment of indecision, Helene took charge of their retreat. "It's breathless in here. I can't stand it." As she spoke she started back up the stairs, pushing Robbie gently before her. Stuart followed gratefully, to the accompaniment of a chorus of obscene witticisms and more laughter.

"What was the matter?" Robbie asked. "Was it too hot? I didn't get down far enough to see." He felt better as soon as he had uttered this falsehood. He had been to school in Cannes for two years. He had heard of such places. Witnessing the scene in his parents' presence had been a moment of horror for him.

"It was absolutely stifling," Helene said hastily. "For a minute I thought I was going to faint." She was shocked and troubled. She had gathered from a line in a newspaper, from a chance remark, from her own observation of the people on the port, that St. Tropez prided itself on the laxness of its morals, but this was worse than anything she had imagined. Robbie apparently hadn't understood any of the things those unspeakable creatures had called out to them. Thank heavens the house would soon be ready and they could entertain friends of their own choosing and avoid the town.

"No more cellars for me," Stuart said. "I didn't think much of the Pêché Mignon or whatever Boldoni's place is called, either. The port's probably the place to stay." He suspected Robbie's lie but understood the embarrassment that had prompted it. The young were always anxious to shield their elders from the sordid facts of life.

"I think all these places are stupid," Robbie said loftily. He was shielding his parents, not from anything they might know already but from noticing that his curiosity had been aroused. They were so nice, so proper, so decent. At sixteen, Robbie was aware of an emptiness in the life at home. He supposed that his parents had never known this other thing, this excitement, this—whatever it was that was beginning to stir in him. He had been stimulated by all that he had seen this evening and he had thought how interesting it might be to come into town alone, but for his mother's sake he resolved never to propose it.

"I bet you won't think that when you know some girls," Stuart said. "You'll be wanting to come every night to dance."

"Fat chance." Robbie took Helene's arm and in another moment they were back on the brightly lighted port.

"Well, now what?" Stuart asked. There was a party in progress on one of the bigger yachts. It looked very gay with the lights strung out above the deck. "Just a few of the people who've bought our land," Stuart said sardonically.

They were soon ready to go home. The first evening in town had offered no great surprises and Stuart couldn't imagine repeating it often. He hadn't gone through these harassing years for the pleasure of having dinner with Mrs. Rawls.

On the way home Robbie went out of his way to say again how pointless he found such diversions and Helene seconded him. After what she had seen, she was prepared to do anything in her power to keep him away from the place, but she knew she needn't worry. His tastes were essentially artistic and intellectual.

Robbie sat in the back of the big car with his hand in his pocket, his fingers straying along his cramped erection. He longed to get to bed and do something about it. He was tormented by all sorts of unfamiliar urges; he supposed it had something to do with the amount of wine he had drunk. Everything he had seen tonight had carried with it the implication of dizzying freedom. Freedom to do what? Sexually, his only points of reference remained Michel and the dirty little girl; he hadn't learned as much at school as he had expected to learn. There was a lot of bawdy talk about girls but when the boys were allowed out on Saturday night, Robbie never accompanied the ones who pretended to be in pursuit of carnal adventure. His classmates were rather in awe of him; a rumor had somehow got about that he had an older woman as a mistress. He and Jean-Marie, his one close friend, sometimes exchanged a kiss, chaste and poetic meetings of lips that had nothing to do with the nastiness Robbie associated with making love. If a random hope strayed through his mind that something more might come of their kisses, he had always suppressed it. He withdrew his hand from his pocket as the delicious tingling threatened to get out of control.

In the moonlight he and his parents picked their way down through the ravaged land. At the house, Robbie kissed his mother goodnight and shook hands with his father in the French way he had learned at school and continued on down to the cove where he was temporarily occupying the beach shelter. His renewed erection clamored for release. He dropped his clothes and it swung up and seemed to become the embodiment of his whole being. He pulled a deck chair out under the sky and lay with his legs spread and gave his body up to the caress of the moon and the night.

He thought of Michel. He had seen him recently. He had turned into a tough-looking but handsome boy. Several times after the episode with the little girl, they had made each other hard and given each other pleasure. Robbie had started to have meager emissions. Michel had explained that that was what made babies but Robbie had pretended extensive knowledge of the subject so he hadn't found out how at the time.

Their play had ended with the move to the house but Robbie wished now that it hadn't. There wouldn't have been anything grotesque about it like the people tonight, only a simple manifestation of enduring comradeship. He wondered if Michel ever had similar thoughts about him. He wondered if Jean-Marie would like to lie in his arms and get hard with him. There were so many things he didn't know how to find out about people.

He tried not to let sex become a preoccupation—it was unworthy of his mother's concept of him—but it would be much easier if he had a friend with whom he could relieve the uncontrollable urges. He had never had any desire to have anything to do with girls. He had easily adopted his mother's attitude that it would be debasing. When he imposed a beautiful girl on his fantasies, for even his mother conceded that there would be one in his future, they were always static and uneventful. The girl was usually vaguely reminiscent of his mother and he couldn't think of anything he wanted to do with her. She had a tendency to merge into a plump little girl

with her legs pressed together, which made his erection wilt.
To revive it he sometimes saw a handsome young man
running up out of the sea, naked like his father, but with his
sex standing up rigidly in front of him. His face was provided
by young film actors Robbie kept on file in his memory,
frequently Rudolph Valentino, whose old movies he had seen
before sound came to St. Tropez. They ran to meet each
other. They touched. This was usually enough to accomplish
his purpose.

Tonight, he had no need of fantasies. He lay back and
caressed himself all over and writhed in his own embrace. He
longed for somebody beside him to share his caresses.
Nothing more. The evening had left him highly charged. The
slightest move promised to bring relief. He sprang up and
moved down toward the water, and stood with his hips thrust
forward and his hands on his buttocks, offering himself to
unknown desire. Would anybody ever worship him as he
longed to wor— His thoughts were cut off abruptly as his
body was shaken by spasms and his ejaculation leaped into
the sea.

The summer was devoted to building. None of them had
time for the life of the port. Except for a visit from Mrs.
Rawls, they were left undisturbed. From time to time, Stuart
caught sight of Odette, smartly dressed, getting in or out of
an expensive car. She could afford it. It was wonderful what
fifty francs a week could be turned into. Stuart asked Robbie
several times if he'd like another night on the town but
Robbie dismissed the suggestion with one of his odd eccentric
gestures. He was occasionally tempted to sneak off on his
own but the thought of getting caught deterred him.

He took an active part in the construction projects, super-
vising the workmen, deciding on details of design, spending
hours sketching the men as they worked. Stuart occupied
himself with the more practical problems of water, heating,
and electricity. He often wandered off down the rocky path
around the ridge in back of the old house to his abandoned
vineyard. There, although they no longer belonged to him, he
would spend an hour weeding and lovingly handling the
maturing grapes. He toyed with the idea of arranging with the
new owner to have one final vintage, until he arrived one day
in August and found tractors running through the vines. He
watched for a moment and then turned back toward his own
property. In the distance, down on the long beach, he saw

men working on the foundations of the new hotel. He stood for a moment with the sense of being witness to an outrage, and then continued on his way home.

The sight of the tractors was a greater wrench than he realized and from that moment he began to think of getting away for a while. The arrivals and departures of the yachts in the port fixed them in his mind as the ideal means of transport. He began talking of a Mediterranean cruise. The rich went in for yachting. The Coslings should have a taste of it. The building would be finished by winter. Landscaping and planting would be done in February and March. They could leave it then. Helene was willing, as soon as she was sure Robbie liked the idea. Talk of Greece made his eyes light up with real excitement.

When they drove him back to Cannes early in October, in a new Citroën, they chartered a sixty-foot yawl with a crew of three for two months beginning the first of May.

By then, the house was well advanced. In the area around the site of the old house stood garages, servants' quarters, guest rooms and baths, all planned to look like separate but connected buildings with irregular frontages and varied roof lines so that one arrived before what appeared to be two sides of a village square. In the middle of it was an arch giving into the glade of olive trees and the airy colonnaded pavilion of the new main house. It was set on the rocks that dropped down to the cove, where a substantial beach house had replaced the palm-frond shelter. The whole was a maze of unexpected passages and breathtaking vistas. It would be easy to get lost in it. The living rooms, the dining room, the master bedroom, gave onto terraces and an expanse of sea. The enormous kitchen was equipped to entertain multitudes.

Behind, dominating the whole, partway up the hillside, the house Stuart referred to as Robbie's Folly was nearing completion, consisting of studio–living room, bedroom, bathroom, and tiny kitchen. Stuart hoped that Robbie would be encouraged to bring friends to his own house where he could be completely independent. The better part of the legacy that had made it possible for them to come here originally had been swallowed up by the vast spectacular playground. Money well spent, if they learned how to use the place.

Stuart figured that a staff of four, plus a gardener, would be sufficient to run the place. He turned naturally to Boldoni to talk over the question of personnel and was delighted when Boldoni proposed himself as cook.

"Yes, it would give me something to do," he said. "My wife and I sit here all day long. She's a good worker. If you plan to entertain a lot, it would be like the old days running the inn." The proposal suited Stuart perfectly and in November the Boldonis took up residence in the servants' wing. A friend of theirs, a bachelor waiter named Felix whose hobby was gardening, would join them in late winter. Madame Boldoni undertook to find two reliable women to help her in time for the following season.

Time began to pass very quickly. Felix arrived and he and Stuart plunged into plans for extensive planting. He turned out to be a perfect prototype of a Parisian *garçon* but he talked knowledgeably about flowers and trees and vines.

For a tense week or two, it looked as if their cruise was going to have to be canceled on account of war. Hitler decided he wanted Austria. Would nobody in Europe object? Even Stuart, who had never taken the prophets of doom very seriously, suspected that the German maniac had gone too far. He hadn't. He was allowed to have Austria once he'd promised not to take anything else.

The danger of cancellation having past, the first of May seemed to rush at them. Felix was after him to decide about the cypresses that were to flank the steps down to the sea; electricians, plumbers, and carpenters had to be dealt with; colors had to be agreed upon with the painters. Stuart and Helene scoured the countryside for old furniture. He loved every minute of it.

Meanwhile, they had to purchase clothes and provisions for the trip and here they had no experience to guide them. They didn't even have a very clear idea of where they were going. They spent the last day of April rushing hither and yon, trying to pack, giving last-minute instructions, quite unable to believe that their boat, *Northern Star*, would actually be in the port the next day to carry them away. They went to bed very late and awoke at dawn to a beautiful spring morning.

When they reached the port, *Northern Star* was there, tied up beside the British admiral's yacht. It was, in fact, the British admiral who greeted Stuart as he crossed the gangplank to the stern of *Northern Star*, Felix at his heels with baggage.

"I say, isn't that Harry Middleton's boat," a deep rich baritone boomed at him from alongside. Stuart looked over and saw half of the British admiral emerging from the main hatch. He was a handsome man with a great mane of snowy hair, a jutting nose and a fine full mouth. He was wearing a pale-pink shirt of some soft stuff and a mauve scarf looped through a ring at his throat.

"I think that's the name," Stuart said as the admiral came up out of the hatch. "I've just chartered her."

"Fine boat. Come aboard. Cumberleigh's the name. Have a drink. You're Cosling, aren't you? Should've met before this. Used to know your uncle. Daresay I must've met your father, too, in the old days, though I can't say I remember him." They addressed each other from their respective decks.

"I've heard of you, too," Stuart said. "You've been here for some time, haven't you?"

"Three years, in and out. Suits us here. Come aboard." The admiral held out his hand and Stuart threw a leg over the rail. Standing beside him, Stuart saw from the skin around his eyes and chin that the admiral must be very old but his erect bearing and the jauntiness of his movements belied his years.

"What'll it be?" the admiral asked, going to a rack of bottles in the wheelhouse. "A spot of brandy? A bit of brandy never did anybody any harm." It was just past nine in the morning so Stuart found the suggestion a trifle alarming, but since this was a special day he accepted. The admiral asked after his wife and Stuart explained that Helene had stopped in the town to do some shopping but would be along shortly.

"Grand," the admiral exclaimed. "We'll have a bit of a party, what? Beautiful woman, your wife. At least, at a distance. Never been close enough to make sure. Always wanted to meet her. There you are. Make yourself comfortable." The admiral poured himself a drink and drank off most of it in one swallow.

"You're here with your family or friends?" Stuart asked conversationally.

"Oh, family for the most part. Mrs. Cumberleigh's aboard. The fourth Mrs. Cumberleigh, that is. Charming girl. You'll like her."

"I've noticed a lot of young people on your boat."

"I like young people. My children, for the most part. I've had seventeen, all told. Not bad, eh? Don't see much of them anymore. Like to keep the young ones around as long as they'll stay." He poured himself another drink. As he did so a dark plump woman with a large nose climbed through the hatch. He waved a hand vaguely in the air. "Oh, this is the Countess Danski or some such damn-fool name. Can't speak a word of English. Says she's in love with me. Silly woman.

Won't go away." Stuart struggled to his feet and shook hands with the countess, who drifted on past him and down the gangplank. The brandy was taking effect, making everything seem improbable. He was suddenly seized with uncontrollable laughter.

"Eh? That's it. Enjoy yourself while you're young," the admiral roared heartily in approval. "Here. Let me tidy up your drink a bit."

"You know I shouldn't really stay. I'm supposed to be going to Greece today. I should be getting things shipshape or something."

"Greece, eh? Charming little country. Know a lot of people in Greece. Must let me give you some names. Not much you can do till your men come back. I saw them go ashore about half an hour ago. I say, isn't that your wife coming? And there's my daughter Anne just behind her. Daughter by my third wife, I think. Married to Binkie Squires now. My third wife, I mean. Know him? Silly ass. Serves her right." The admiral went back to the gangplank and made a theatrically welcoming gesture to Helene. "Come aboard, dear lady," he boomed. "I have your husband here."

Helene was followed by the daughter Anne and the deck seemed suddenly crowded with people. A slender, sensible-looking young woman climbed out of the hatch and was introduced as Mrs. Cumberleigh. A tall young man appeared from somewhere up forward and was introduced simply as Edward and for a moment there was a good deal of milling about as the company seated itself.

The admiral dominated the proceedings with jovial authority. He paid Helene extravagant compliments, greeted his wife as if her appearance were a delightful surprise, was gallantly ceremonious with Anne, a pale frail girl with lank pale hair. He managed at the same time to communicate to Stuart and Edward, who turned out to be his son, a feeling of hearty male camaraderie. It was, nevertheless, a curiously impersonal performance. He was like a great, aging actor, given to forgetfulness, whose supporting company is dependent on him for its livelihood and will, therefore, do anything in its power to cover up any slight lapses.

This created an electric atmosphere. Its effect on Helene surprised her. For the first time in years she felt as if she might have been missing something; people still had the power to attract and stir her. She thought of Robbie and was sorry he was waiting for them in Cannes so that they couldn't delay their departure. She found the old man fascinating, his wife charming, and the young people most sympathetic, and she wanted to make a good impression on them.

When the crew of *Northern Star* was seen coming back on board, Helene remained behind while Stuart climbed over the rail to make whatever arrangements were necessary to leave. He introduced himself. The captain was a competent-looking Italian of about his own age called Angelino. The dark husky youngster at his side was called Rico. The third member of the crew was a crumpled little old man called Beppo, who was the cook and deckhand. They were dressed alike in dark-blue trousers and jersies with NORTHERN STAR in white lettering across their chests.

Stuart tried to think of intelligent questions to ask the captain who, by addressing him as *"patron,"* placed him in a position of authority. Everything seemed to be in order. Angelino advised putting on supplies at Cannes, which made sense since Robbie was waiting for them there. He called across to Helene that it was time to leave. The admiral insisted that he come back for a final drink and when Stuart saw that Helene seemed happy to linger, he did so. Finally the admiral escorted Helene down one gangplank and up the other while the rest of the group lined up along the rail.

"Sound craft," the admiral asserted, gazing up into the rigging in a nautical fashion. There was much handshaking all around, the engine started, the admiral climbed back onto his own boat, the anchor chain rattled, and Rico leaped about taking in lines. The Coslings stood in the stern and waved as *Northern Star* slid gracefully out of the port. This was the clean break Stuart had been waiting for. When they returned, all ties with the land would have been severed and they would pick up a new life in a new environment.

He made a point of finding out how to handle the engine, how to turn it on and off, the maximum speed at which it should be run. He and Robbie were going to have to do their share when they were at sea for several days at a time. He had done quite a lot of small-boat sailing years ago but knew nothing about cruising in the open sea on a yacht this size. He and Angelino discussed getting some sail up but decided there wasn't enough wind to make it worthwhile.

The Coslings had a light lunch under an awning in the comfortable cockpit, with Rico at the wheel beside them. Stuart had taken an immediate liking to the youngster. He was bright and lively, with a winning smile. He had a gold tooth quite far back in his mouth but it flashed when he uttered full-throated laughter. Stuart was glad that there was somebody on board who wasn't too far from Robbie's age—five years or so, no more.

He and Helene went below after lunch to inspect their quarters. There was a pleasant saloon and a comfortable master's cabin aft, and a choice of two cabins forward for Robbie. Old Beppo showed them how to use the rather complicated system of pumps and sea cocks for the washbasin, the head, the shower.

They sailed past Ste. Maxime and St. Raphael and pulled into the yacht harbor of Cannes in the late afternoon. Robbie was waiting for them on the quai.

Stuart was impressed by his appearance. He had just turned seventeen and had filled out considerably since Christmas. He seemed to have lost some of his funny fey quality and moved with a more mature assurance. He was strikingly beautiful. In another year or two, handsome would undoubtedly be the right word, but now his looks still had enough of feminine youthfulness to qualify as beautiful.

The next morning, Stuart went off with Angelino to be introduced to the complications of a yachting life, which turned out to be considerable. By the end of the afternoon Stuart felt as if he were in charge of an ocean liner. Helene, too, had been busy. There was a collection of waterproof suits laid out on deck when he came aboard.

"She seems to think we're going to the North Pole," Robbie said. Angelino, who had suggested the suits, looked at them approvingly. By noon the next day they were ready to go. The sun was hot and clear; the sea was calm.

They had an early lunch and shortly afterward they cast off their lines and motored out of Cannes' smiling harbor. They expected to be in Corsica the next morning, but for the Coslings who had never before traveled on a yacht, that remained part of a dream. Reality was this lovely bay dotted with other pleasure craft moving back and forth from Cannes to Antibes or the Îles de Lérins. They installed themselves comfortably on deck with Stuart on the wheel while captain and crew disappeared below.

Stuart taught Robbie how to handle the wheel and hold the boat on course. Before they knew it, France was a blue haze behind them and they were alone on the shimmering sea. Stuart felt the air stir against his cheek and his hair was ruffled by a light touch and he looked around him. "By golly, I think we're going to get a little breeze," he exclaimed. The water was darkening ahead of them. "Hold the wheel. I'm going to call Angelino."

Angelino responded to the summons by climbing out of the forward hatch. The wind had moved in from the southeast.

"As you wish, *patron*," Angelino said in reply to Stuart's suggestion that they raise sail. He called Rico and in a moment they were working nimbly around the deck.

"Better let me have the wheel," Stuart said, taking over from Robbie. He explained everything as he held the boat into the wind and the sails went up, jib, mainsail, staysail. At a signal from Angelino he pulled the boat off the wind and waited as the sails flapped and filled, held, began to draw. He snapped off the motor. In the sudden silence, the boat hovered, staggered slightly, rolled over slowly, and with an upward surge bit into the water. Stuart felt his heart beating with exhilaration. He looked at Robbie and Helene, grinning with inexplicable pride as if he had performed a miracle. Helene, stretched out on a mattress a few feet away, was gazing up at the mainsail. Robbie, beside him, was observing everything with interest. Stuart slapped him on the knee.

"Would you like to take it? It's easy once you get the hang of it." They shifted places and Stuart continued his instructions. Angelino came aft and gave Stuart a compass reading for their course and threw the log over the stern. He told Stuart to check the mileage it registered if he was obliged to alter course. Stuart was fascinated. They were navigating in open sea.

When they went on from Corsica the next day, they had become prisoners of the sea. Each morning, something forced them out of their bunks at dawn. The gentle motion of the boat was soporific and they were no sooner up than they went to sleep again. They ate. They slept some more. By the time the sun had set they were yawning. Stuart, who was taking a regular watch on this leg of the voyage, found that it required an enormous effort of will to stay awake until midnight when Rico relieved him.

Stuart drew Rico into the family circle. From the moment of their meeting, Rico displayed a touching admiration for everything Robbie did or said and Robbie accepted his admiration with a show of indifference. This was Stuart's first opportunity to observe Robbie at close range with somebody who was more or less a contemporary and he hoped before the trip was over to understand what lay at the root of his son's friendlessness and know whether there was anything he could do about it. Helene thought Stuart was making too much fuss over Rico. Why would Robbie take any interest in him?

Robbie was enchanted by him. The possibility that it might show in front of his parents overcame him with shy embarrassment. He was supposed to be above anything so commonplace as the boyish fun he felt in the sailor boy's company. He had never known anyone like him, never been treated with the cheerful comradely affection that Rico offered him. When Robbie was alone with him, which he managed to be with increasing frequency as the cockpit became his parents' home base and the forward deck was left to the crew, his manner was transformed. He laughed freely, encouraged physical horseplay, teased as mercilessly as he was teased. He didn't even mind Rico's endless prattle about girls. When Robbie snubbed him in front of his parents, he hoped his eyes told him that he didn't mean it.

Rico's compact body was a marvel of athletic efficiency when he strode the deck dealing with ropes and sails. Robbie wished he didn't always wear a thick jersey and pants. He wanted to see how his body worked. His drawing hand itched to sketch him, not as an artistic challenge—his art teacher at school had told him he had gone beyond life class—but in order to take possession of him in a private personal way. He learned how to be useful so that he could work alongside him. Rico had a way of taking his hand to lead him along the narrow part of the deck that made his knees go weak. He was a good deal taller than the sailor, which compensated somewhat for their age difference. He had found out that Rico was twenty-three. Rico's French was mostly Italian and Robbie's Italian was labored, so they spoke English together; it was part of creating their own world for themselves.

His parents had always told Robbie that he was an American but he knew little of the land of his birth. He felt French, or at least a native of the small part of France that his father owned. With no real nationality, no friends, and a minimal family, his connection with the world around him was often tenuous. Suddenly there was an enormous connection with Rico. The cruise, which Robbie had thought of in a scholarly sort of way as an interesting opportunity to see some of the wonders of the ancient world, had become a dazzling delight.

The weather continued favorable. After an uneventful three-day passage, they arrived at Capri where they lingered several days, the Coslings at a grand hotel on the heights, the sailors on the boat in the little port below. Stuart arranged to include Rico in several of their outings. He was always full of laughter, helpful in saving them from being cheated, and rapturous over every pretty girl he saw, insisting that they were all eyeing Robbie longingly.

They sailed on southward, past Stromboli and the sinister Liparis, through the Straits of Messina. They ran along the coast of Sicily with Etna sloping mistily up and up and away from them. Robbie sat forward staring at it all one morning.

Stuart glanced at him with interest from time to time. The passionate absorption in his gaze was impressive. He wondered what was going on in the mind that he should know so well.

Robbie's mind was gripped by the surge of his emotions. Something about the mysterious soaring immensity of the volcano made a direct connection with his spirit. He felt as if he too were soaring, as if he were being lifted up and out of himself toward some ultimate fulfillment. It was nothing he wanted to express in paint. It was all around him, in him but existing independently of his will. What was it? What made his body feel so sensitized that it seemed to be expanding? What made his heart leap up in strange bursts of exaltation? Why did his mind keep trying to pin down some elusive inexplicable longing? He felt as if he were on the threshold of a final enormous discovery about life, a secret he had shrunk from but which drew him on irresistibly now.

"Have you decided where we're going to put in for the night, *patron*?" Rico asked Stuart during the course of the morning.

"Angelino thinks we might make Syracuse if the wind holds up but it'll make a long day. I think I'd rather stop at Catania and go on tomorrow."

"That so? Very wonderful," Rico said gleefully. "I have girl in Catania. She like me. Very good girl."

"Tell me if there's any place you want to stop along the way. We usually could work it out," Stuart suggested.

"Hokay, *patron*. Is all right if Robbie come with me? Anna has a sister. Family very proud if he come. Just poor peoples, but very good."

"I think he'd be delighted," Stuart said. "It's nice of you to include him." He could imagine Robbie hurting the lad with a brusque refusal. "You mind holding on here for a while?" He left the sailor and went forward to where Robbie was sitting on the cabin gazing landward.

"Rico just told me he wants you to go with him tonight to see some girls he knows," Stuart said. "That is, if we put in at Catania. Do you want to?"

Robbie turned to him vaguely as if he'd been awakened from a dream. "What?" he asked vacantly. "What about Rico?" Stuart explained more fully about Rico's proposal. Robbie wasn't surprised that Rico wanted to take him with him. There was an unspoken bond between them. They would do everything together. "Do I have to?" he asked with his customary show of indifference. "Why can't he go see his girl friend by himself?" Why did Rico have to see a girl? Why couldn't he have suggested their just going ashore together? Robbie hoped his father would urge him to accept.

"Don't go if you don't want to but it might be fun. Anyway, be nice to him. He admires you."

"When you put it that way, I suppose I'll have to go," Robbie said, unhappy that the decision had been left up to him. He would suggest to his mother that he had been given no choice.

Catania was hot, drab, and dirty. Once the port formalities had been taken care of, Stuart returned to the boat to suggest to Helene that they have a quiet evening aboard. He found her in the cockpit, preoccupied with Robbie's outing.

"Why do you insist on his being so friendly with that boy? You don't know what sort of foolishness he might get Robbie involved in."

"Don't be silly. Rico's a decent kid. Besides, I didn't insist. I left it entirely up to Robbie. I didn't even know if he'd decided to go."

"Oh, he's going, but only because you want him to. You know Robbie has no interest in that sort of thing."

"What sort of thing? You make it sound as if he'd fallen in with pimps and harlots. Don't worry about it. The little bird must fly out of the nest some time. Sit here and I'll make us a drink."

Helene responded with a reluctant smile and allowed him to tuck cushions behind her back. While Stuart was getting the drinks, Rico came out on deck scrubbed and resplendent in immaculate white pants and jersey, his curly dark hair plastered to his head.

"I don't want you to be late," she said when he joined her.

"Late? Not late. Nothing in Catania for to be late," Rico said with a laugh.

"Not after midnight at the very latest. You understand?"

"Very good, *patronne*," he said. Stuart appeared with drinks and Robbie followed, looking smart in flannels and sport shirt and scarf.

"By the way," he asked Rico loftily, "what makes you so sure these people are going to be home waiting for us?"

"Where else they be?" Rico replied with simple logic. "Poor people stay home. They wait for beautiful rich boy from yacht."

"Well, if we're going we might as well go," Robbie said hastily, blushing with pleasure. Nobody had ever called him beautiful before. Rico scrambled up onto the quai and offered his hand to Robbie to help him up. They waved to Stuart and Helene and set off, Robbie tall, elegant, and indifferent, Rico trotting happily at his side.

Once they had passed through the gates to the docks, Robbie let himself be carried away by the new delight of being alone with his friend. He wanted to run his fingers through Rico's hair to restore his curls' usual windblown look but restricted himself to throwing an arm around his shoulders. He withdrew it hastily as he felt his knees go weak.

"I'm glad you asked me to come," he said, looking into laughing eyes. His glance dropped to firmly modeled lips. Rico was a film-star bandit, roguish and devil-may-care. "You sure it's all right, your taking me with you?"

"Oh, they so glad to see me they no care who I bring." He roared with laughter. "You. Me. Friends, yes? We go together." He put his arm through Robbie's and hugged it to him. Robbie's head swam. Being with Rico made him feel so free; again he experienced the sensation of soaring out of himself. He wished that the family had moved or the girls had left home, and then they could have dinner together alone. Girls were a nuisance.

Rico turned up a narrow side street and they walked beneath a canopy of crisscrossed clotheslines hung with tattered garments. Bedclothes spilled from windows and hungry-eyed children crouched on stoops, staring as they passed.

"Anna my girl. Gina, she's sister. She for you," Rico told him. "Here we are." He stopped and peered up through the linen at a mouldering building across which was scrawled: w

MUSSOLINI. They entered a dark hall and mounted flight after flight of wide slanting stairs. Sounds and smells emerged from behind every door. The building seemed to vibrate with life. There was a vitality in it so unfamiliar to Robbie that it seemed almost dangerous. They went on up until they reached the top. There, Rico knocked on a door and looked at Robbie with a smile and a wink.

The door was thrown open by a pretty dark-eyed girl in a plain cotton dress. She shrieked and fell on Rico and he and Robbie were swallowed up in a wave of laughing men, women, and children. Robbie's hand was shaken, everybody talked at once, his Italian foundered, and he found himself grinning foolishly. In the confusion, Rico apparently managed to identify his companion and explain their presence, for Robbie heard himself addressed by name and the whole group jostled their way to a table at the end of a big room.

Once seated, they seemed less numerous. There was a small gaunt woman, a fat man, a younger man who was turning to fat, the pretty girl who had opened the door, another girl very like her with the same delicate nose and flower-petal mouth, a beautiful boy, younger than Robbie, and four small children. Robbie was pleased to find Rico still beside him. Glasses were distributed and filled with a black wine from a long-necked bottle, and everybody drank to everybody else. Robbie recognized this gathering as the sort his father would feel at home in and he felt himself stiffening against the noisy laughing group. His mother would find them common.

He looked around and observed the poverty of the place, plaster broken from a corner of the ceiling, paint flaking from the walls, two sprung iron beds with soiled blankets, a tin tub in one corner, cotton underclothes hanging on a line in another, a geranium struggling from a tin can on the windowsill.

Depressing, but he liked having Rico beside him and the others responding to Rico's extravagant praise of his new friend. He launched into his favorite joke about Robbie's devastating effect on all females. Robbie blushed and could think of nothing to say and then, carried away by the atmosphere and the wine, he clapped his hand over Rico's mouth. The instant he felt his lips and nose and cheeks beneath his fingers, he was appalled by the familiarity of the act. Rico pommeled him and everybody laughed and the awful moment passed. Robbie shut his eyes and laughed wildly, too. His hand still tingled with the feel of Rico's face. There was danger here, danger in his wild sense of freedom. He wanted to trace the straight line of Rico's brow with his fingers and the curve of his laughing mouth. He pressed his legs together to subdue the inexplicable stirrings of his sex.

Food appeared, a hearty soup and a mountain of pasta. When the meal was over, Rico suggested a stroll with the girls before the cafés closed and there was another explosion of voices, this time devoted to farewells and promises to return. Rico and Anna took the lead, arm in arm, Robbie and Gina followed decorously. They made their way to the waterfront, bright with the lights from the cafés and busy with strollers.

Robbie tried to make conversation with Gina but found little to talk about. She gazed at him wide-eyed, her charming young mouth slightly open. He was relieved when Rico and Anna stopped at a sidewalk table and the talk became general. They had coffee and sticky liqueurs, which Robbie paid for, and then Rico suggested a walk along the quai. They had to pick their way cautiously in the dark once they'd passed through the gates to the docks. A waning moon silvered the water and the shipping lying at anchor. Rico led them out along the quai where *Northern Star* was moored. A sea wall ran on one side of it and when they came to some steps in it, Rico mounted them. The others followed. He stopped at the top. On the other side, great rocks stretched unevenly down to the water.

"Me and Anna, we go for serious talk," he said to Robbie. "We leave you here. You like serious talk with Gina, yes?" He laughed and gave Robbie a pat on the shoulder. Robbie's heart began to pound. What could he say to stop him? Something about the way he stood close to him urging him toward the girl stirred in him a memory of the afternoon long ago at Boldoni's.

Rico and Anna slipped off, hand in hand, down the rocks. Robbie heard Anna giggle and then their shadows melted into the night. He stood helplessly on the wall, avoiding any contact with Gina, praying for the pounding of his heart to subside. The intense and perilous excitement of the evening drained away as he felt Rico's absence.

The girl moved closer to him, smiling softly. Invitingly? "It's cool here by the water," she said.

He had been imagining things. They would just have a little

talk until Rico came back. "Yes, it is," he agreed in careful Italian. "It is hot there where you live?"

"Oh, it's not too bad. It's quite high. There's always some air."

"Yes, that's true. It is high." She made no answer and Robbie searched frantically for another topic, but the longer the silence lasted the harder it was to break. What was he supposed to do now? Put his arm around her? Would he be obliged to kiss her? And after that? What if she let him . . . ? This was the first time he had been in a situation where it could happen and he knew he didn't want it. The girl was pretty but he hardly knew her. He felt paralyzed from the waist down. What if he made some false move? What if nothing worked the way he thought it was supposed to? It was beneath him, indecent. He abruptly turned his back on the rocks. "Come on," he said, and started down the steps without looking back. He heard her scrambling after him. When they reached the foot of the steps she stopped.

"Where are you taking me?" she asked breathlessly.

"Home, of course," he said, turning to her but looking over her head.

"Oh!" she gasped. She seemed to shrink from him and then she gathered herself together and sprang away and went running off along the quai, her feet padding lightly into the night. Robbie stood for a moment, feeling a stinging heat behind his eyes, a crushing sense of failure in his chest. I didn't want to, he told himself, conquering the turmoil of his thoughts. If I'd wanted to I would have. And how did he know she would have let him? He would never do it. It was disgusting, lying on top of a girl he didn't even particularly like and pumping his bare behind up and down in the air. It was apparently a responsibility of manhood that he would be expected to assume some day. He dreaded it. He turned and walked rapidly back toward *Northern Star*. Rico had betrayed their newly declared friendship. He had said they were going to spend the evening together. He could get along without friends. His mother understood; she hadn't wanted him to go with Rico.

Stuart had decided to take a stroll before turning in. He walked up to the gates and turned back. A girl ran past him and for the few seconds she was visible he admired the fleet movement of her young legs. When he came to the steps in the sea wall he mounted them to contemplate the sea and the sky. As he stood there he heard muffled laughter on the rocks below and through the still air he recognized Rico's voice. Was Robbie down there somewhere with the sister?

Stuart smiled to himself and discreetly descended the stairs and headed back to the boat, thinking of Marguerite and his first love. Had he been even younger than Robbie when he had proposed marriage? He laughed at himself, envying Robbie the fire of his youth.

Early the next morning they set out across the Ionian Sea for Greece. Robbie was determined to snub Rico as a punishment for abandoning him but he couldn't make much of a dent on the sailor's happy-go-lucky affectionate nature. He soon gave up and carried cushions forward to the open deck and lay out in the sun, wearing the swimming trunks that had become his uniform on board. He was turning a dark mahogany brown. As usual, Rico flopped down beside him during breaks in his nautical chores. He pinched and punched him and made him laugh. He was full of talk about girls, in particular last night's girls. For some reason, Robbie insisted on the fact that nothing had happened with Gina.

"Why not? Gina good girl. Why you no take her?"

"Why should I?" Robbie said with a superior shrug. "We didn't fall in love with each other or anything. Why bother? She didn't want it, either."

"Sure she want. I no understand." Rico shook his head with perplexity. "You got beautiful body. You got beautiful face. You very fine man here too, I bet." Rico dropped his hand on Robbie's cock and gave it a squeeze. Robbie's body gave a great leap and he rolled over hastily onto his stomach to conceal his immediate erection. He hoped Rico wouldn't think he minded being touched there. The gold in Rico's mouth flashed as he laughed. "Sure. You take every girl you want with that."

Robbie wondered if Rico had felt it getting hard. Everybody told him that he was just entering manhood and he was still prepared for surprises. Maybe all guys got like this when they were with somebody they liked. Every time he thought he had discovered something special about his body, it turned out that everybody was the same. Like masturbating. Or before that, when he'd had the odd thrilling spasms without much coming out, unlike Michel's performance. He'd discovered that it was just a matter of time. Or when hair had started growing around his cock. He'd thought it was some weird throwback to the beast. His father had hair there but it had never occurred to him that he would. Michel hadn't. His father had some hair on his chest but he hadn't grown any there. Maybe it would come later. Live and learn. "You never think about anything but girls," he said in his most world-weary manner.

"Sure. I very sexy. I take any girl she want me. Next time, I stay with you till I sure you get the girl."

There wouldn't be a next time, Robbie thought firmly. They were embarked on a long passage across open sea; they wouldn't reach port for several days. By then, perhaps they would have become such close friends that they could do things together without bothering about girls.

If not, he would stay with his parents. He turned over and sat up and pulled his knees up and put his arms around them, keeping his erection out of sight. It brought his face close to Rico's. "Wouldn't you be more comfortable if you didn't wear all those clothes?" he asked.

"What you want I wear? Much sun very bad. You be careful." He pressed Robbie's shoulder with his fingers. "You no burn?"

"No." His erection grew achingly rigid. He closed his eyes, longing for him to put his arms around him. He wanted them to lie in each other's arms. There was nothing ugly about that. Rico acted as if he might want it too, always touching him. How could you tell what people were thinking?

"I got work. I come back." He gave Robbie's shoulder a pat and Robbie opened his eyes as Rico rose and moved forward with an athletic spring in his compact body. If you liked somebody, wasn't it natural to hold each other, perhaps kiss gently, as he and Jean-Marie had kissed? There was nothing wrong with wanting it. He had heard plenty of crude jokes about boys doing things together but he didn't mean anything like that. That was some sort of insane depravity that couldn't happen with decent people. He wanted only something he had caught hints of in an E.M. Forster novel he had read that winter, nothing explicit but something that seemed to quiver beneath the words, a sense of a deep passionate masculine love that could light life with joy, as if friendship were almost like falling in love. He could love Rico like that if he would forget about girls. Thinking about it made his spirit soar again. The vast discovery was almost within his grasp.

Time slipped out of focus as it had a way of doing on board. Day melted into night and became day again without any change in the routine. The wind stiffened and subsided. Sails were trimmed and eased. The course was altered. Robbie lay in the sun, with Rico always near at hand. Nobody else existed; they were alone together in the isolation of the empty sea. Robbie felt something suspended between them that a word or a gesture might precipitate into an expression of the love that he knew was growing between them. Thinking of his father's casual attitude toward nakedness, he stripped off his trunks one day and lay on his stomach to tan himself all over. It was thrilling to expose himself totally, knowing that his friend would soon find him. He hoped his example would persuade Rico to shed some of his clothes. It would be bliss to be able to fool around naked together.

Rico came upon him with a shout of laughter and a flash of gold. "You gotta pretty bottom like a girl. You watch out who you show."

Robbie looked up, giggling delightedly. "I suppose you'll want to pinch it next," he said, resorting to schoolboy banter.

"You watch out. I spank pretty bottom." He leaned over and gave Robbie's behind a resounding smack. The rules of horseplay demanded retaliation. Robbie made a grab for Rico's bare foot and caught him off balance and brought him tumbling down beside him. "You get good spank for that," Rico cried, entering into the spirit of the fray. He snatched up Robbie's trunks and gave them a whirl and sent them sailing along the deck. "Now you got no clothes." He tried to wrestle Robbie over onto his back, yanking at the towel he was lying on. Robbie was so accustomed to what happened when Rico touched him that he was scarcely aware of it. He felt an intense ecstatic physical freedom that made him want Rico to know all of him. He wriggled free and clutched the towel against himself and started crawling toward the forward hatch. Rico pulled his knees out from under him, bringing him to a painful halt. He fought him off, kicking and squirming out of his grip, and reached the hatch.

He rolled himself through it and slid down steps and landed on the lower deck. He still had the towel as a haphazard shield for his upright sex. Rico was on him. They sparred and wrestled along the passage, laughing into each other's eyes and spurring each other on. Robbie retreated into his cabin. Rico crowded in after him. This was the exuberant expression of friendship Robbie had been hoping for. He was swept up on a wave of dizzying abandon. Hands were on him everywhere, playful and affectionate. He let the towel go. With a

142

shout of triumph, Rico made a grab for his erection and held it.

"No," Robbie cried. His orgasm almost knocked him off his feet. It was so unlike any he had ever experienced that he didn't immediately identify it for what it was. He pitched in against Rico for support and was plunged into an appalled awareness of what was happening. The disgrace of his ejaculation shot out across the cabin. Rico held him with an arm around his waist and a hand on his heaving chest. Robbie stood aghast while his erection subsided in the sudden silence, all movement suspended except for the roll and sway of the boat.

"I didn't—" he began in a spent voice. "Why did you do that?" He had to blame Rico to exonerate himself.

"I no do nothing, Robbie. You do. I know boys like you. You maybe no want girl. You want big man like Rico? Sure. You come see me when I watch. Midnight. I show you something you like." He withdrew his support and turned toward the door.

"But, Rico," Robbie implored. "I didn't—"

Rico turned back with a wink and a flash of his smile. "Sure. I know. You no worry. You and me friends. Hokay? You come see me later."

As the door closed behind him, Robbie struggled to find excuses for himself. Rico had taken the initiative. Rico had encouraged him. He was suddenly rocked by a great burst of euphoria. Rico had held his naked body and seen his erection without any sign of disapproval. They were still friends. Rico understood his not being interested in girls although Robbie didn't understand the distinction he was making about "boys like you." Rico had seemed to think no more of his having had an orgasm in front of him than Michel had. Perhaps that was just another of the things that happened to everybody. It had been tremendous but he felt as if there were still something missing. He wished Rico had stayed and taken his clothes off and let them lie together and laugh and talk in total intimacy. He had promised something more for later. He felt that he was getting very close to some ultimate secret; tonight might offer the revelation that still eluded him.

He rode the crest of his euphoria throughout the rest of the day. He soared with the promise of midnight. When he joined his parents for their usual early dinner in the gently rocking main saloon he was aware that his friendship with Rico was turning him into somebody neither of them knew. He felt a new identity emerging, a sense of a personal existence that for the first time had no reference to them. Although he knew his mother would find it uncharacteristic of him, he couldn't resist telling them that he might keep Rico company during his watch that night.

"That should be fun for you," Stuart said approvingly. "It's exciting sailing at night."

The sea grew rougher during the evening. When his parents were ready for bed, Robbie lurched to his cabin and stretched out in his bunk. He knew Rico slept during the early part of the night. He wished he were sleeping alongside him. Would he be able to suggest it after tonight? The thought of their sleeping together gave him an erection but Rico didn't mind that. He hoped he had the same affect on Rico. If he did and they did something about it, there wouldn't be any more nonsense about girls. He had found the friendship that was like falling in love.

Robbie opened his pants and freed his erection for his customary play but he realized that by himself he couldn't achieve the prodigious sensation he had experienced with Rico and simply let his hand rest on it. He wondered if Rico would like it; he knew he would be enthralled by Rico's. He had no idea how his compared to others and had never particularly cared. He held it upright and gazed at it. Boys boasted about their size. His looked quite big. When he let it fall, its head just touched his belly button. He wondered if Rico's was much bigger. He wanted to know. There could be no greater intimacy than knowing this private part of a friend. He had always wanted to hold Jean-Marie's. He would never do so now; Jean-Marie wasn't coming back to school in the fall. Thinking about what he'd missed almost gave him an orgasm. He took a deep breath and made his mind a blank and waited.

The boat was still pitching when midnight finally came. He wished he could go to Rico naked or wearing only the trunks he had retrieved from the deck, but it was chilly at night. He got a sweater out but only put it around his shoulders; he didn't want them to be separated by layers of cloth. They could put their arms around each other to keep warm. He swayed and staggered to the aft companionway and climbed up on deck. The wind wasn't as strong as he'd expected and it wasn't cold. The binnacle light astern created a wall of darkness. He couldn't see the wheel or whether anybody was manning it, although he knew somebody must be there. He adjusted his balance to the roll of the deck and made a dash for the light. A hand reached out and pulled him down to the cushions behind the wheel. He let himself drop and landed almost on top of Rico, with one hand on his chest and the other on the back of his neck, his fingers immediately caressing it.

"You no forget," Rico said. He gave a sort of shrug that had the effect of a little push and Robbie drew back slightly to permit him more freedom for handling the wheel. "You come at just good time. I think about girls."

"I've been waiting. You said midnight," Robbie said. He dropped a hand daringly onto Rico's thigh. The dark would excuse his touching the wrong places. Rico laughed and moved it up to the hard, tightly packed curve of his crotch. Robbie's heart leaped up and began to hammer against his chest. Rico was letting him feel it. Rico liked girls but he seemed to think it natural for Robbie to want to feel it. It swelled under the heavy fabric. He was making Rico's cock hard. It was the most thrilling moment of his life.

"You like. You wanta see, I bet. Lotsa crazy guys want but I no let. You and me friends. I show you." He unbuttoned his fly and Robbie's heart gave another great leap as he saw the dim shape of Rico's erection lift from confinement. Rico wasn't ashamed of getting hard with him. Robbie moved his hands over his friend's cock with wonder, learning its dimensions. It felt shorter than his own but filled his hand more bulkily. "Is pretty big, yes?"

"Yes. Wonderful." He leaned over to see it more clearly in the feeble light.

"*Chope et fume,*" Rico said jauntily. Robbie's blood ran cold. He had heard the expression, always accompanied by laughter and obscene gestures, but never dreamed that it referred to something that people might actually do. Rico's hand was on the back of his head, pushing it down until his face was pressed against the rigid flesh. His senses recoiled from the contact. Tears sprang to his eyes. He couldn't do it. It was vile. In spite of himself, his tongue moved to it and touched it.

"Suck. Make Rico feel good," Rico ordered. Robbie's stomach turned over. The fires of Hell would consume him if he obeyed. He would be damned, a criminal for life. His lips moved furtively on it, obeying some impulse he couldn't control. The smooth taut skin felt rubbery and artificial, unlike anything he had ever touched. His mouth opened and thick flesh filled it. The most secret part of Rico was in his mouth.

Some blockage of his mind or spirit suddenly gave way. Revelation flooded him, bringing with it a rushing tide of desire. He wanted it. He had always wanted it. His passions were ruled by the hard phallic thrust of male beauty. Rico was offering himself for his worship. Robbie uttered a strangled cry and his orgasm toppled him from his seat and brought him to his knees in front of his friend. His hands and mouth became avid. Rico chuckled approvingly.

"You suck good, like a girl."

This was the way he could make a friend his own. His worship could transcend the ordinary limitations of sex. He could feel the excitement he was generating in Rico with his lips and tongue. He heard a little yelp above him and a surge of dense warm fluid spilled into his mouth. It took him a stunned instant to grasp what had happened and the radiance of his worship turned to horror. He retched as the fluid overflowed and dribbled down his chin. He tore his mouth away and made a lunge for the rail, gagging and spitting into the hissing sea. He sank back onto the cushions, his head reeling with revulsion. Rico had betrayed him by defiling them both. He hated him. There was nothing left of love but black guilt for the loathsome deed he had done. He would never be able to cleanse himself of it.

"Why you no swallow it?" Rico asked with laughter in his voice. "Is good for you, like spinach."

Turning it into a joke made it even more repellent. He began to shake from head to foot. He hugged himself, feeling as if he might still vomit. "I've got to go." His voice sounded hollow as it issued from the depths of his horror.

"Sure. You suck good. I like. I fuck you too. You be my girl. You go now. I come after watch."

Robbie didn't hear the words, only the blithe confident notes of the voice coming to him out of the dark. He struggled to his feet and careened across the deck and almost fell down the companionway. He tore his clothes off in his cabin and washed and dropped onto his bunk feeling doomed and half dead. His body ached as if he had been beaten and he felt he'd never again find the peace of sleep. He was gripped by the horror he had committed. He would never be free from the memory of it. What absolution could he hope for? He would have to face his mother as if nothing in him had been soiled or corrupted. She would never suspect the depths to which he had sunk. At least he still hadn't been tempted to do anything with a girl. He would never be untrue to her and to the unspoken pact between them. He dozed.

He awoke with pale light filling the cabin. Rico stood palely naked near the washbasin. His friend had come to sleep with him. His heart bounded up with welcome. His erection locked rigidly against his belly and he let the sheet slide off him. The torment he had gone through earlier was relegated to some corner of his mind where fragmentary nightmares lurked. If Rico did it with his mouth, he might be able to do it again for Rico. Something in him cringed from the act but he was consumed with the desire to worship proud masculinity. He was torn by the violence of his conflicting emotions, caught between the sublime and the physical degradation of achieving it.

He sat up to absorb the wonder of seeing Rico naked at last. His body looked slighter without the bulky clothes, compact and muscular but unexpectedly boyish. Hair formed a cross on his torso, rooted in his shadowed groin. He turned from the washbasin and approached with a carefree spring in his step. He had an erection; he made a swaggering display of it. Robbie's trained eye confirmed that his own was longer. If Rico could boast about his, Robbie had something to boast about, too. Rico's had a slight upward curve and looked confident and aggressive. He caught his breath and began to tremble as Rico took a final step toward him. He was going to find out for the first time what a naked body felt like against his; he was going to learn what to expect of a man who was hard with love for him. He reached up for him but Rico brushed his hands aside and pushed him back and rolled him over onto his stomach. A hand moved over his buttocks and greasy fingers probed between them. Terror struck, making the soles of Robbie's feet contract. He knew what Rico wanted. He had heard of it without believing it possible. The moment on deck wasn't a nightmare but the prelude to this culmination of horror.

He wanted to shout with protest; he wanted to leap up and fight off his assailant and escape but he didn't dare make a sound. The creak of the hull and the slap and rattle of gear above drowned small sounds in the cabin but he couldn't risk an outcry that might bring others running. Fingers continued to probe into him and apply some greasy stuff. He must stop him somehow. He would never survive it.

Rico dropped down over him, straddling him on his knees, and pulled his hips up to him. The contact of their naked bodies seemed to drain all the strength out of Robbie's muscles.

"No," he gasped as he felt a nudge of entry. He tried to tense his muscles to prevent a further advance. He tried to twist his hips away but he was held in a powerful grip. He clamped his teeth onto his arm to suppress a scream and prepared for the claw of pain. Rico seemed to become enormous as he slid deeper into him. A flash of pain seared him and shattered his remaining resistance. His body went limp with a groan. Rico was tearing him apart. He felt as if all his insides were going to spill out of him. If he suffered some hideous damage he would never be able to tell anybody, never dare have himself healed. He sobbed uncontrollably as pain ripped into him with the endless enormous penetration. For an instant's pause, he thought Rico had reached his limit and then he made another lunge into him. Rockets seemed to burst in his brain. It had happened. He had been destroyed. His death throes were an orgasm that spun off to infinity.

Pain was bliss. He hovered on the outer edge of ecstasy. His fingers opened and closed to cling to it. His toes stretched. Rico's cock was in him. It made him a part of his friend. He acquired identity with every thrust of it. He was wanted, he existed. He knew absolutely and irrevocably who he was.

"Oh God. Yes," he murmured. "Yes, Rico. Do it. I'm yours."

Rico chuckled contentedly without breaking the rhythm of his masterful drive for conquest. "Sure. I fuck you good. Is plenty big, yes? I know. You want big man."

Robbie's orgasm had no ending. It shook him anew, spreading ecstasy into every particle of him. Rico had taken possession of him and was finding satisfaction in him. All of him melted with submission. He wanted to be taken. He wanted to offer himself without reserve. The revelation was complete. His body was a receptacle to be filled by a man's desire. He wanted Rico to feel how total his possession was, joining them and making them one. He moved against him, shaken by paroxysms of rapture, inciting him to an unrestrained exercise of his will.

Rico gripped his shoulders and threw all his weight on him and drove into him with redoubled force. Robbie wanted to be punished for exulting in his subjugation. He had discovered the ecstasy of pain. Briefly, they were warriors locked in mortal combat and they both cried out with victory as they were rocked by orgasm. Rico drove his triumphantly into an adversary whose victory consisted of surrender and lay on him, breathing heavily. Robbie drifted in a stupefied daze of fulfillment, not daring to think how far he had moved toward accepting his future. He felt the hard power within him diminishing and he flexed newly discovered muscles to retain it.

"Some boys almost good like girls," Rico said against his ear. "You very good, very wanting. Why you no got tits? You be perfect then." He laughed. Robbie could feel it inside him.

"Have you done it with many boys?" Robbie asked hesitantly, still trying to fathom the mystery of what this meant for him.

"Sure not. Not many. Five, six maybe, when no girl. You the best. You be my girl. You give me present, show Rico how much you like fuck. Other boys give me present."

"What kind of present?"

"Nice present. Money. I got no money. You no want to give me money?"

"Sure, but I haven't got any, either." He knew Rico didn't mean it the way it sounded. He wasn't asking to be paid for what had happened. It was just sharing between friends. "Don't worry. I'll get some. I promise." He uttered a little cry as the power surged into him and filled him again.

Rico chuckled. "You want very much, you make me strong. I fuck you good again."

"God, yes. I want what you want."

"Sure. You my girl. Beautiful like girl. You give me nice present, maybe I give you a kiss." He laughed as if he'd made a great joke.

Offering himself again for Rico's satisfaction confirmed everything he was discovering in himself. He had never guessed that his body would some day be capable of such rapture. He had never imagined that he would arrive at such sexual freedom. His mouth tried to join Rico's but it evaded him. He was aflame with love and untried sensuality but resigned himself to what he supposed was the normal restraint imposed by their being the same sex. As they approached another climax, he sensed the restraint being overcome, as if Rico had forgotten that he wasn't a girl. He doubted if a girl could bring his friend to more impassioned orgasm. Rico wanted him.

When they lay still, Robbie felt as if he were cradled in a great healing peace after surviving a violent storm and he plunged into a deep sleep with Rico still sprawled on top of him, slackly joined to him. He awoke alone and squinted against the glitter of sun in the light that filled the cabin. He was seized by panic at the memories that crowded his mind but was instantly lulled by the peaceful fulfillment that seemed to have seeped into his bones. His new sense of identity was strong. He was somebody at last. He was embarked on a life of his own. He would have private joys, private disappointments. He was alone but he knew what it was like to be wanted. It dispelled the loneliness that had always haunted him.

He became aware of the mess he had made of the sheet and rose, pulling the sheet up with him and tossing it into a corner. He replaced it with the top sheet. He must be sure to have a towel with him in the future. Rico would know how to dispose of soiled linen.

He went through his morning routine at the basin and crossed the passage to the cramped shower to wash thoroughly. The boat was moving smoothly through the sea and it was another brilliant day. He wanted to go above to join Rico but he also wanted a little time to himself, to grow accustomed to everything that was new in him. His body had become precious to him in a way it had never been before. He saw for the first time that it was beautiful.

He dried himself slowly in front of the mirror in his cabin, gloating over his tan and the smooth flow of muscle under his hairless skin. Now that he'd seen another to compare it to, he was impressed by his cock. Wondering if Rico would ever want to take it in his mouth made it lengthen and a little encouragement from his hand and the towel made it rigid. He swayed his hips, studying it. As pure form, he found it spellbinding—long and straight, the convoluted head suggestive of plant life, with an indefinably imperious lift unlike anything else he knew in nature. The more he studied it, the more conspicuous it appeared to be, more worthy of Rico's attention.

He dropped to the bunk and stretched out and caressed himself idly where he wished Rico would caress him. Although his mind shied away from the word, he knew that the monstrous thing called homosexuality was a threat he must beware. He wasn't a homosexual and could never become one, but apparently it happened to some people. Things he had thought and felt last night—this morning—might be deeply troubling if it hadn't happened with Rico. Finding a substitute for girls wasn't homosexuality. Rico would probably kill him if he suggested there was anything homosexual about it. If he could be transported to an exalted level of pure emotion and selfless adoration by acts that he had been taught to think of as abhorrent, he couldn't accept anything as truth without testing and re-examining it for himself.

Most people didn't really know very much. There was so much to learn. He had discovered that with his painting. For the immediate future, he had to learn how to make his friend so happy with what they had found with each other that he would forget any limits that two boys might ordinarily impose on themselves. He thought of Rico's "nice present." He must find a reason for asking his mother for money.

He sprang up as his erection subsided. It was time to go out and discover how he would actually function now that he had acquired a whole new self. As a start, he could dispense with his confining trunks. He hitched a towel around his waist. His cock felt good swinging about freely as he headed to the aft companionway. Rico could get at it easily if he should suddenly take an interest in it. He found his mother writing a letter in the saloon and paused to greet her. She looked up serenely, her eyes gentle with love.

"How enchanting you're looking, my beloved. That tan is heavenly. Are you just getting up? What a lazybones. It's almost lunchtime."

"Mercy. How decadent. I suddenly felt like sleeping my life away. Did I miss anything? Any sign of Greece?"

"Angelino says we'll sight land in the morning. We should be in by midday. It's really quite exciting, sailing all the way to Greece. I don't see how they know where we are in all this water. Your father thinks he's Odysseus."

"I hope he has a better sense of direction. I wouldn't want to be out here for the next forty years or whatever it was. He's a great one for battling the elements. We're going to have to arrange for things to go wrong at home every now and then—power failures, water shortages—something for him to cope with now that he hasn't got his grapes."

"That's very perceptive of you, my darling. Heaven forbid that we should simply relax into the lap of luxury." They laughed at the head of the family.

"We'll have to tip the crew, won't we, Mum?" Robbie asked.

"I think that's the usual thing."

"I thought it would be nice if I give Rico his. We've become good friends. It would make it more personal."

"That's very thoughtful of you, darling."

"Do you have any money? If I give it to him now, he'd be able to have some fun ashore. I'm sure he has a girl in every port."

"What an odd life a boy like that must lead. I have some leftover lire. About fifty dollars, I think. Is that too much?"

"We'd better ask somebody but that sounds all right for now. Maybe we should give him more at the end."

"It's very sweet of you, darling." She was surprised by his thought. Over the last few days she had noticed a change in him that seemed to be growing more pronounced. He was more open, more easygoing, more—"ordinary" was the word that came unexpectedly to her mind. She loved his aloof, superior manner. It kept people at their distance. Was he going to turn into just another amiable boy, popular and easily absorbed into the herd? With the customary pang, she thought of girls. She hoped his sailor friend wouldn't try to include him in all his escapades.

"I think I'll go above and take a turn around the deck before lunch," he said in mockingly hearty nautical style.

"You're too absurd." She trilled youthful laughter and gathered up her writing things. "I'd better let Beppo set the table for lunch."

Robbie let her precede him up the companionway. He had made another major discovery during the brief conversation. He was safe. If he had suggested making a gift to a girl he would have had to put up with jocular innuendo from his father, reproachful warnings from his mother. He could suggest giving money to a boy without sacrificing his privacy. Whatever took place between them, there were certain things that people didn't mention or even think about. He was free to be himself. Everybody didn't have to be silly about girls. What about bachelors? He could ask his mother for money again and give Rico lots of presents. His friend would be pleased.

His father was sitting at the wheel behind the binnacle where Rico had been last night. Robbie blushed and his eyes slid past him as they exchanged the usual pleasantries. He caught sight of Rico forward, bent over one of his ceaseless chores. He gave his towel a hitch for security and stepped up onto the narrow deck. Rico looked up as he approached.

"Hey, Robbie. What you do? Why you no come see me?" His smile was merry and his eyes full of familiar admiration. He radiated health and wholesome high spirits. There was no shadow of shame between them. They loved each other. He dropped down beside him.

"I just woke up."

"We have big night." Rico's teeth flashed with his laughter and he winked. "You like? You want again?"

"God, yes." Rico had a big needle in his hand and was repairing a sail. They sat side by side on the deck, facing in opposite directions, their thighs touching. The freedom of Robbie's cock permitted it to swell deliciously at the contact. They were out of sight of the cockpit. "I just asked my mother for some money. I'll have a present for you."

"You get?" Rico beamed with pleasure. Robbie soared giddily; it made him almost burst with happiness to see his friend happy. "You good friend. Nice present?"

"Fifty dollars."

Rico's eyes sparkled with cupidity. "Very fine. You *very* good friend. I give you kiss for that." He slipped a hand under Robbie's towel and ran it along his thigh. Robbie's cock leaped up when the work-roughened hand reached it and moved on it with playful familiarity.

Rico didn't seem to find it particularly exciting but he was getting more interested in it. His hand was really feeling it for the first time. "You plenty big, Robbie. You crazy notta want girls. You change, I bet."

"There's nothing to change. You're the one who says I don't want girls. I just don't think about them."

Rico chuckled. "You get big hard cock when you think about me." He moved his hand along it, exerting small pressures. When he reached the end, Robbie was shaken by a little shudder.

"My God, Rico. You're going to make me come."

"Sure. You suck me. We come together. Nice. Hurry." He pushed the sail aside and scrambled to the hatch. Robbie followed, trying to keep his erection under cover. He

153

dropped down into Rico's arms where he was content to remain but Rico hustled him along the passage to his cabin. Robbie tossed his towel onto the bunk. Already he found it natural to be naked with his friend. His erection lifted shamelessly toward Rico as he stripped. They loved each other. They liked to be naked together. Rico reached for him and ran his hands over him down to his buttocks and pulled him in against him. Their bodies moved against each other, their joined erections prodding them into closer union. Rico chuckled.

"You got skin like a girl. Beautiful." Their mouths met. Staggeringly, Rico darted his tongue out along his lips. Robbie's heart almost stopped. Was that the way to kiss? The caress of hands on him and the tongue against his lips overcame him. He dropped back onto the bunk and grabbed for the towel and was shaken by orgasm.

Rico stood over him and laughed. "I make you come quick. You do me now."

Robbie was seized by a final spasm and he lifted his head. Rico's aggressive cock stood in front of him, demanding his attention. Could he do it again? If it was something that boys usually did together, why hadn't Rico done it for him? He supposed he hadn't given him much opportunity to. He shook off what seemed now like only token reluctance and lifted his hands to him. This rigid virile flesh had joined them to each other this morning. He mustn't think about that. His mouth was compelled to celebrate its phallic splendor. His tongue rolled over taut skin. His lips caressed it. He opened his mouth wide to allow its mysterious power to enter and claim him once more. How could he have thought this act was ugly or abject? It was sublime, the hard purity of male serving male, male obeisance to male supremacy. His hands roamed over Rico's chest. The hair on his body was a light froth of curls scattered over clean muscle and swarthy skin. His hands caressed all Rico's body and felt tremors of response racing through it. He held small tight buttocks and drew him closer in an ecstasy of worship, filling his mouth and stretching his jaws until his lips were brushed by hair. Rico gripped his head and put a hand under his chin and drove into his mouth with mounting urgency. His body was tensed and strained with lust, muscles and tendons as taut as his swelling cock. The imminence of Rico's climax made Robbie shake with excitement and his own cock filled out and lifted again. His hands flew about erratically over his agitated partner. He moaned with anticipation.

"You swallow now," Rico commanded. His hips gave a great lurch, his knees buckled momentarily, and Robbie reeled with a second orgasm. His mouth was flooded once more with the pungent essence of his friend. He swallowed it avidly, grateful to receive it. Why had he wanted to spit it out? He continued to suck on dwindling flesh while Rico made little sounds of satisfaction in his throat. He had done it right this time.

"You good, Robbie," Rico said when tension had drained out of his body. "No girl do it good like you. You got beautiful mouth." He ruffled his hair and stroked his cheek and pulled away and turned to his clothes. "I go quick. I get clean sheets and towels. You come talk with me this afternoon. I fuck you later. Hokay?" He settled the jersey around his hips and was dressed. His dark curls were tumbled about boyishly on his forehead. He stepped back to Robbie and touched his cheek again and flashed him a dazzling smile. "You too beautiful, Robbie." He left with a swaggering little roll in his gait.

Robbie dropped back on his bunk, tingling with ecstasy, and waited for his excitement to subside. He could taste Rico in his mouth. He had fed from his body. Life was too exciting to grasp all at once. They were together, within reach of each other all day and all night; he worshiped Rico's body and could feel Rico succumbing to his. He knew everything now, or almost everything. He still wanted to feel Rico's mouth on him but accepted the possibility that it was something Rico didn't like to do any more than he wanted to take somebody the way Rico took him. He had been wrong about some things but he knew that that would always horrify him.

His mind hovered and strayed around a puzzle. There was a difference in the things he and Rico wanted from each other. Were his desires girlish? He didn't feel girlish. Nobody had ever called him a sissy at school. If anything, his classmates were a bit frightened of him. Nobody was frightened of sissies. He would probably discover in time how it all fitted into a pattern of normal human experience.

At lunch, he felt his idyll threatened by land. He and Rico had been isolated together on an eternal sea. Now there was talk of the hotel in Athens where he would stay with his parents for several days, of people whose names the admiral

155

had given them to look up, of the sights they would see. Robbie's sense of time was restored and he was stunned to realize that their physical intimacy had started barely twenty-four hours ago. It had seemed a lifetime. With the dawning of a new perspective, he was able to convince himself that the revelation of the last two days was the product of circumstances that could never be repeated. He had probably already had the best the experience could offer him. He knew who he was. He loved Rico but he knew he couldn't hope to be with him forever. The dark unimaginable spectre of homosexuality had to be kept at bay.

Rico was reassuring. He spent the afternoon speculating about all the girls he would find in Greece. If he didn't have a girl soon, he maintained, he'd go crazy or fall in love with Robbie. This was accompanied by uproarious laughter. He patted Robbie's bare bottom when it was available during the sunbathing ritual and continued to say that it was as pretty as a girl's, but he didn't touch his cock again even when Robbie let him see that it was hard.

During the night Rico came to him and took him vigorously, but now that Robbie knew the wonder of being able to give himself to a man, he was beginning to feel lonely again. He really was a substitute for a girl and not a completely satisfactory one. Rico didn't want his kisses. Rico would keep him within the bounds of normalcy.

The next morning was filled with the adventure of arriving in a distant and legendary land. After the long days of open sea, there was a touch of the miraculous about seeing it rising on the horizon ahead of them. They were soon part of an island landscape with a great mountainous land mass taking shape beyond.

"Do you suppose it's really Greece?" Robbie wondered. He was sitting with his parents in the cockpit. Rico was busy performing obscure chores with lines and chains and anchors. "What if somebody's made a mistake? We could be almost anywhere."

"I hope it's not still Italy," Stuart said with a grin. "Wherever it is, it's pretty exciting. That was quite a sail. You've enjoyed it, haven't you?"

"Lord, yes. It's been marvelous."

Stuart had never heard him speak with such simple enthusiasm. He was delighted with the boy. He had been a good sport all the way. He had shed his standoffish superior airs and become an inseparable friend of the cocky Italian kid. He had acquired a new alert manliness, in sharp contrast to the dreamy poetic quality that Stuart thought of as his dominant characteristic. The cruise had paid off in a way that he had hardly dared hope for. After the years of his own consuming preoccupations and the estrangement he had felt as Robbie became a mother's boy, he hoped that he and his son would recapture the closeness they had had before Robbie's illness.

The days in the sun had turned him stunningly handsome. Or at least Stuart could see that he would be handsome when his beauty matured. He leaned across to his son and slapped his knee. "I don't know about you, but I'm not going to wait much longer to celebrate. There's just enough ice left to chill a bottle of champagne. How about you, old girl?" He turned to Helene and his approval of Robbie spread out to embrace her; she was largely responsible for the way the boy was turning out. She was looking stunning too. After the bad years, things were beginning to go right again. He hadn't forgotten the morning of their departure, when she had responded to the world outside her home for the first time in years. It was a development he intended to encourage. There had even been a touch of eagerness in her lovemaking on board. Something about being at sea seemed to strengthen bonds between people. He felt as if she were awakening from a long sleep. As usual, she turned to Robbie for her cue.

"What about it, my beloved?" she asked. "Shall we let him get us drunk at eleven o'clock in the morning?"

"Why not? We don't sail to Greece every day of the week."

She had expected him to refuse loftily. He didn't usually enter into his father's games. There was definitely a change in him.

They were where they expected to be, at the mouth of the Gulf of Corinth. When they had dropped sail and the anchor and tied up to a dusty stretch of cement, Rico put the gangplank over the stern and Angelino played host below to a procession of shabby-looking officials while the Coslings drank champagne and sweltered in the airless somnolent port. There was no town of any consequence in sight, only a few decrepit buildings. When the champagne was finished, Robbie stood.

"I'm going to set foot on Greek soil," he announced. He teetered out to the end of the gangplank and stood on shore. "My God," he called back. "It's either the champagne or the motion of the ocean. I can hardly stand up. Greece is rocking." He returned to the relative stability of the boat. Greece. Athens. He was suddenly overwhelmed by a sense of where they were. He felt a vivid new immediacy and meaning in things he had read in classic Greek literature. It was full of heroic friendships in which passion could be implied. It was probably the champagne that was playing tricks on him. He felt oddly excited and languid and amorous all at the same time. His mind was filled with thoughts of somebody who would worship his body with the fervent abandon that he had been ready to offer Rico. He dreamed of eager lips on his, of a tongue darting into his mouth. If you knew the delights of kissing, why not enjoy them? He almost wished they hadn't shared that staggering moment so that he wouldn't know what he was being denied. If there was anything wrong with what they were doing, all of it was wrong, not just some of it. He couldn't repress the special element in him that craved more than Rico would give him. Who would he find to satisfy it? Probably nobody. He was dreaming of the impossible—of finding a complete passionate love with a boy without sinking into the unspeakable depravity of homosexuality. Greek love. He had heard it mentioned without knowing what it meant.

Ice was delivered to the end of the gangplank. Rico and Beppo came and went on purposeful errands. Angelino saw off the last of the officials and water was brought on board. They were ready to go to sea again.

They went through the Corinth Canal at dawn and they were all on deck to see it. When they emerged from the incredible ditch, Rico touched Robbie's shoulder and the younger boy dutifully went below and undressed. In a moment, Rico joined him and took him.

Robbie found the act growing more mechanical and perfunctory. For the first time it didn't even give him an orgasm, not that Rico noticed in the throes of his own satisfaction. Was it only novelty that had seemed to fill it with glory at first? He felt increasingly safe from any unnatural tendencies that might be lurking in him. He had dreamed of much more than sex with Rico. Perhaps his mother had been right in dismissing lust as beneath him.

Athens was a welcome release from Rico's constant presence. There was so much to see. The Coslings met people. They were introduced to the King at a party. There were discussions of the ancient world with cultivated new acquaintances during which Robbie could display the refinement and sensitivity that his mother valued so highly in him. They played up to each other in public, drawing each other out to display their best sides. Helene found that he was helping her recover the social gifts that had grown so rusty with disuse. Stuart observed them affectionately, fascinated by their resemblance to each other and delighted with their popularity.

One morning at the Acropolis, whose eerie magic had drawn Robbie back several times, a good-looking young American engaged him in conversation. Small things about the stranger began to make Robbie nervous—an insinuating look in his eye, slightly effeminate mannerisms of speech and gesture, a tendency to touch him unnecessarily. When he invited Robbie to come back to his hotel with him ("I think we might have rather a divine time together"), there was no further doubt about what he wanted. Robbie was indignant. How could anybody suppose that he was "like that"? (The French expression for homosexuality, *comme ça*, was the first that occurred to him.) It made him feel dirty and cheapened the unique and beautiful things he had dreamed of with Rico. He brusquely left the young American and went back to the hotel and took a shower, studying his body for flaws that he hoped time would correct, and wondering whether he should have found out what sex was like with somebody who was *comme ça*.

Athens was beginning to make him wonder if the dread stigma attached to being *comme ça* might be a recent step in human evolution. It apparently hadn't existed in ancient Greece, and perhaps didn't even today. He saw young men holding hands in the street. Plato had advocated the sublimation of love onto a purely spiritual plane. The point that Robbie's teacher at school hadn't dwelt on was that the love Plato was talking about was love between men. If Plato had felt the need to make a case for sublimation, sex must have had something to do with it. The classic idealization of the male form in sculpture stirred him deeply.

The Aegean awaited them. If they went to all the places that everybody said they mustn't miss, they would have to stay a year. They set off rather aimlessly, planning to include the major sites of Santorini and Rhodes and Crete and Delos in their itinerary. A study of the charts with Angelino indicated that they could put into port every night at different islands along the way. Rico greeted Robbie with boisterous affection after their brief separation and told him all about his triumphs with girls. He wasn't going to need a substitute if he could go ashore every night.

An island called Poros had kept coming up in conversations as a pretty place within easy reach for their first day's sail so they put in there in late afternoon after having been amazed along the way by the dimensions of the ancient world. Salamis, the scene of a great naval battle, was just outside the port of Piraeus. Aegina, once an important power and a respected ally of Athens, was a small humpy island they passed during lunch. Sparta, the capital of a great nation that had overpowered Athens, lay across a few misty hills on the Peloponnesos. The heroic events of antiquity had been enacted on a very small stage. Stuart wished that the European war everybody spoke of as inevitable could be reduced to such a modest scale.

A crowd of children gathered on the quai as they tied up in what appeared to be an inland lake but was in fact a small pocket of sea formed by the island's proximity to the mainland. In front of them, a whitewashed village sprawled haphazardly against a hill. For a few moments they were soothed by the sense of total peace that descended on them when the lines were secure and the sails down and the engine was off. They became aware of the crowd making way for a simply dressed elderly woman of commanding presence and enormously distinguished looks who approached the end of the gangplank and came to a halt.

"Welcome. Have you come from far?" she called in a rich cultivated voice.

Stuart moved out along the deck to meet her. He was immediately intrigued and impressed by her; she was such a grand lady to emerge from a crowd of urchins. "We sailed from France," he said across the gangplank. "We've just come from Athens today. Won't you come aboard?"

"How kind of you." She showed no signs of age as she stepped nimbly down the gangplank. "I'm Mrs. Dianopoulou. We don't get many foreign yachts here. You're a major event in our placid lives."

Stuart introduced himself and turned to include his family. "There aren't enough of us to make much of an event."

"The three of you? How charming. You're such extraordinarily handsome people. I have a house here. You must come and let me give you a glass of *ouzo*. I have friends with me. You'll give us an excuse to make an evening of it. Our pleasures are simple but we can give you a taste of Greek island life. It has a certain enchantment." Her beautiful eyes gazed through and beyond them as she chose her words carefully and enunciated them with great precision. Her presence made everything a major event.

It was the beginning of an evening of sharp but dreamlike impressions. A small sputtering motor launch transported them across the inland lake. They headed into the setting sun and were deposited at a rocky promontory and clambered up to a garden on various levels planted around a rambling old mansion. It appeared to be imbedded in trees. Mrs. Dianopoulou flitted gracefully through the foliage as she came to meet them. The terraced garden was bathed in golden light. They sat in garden furniture under a tree and were served *ouzo*. Others joined them. There was an English couple. There was a rather droopy young Englishman called Johnny Metcalfe who turned out to be a painter. He appropriated Robbie to discuss their work. A boy and a girl, both younger than Robbie, joined them. There was, most notably, Carl von Eschenstadt. The atmosphere of the gathering altered slightly with his arrival. He seemed to put them all on their mettle.

He was a strappingly handsome man, golden blond, blue-eyed, with gleaming white teeth. He immediately singled Helene out for his attentions though he wooed them all with easy charm. His manner and appearance were youthful but he quickly made a point of being almost forty. Helene blushed, suspecting that he did so to put them on an equal footing before launching a flirtation.

"Incredible that Mrs. Cosling should have a grown son, eh, Carl?" the married Englishman remarked.

"No, Harold, no. You English have no perceptions. No woman can be truly beautiful *unless* she has a grown son," von Eschenstadt replied.

"I know what you're going to say next, Carl," Mrs. Dianopoulou said, gazing out across the bay as if she could wrest secrets from the gathering night. "You are going to say that twenty years ago when I was already older than Mrs. Cosling is now, I was the most beautiful woman you had ever seen."

"You are still beautiful," the German declared gallantly, "but you are now also a mind reader."

"I know you, my friend. You are incapable of talking to a woman without trying to make her feel that she has never been appreciated as you appreciate her." Mrs. Dianopoulou looked at Helene. "It is my warning, Mrs. Cosling. I always warn women I introduce to Carl."

"Now I won't be able to say a word to Mrs. Cosling without her suspecting my sincerity," von Eschenstadt sighed. "No matter, I shall tell her that her husband is very handsome, that her son is most handsome, too. She can't question that."

Mrs. Dianopoulou smiled serenely. "You see, he is incorrigible," she said.

Helene remembered from the old days that some men couldn't discuss the weather without turning it into a flirtation and it had always annoyed her. Von Eschenstadt had a sort of devil-may-care *joie de vivre* that saved him from being annoying. While they drank and chatted, he was all meaningful glances, silent appeals, veiled challenges, as insistent as hands touching her, but she was enjoying herself as she had enjoyed that faraway morning with the admiral's family. She was recovering her social aptitudes and was able to parry his attentions lightly without completely discouraging them. It was fun being courted again though even Carl, in the presence of her husband and son, would know that it was only a game.

It was dark when servants with lamps lighted the party down over the rocks to two waiting boats. Robbie stood back and watched while the German helped Mrs. Dianopoulou and the English lady onto the first boat, keeping his mother at his side until last. He gave her a hand and clambered quickly aboard after her, followed by his father and the Englishman called Harold. The boat circled away, its motor popping, and the second nosed in with the boatman standing in the bow.

There was enough light coming from somewhere for Robbie to see that he was the same one who had brought them out, young and good-looking. Robbie had been instantly attracted to him but had been careful not to pay any attention to him in front of his parents. The boatman beckoned to him and held out his hand. Robbie picked his way over the last few rocks and made a leap for the boat. He grabbed the extended hand and was pulled down into the boatman's arms. The tenderness with which he was briefly held caused his heart to skip a beat. He felt a shock of recognition pass between them.

The boatman laughed and gave him a little hug and took his hand and led him to the stern and seated him beside the tiller as if he knew they belonged together. He returned to the bow and helped Johnny Metcalfe and the younger pair safely on board and came back and did something with the engine. They reversed and Robbie pulled the tiller toward him to bring them around, inaugurating a collaboration that they both seemed to expect.

The boatman patted his shoulder approvingly and dropped down beside him and put his arm around him and hugged him close. He put his hand on Robbie's where it held the tiller and moved it back and forth on the wood. He said something and laughed. An image sprang to Robbie's mind. Did the young boatman mean what he seemed to mean? Even though he couldn't see him clearly, Robbie had the impression that he was only a boy, probably about his own age. The boy lifted his hand from Robbie's and pointed at himself, leaning his face in close. "Theo," he said.

"Theo," Robbie repeated. Theo nodded vigorously and pointed at Robbie. Robbie said his own name.

"Roddy?" He pronounced it almost as if it were spelled with a "th" and Robbie didn't correct him. He liked having a special name for Theo. He replaced his hand on Robbie's and squeezed it as he shifted the tiller to alter their course slightly. "Roddy," he repeated delightedly. They moved slowly and noisily out across the still lake. Stars pulsated in the sky. The lights of the town were strung out along the hillside like a fallen constellation. The arm held Robbie firmly as if it weren't going to let go. Robbie had an erection.

He told himself that he was imagining things. Theo was simply being affectionate in a way that was permitted here. The other three passengers were dark shapeless forms only a few feet away. Robbie moved his thumb in a tentative caress. The hand on his waist moved up amorously along the side of his ribs, pressing him closer. Robbie slipped his free hand over onto Theo's thigh but didn't dare let it go exploring. Theo clasped it between his knees and brushed his mouth against the side of Robbie's face. Robbie turned and Theo kissed him quickly on the lips. Robbie was barely able to stifle a cry of incredulous delight.

They both drew back but Theo's arm remained around him and their fingers played provocatively together on the tiller. Robbie was breathing rapidly. He didn't see how they could

163

go any further but they had declared themselves. They were making love to each other. It was perfectly simple and open and natural. Why couldn't everybody be like the Greeks?

They rounded a point and headed in toward a big, brightly lighted house set just above the sea on a wide terrace. As they drew closer, Robbie could see tables set out on the terrace with people sitting around them. Light began to dart and flicker into the boat and he gave Theo's knee a squeeze and reluctantly withdrew his hand. Their hands remained on the tiller but with their fingers spread out on it, touching but no longer holding each other. Theo continued to stroke his back down to his buttocks and up along his side. He surely had an erection too; Robbie longed to touch it before they were parted.

They approached a short jetty and Theo cut the motor. It was light enough now for Robbie to see his companion clearly. He was as young as he had thought and very handsome, with wide-set eyes and broad cheekbones and a marvelously expressive and mobile mouth. It was a northern face and his hair was light brown instead of the standard Greek black. Theo stood as they drifted in close to the jetty and he and Johnny exchanged a few words in Greek. Robbie's eyes were fixed on the swell of his crotch, startlingly bulky in tight cotton pants.

He started to rise but Theo put a hand on his neck and ran his fingers through his hair, keeping him beside him the way Carl (Robbie thought unexpectedly) kept his mother with him while he helped the others. When Johnny and the young pair had climbed onto the jetty, Theo gave his shoulder a pat and Robbie rose, finding the courage to let his hand brush against the splendor he had been admiring. A shiver of excitement ran down his spine; Theo wanted him. They stood close together, holding hands. Theo had wide shoulders but was shorter than Robbie. Their eyes met and Theo's mouth formed a suggestion of a kiss and his eyes filled with laughter and desire.

"Here? Later?" Robbie asked, pointing down at the boat. It had to happen, although he couldn't imagine how they would manage to be alone together. Theo laughed and nodded and waved toward the town. He exerted pressure on Robbie's hand and led him forward. He made a thorough loving exploration of Robbie's behind as he gave him a boost onto the deck. Robbie put his hand on the top of his head in a final caress as he jumped onto the jetty. They waved to each other and Robbie turned to Johnny Metcalfe. The two adolescents were mounting the steps ahead of them.

"I'd say young Theo rather fancies you," Johnny said in a subdued voice.

"He seemed to want to hold my hand," Robbie said in case Johnny had seen them.

"A friendly custom, if sometimes misleading. He's one of the Five Brothers. They enliven our days—our nights, too, as far as that's concerned—with their charms. Theo's the youngest. The others are all married. He's something of a celebrity in his own right. If you're interested, you'll doubtless find out why."

"What do you mean?"

"Never mind. I have it only on hearsay. You'll doubtless find out for yourself. You're inclined that way? They're an extraordinary family. Not typically Greek. You run into these unexpected strains here that date back to before the Turkish occupation. There's Macedonian blood there somewhere. I like to think of them as descendants of the Great Alexander. I can easily see you as Hephaistion."

Robbie blushed as he picked up the reference and began to like this mournful-looking young Englishman. "Is he going to be waiting for us after dinner?" Robbie dared ask.

"For you. Don't worry about that. Greek boys are very faithful when they find someone they like."

"He made some sort of gesture toward town."

"I dare say he meant he'll be taking us all to the taverna later. We'll see some dancing. His twin brothers are famous dancers."

They were going to see each other again. Robbie could get through dinner without the anguish of not knowing.

They found the older members of the party already seated at a big table when they climbed up to the terrace. They all exchanged greetings and the newcomers took the chairs left for them at the end of the table. Helene noticed that Robbie was looking particularly beautiful tonight, all vibrant and alive, rather as if he'd just fallen in love. She smiled fondly. That would happen one day soon. For the first time, she thought of it without dread. It would be rather sweet and exciting to watch him with his first girl. Something about the novelty and beauty of the evening engendered romantic thoughts. She turned back to Carl to answer some question about the house in St. Tropez. He had "placed" them very quickly. He knew of Stuart's father and other members of his family and had even met a cousin of Helene's late husband. He was now familiarizing himself with their house.

"It's so difficult to describe," Helene said. "We lived in a little sort of cabin and then when we sold some land Stuart decided to build a showplace. I hope it isn't too showy but it *is* extraordinary."

"Not extraordinary enough, I'm sure, to house the extraordinary beauty of its mistress."

"Oh really, Carl. You're such a fool," she said with flustered girlish laughter. She was astonished that they should be on such easy terms so quickly. She enjoyed looking at the handsome blond German. His smile rose in his eyes before it burst across his face in a way that was quite beguiling.

He leaned across the table to Stuart. "Your wife says I'm a fool because I tell her she is beautiful. Why have you kept it a secret from her?"

"For a while, we couldn't afford a mirror. It's high time somebody reminded her. It's something husbands sometimes forget to mention. I don't think I've been too remiss." He smiled across at them. He had fallen in love with Greece. He hadn't seen Helene so playful and happy for years, momentarily freed from her doting absorption in Robbie. He liked Carl; he was a man's man, for all his elaborate flirtatiousness. He was pleased for Helene to have an admirer after the years of isolation. The evening had been given a mystic significance by the oracular presence of Mrs. Dianopoulou. She seemed to have accumulated into herself all the wisdom of the race. He felt as if she were about to give utterance to the ultimate secret. He listened attentively to every word she said, even if it was only to order dinner. More than anybody he knew, she struck him as being rooted in some timeless reality that had so far eluded him.

Robbie fidgeted with impatience. Why did he have to be here instead of with his friend? It was time to strike a blow for his independence. He couldn't spend every waking moment for the next month with his parents. He and Johnny talked about color and form and he began to find Johnny's long nose and almost total lack of chin more entertaining than depressing but he couldn't forget the handsome boy. They drank plentifully of *retsina* on top of the *ouzo* but instead of dulling his senses it inflamed his desire. Johnny seemed to understand and approve his interest in the young Greek, which reassured him. Things could happen here that might not anywhere else. But how? He was tied to his parents.

Halfway through the meal, Theo appeared at the top of the steps. Robbie wanted to let out a whoop of welcome. He was too well trained to give way to the impulse but he felt something happening in his face, as if a hundred lights had been turned on inside him. Their eyes drew each other as Theo advanced partway across the terrace and stopped. They beamed at each other and Theo pointed at himself and down below where the boat was waiting and nodded. Robbie nodded in reply and watched the boy turn and head for the corner of the house. Robbie glanced hastily around the table to see if he had been observed but everybody was engaged in conversation. Only Johnny smiled at him with mournful comprehension.

"My word," he commented. "Anybody who can make you look like that should have you."

Johnny had been right. Theo was here, watching over him, waiting for him. Robbie finished the meal in a state of almost uncontrollable excitement, in love with Greece, in love with Theo, almost in love with Johnny. He remained at a loss as to how he could free himself for the Greek boy but Theo would think of something. They had kissed. Theo would know how to get what he wanted.

When the party rose to go down to the boats for town, Robbie hung back, hoping they would divide up the same way as before. When he reached the head of the steps, he looked down for Theo and saw him waving at him. He waved back. He was keeping his boat clear of the jetty.

The others climbed into the first boat. Johnny deftly steered the young people into it and stood beside Robbie as it pulled away and Theo moved in toward them. "I'm your chaperone. Pay no attention to me. I'm going to look at the stars."

Robbie was flooded with gratitude. He would have a few minutes with Theo. "You're wonderful," he exclaimed.

"Think nothing of it. I like to see the course of true love run smooth." He gave Robbie a little push, which sent him into a flying leap for the boat. Theo hurried to him and conducted him aft, guiding him around the engine housing with his arm around him and repeating his name like an endearment. All his movements were youthfully impetuous but filled with remarkable tenderness. He handled Robbie like some precious fragile object.

The boat gave a lurch as Johnny jumped aboard and they exchanged a few words before Theo accelerated and turned in a wide arc and headed out away from town. Robbie was suddenly alarmed. What would everybody think if he didn't join them?

"Where're we going?" he called to Johnny.

"He wants a private moment with you. I can't see what you're doing even if I wanted to, so don't be shy."

Theo remained standing at the motor, his shirt unbuttoned and shirttails flapping, revealing a deep chest and muscular abdomen. As soon as they reached dark water, he cut the motor until it was idling, with an occasional pop and stutter. He dropped down beside Robbie and drew him close with his lips parted. Robbie's heart began to pound. Somebody wanted to really kiss him at last. Their mouths met. It wasn't a tentative touching of lips but a deep devouring possession of each other, their tongues plunging against each other. Robbie was swept up in a storm of passion. They gripped each other's biceps and their bodies writhed and strained to each other across the tiller. He wasn't a substitute for a girl. Theo wanted him for himself. They broke apart gasping and Robbie dropped his head to a broad shoulder and waited for the pounding of his heart to subside.

Theo spoke to him gently against his ear. Robbie wanted to cry with frustration. For all he knew, Theo might be saying that they mustn't make love anymore. It didn't seem likely. He was working his hands inside the back of Robbie's slacks. Robbie unfastened the top two buttons and the hand slid in under his shorts and roamed over his naked skin. He shifted his weight onto one hip so that fingers slipped between his buttocks and exerted pressure. Robbie closed his eyes and uttered a little cry of delight.

"Help me, Johnny," he called in desperation. "Tell me what he's saying."

"I don't want to intrude but—" He addressed Theo and after a brief exchange he reported, "He says he wants to be with you later."

"I want to, too, but I don't see how it's possible. Explain that I'm with my parents. I'll do anything to get away. Oh God." Theo had moved his hand around to the front of his slacks and found the head of his erection. He fondled it lovingly. More Greek was spoken while he pulled Robbie's shirt out of his trousers and unbuttoned it. Their hands moved over each other's torsos. Theo's chest was voluptuous, twin slabs of muscle, deeply defined. It was as hairless as Robbie's.

"I'd make a rather special effort if I were you," Johnny said. "He says he loves you. They use the word loosely. *S'agapo*. I love you."

"*S'agapo*, Theo," Robbie repeated.

"He says you're the most beautiful boy he's ever seen," Johnny added. "I'll second him on that."

"Tell him that if my parents will let me, I'll go anywhere he wants."

"I'll tell him but I'm afraid he'll find it very peculiar. To him, you're a grown man who wants to spend the night with a friend. He'd never understand why your parents would object. On the contrary, he'd expect them to encourage you. You're not running the risk of getting into trouble with a girl."

The dialogue in Greek continued while Robbie leaned over and ran his lips and tongue over the deep curves of Theo's chest and drew hard nipples into his mouth. Theo's excitement matched his own. He had pulled Robbie's pants down and was stroking his erection and caressing his buttocks and urging him in closer against him. Robbie's hand was drawn irresistibly downward but lingered on the ripple of muscle of his abdomen. There was so much of him he wanted to touch and know. This boy wouldn't impose any restraints.

"He says he'll arrange it, " Johnny said. "Perhaps he's planning to kidnap you. I've made some practical suggestions."

Robbie's hand moved on to its goal and tugged at buttons that were locked into place by the rigid pressure against them. Theo laughed and helped him by shifting on the bench. Pressure was eased and Robbie was able to open his fly with growing thrilled amazement at what he was uncovering. Theo's erection swung heavily into his grasp. His hand was jolted by the size of it, as if he had received an electric shock. It was bigger than he had imagined a cock could be; his hand encircled its imposing girth and moved down to its base. His fingers strayed through pubic hair and he hooked his thumb around the shaft, swaying it slightly to define its dimensions in the dark. It was a long pale form that seemed to have no beginning or end. He crouched down and opened his mouth on it and curled his tongue around its head. After a moment, Theo drew him up to him again and began to make love to his face—eyes, nose, lips—with gentle openmouthed kisses. Their hands moved slowly and lingeringly on each other's erections, telling each other that their bodies were pleasing.

169

Robbie's heart seemed to overflow with the tenderness he felt in the boy. Theo spoke with his mouth just touching Robbie's.

"He says you've got a wonderfully big cock," Johnny said. "He'd like to know if you want him to fuck you or whether you're thinking of the other way around."

"Oh no. I want what he wants." He looked at Theo and nodded while Johnny translated. Theo put his hand on the back of his head and stroked his hair and said something else.

"This is getting a bit sticky," Johnny said, "but here we go. It's to do with oral intercourse—uh, sucking cock to put it bluntly. He wants to know if it's what you prefer."

"Not necessarily. I want everything."

"Naturally, but it's not the done thing here. I find that every country has these odd taboos. I'll tell him you have an open mind on the subject. Fucking is all they're really interested in."

Theo replied at length to Johnny's brief remark while he and Robbie continued to stimulate each other's erections. Robbie was hardly conscious of revealing his most secret and unmentionable desires to a comparative stranger. Johnny took everything for granted.

"He says he doesn't usually like it but he wants you to," Johnny reported. "No, that isn't quite it. He says that he doesn't usually like boys who want to do it but he doesn't mind if you do because you're different. He wants you to have everything you want."

They tried to see into each other's eyes in the dark while Johnny spoke. Their mouths met and opened to each other again and they exchanged another tumultuous kiss. Their hands became more agitated on their erections. Robbie could feel that they were both close to orgasm. He broke away with a cry and dropped to his knees between Theo's legs and measured the soaring flesh with both hands and stretched his mouth wide to receive it. He thought of Rico and acknowledged his debt to him for having shown him what he wanted. He was worshiping at the source of life, paying obeisance to a primal force greater than his own. Theo pushed a cloth into his hand and made a low growling sound in his throat. Robbie hastily moved the cloth to his erection and ejaculated into it while Theo's body gave a leap and Robbie's mouth was filled with sweetish aromatic fluid. He tasted the thrilling mystery of it and swallowed it with joy. He continued to suck on the superb flesh until it began to dwindle. He lifted himself back onto the bench and Theo put his arm around him and drew him close and kissed the side of his face and spoke.

"What's he saying now?" Robbie asked the dark shape forward.

"Why he doesn't know is best known to yourselves, but he wants to be sure you came."

"God, yes." He turned an ecstatic face to his lover and nodded. Theo hugged him and laughed.

"Forgive my asking but you must make allowances for my curiosity. Is his cock enormous?"

"Yes. Unbelievable."

"So we've all heard. He's famous for it although I've never known anybody before who can speak with authority. You're one of the elect. With your looks, I'd expect you to be. I've heard ten inches."

"I don't know but it could be. Maybe more."

"Lumme. If the first fine frenzy has passed, shouldn't we get back? I don't want everybody to think I'm aiding and abetting an elopement."

"Yes. Just tell him I don't care what I have to do. I'm going to be with him tonight."

Greek was spoken while Theo's arm tightened around him. "He's glad you agree because he wasn't going to give you any choice," Johnny explained. "He says that the moment he saw you he wanted you more than he's ever wanted a boy in his life."

Robbie settled back against his lover with a sigh of profound contentment. He'd made love to the great cock. If anything went wrong later, at least he'd had that.

Theo kicked the engine into noisy activity and turned and headed toward town. Robbie trailed the cloth he had used in the water and kept his other hand on Theo's quiescent sex. He felt it stir whenever they exchanged a kiss. He could still feel his hands on him everywhere, wanting all of him. His arm around him now was so possessive that he felt as if he could never give himself to anybody else. As they neared the lights of the town, they arranged their clothes and fastened buttons. They looked into each other's eyes when there was light enough to see the desire burning in them, promising them the ultimate union.

When he could see him clearly again on the bright water-front, Robbie was stunned anew by the Greek boy's looks. He was boldly handsome. His strong straight nose gave force to an otherwise endearingly gentle face. His generous mouth

171

was a composition of fluid, enticing curves. When he turned his wide-set eyes to Robbie, they contained depths of slightly awed, amorous devotion. Robbie could scarcely believe that he knew the stalwart body almost as intimately as anybody could. They strolled along the waterfront toward the sound of music with their arms around each other.

"Do you all have the boys here?" Robbie asked Johnny. After what had taken place, the question seemed no more than politely conversational, although it was hard to imagine the Englishman as anybody's bedmate.

"How charming of you to ask. The boys all have each other. I'm not very keen on sex myself. I'm a very visual person. You doubtless are too, but you're a supreme beauty. I dare say that affects one's responses to life. You can't keep it all to yourself. Given the choice, I'm inclined to like the occasional girl. The poor things are usually so grateful, unlike you dazzling boys."

"But then—" Robbie felt hopelessly out of his depth. Here was another man who preferred girls but who took it for granted that boys made love to each other. He would never get it all straight. "You didn't mind talking about those things?"

"I minded not being able to see more. It's very sensible to settle the basic questions beforehand. In this particular case, I think I envy both of you."

"I can't thank you enough. You've been awfully damn understanding."

"Why not? All these boys are my friends. People talk a great deal of nonsense about sex. Try not to let it confuse you. You're still very young but old enough to get away from your parents when you choose. They're surely more understanding than you think."

The music was growing louder, an odd Eastern wail. They turned in at an arched door and were submerged in a din of shouting voices and the insistent music. A small orchestra played at the end of a wide, bare, harshly lighted room filled with long tables set around a clearing in the middle. Robbie caught sight of Mrs. Dianopoulou's party at the end of one of the tables. There were no women at any of the other tables in the room. When he looked around, Johnny had disappeared. Theo took his hand and led him in among the tables and seated him between two handsome youths who looked so much alike that he assumed they were twins. They greeted

Theo exuberantly with much handclasping and patting of each other's backs. Theo squeezed a chair in beside Robbie and spoke at length. Robbie heard Theo's name for him being repeated and caught the word *"adelphos."* These must be two of Theo's married brothers. There was a family resemblance and they were as fair as Theo. The latter pointed first at one and then the other and repeated names. "Niko. Tassos." Niko had wavy hair. Tassos's was straight. Otherwise Robbie couldn't have told them apart.

"Niko. Tassos," Robbie said, looking from one to the other. They all laughed and nodded and Niko put an arm around his shoulder and hugged him. Theo took Robbie's hand and put it on his cock. It was hard again. So was Robbie's. Theo put an arm around his waist and moved his other hand slowly over him, up along his ribs and across his chest and down to his groin where his erection was imprisoned. He was making it clear to everybody that he had chosen Robbie; they were pairing off publicly. It amazed Robbie but he loved it. He wished he could stay forever. Copper tankards of *retsina* were set out along the table and Theo filled a glass and held it to Robbie's lips for him to drink. As soon as he had done so, Robbie took the glass and held it for Theo. They continued to share the glass, refilling it constantly and feeding each other wine. When their eyes met, they became inextricably fixed in each other. Sometimes they were able to break the contact by laughing at themselves, Theo's laughter so joyously youthful that Robbie wondered if he might be younger than he, and sometimes their gaze grew so intense and their hands moved with such urgency on each other that he didn't think they could stay out of each other's arms a moment longer.

He had time to observe that in the exclusively male gathering, except for the Dianopoulou party, they weren't the only pair exchanging physical endearments. A good many arms were around a good many shoulders. Couples sang as they looked yearningly into each other's eyes. Groups danced together, lined up on the floor in a row linked by the handkerchiefs they held in their hands. They dipped and stamped and leaped in skillful unison to an elusive beat. There were slow dances and fast dances, sometimes with a leader, always in a row. This pattern was broken when two boys moved onto the floor and performed a dance of astonishingly explicit eroticism. To Robbie, it appeared to be a mating rite and he hoped his parents wouldn't be shocked. Occasionally, he caught his mother's eye from several tables away and smiled and nodded distractedly at her before he returned his enthralled attention to Theo.

Helene felt guilty about leaving the boy to his own devices. It wasn't the sort of evening he was apt to enjoy. He would find the noise and the rough boys irritating, although he seemed to be playing some sort of game involving a wineglass with the handsome lad beside him. She didn't quite know how he'd been separated from the party. She'd thought he was with the young English painter and then they'd both disappeared. She really shouldn't have let herself get so taken up by Carl. The music grew faster and suddenly Mrs. Dianopoulou was on her feet and whirling into the lead of a row of dancers. She moved with charming grace and assurance.

"You see?" Carl said, leaning close to Helene to make himself heard. "She is wrong to make fun of me when I tell her she is beautiful." He spoke with disarming affection. Helene thought he was really very nice but wished he didn't make her feel that he was about to pounce.

They were all a bit giddy from the long evening of *retsina*. Robbie swayed and propped himself against the table as Theo disengaged himself from him and rose. He stood with a hand on his shoulder and spoke to him. The hand seemed to be telling him to stay where he was. Their eyes gazed lingeringly at each other. Theo gave his chin a tender little tap and turned away. The twins stood and patted Robbie's shoulders and followed. Robbie's eyes roved admiringly over their wide shoulders and slim hips. All three had similar builds, the twins more developed and mature, too compact and muscular to be graceful but sexually compelling. He wondered if they were alike in every detail.

The music came to a halt and the musicians began to put away their instruments. There was a general movement toward the exit. Robbie searched for his interpreter and saw him standing at Mrs. Dianopoulou's side. He hurried to him and drew him aside while the party prepared to leave.

"He's gone. What do I do now? He seemed to want me to stay here," Robbie said in an undertone.

"I doubt it. They're closing. Don't worry," Johnny reassured him. "One thing about an island is that you always know where everybody is. He'll turn up at the right moment."

They all drifted out, Robbie dragging his feet beside Johnny in case Theo came back for him. He knew they would find each other somewhere. Their hands on each other all evening, the last look they had exchanged were guarantees that Theo wouldn't let him get away.

They wandered along the waterfront, everybody telling Mrs. Dianopoulou and each other what a fascinating evening it had been. Johnny nudged Robbie and nodded ahead of them. Robbie saw three familiar figures standing under a streetlight and he was instantly afire with the need to be at the Greek boy's side. He was disappointed that the twins were still there but realized that he would never dare go off with Theo if they weren't. Numbers lent innocence. He said a polite goodnight to everybody and murmured another word of gratitude to Johnny and moved on toward Theo, trying not to hurry. The three brothers gathered around him, all talking at once, and pointed at a boat. Robbie supposed they were putting on a performance for his parents' sake. He looked into Theo's eyes and laughed and touched his hand. He heard a motor start and voices calling, among them his mother's, and the motor went puttering off across the water. Robbie turned as his parents approached.

"These are friends of Johnny Metcalfe. They want me to go somewhere with them," he explained. "I think they want to show me where they live. Do you mind? They're brothers."

"Run along," his father said. "Go see something of the real Greece. You can tell us all about it in the morning."

"Aren't you tired?" his mother asked. She wondered if he really wanted to go off with these simple good-looking boys or didn't know how to refuse and was waiting for help from her. She had shirked her responsibility to him enough for today. "Don't you want to tell them you've had a pretty long evening?"

"I'm not remotely tired. I don't suppose I'll be very long." He held his breath, ready to do battle, but she only gave him a thoughtful look and nodded and they both said goodnight and strolled on. At least he could count on his father not to interfere. He expelled a long liberated breath and Theo seized his arm and they leaped together onto a bigger boat than the one Theo had been running. Theo moved purposefully along the benchlike seat, pushing cushions onto the forward floorboards. A lamp on the short mast cast a shadowy shifting pool of light on the forward area, too bright for privacy. The twins edged past them, gripping their arms from behind and shoving them toward each other, and continued to the stern. The engine started and Theo made a grab for Robbie and pulled him down onto the improvised bed. Privacy was forgotten as they came together with the breathless urgency of lovers who have been interrupted in an act of passion. Clothes were flung aside. They were gloriously naked together. Their hands grappled with their bodies while their mouths devoured each other. They rolled about, clasped in each other's arms, in a passion to get into each other's skin. Their hands and mouths were everywhere on each other. The motor drowned their shouts and moans and laughter. Robbie saw that the engine housing offered some shelter from onlookers but he didn't really care. They were all brothers. Theo's cock slammed about against him as Robbie twisted and turned to feel it all over him. They had sudden uncontrollable orgasms against each other's bellies, clamped together to subdue the ecstatic convulsions of their bodies.

They lay quietly in each other's arms, their mouths loosely joined and their tongues indolently playing together. "S'agapo, Roddy. S'agapo," Theo murmured against his lips.

"S'agapo." It was an odd outlandish sound but Robbie loved saying it. His body was still tingling with what he thought of as an initiation. Nothing that had happened with Rico could compare to it. He had entered a world of adult passion and found a partner waiting to welcome him. He wasn't the victim of some strange private sickness. Theo had held his cock in his mouth, briefly but without aversion. The thought of any of this happening with a girl shocked him; it would be obscene, a desecration of what he thought of as feminine refinement. Male needs demanded male satisfaction. No girl could offer him the complete physical abandon he had shared with Theo.

Theo stirred and pulled a cloth out from somewhere and wiped them off. Robbie looked at the straight nose and the bewitching mouth and stroked his hair and tilted his head so that he could look into the gentle wide-set eyes. A paragon of masculine beauty. His lover. They wanted each other equally, insatiably. Their hands and mouths became active again and their bodies moved against each other as Robbie's erection revived. Theo stroked it lovingly and laughed while Robbie felt Theo's cock lengthening and filling out. Robbie moved to it and Theo acknowledged his desire by holding it and shifting about so that he could stroke Robbie's eyes and nose and cheeks with it. He laughed again and scrambled to his knees and backed up against the forward bulwark. He spread his knees wide and thrust his hips forward and dropped his hand away from it. It lifted with its own power. Light fell on it and isolated it in space like phallic sculpture.

Robbie lifted himself to it with his hands on Theo's thighs and his mouth offered it all the adoration he had discovered in himself; he worshiped proud masculinity. He had found his god. Theo ran his hands through his hair and murmured gentle words to him.

"*S'agapo*," he repeated. "*S'agapo.*"

He called out something to the twins, whose presence Robbie had almost forgotten.

In a moment, he felt the cushions give under a new weight and his daze of adoration was shattered by somebody moving around close behind him. His heart suddenly raced with excitement as it dawned on him that Theo wasn't going to keep him exclusively for himself. By sharing him, he would extend his conquest of him. Robbie was seized by a passion of surrender. Theo pulled his head up against his chest and put his arms around his shoulders and held him firmly, a captive for his brother's pleasure.

A hand moved over his buttocks and oiled fingers prepared him. Robbie's heart pounded as he wondered again if the twins were as magnificently equipped as their brother.

Hands held his hips and lifted them and hard flesh entered him easily. It felt no bigger than Rico's but the hands were filled with desire to know his body. They moved over him eagerly and found his erection and fondled it as if they enjoyed feeling it. Men, even married men, didn't have to pretend to be indifferent to a boy's body.

He broke Theo's hold on him. If they were all going to take him, he wanted to participate in his surrender. He wanted men to want him. He wanted to give them pleasure.

He swung his shoulders around and looked up at the man who was joined to him. He recognized Niko's wavy hair. The handsome young Greek smiled down at him. Robbie lifted a hand and moved it slowly up over the compact body, lingering to caress the muscles of his chest and toy with his nipples. He felt the flesh within him grow harder and slip deeper into him. He reached for the back of Niko's neck and pulled his head down and opened his mouth to this unex-

177

pected lover. Niko's kiss was reticent until Robbie aroused it to passion with his darting tongue. He was gathered into strong arms and Niko began to move in him with a conqueror's thrust. He wasn't just being used as a convenience; they were making love together. He seemed to be filled with a vast reservoir of love that was finally being tapped. Sex was the key to all of life's rewards.

Niko's thrusts accelerated as he drove toward orgasm. His hands were intent on bringing Robbie with him. Their mouths broke apart and they both cried out with the approaching climax. Robbie found the cloth and held it in readiness. They achieved simultaneous orgasms and Robbie let himself drop down betwen Theo's legs and laid his face against the object of his adoration. Theo smoothed his hair. Niko clung to him while his erection diminished, then withdrew from him slowly and was gone.

Theo sat propped up against the bulwark. He leaned forward and turned Robbie's face up to him and looked at him with solicitous eyes. He spoke to him questioningly. He pronounced the twins' names. Asking if he minded being shared by the brothers? Robbie smiled and rubbed his cheek against the magnificent erection. He hoped to convey his acquiescence to anything his lover proposed.

Theo called out to the stern and a voice answered from nearby. Tassos stepped into the pool of light, naked and erect, and dropped down beside them. His body was a duplicate of Niko's, his erection much as Robbie had imagined the other's, more or less the same as Rico's. He was pleased that his was bigger than three of the four he had seen so far. The brothers spoke to each other and laughed and Tassos ruffled Theo's hair. He reached for Robbie and pulled him over onto his back. Robbie was reluctant to be seen without an erection but supposed his cock wouldn't remain inert for long. Tassos held him sprawled out across his thighs and both brothers stroked it. It began to burgeon under this double stimulus. Theo leaned forward and kissed it again with a little flick of his tongue and Robbie gasped as it sprang up into full erection. The brothers laughed and Tassos turned and drew him closer. His mouth was sweetly passionate the moment their lips touched. The twins were different. Tassos was more outgoing, more playful, more affectionate. He stroked all of Robbie's body as if he were making a delighted discovery of what a boy's body felt like. He caressed his erection as if he had never known anything so agreeable to the touch. Robbie was a child being cuddled against the massive chest. When their mouths parted, Robbie slid down over him and gratefully drew his erection into his mouth. Its more modest size after his jaw-stretching efforts with the adored one gave him more freedom to demonstrate his hunger for this part of a man's body and he applied himself to making it exciting for his partner. He was getting good at it and he loved feeling so close to the core of a man's desire. Tassos obviously liked it even if it wasn't the done thing here. He made little murmuring sounds and fell back on the support of his arms in order to move his hips to the promptings of Robbie's increasingly skillful mouth. Again, Robbie felt the bond of shared desire. Robbie could feel him approaching orgasm. He was nearing a climax himself when the Greek uttered a cry and his hips convulsed and Robbie swallowed his ejaculation. Tassos stroked Robbie's face as he completed the act with a final little play of his tongue on softening flesh.

The brothers pulled him up between them and spoke to each other cheerfully. Tassos reached over and held Theo's cock for a moment and they both laughed. He pulled himself to his feet and Theo rolled up on top of Robbie and they kissed and moaned and writhed against each other with the need to reclaim each other. Robbie was glad he hadn't had an orgasm with Tassos. All his desire was aroused and focused again on Theo. He was sure he would never want anybody so much as long as he lived. He belonged to him. Theo could give him to anybody he liked; nobody could make him stop belonging to Theo. His cock felt bigger than ever. Robbie didn't know how he had been able to wait for it for so long but the wait was ending.

Theo tore himself out of his arms and reared up over him and backed away on his knees. Robbie tried to turn over but Theo held him on his back by seizing his legs and placing himself between them and lifting them over his shoulders. He pulled his hips in to him. Robbie had barely grasped what was happening before Theo had entered him. He shouted his welcome and moved his hips to draw him in.

After the initial pain, it became the most sublime sensation he had ever experienced—the godlike instrument advancing smoothly into him, deeper, always deeper, filling him with its glory. It was thrilling to be able to look at the boy who was

179

taking him. There was an exultant light in Theo's eyes and his smile gloated down at him as he completed the long penetration. Their orgasms were quick. Theo's weight went slack on top of Robbie and they murmured repeatedly the one word of love they both knew.

The engine was cut to half-speed and they stirred and Theo withdrew gently, still feeling huge and hard. He pulled himself to his knees. His cock slanted out at a downward angle, long and heavy with latent power. Robbie lifted himself and knelt beside him and they put their arms around each other and looked ahead.

They were approaching a short strip of beach backed by a stand of tall reeds. A segment of moon cast pale light over the peaceful scene. Theo gave him a hug and sprang up and dived into the sea. Robbie followed him and they romped about in the water while the twins cut the engine and beached the boat. They were in their clothes again. They waved as they jumped ashore and disappeared into the reeds. Robbie supposed the evening had some logic but he had no idea what it was. As long as he and Theo were allowed to remain together, he felt no need to understand. They revived each other's erections and clambered back into the boat and Theo took him again. They dozed in each other's arms and awoke with erections once more. Robbie could feel their bodies attaining new heights of ecstasy with each confirmation of their passion for each other. They were growing together into perfect physical union, each alert and responsive to the other's slightest touch or move.

The twins returned during an exquisite lull filled with secret caresses and the yearning pledges of their eyes and loose, openmouthed exchanges of saliva. They put a bottle on the bow and stripped off their clothes and tossed them into the boat and plunged into the sea. Robbie and Theo laughed softly together and teased each other with their eyes and disentangled themselves and jumped in after them. They played together in shallow water until all four had erections. The brothers were remarkably free with each other's bodies. The twins made much of Theo's cock and held Robbie beside him to compare them. To Robbie, this seemed a pointless confrontation, but the twins seemed impressed by him. He was beginning to be proud of it. Maybe it was bigger than most.

They all scrambled back into the boat and rolled about

together on the cushions, kissing and fondling each other indiscriminately. The bottle contained more *retsina*. They passed it from hand to hand and drank. Robbie displayed the skills of his mouth to sustain the erotic play and made them all laugh with pleasure. He was aware of a miracle taking place. Lust had provided him with a family. They really *were* all brothers; a lifetime of solitude had been wiped away. He was cradled in an interlocking web of warmth and affection and desire. It could happen only in an atmosphere of male camaraderie. Tears of happiness gathered in his eyes.

When the wine was finished, the twins rolled him and Theo over onto their stomachs and took them. Robbie was so stunned by the sight of the brothers copulating that it took him a moment to realize that he had been chosen by Tassos. The circle was complete. They had all had him. Shock was replaced by almost uncontainable excitement, the strange excitement of witnessing the act of incestuous love but above all the excitement of sharing with Theo, the extravagant embodiment of triumphant masculinity, his surrender to a man's desire. Theo wanted to be taken too. Each knew intimately what the other was experiencing. They were indissolubly one. They reached out to each other and wound their arms around each other and locked each other in an iron grip with their mouths joined while the twins found their satisfaction in them.

As soon as Robbie and Theo were free, their bodies lunged to each other and Theo was on his young partner, driving deep into him. They lay motionless together, joined and suspended in the profound harmony they could find in each other's bodies. The engine started and the twins moved around them and the boat began to back away from land. Robbie felt its balance shift as the twins returned to the stern. He lay under Theo's weight, welcoming it with all his soul, feeling the divine flesh swelling and throbbing deep within him, scarcely daring to breathe for fear of dislodging it, and tried to fit tonight's events into the confusing picture he was assembling of a life he hadn't known existed a few weeks ago and yet to which by nature he seemed to belong.

Dark hints of obscene jokes and schoolboy innuendo told him that everything he'd done this evening was vile and unspeakable but his three brothers had participated openly and unashamedly. If everybody here was *comme ça* all it meant was that he was like everybody else. He had known there was nothing strange about him; he had only to find the right place to be understood and accepted.

Why here and not elsewhere? Perhaps school wasn't life in a microcosm, as everybody liked to pretend, but a queer hermetic enclave in a world of freedom and tolerance. A boy as simply wholesome as Theo could enjoy being taken for another's pleasure. Only his own craving to worship the source of masculinity with his mouth still seemed an aberration. He didn't understand why he was different in this respect. It seemed such an integral part of everything that tonight had offered him. "Naturally," Johnny had said when he had admitted that he wanted to suck Theo's cock, but it evidently wasn't natural to his brothers.

He supposed it wasn't important so long as he wasn't despised for wanting it. His brothers had encouraged him. He suspected that Theo might share his worship if he allowed himself to; maybe he didn't want his brothers to see him do it. Always an element of secrecy. It seemed to him that everybody was awfully mixed up about the whole matter.

He wasn't. He was sure that being joined to Theo and becoming one with him was a manifestation of some universal brotherhood of love. When Theo began to move in him, slowly and with total mastery of him, it was a culmination of the evening's joy, peaceful with the proven knowledge of each other's needs, brimming with acknowledged desire. They prolonged it, heading off the wrench of an unbearable ending, while the sky paled above them.

Eventually, a call from one of the twins intruded on their breathtaking absorption in each other. Robbie understood that their time had run out and they led each other to the ultimate overwhelming orgasm. The engine was cut back and they sat up, dazed that the world still existed outside themselves. They tidied themselves up with wet cloths. Theo looked into Robbie's eyes with smiling tenderness and they kissed gently and murmured their word of love as the twins brought the boat into the quaiside near where *Northern Star* was moored. Robbie had no sense of parting. He couldn't give any coherent thought to the day that was dawning. They belonged to each other forever.

He slept late and profoundly while life on board went on without him. When Stuart went ashore during the morning, he ran into von Eschenstadt at a waterfront café and joined him.

"Is it too early for beer?" Stuart asked. "I'm dying of thirst. It must be all that resinated wine."

"Yes. Yes. An acquired taste, as I imagine all tastes are."

"Come to think of it, I suppose you're right." Stuart was intrigued by the German. He had been everywhere and done all sorts of things. Stuart saw in him a reflection of his own old ideal. He was a wanderer, rootless, self-sufficient, in contact with life itself, not with somebody else's idea of what life should be. They discussed their respective plans for the next month or two. As Stuart expected, Carl's were amorphous.

"I live where I find myself," he said. "Is that not the best way?"

"I used to think so. I couldn't afford it."

"Money comes," Carl laughed and smoothed his thick yellow hair with a well-manicured hand. "People think I must be a rich man but I'm not. I think it has made my life more interesting."

"And you've never married? That makes a difference."

"Yes, but I've not always been alone. I've had some charming interludes. I would have made a poor husband. I am too much in love with the world."

"You don't think you'll stay in Greece much longer?"

"Who knows." His shirt was open down to his waist and he scratched his broad chest reflectively. "Another day. Another week. What you tell me about St. Tropez interests me. I am bored with the rest of the Riviera. Perhaps I will go to St. Tropez later in the summer."

"You could always stay with us." Stuart was pleased with the idea and thought Helene would be too. They still had to populate their mansion. "You could even go back with us on the boat."

"Ah, my friend. I never travel on yachts with people I want to remain friends with." He slapped Stuart jovially on the shoulder and tapped his glass on the table for another drink. "I have made my worst enemies on boats. To stay with you on dry land would be charming. I have another idea. You want to get on your way. It's getting late for a long sail today. Why don't you go to Hydra this afternoon? If you like, I'll go with you and introduce you to friends. I think we can risk a few hours on board together."

They laughed. Stuart had never heard of Hydra but listening to Carl he gathered that it was another of the places that couldn't be missed. Carl admitted that he wanted to go there anyway and that the passenger boats were unpredictable. The Coslings would be doing him a favor as well as getting farther along their way. Stuart agreed.

"It's a lovely day for a sail, just enough breeze," Carl said authoritatively. "You're planning to go to Delos of course."

"Delos? Right next to Mykonos? The one they call the birthplace of Apollo?"

"Yes. One of the wonders of the Aegean. I know it well. We must plan to meet there."

"I thought we'd make it one of our last stops, along about the middle of next month, before we have to head for home."

"Perfect. Most tourists see it only during the day when boats bring groups over from Mykonos. I love it in the evening and early morning when it's deserted. There's no place to stay except for a few houses for the archeologists who work there. Fortunately, I have a friend working there now who has asked me to visit him. I'll accept his invitation for the first part of June and be there to welcome you. We will be friends. I've fallen in love with the Coslings." He smiled his youthfully winning smile.

Stuart chuckled. "You're quite a fellow, Carl. I wish all Germans were like you."

Carl winced. "Please. Must you remind me? I haven't gone back to my country for four years. Do you think me irresponsible? Should I go home and make a stand against dictatorship?"

"I don't know. I've had twinges of conscience myself. I even thought of joining the Loyalists in Spain a year or two ago. What do you think's going to happen?"

"Nothing, I hope, that will end by making us shoot at each other, my friend."

"It sounds absurd, doesn't it? All the same, I think if we had a Hitler at home I'd feel obliged to go and try to do something about it."

"Then you condemn me? Everybody tells me that there is no resistance to *der Führer*. If a leader has the undivided support of his country, what is one man to do?"

Everything, Stuart was inclined to reply but he was brought up against the imponderables of his own life. He had fought for and won greater freedom than he had ever bargained for. What was he going to do with it? This cruise was a time-killer, just as building the house and furnishing it and planning the gardens had been time-killers. Eventually he would have to come to grips with a life of leisure. What would he find to give some importance to his existence? Helene was finding a happy new equilibrium. Was he essential to it? Robbie had obviously outgrown whatever it was that had left him friendless for so many years. He had taken an interest in the boys last night and evidently got along easily with them. His painting gave him a direction in life. He was ready to get out on his own. Fathers quickly outlived their usefulness. He smiled ruefully at his new friend and shrugged. "Perhaps we'd better stick to our plans for Delos. When you come to see us in St. Tropez, I might've thought of all sorts of things one man can do."

"I don't wish you to think ill of me. The world is complicated. Your Loyalists were communists. Surely Western Europe is anticommunist. America, too. We should all unite to fight communism. Wouldn't that be best for all of us?"

"If Hitler really wanted to fight communism instead of trying to grab all of Europe, it might be worth discussing."

"It looks very bad, I admit, but I must go on believing that Germany will once more emerge as a great civilizing force in the world."

"That's something we can all hope, but if I were you I'd find it pretty hard to believe as long as your compatriots tolerate Hitler. What about the Jews?"

"I can hardly bear to think of it. I have many dear Jewish friends."

"I'm glad we agree about that. To me, that's the most appalling part of it. The rest could be considered old-fashioned power politics on a more or less brutal scale." Stuart was glad the German had come through the touchy conversation without damning himself. He too had been rather friendless for the last few years. "If you're coming with us, do you have to pack or anything?"

"No, no. I'll run out to Mina's house and pick up a few things."

"Then why don't you plan to have lunch on board? We can take off whenever we're ready. I'd better go speak to the captain." They had the usual little squabble over paying the bill, which Carl won by pointing out that he was about to be Stuart's guest. Stuart thanked him and rose and gave his shoulder a friendly clap. "Come along whenever you feel like it."

Von Eschenstadt was delighted with this development. He

had hoped for an opportunity to cultivate the Coslings; they were the sort of people who might prove useful as time went by. Their family connections were interesting. They were well located geographically, affluent, with no fixed social ties. The wife was beautiful and obviously restless. The poetic-looking son was more beautiful than a boy should be. Carl had his suspicions about what he'd been up to with the young Greeks the night before. He found Stuart something of an enigma, an innocent who yet seemed at home in the world. His gentle, slightly distant manner masked what he sensed was a tough center of passionate convictions. He was the sort who could easily lull an adversary into thinking that he was unaware of anything going on around him and then suddenly strike. He would keep a wary eye on him.

He paid and strolled along the waterfront looking for a taxi boat to take him out to Mina Dianopoulou's house. It was a nuisance having to go to Hydra but he thought the trip might be worth the inconvenience. He found the handsome Theo and jumped into his boat.

"Mrs. Mina's house?" the boy asked. "I can't wait for you there. You found me just in time. I'm taking the boat to Methana for two days."

"I must find another boat," Carl said in his rough but serviceable Greek. "What if I go for a minute and come right back?"

"You'll be quick? Okay. For you, I'll do it. I should be going."

"You had a fine time last night, I hear," Carl said to test his suspicions after they were underway.

The handsome boy grinned and squeezed his famous crotch. "Very fine. Did he tell you? He's the most beautiful boy I've ever had. You tell him I won't forget him. He's my friend. Tell him to come back."

Carl filed the message away in the back of his mind for possible future use. . . .

When Robbie came out on deck, blinking in the bright light, he found a party in progress. The good-looking German was there and doleful Johnny and their hostess of the night before. His appearance gave rise to playful remarks about sleeping his way through Greece.

"I suppose I was quite late," he said. "We went over there somewhere to a house where there were other people. We had more wine and swam." And made love, he almost added, looking at Johnny. His father gave him a beer and Johnny indicated discreetly that he had something private to say to him. Robbie stepped up on deck and led him forward.

"He asked me to give you this," Johnny said, handing over a small object wrapped in crumpled brown paper. The loose paper fell away from a blue glass disk with a bull's-eye bead set in it. It was strung on a leather thong. "It's to ward off the evil eye," Johnny explained. "He wants you to come back. Was it lovely?"

"God, yes. Wonderful. Where is he? I've got to see him."

"He's gone across to the mainland till tomorrow or the next day. That's probably best, don't you think? What could you say to each other except good-bye?"

"Yes, I suppose so." Robbie looked at the curious little pendant and felt warmed and loved and protected by his family of brothers. He had yet to acquire any sense of continuity in his lovemaking. Things happened with the sudden force of a bolt of lightning. Last night it had been forever, but it was no great shock to him to realize that he might never see the boy again. He supposed it had been the wine that cloaked it in a dreamlike haze but he could still feel Theo in him. They loved each other. "I wish I had something to leave him," he said, his eyes misting slightly.

"I'll get some little thing for him and say you sent it."

"I haven't any money."

"Never mind. I shan't spend much but he'll be pleased. He was very sweet and affectionate about you. He'll probably always remember the beautiful American boy as one of the highlights of his life."

"Tell him I'll try to come on the way back. Tell him to watch for the boat in about a month."

Robbie put the thong around his neck and they wandered back to the others. If anybody asked about the trinket, he'd say he'd found it on the beach.

Drinks were replenished and drunk. Robbie learned that Carl was coming with them. Johnny escorted Mrs. Dianopoulou to the end of the gangplank. "I think perhaps you will regret taking a passenger," she said oracularly as she bade Stuart good-bye.

"Why? Is he badly behaved at sea?" he asked.

"Oh." She lifted her hand in an odd benediction. "I am an old woman and see evil everywhere."

The newly constituted foursome had lunch under the

awning in the cockpit. The guest was so much the center of attention that not even Helene noticed Robbie's pendant. He resented Carl's preoccupation with her. He resented her appearing to enjoy it. He couldn't understand why his father encouraged them. He felt Carl's charm but thought him too slick and overconfident.

From time to time the German caught his eye and looked at him with amused complicity, as if they shared a pleasant secret. It made Robbie nervous. There was a reference to some plan to meet Carl later at Delos. Stuart even tried to persuade him to stay with them until then.

"No," Carl said with robust good humor. "I shall go to Delos and wait impatiently for you."

"Not too impatiently, I hope," Helene said lightly. "It's so difficult for us to make any fixed plans."

"Oh, we'll be there, all right," Stuart put in.

"Darling, you've said all along we don't want to follow a schedule," she protested.

"No matter," Carl said. "You can't leave without seeing Delos. I shall be waiting." His eyes met Robbie's again and this time seemed to contain a promise that sent a shiver down his spine. Was it possible that they understood each other? Could an older man be interested in a boy in that way? Was his interest in his mother only a camouflage?

He was suddenly swept by a wave of condemnation of his father. He had practically forced him to be friendly with Rico. He had let him go off last night without paying any attention to where he was going. If he had done anything wrong, it was his father's fault for not using his imagination. If he'd been running after girls he would have teased him unmercifully. Because everything had happened with boys, he ignored it. He remembered their embarrassed flight from that place in St. Tropez during their big night in town last year. If it was so terrible, why hadn't his father warned him about such things? What had become of the paternal authority he had been taught to honor and respect? Maybe it didn't matter if his mother behaved foolishly but what if the German's attentions were really directed at him? He tried not to let himself be excited by the possibility. Couldn't his father see the danger and take steps to eliminate it instead of befriending Carl? His father was all for freedom; maybe he didn't care.

Last night, everything had seemed so simple and natural, thanks to Johnny and the Greeks, and his whole being had responded with joy. Now, the initial guilt he had felt with Rico was getting a grip on him again and threatened him once more with despair.

Was it possible to renounce sex? It would never again be so wonderful as it had been with Theo. He couldn't imagine wanting to do things with a girl, and homosexuality, which hadn't seemed to mean anything last night, was too abhorrent to think about, an affliction that would have already marked him as indelibly as leprosy. He couldn't be that way. His three brothers were strong healthy men, not homosexuals.

He would close his mind to whatever evil acts he had committed and the ecstasy they had offered him, cease to count on his father's guidance, freeze out this insidious stranger, and live in peace for his mother and his work.

When they had cast off lines and hoisted sail Helene and Carl usurped Robbie's place on the forward deck. Stuart started to join them but was arrested by the sound of Helene's full-throated laughter. He hadn't heard her laugh like that for years. Would he be an intrusion on their enjoyment of each other's company? Nonsense. He started forward and stopped again. What was this? Jealousy? He made himself go back to Rico and take the wheel, thinking of Mrs. Dianopoulou's last words, and wished the woman hadn't put ideas in his head.

They were all back in the cockpit having drinks when they sailed into the amphitheater of Hydra's port in the late afternoon. Because of the way it was situated, they didn't see it until they were in it. It was an impressive ruin. Mouldering carcasses of houses were strewn over the highest hillsides. Carl knew its history and told them about its eminence during the Napoleonic Wars and the War of Independence against the Turks when it had been an important maritime power. He pointed out the remains of fortifications on both arms of the port and the great stone mansions along the waterfront that had been built by pirate princes. He made it a colorful story.

The alchemy of a small boat at sea had forged ties between them as strong as if they'd known each other for years. Even Robbie found it difficult to hold himself aloof from the guest. Their frequent insinuating eye contact was wearing down his resistance. He was almost sure now that Carl wanted him. He had the air of a man who usually got what he wanted. He couldn't help seeing, in the light summer clothes Carl wore, that his body was still youthful and handsomely desirable. His crotch was bulky with promise. Robbie began to see in him the father he would have liked to have, dashing, playful, full of hearty laughter, vividly authoritative. He accepted his flirtatiousness with his mother as he grew more confident that he was the real object of his pursuit.

There was no quai they could tie up to, only a steep pebble beach on which lay a number of *caïques*, similar to St. Tropez's *tartanes*. They dropped anchor while a crowd gathered on the paved waterfront and Robbie helped Rico get the dinghy over the side.

"You no come home till morning. I watch," Rico said, taking advantage of the private moment. "Greek boys crazy. They like each other. No girls. You fuck with friend, I bet."

"Yes," Robbie admitted, blushing.

"Sure. You and me, too much danger in port. We wait. Hokay?"

"We'd better." He was glad to shelve that problem for the time being. If Carl stayed aboard for the night, he would be free for any eventuality.

Carl pointed out a dilapidated house high up on one arm of the port and told them that he wanted to take them up to meet the Hamiltons, an English writer and his wife. As far as he knew, they were the only foreigners who lived on the island. When the time came to go ashore, Helene emerged looking radiant in a simple summer dress. She was more carefully made up than usual and had arranged her hair softly around her face in a way that made her look younger. Carl was carrying the small bag he'd brought with him.

"Why're you taking that?" Stuart asked. "Aren't you spending the night with us? There's an extra cabin."

"No, no, my friend. You want to get off first thing in the morning. The Hamiltons will always give me a bed. I'll make my way back to Poros in the next day or two."

"Suit yourself." Stuart admired the German's independence. He would never be a nuisance to have around.

Robbie felt cheated. What had Carl's eyes meant if he wasn't waiting for a chance to have him? He had filled his mind with unwanted thoughts and led him to the point of acquiescence. That settled it. He wasn't going to let himself think about sex anymore.

They were rowed ashore by Rico and climbed a steep difficult path to the house. Carl was as agile as a goat; the others labored in his wake. He was greeted by the Hamiltons like an old and valued friend. A man identified as a famous Greek painter with a house on the island had also brought a group, including the startlingly glamorous Lady Diana Cooper. *Ouzo* and *retsina* flowed. Food kept appearing in a succession of exotic appetizers. Lamps were lighted as it grew dark. There was no electricity except around the port, no telephones, no cars, no daily papers, only spasmodic mail. The Coslings had the impression of an enchanted outpost of civilization, remote and timeless. Stuart issued more invitations to St. Tropez. Lady Diana knew the admiral and expected to be there in August if there wasn't a war.

Robbie was much younger than the others and Helene watched with delight as he charmed them all with his good looks and quiet intelligence. His fastidiousness, which she credited herself with cultivating in him, was in marked contrast to Carl's slightly coarse if beguiling geniality.

"For me, this has been the most momentous encounter of many years," Carl said to her when the party was showing signs of breaking up. "I can't wait for our reunion in Delos "

"I wish you wouldn't make it sound as if you were arranging all your plans around it. So many things can change on a boat. Everybody says we've been lucky with the weather. Our luck might not hold."

"No, no. The Coslings lead charmed lives. The weather will be perfect. If you don't meet me, I will know you are afraid of me."

"Oh really, Carl," she said with exasperation. Nothing had occurred between them to justify this challenge. She found him attractive but he was a fool.

He had a private word with Robbie during a general move toward departure. "You must make sure your parents keep our date in Delos. I'll expect you in no more than three weeks. It is a place of special meanings for you. It will be exciting to share it with you." His eyes were once more full of promise.

Robbie didn't understand what it was supposed to be leading to. It made him impatient of his own lack of comprehension. "It's one of the places we've planned to go to all along," he said dismissively. "I don't think there's much doubt we'll get there."

Carl lighted them down the hill with a flashlight and waited with them while Rico brought the dinghy in for them. They thanked him for a charming evening and exchanged pledges of future friendship. Stuart told him that he would expect to fix dates for his visit to St. Tropez when they met next. They stepped into the dinghy and waved as they were rowed off into the night.

They wandered on across the legendary sea, through days of reverberating light, past bare islands of rock, putting in at gleaming whitewashed villages where the natives received them with grave kindliness and offered them glasses of water and little dishes of sweets.

At the classical site on Santorini, high on a windswept hill, an attractive young guide with impudent eyes managed to separate Robbie from his parents to show him a stone plaque covered with crude lettering with a phallus incised at the bottom. The guide explained that it was a dedicatory offering from a rich merchant to a beautiful dancing boy. He ran his forefinger along the phallus.

"You like?" he said. "I show you."

Robbie's heart was beating rapidly as he followed the young guide around ruined walls and along a weed-choked path to a pile of masonry that formed a sort of enclosure. The guide opened his fly and showed him the real thing, not very big but commandingly erect. Robbie unbuttoned his shorts and displayed his conspicuously bigger one. The guide smiled approvingly and put a hand on Robbie's shoulder and exerted pressure. Robbie dropped down and worshiped male potency with his mouth. If it wasn't the done thing here, he wondered how the guide had guessed that he was willing to do it. Maybe it was expected of foreign boys. Receiving the copious ejaculation gave him an unassisted orgasm.

At Crete, they left the boat for a few days because the harbor was hot and hideous. They stayed in a seaside hotel. Late one afternoon, back at the hotel after a long day of sightseeing, Robbie took a refreshing swim and lay out on a deck chair to dry off. He was aware of a man pulling a deck chair over quite near to him and facing it in his direction. He sat and Robbie felt eyes on him. Robbie's cautious glances took in a mature body that was still fit and trim and a cock that was clearly outlined in brief trunks. His eyes lingered on it, enthralled as he watched it lengthen and thicken. Robbie's responded. He lifted his eyes and met a gaze of magnetic intensity. The man's features were clean-cut, with an unsmiling air of command; he inclined his head slightly toward the row of little bathhouses provided for changing.

Robbie consented with his eyes. The man rose with a little nod at him and strode away. He watched him unlock one of the bathhouse doors and leave the key dangling outside as he went in. He waited for the beating of his heart to subside and tried to resist the temptation that had been offered him. He had promised himself to stop thinking about sex but he couldn't help it if his cock was straining for satisfaction. The man had singled him out and was waiting for him. He gathered up his towel and rose and followed him.

He pulled the key out of the lock and handed it to the naked figure standing behind the door of the tiny cubicle. A crisp white uniform with a great deal of gold braid was hanging on the wall. He felt a little shiver of awe at having been chosen by a man of high rank. The officer's erection wasn't as impressive as he had expected; it conformed to what he was beginning to think of as the norm—about the same as Rico's and the twins'. It was already oiled in preparation for him. Robbie stripped off his trunks and delivered himself into the hands that reached for him, one completing the preparations, the other making an appreciative assessment of his cock.

The officer nodded at the floor where a towel was spread. Robbie dropped down to his hands and knees. The officer moved in behind him and inserted himself and drove fully into him. He gripped Robbie's hips and pulled him back with him onto the floor and straightened his legs and lay out full length with Robbie seated on him, impaled. Hands still guided him and Robbie swiveled around and threw a leg over the body beneath him and straddled it on his knees. The officer sat up and lifted Robbie's arms and folded his hands on top of his head. He held Robbie's hips and moved him up and down on himself. In this position, being arranged like an object for the other's use, Robbie felt indecently naked and exposed. Compelling eyes seemed to burn into his soul. He choked back his shame and moved his hands to the back of his neck and lifted his chin and arched his back to display his cock, offering himself wantonly.

He swayed his body and ground his hips down in lascivious surrender. Grasping hands moved on him, not caressingly but with a craving to seize every part of him, his armpits, his chest, his cock, his buttocks. It made Robbie feel as if his youth were being torn from him. The officer pulled him close and lay back and opened his mouth with his tongue. Their teeth clashed as the tongue lunged for his throat. Robbie let his mouth go slack to become the passive prisoner of the other's. They writhed against each other and Robbie's body grew frenzied in its service to his master. They were engaged in a conspiracy to goad each other to the limits of their endurance. The body beneath him bucked and jolted him with the power of its thrust. He could feel them rushing toward orgasm. At the last moment, the officer pushed Robbie up and seized his hand and moved their joined hands rapidly on Robbie's erection. The supine body leaped and a shout broke from it and Robbie could feel its spasms in him as his own ejaculation was scattered on his partner's face and shoulders and chest. The officer lifted his knees and Robbie sank back against them with his eyes closed, feeling sick with shock. They had shared in each other's degradation.

He lay inert for a moment while their erections subsided and then disengaged himself and rose. He wiped himself with a towel and pulled on his trunks and left without looking at the body on the floor. Not a word had been exchanged between them.

Robbie returned to his deck chair, drained and shaken. He had left it barely five minutes earlier but his world was irrevocably altered. He had made a deep commitment to a forbidden side of him that he had refused to acknowledge until now. He could no longer pretend to himself that all he wanted was a complete expression of romantic friendship, including the affectionate fondling of bodies. With Theo and the twins, sex had been a celebration of physical well-being and fraternal love with no clear distinctions of gender, but something in him set him apart from them. Was it only that he wanted to put their cocks in his mouth? Johnny had made him feel that there was nothing unnatural about that. Girls apparently did it. He wasn't a girl but lots of the boys at school had what were regarded as feminine tastes. Needle-point, for one. There was something else that he still hadn't been able to grasp. The bathhouse had offered a frightening confrontation with all his darkest yearnings. He still shied away from the word, but he had engaged in an unequivocally homosexual act. He had wanted the officer to humiliate him and force him to acknowledge his abject enslavement to men.

Homosexual. His mind could barely contain the word when applied to himself. Vile, corrupt, depraved, damned by all decent people. A pervert. What of Theo, glowing with wholesome masculinity, his eyes filled with untroubled tenderness? He seemed to be confronted with two different worlds between which he could find no bridge. He knew only that he must save himself from the shameless, perverse world he had glimpsed at St. Tropez.

He wished he could talk to somebody who could explain what he was going through, somebody with experience who knew what it was like to love boys. Carl? Delos was getting closer every day.

At Rhodes, he almost succumbed to temptation when a blatantly willing and spectacularly attractive young shopkeeper invited him to look at some special merchandise in his back room. Somehow his resolution held, possibly because the shopkeeper reminded him of the American on the Acropolis. He was beginning to recognize something in people to which the appalling word could be applied. The shopkeeper had been a homosexual. The pilot book indicated that the few stops that remained before Delos were small villages where he was unlikely to run into trouble.

When they sailed into the deep natural harbor of Ios, the place looked uninhabited. One end of a house just visible at the edge of a fold in the surrounding hills was the only sign of humanity. They had encountered some heavy seas during the day and the sudden late-afternoon stillness was profoundly soothing. Stuart reported that the pilot book described a village on the hill. The bit of house they could see must be part of it. Robbie decided to row ashore and look around. He was nearing the beach when the silence was shattered by the roar of an engine. He glanced over his shoulder and saw a slim young man on a motorcycle hurtling toward him along the road that circled the harbor. When he climbed out of the dinghy and beached it, he saw that the man had stopped, sitting astride the machine with the engine running, watching him. Robbie's interest quickened. At least there was somebody to talk to.

He gave the dinghy a final tug and strolled across the beach toward the stranger. As he drew nearer, Robbie saw that he was about thirty, lean, and hard-looking. A lock of dark hair fell across his forehead. He was attractive and had no trace of the special something that Robbie was beginning to recognize.

"You American?" the man called in greeting.

"Sort of," Robbie replied.

"I seen you come in. I been watching if anybody come ashore." Robbie stopped in front of him. Their eyes met. "You're a helluva good-looking kid."

"Thanks." His elders said that to him in a completely impersonal way. "You speak good English."

"Sure. I work on ships. I speak English, German, lotsa languages. I'm Yanni."

"My name's Robbie." He shook the calloused hand that was offered him. Yanni had hooded eyes and a sensual mouth with a hint of cruelty in it. There were interesting hollows under his cheekbones. He looked freshly scrubbed and meticulously clean. He was all bone and sinew under a shirt and pants so tight that they left little to the imagination. Robbie wasn't indifferent to the hard body or to the thought of seeing the slightly menacing eyes soften with desire. He was Greek so anything could happen. He still expected others to make the first move. He let his eyes linger on the hard curve of red lips.

"Where are you going?" Yanni asked.

"Nowhere in particular. I was just going for a walk."

"It's good I'm watching. You get on. I take you wherever you want to go. It's too hot to walk."

"Thanks again." Robbie looked into his eyes and saw a glint of what might be lust. He put his hands on Yanni's shoulders and swung a leg over the machine and sat behind him. The seat was a single oblong pillbox with no division for a passenger. There was nothing to hold on to except the driver. Their bodies were against each other, Robbie's hands finding out what the hard flat chest felt like. It was exciting. His cock began to harden, pressed against the small of his companion's back. There was no way to keep Yanni from feeling it. It continued to harden, making clear what it wanted. Robbie was making the first move after all.

"All set?" Yanni asked, gunning the motor.

"Okay. Where're we going?"

"There ain't no place to go around here unless we just happen to think of something. Here goes." They were off with a burst of speed.

When he had found his balance, Robbie moved his hands down slowly over the spare torso and gripped Yanni's hips, with his fingers directed toward the Greek's groin. The friction of their bodies against each other was bringing him close to orgasm. He wondered if he should pretend to lose his balance and ask his chauffeur to stop.

"You like it?" Yanni called over his shoulder.

"What?"

"My body. You've given it a good feel. A pretty kid like you, I'm flattered. You put your hands in the right place, you'll find something to hang on to. It's as hard as yours."

It took Robbie a moment to react. He was still amazed at how easily and naturally it happened and at the widespread acceptance of it. "I don't want to interfere with your driving," he objected for the record.

"Don't worry. Go ahead. You want it, don't you?"

"I'll say." He leaned forward so that his face was beside Yanni's and moved his hands over a long slim erection. He gripped it and felt it respond.

"I'll take you somewhere and let you have it. I figured we'd think of something to do. Okay? You wanna get fucked?"

"Yes."

"That's good. That's all I want with guys—a good fuck. Nobody fucks me, in case you had any ideas. Is it big enough for you?"

"It feels fine."

"Yeah. It's pretty big. Yours feels a helluva lot bigger. That's okay with me. I like to see a big cock. It gives me a kick. You like to suck? American guys are usually good cocksuckers, better than girls."

"I'm an American." Robbie laughed at his bold admission. Maybe Johnny had been right. Maybe it had to do with nationality, part of his heritage.

"It's not for me but I like guys to do it to me. Hey. You better watch it. You're going to make me come."

Robbie let go of the erection and moved his hands up over his torso, unbuttoning the tight shirt as he went along. There was only a light scattering of hair on Yanni's chest. He planted his hands on it and pressed himself against him and ran his tongue up his neck and around his ear.

"You're a helluva sexy guy," Yanni said. "You like me, hunh?"

The question was touching. He had imagined menace; Yanni just wanted to be liked. He kissed the hollow of his cheek. "You're damned attractive."

"You, too. When I seen you coming, I thought, Boy, there's a piece of ass I wouldn't mind having. There ain't no kids like you around here. Frankly, you're the most beautiful guy I ever seen."

The road was deserted, winding through trees. Yanni was

so nearly naked that Robbie couldn't see any reason not to go further. He dropped his hands and unbuttoned his pants and pushed them down as low as they would go. He ran his hands over the hard flat belly and reached in under his balls and lifted everything out.

"Wow," Yanni cried. "I'm Superman. Here I come." He put on a burst of speed.

Robbie swept his hands up over his body and pulled his shoulders back and looked down at his handiwork. The long slim erection was airborne, flying as straight as an arrow to its destination. It pierced the air. Robbie nuzzled his neck and moved his hands everywhere on the naked body and laughed.

"Jeez, I never been so excited," Yanni shouted. "We better stop fooling around on this thing." He veered off the road and roared up an incline into the trees and came to a jolting halt. "Okay. Nobody'll bother us here."

They dismounted. Yanni did something to the motorcycle that made it stand and wait for them. He looked outrageously naked in the loose disarray of his clothes. Robbie was seized in a wiry embrace and his mouth was invaded by a lively tongue. Yanni opened his shorts and withdrew his erection and pulled back.

"Jeez. You got a cock. I never seen a bigger one. Take your clothes off. I want a good look at you."

Robbie shed his brief garments. He loved being naked out of doors. He loved being told he had a big cock. "I'm about to come," he said urgently.

"Good. You come when I do." Yanni moved around behind him and squeezed his buttocks. "What a body. I've got myself an ass. Quick. You suck me off and then I'll take you somewhere I can fuck you silly."

"I hope so."

"No problem. I can make it five times in a row easy, specially with a guy like you."

When Robbie was returned to the beached dinghy, he didn't feel that his education had been much advanced by the experience. He still didn't know the difference between homosexuality and what they'd been doing, although there obviously was one. Yanni had said enough to indicate that girls weren't excluded from his life but Robbie couldn't imagine a more satisfying lover except for his Greek refusal to take his cock into his mouth. He no longer needed any confirmation of the fact that men who seemed normal wanted him. Why? He still needed somebody to talk to. He needed Carl. At least Yanni hadn't made him feel guilty. They had had a nice friendly time together.

The weather turned unfavorable. The Coslings continued to run into stiff winds and rough seas that slowed their progress. They were close to Delos but it was taking forever to get there. Carl was on all their minds although his name wasn't mentioned. Stuart was afraid he'd think them unfriendly if they didn't show up. Helene thought of his last outrageous remark. If it weren't for that, she wouldn't want to see him again. Robbie simply wondered. They all agreed that they couldn't miss Delos.

They finally sighted it across a tumultuous sea and the first person they saw as they pulled in beside the protection of its dock was Carl von Eschenstadt in crisp white shorts and shirt.

"You're late," he called. "I've been waiting for weeks."

Stuart was too busy helping to tie up the boat to notice the slightly wild note in Helene's laughter.

"We've had the most awful weather," she said when the flurry of arrival was over and Carl was waiting for the gangplank. "We planned to get here four days ago."

"I've always thought she was a good sailor until the last few days. She's been as nervous as a cat," Stuart said jokingly as he gave von Eschenstadt a hand to help him aboard.

"Ah, so?" He glanced quickly from one to the other and then gave Stuart a hug, shook hands with Helene, smiled at Robbie, and mussed his hair. "I'm sorry. However, you are here. I was afraid you weren't coming. Ah, the beautiful handsome Coslings. I am so happy to see you again." It was a joyful reunion. He told them that he had decided to go to France the following month and that if he liked St. Tropez he might try to find a small house to rent. The friend he was staying with here was away for a few days so he was completely at their disposal. He was eager to show them the sights.

"It is fantastic," he exclaimed. "Wait till you see the wonders that are here. They keep stumbling on more every day. Robbie specially—you will go mad about it." He looked at Robbie in his tantalizing way.

Robbie felt a lift of excitement. He was aware of the knowledge he had acquired in the last few weeks. He was no longer daunted by an older man and was confident of being able to take him on as a sexual partner. Carl wasn't a homosexual but he was sure his sexual experience had been varied. He would be able to explain the things that were troubling him.

They lounged away the evening with tall drinks and a meal and talk. Helene frequently felt the German's eyes on her and she had to make an effort not to turn on him the look of withering scorn he deserved. Afraid of him, indeed! When he got caught up in a conversation with Stuart, she could allow herself the pleasure of watching the sparkle of his eyes, the flash of his white teeth, the gestures of his powerful hands, and the play of muscles in his arms and shoulders. He was a superb creature. It was somehow appropriate to find him here at the birthplace of Apollo. Robbie waited for the moment he was sure would come.

Carl came for them the next morning to go on a tour. As they approached the site, Robbie noticed a broken marble column that rose some ten feet against the sky. He did a double take before he felt the shock in the soles of his feet. It was a colossal phallus with giant testicles for a base. The others paid no overt attention to it and he hurried past. He was going to have to do some exploring on his own.

They saw all the major sights and then Carl led them on to the recent excavations in the less ancient area of the Roman resort. He made an admirable guide, a touch of poetry enlivening plentiful facts and figures.

"Now, look here," he exclaimed. "Imagine the perfection of this patio and this row of columns when they were standing. Such harmony and space. This was a relatively modest private house. What do we have to compare to it today?"

"It reminds me a bit of home," Stuart said with a wink at Robbie. "What does the master architect say?"

Robbie burst out laughing, imagining a giant phallus at the entrance to their property. Carl had been right: the place fascinated him. The cult of Apollo, the worship of beauty with its overtones of frank pagan eroticism, was everywhere in evidence. He felt a meeting of the sensual and the spiritual that reflected his own almost religious awe of the male body. He wasn't alone in worshiping at the phallic altar. The spiritual and the sensual—would he eventually find a balance that would absolve him of all guilt?

As they approached the entrance to another enclosure of tumbling walls, Carl stopped and held up his hand. "Now you shall see something," he said impressively. "This is the sort of thing they turn up all the time." He stood aside and gestured them in. There, propped up in a corner against some blocks of stone, was a superb marble male figure. "You see how like it is to the Belvedere Apollo?" Carl said. "Probably a contemporary copy on a small scale although the head is different and the cloak has been left off. The tragedy is that it will probably lie here indefinitely. We need another Napoleon to gather up the treasures of Europe and give them proper housing."

"You might suggest it to Hitler," Stuart remarked.

"He would put a fig leaf on it," Carl said, making a face. He went to the statue and ran his hand lovingly over the neck and shoulders. Robbie's cock stirred. "Come, you must feel it. Beautiful creature, how I should love to own you." They gathered around it in silent admiration.

"Do they really let things like this lie around here?" Stuart asked. "I should think they'd get stolen."

Carl uttered his hearty laughter. "Try to lift it," he said. "Of course, things do disappear and they call it stealing. The Greeks are poor, after all."

"You mean they sell off things like this?"

"It happens. This isn't even classified yet. Do you want it? You could probably have it."

"Shocking thought," Stuart said with a smile of disbelief.

"That is one's first reaction. But I confess that if I had a home, I should make a serious effort to acquire it."

"Why don't we take it?" Robbie said eagerly. The thought of owning it took his breath away.

"There is the realistic voice of youth," Carl said, not disapprovingly.

"Darling, things like that are public property," Helene objected.

"But Carl says—"

"I'm sure Carl doesn't mean half of what he says," she said.

Carl met her eyes for an instant. "Ah, my dear Helene, I do," he said. "I always mean exactly what I say."

Stuart broke in. "If what you say is true, how would you go about getting hold of it?" The eagerness in Robbie's voice had prompted him to speak. He wanted to share the boy's enthusiasm; it was a reminder of the larks they had enjoyed together long ago.

"Are you serious, my friend?" Carl asked.

"Why not? Would it be expensive?"

"I would have to inquire. You know, you could get in

trouble. Its disappearance might not be noticed at once but if it should be, any yacht that had been here would be suspect."

"What would they do? Send a battleship after us?"

"Nothing as sensible as that. But they would certainly send out an order to every Greek port to search you."

"What if we didn't put in at any Greek port?"

"That would be the best plan. Then your only problem would be to explain yourself to the customs of other nations. The Italians would undoubtedly think you had stolen it from them. I believe Mussolini is very touchy about such things."

"Well, I suppose we could go straight home without stopping. I'd have to talk it over with Angelino."

"Ah, I hope you do it. It would be like having another friend to visit at St. Tropez."

"I think you're both mad," Helene commented.

"Go ahead and see what you can find out about it." Stuart turned to Robbie with a grin. "I hope this isn't going to start you off on a career of looting and larceny."

"All it needs is 'Souvenir of Athens' written on its stomach," Robbie replied, laughing delightedly. It had occurred to him that making an uninterrupted run for home meant not seeing Theo again but that was already long ago. The statue was now. Carl was now.

They left the statue but it remained uppermost in their minds as they continued their tour. Robbie went back to look at it again before they returned to the boat for lunch. That evening, Carl reported that nine hundred dollars distributed judiciously among a few guards and an archeological official in residence would assure their safe departure with the treasure. They were all suddenly involved in a plot.

Angelino made no objection to sailing directly home, beyond pointing out that they would have to do without fresh food most of the way. Stuart decided that it would be unfair to implicate the crew in the theft so they had to work out a plan for getting the statue on board in secret. He and Robbie went over the boat, looking for a hiding place. Robbie, who knew the sculpture by heart now, assured his father that it would fit into a locker in the master cabin behind some clothes. Stuart had brief misgivings. What if bad weather or some breakdown forced them into a Greek port? Of course, they could always give it back and pay fines and treat it all as a joke—money would eventually smooth everything over—but mightn't it be more unpleasant than it was worth?

Robbie and Carl, as the chief instigators of the theft,

wouldn't listen to objections. Their alliance was growing more pronounced. Helene observed it with displeasure. There was something vaguely troubling about a mature man behaving like the contemporary of a teenager. Why didn't Carl act his age? His innate flirtatiousness seemed to include everybody, even the boy. Only the fact that Robbie's heart was so obviously set on the statue kept her from rebuking Carl for encouraging him.

Over dinner, the two discussed their plan for taking on the illicit cargo. Carl knew a cove at the southern tip of the island. He thought he could arrange, for the fee agreed on, to have the statue delivered to the beach there in the next day or two. Once there, they could sail down and collect it.

"Dad doesn't want the crew to know about it," Robbie pointed out.

"No, no. We'll say that we want to have a farewell party and leave the crew here for the evening at the tourist café. You come back and pick them up and sail away."

"That sounds perfect." Robbie directed all his delight at him. Their plot was giving them constant excuses to address each other, look into each other's eyes, even to touch each other to underline a point. Carl's eyes had become as easy to read as his own apparently were. Robbie didn't think he'd have to wait much longer.

Stuart wondered aloud if the whole deal might not be a setup in order to denounce them for a reward. Robbie found it typical of his father to propose the daring scheme and then vacillate when it came to carrying it out. He never seemed to know his own mind.

"What do you think, Carl?" Robbie asked.

"It is understood that no money will change hands until you're gone. I remain as a hostage for you." He smiled around at the family circle and his eyes settled on its youngest member. Robbie felt as if he were being ensnared in bonds of steel. The eyes hypnotized him and bent him to their will. He knew that he would surrender to them even if it weren't in his nature to want him. His parents were witnesses to an indestructible pact. The eyes shifted from him. Talk continued, punctuated by Carl's easy laughter. Robbie felt a void where what he thought of as himself had been. The eyes returned to him and the void was filled.

The next morning, Robbie returned to the site to gloat over the statue. He could look at it with proprietary eyes now; it was all but theirs; nothing could go wrong. He shifted it carefully on its makeshift base to test its weight. It was heavy but the three of them could manage it. Its head came to his chest. He stroked the shoulders as Carl had done and the cool perfection of the marble seemed almost alive under his hands. He wondered where they could show it to its best advantage. Out of doors somewhere. It had to stand free so that it could be seen from every angle. The flowing line of the back was lovely.

He heard a sound behind him and turned. Carl was standing at the entrance to the ruined enclosure. Their eyes met. Robbie surrendered to them. Carl was smiling with confident affection. "So. Have you fallen in love with him?" he asked.

"Yes. Any news?"

"The plot is afoot. He will be moved tomorrow night when the right people are on duty. That means you can collect him day after tomorrow and be on your way. Your father is anxious to leave. If it takes you a week to get back, it will be very nearly time for your charter to expire. I suggested a swim but they prefer to wait till after lunch. I knew where to find you. Your mother sent these." He was carrying a straw basket. He pulled Robbie's trunks out of it and tossed them to him. "You won't need them where I will take you. Come."

Robbie's wait was over. He dropped his hand from the statue and moved to Carl. They set off side by side. His heart was beating rapidly but he felt surprisingly calm and self-assured. He would let Carl choose the time and place. He wanted to find out how an experienced man of the world went about it.

"I think you mustn't go back there again," Carl said. "You'll attract attention if you go too often. The next time you see him, he'll be yours."

"Thanks to you."

"I will have my reward. We're going to my secret cove."

"The cove where we pick up the statue?"

"No, no. Another, very private."

They crossed fields sloping upward and reached a crest and started down the side of high land that dropped to the sea. They picked their way over rock formations and clambered down to a small cove similar to the one where the Coslings swam at home, enclosed by two short rocky points. There was a short beach of hard-packed sand and behind it an outcropping of rock that formed a shallow cave screened from above by pines. If nobody else came along, they were as private as if they were behind locked doors. Robbie felt totally cut off from the world.

"So," Carl said with satisfaction. "My private outdoor pool. We will make ourselves at home." He emptied his bag of towels and suntan lotions and pulled off his shirt.

Robbie knew his handsome torso but was unprepared for the sensual shock of seeing it totally naked. He turned away, faced with a dilemma. He didn't think he could be naked with Carl without getting an erection. It was already well started. Would it be permissible? It struck him as forcing the issue until some preliminary contact was made. He was saved further uncertainty by Carl darting past him and running naked down to the sea. His back was more stunning than the statue's, as massive as a Michelangelo. Robbie stripped with relief and followed him slowly, holding a towel in front of himself. Carl was swimming vigorously out beyond the cove's enclosure. Robbie dropped the towel and plunged in but stayed close to shore. He was learning a lesson in adult timing. There was no need to fling themselves on each other like kids. Carl would take him when he was ready for him. He climbed out and dried himself and returned to where Carl had left his bag. He spread the towel and lay on it on his back with one end draped across his midriff.

He saw Carl swimming toward shore and his heart accelerated again. He lay without moving as Carl emerged from the sea and strolled toward him, unconcernedly, masterfully naked. Robbie watched his not unexpectedly big cock swing as he moved. He stood over Robbie and shook out a towel and gave himself a brisk rubdown. When he was finished, the big cock was considerably bigger. Robbie's grew with it. He adjusted his towel to cover it as he gazed up at the golden body. Golden curls glinted on his chest. His cock hung from a froth of fine-spun gold. Carl dropped the towel and knelt on it with one knee touching Robbie's side. He found a comb in his bag and ran it through his thick golden hair. All his movements were calm and deliberate; he was approaching love-making as something simple and relaxed and expected, as natural between them as conversation. Robbie's erection was complete, lying on his belly under the towel. Carl's cock continued to burgeon, developing a pronounced jut, but he finished combing his hair as if he weren't aware of it. Nothing could shake his self-possession. Robbie had never watched a cock go through the transition from repose to erection. His eyes were riveted on it. Carl dropped the comb into his bag and sat back on his heels. His cock lay along his thigh.

"So. Do you think anybody suspects what we've been waiting for?" he asked playfully.

"What do you mean?"

"You can see for yourself, you wicked child." He put a hand on Robbie's chest. "My, how your heart is beating."

Robbie watched his cock surge out like a great snake uncoiling and swelling for an attack, curving across his thigh. His heart beat faster. "I'm not a child," he said.

"But wicked, eh?"

"If you want to call it that." He gave his towel a little push and it fell away to his side, uncovering his erection. Carl's hand went to it and raised it and moved over it appreciatively.

"No, not a child. A very splendid young man." His cock lifted. Robbie watched as it straightened and swung out and stood upright. It was on the heroic scale of all his heroic body, not quite the equal of Theo's but nearly so.

"Oh my God," Robbie murmured. He pulled himself up and fell on it, grasping it with both hands and working his open mouth over it. Carl stroked his head and shoulders for a moment and laughed.

"Such a hungry boy." He gripped his arms and pulled him up against him and kissed him. The pressure of their erections against each other gave Robbie an immediate orgasm. He snatched for the towel to contain the ejaculation and lay gasping in Carl's arms. "Youth's hot blood," Carl said with a chuckle.

"I'm sorry. I couldn't help it. It doesn't matter. You know what I want. Take me."

"It's not too big? Some boys are frightened of it."

"No. I've had one like it."

"Theo? At Poros?"

Robbie looked at him and his eyes widened. "Does everybody know?"

"I doubt it. I made it my business to find out. I've heard there might be some similarity."

"You haven't found out for yourself?"

"How could I? I don't pick up boys, my dear. Sometimes some chemistry occurs and then not making love would be as forced and foolish as not breathing. That's what has happened to us, my darling boy." Carl drew Robbie closer and the boy gave his mouth to him. The kiss became breathless as

Robbie was once more aroused and he struggled away and flung himself down on his stomach.

"Take me. Please," he begged. Carl did so superbly.

Robbie lay where Carl had left him, taking stock of the momentous event. It was another initiation. Carl was somebody he knew with his parents; he would go on seeing him in the future. It hadn't been just sex, but the consecration of a relationship that would become a part of life. It was a relationship that hadn't been imposed by outside circumstances, family or school, but had to be created out of himself. How were they supposed to behave in public? He had somebody at last who could tell him everything.

He rolled over and scrambled to his feet and went down to the sea and washed all over in shallow water, watching Carl's head bobbing about far beyond the cove. He could feel the bond between them spanning the distance; he belonged more to Carl than to his parents. He saw him heading in finally and he lay with the sea washing over him and waited for him. They put their arms around each other and walked back to the towels. Carl wasn't much taller but so much bigger that Robbie felt swallowed up by him. They stretched out again, Robbie on his back, Carl against him on his side, propped on an elbow so that they were touching everywhere.

"Is anybody going to know about this?" Robbie asked with a hand on Carl's hair.

"No, no. It's our secret. We're allies. We will tell each other our secrets. I'm in love with the Coslings. You must make your mother like me. I don't think she trusts me."

"I'll make her love you if you promise to take me whenever I want."

"Will that be often?"

"All the time."

Carl laughed. "There might be difficulties. Perhaps it will be easier in St. Tropez."

"You have women too?"

"Of course, as you will soon, if you haven't already."

"No, never," Robbie asserted. "I'll never want a girl."

"You consider yourself a homosexual?"

"No." It was a terrified denial. "I want to talk to you about it. Is it possible? I don't want to be. Isn't homosexuality some sort of insanity? I mean, I know there's a place in St. Tropez where boys go dressed as girls. I'd never want to do that."

"Why should you? Homosexuality is simply preferring your own sex. There's no need to dress up for it."

"You mean, because we've made love together, we're both homosexuals?"

"Of course not. I said *preferring* your own sex. I've never felt the need for boys as I have sometimes for a woman, although they've given me much pleasure. Is it vicious of me to indulge myself or is it only a normal response to physical beauty not unlike what I feel for our statue? Who could resist beauty such as yours?"

"No. Tell me. I've got to know." He was suddenly desperate for reassurance, to be told the difference between him and the damned. "Do you think I'm a homosexual?"

"Oh, my dear Robbie, how can I know? It's probably too soon for you to know. We should talk about this in a year or two."

"No. I've got to know now. You say I can tell you everything. I will. I like to suck cocks. Is that insane?"

"I don't think the women who have enjoyed doing it would think so. You probably have a strong feminine streak in you. For a man to want it is considered a perversion."

"You don't want to suck mine?"

"In sex, everybody has their preferences. That has never been one of mine but I have no hard-and-fast rules. I have done it. Things happen unexpectedly. Do you want me to?"

"No, not if you don't want to. Nobody ever has. Have you ever been fucked?"

"No. That, never."

Robbie was seized by panic as he realized that he wasn't going to be offered any reassurances. His heart began to pound so violently that he could hardly breathe. He turned in against Carl and clung to him and forced himself to speak. "I wanted you to fuck me. I begged you to. I want men to take me. I want to suck their cocks. What can I do about it?"

Carl hugged him close. "Did anybody teach you these things?"

"You mean, force me? There was a first time, of course. I was horrified and then I discovered that I wanted it. I wanted more than the first boy would allow. I wanted to teach *him* things."

"Then only nature is to blame."

"Blame? Why is it wrong when so many people want it? It doesn't seem wrong with you. It didn't with Theo." He felt their cocks hardening against each other. Only that could keep panic at bay.

"Theo isn't a homosexual."

"That's what I thought. Then what's different about me? That's what I don't understand. We did everything together. He didn't really suck my cock but he put it in his mouth. He let his brother fuck him. Doesn't that make him a homosexual?"

"No. Very few Greeks are homosexuals. Why should they be? Their attitude toward sex is very different from ours. I didn't mean that you are to be blamed. How could I? You noticed the broken column over there at the entrance to the site. It was put there by men. The difference is that women were included in their lives. Christianity has made us sexual bigots and forced us to make an unnatural choice."

"You mean, I've *chosen* to be a homosexual and you haven't?"

"No, no. I speak of pressures we usually know nothing about. Something has happened to you that makes you exclude girls. I was lucky, I think, more the way we're meant to be. I'm in love with people, not with one sex or the other, though perhaps a little more with women."

"Then that's the difference? Men can make love with men without being homosexual? I'm doomed if I don't want girls? I've had sex with seven men in the last few weeks. You're the eighth. It's always the same." Panic still pounded in his veins as he drew the unavoidable conclusion. "I wanted them to take me like a girl or let me suck their cocks. They didn't suck mine. I didn't understand but I'm beginning to. I'm all the things people are disgusted by. I'm a cocksucker, a boy who wants to be fucked. Big cocks thrill me—yours, Theo's—but I even worship smaller ones. I'm growing up to be more of a girl than a man, even if I don't want to dress like one. Not yet. It's horrible and terrifying but I've got to face it. I'm a freak. Could you like me if I'm a homosexual?" His eyes filled with tears and he choked on his words.

Carl lifted himself over Robbie and kissed his eyes and hair and cheeks and cradled him in his arms. He found this outburst surprisingly childish but it suited his purposes. The boy was his for life. "My dearest Robbie. My poor darling boy," he said. "You mustn't be frightened of life. I'm not a very good man in many ways but I do know the world. There are millions of men who share your feelings—as you said yourself, some very great men. Why do you think da Vinci and Michelangelo were so obsessed by the male body? If nothing changes in the next few years, you will fall in love with a boy your own age and he will love you in return and you will discover how happy life can be even for a freak. No, I mustn't joke. I won't have you think of yourself in such a way. Do you think I would want you if you were a freak? Feel my cock, how much I want you. You are a beautiful brilliant boy and we will be friends for always."

"Do you mean it? Oh God, I want to stay with you. I wish you were my father."

"I doubt if this would be happening if I were."

"Why not?"

"Do you want to make love with your father?"

"No, I don't suppose so. Not really, but it might be better than nothing. He doesn't know I exist."

"Nonsense. Why do you think he's taking all this trouble for the statue? It's for you."

"He may think so but it's really because he likes to make unconventional gestures. He wants to be unconventional but he isn't. What do you think he'd do if I told him what I'm finding out about myself?"

"I don't think I'd risk it, if I were you."

"That's just it. He talks about freedom but look what happens. I've done things I'm ashamed of. Maybe I wouldn't if I could talk to him and understand why I shouldn't feel free to be myself. Now I have you. I'll tell you everything and you'll help me to be decent, if there are any decent homosexuals."

"Of course there are. Homosexuals are like everybody else, some nice, some not so nice. I am very fond of quite a few."

"You *know* some? I mean, they're friends?"

"Of course. Like you. Can you get away from the boat at night without anybody knowing?"

"Sure."

"Then you'll come to me tonight and tomorrow night. You will become my boy. You will be waiting for me in St. Tropez."

"That's what I want, to fall in love, to keep myself for one person." He discovered a new truth as he spoke. "Am I really beautiful?"

"One of the most beautiful people I've ever seen of either sex. Don't you know?"

"People have said so recently. If you think so, maybe I really am."

"Does it make you vain?"

"How could it when I've been with boys who're much more beautiful? Is my cock big enough?"

"For what?"

"To interest boys who feel the way I do."

Carl chuckled. "I think you won't find many bigger. It is very pleasing—a beautiful boy with a very big cock that is always erect for me."

"Then show me everything that people do together. I'm not sure I know."

Carl complied. Robbie stretched his body to open every cranny of it to sensual delight. He let it go slack to sponge up every new sensation. When Carl entered him again, it wasn't an isolated act of possession but the culmination of a pattern of physical pleasure that they had evolved together.

"That's what I thought," Robbie murmured when they were lying at peace. "I can't deny it. It's a necessity. Being taken by a man makes me feel alive. That's the first time that anybody's made love to me all the way. You sucked my cock just enough to show me how lovely it must be to come that way. I'll have to find a boy who likes to do it as much as I do. I know what everything's supposed to be like now. Is it better for you with a woman?"

"You're a very passionate boy, my darling. Very few women have made me feel so wanted. That, after all, is what we all crave."

"I'm your boy. You make me feel as if you want me—more than the others did."

"You said it was good with Theo."

"Oh yes, heaven, but I didn't know then what I know now. He let his brothers have me. I'd never do that again. I'd want him to keep me for himself."

"But, you see, you're thinking of him as a homosexual, my dear. He wouldn't see any reason not to share you."

"Yes, I keep forgetting. I'm a freak. I'm a homosexual. Will everybody know?"

"There are important men in public life who prefer to keep it a secret. They've succeeded."

"I'll try not to let people find out. I couldn't stand it if my parents did. I don't see how I'm ever going to get used to it myself."

The ghastly fact kept crashing into his thoughts all through the rest of the day. I'm a homosexual. It made his arms and legs feel numb He felt it must show in his face. How had it

211

happened to him? He was sure of one thing: he had had no choice. It had always been in him. He was Carl's boy. Did that mean that he filled a need in Carl's life? To feel needed, as he needed Carl, might make his condition more bearable.

He fell back on an earlier comfort; his mother would think he was too pure for sex. If he always let others make the first move, there would be no risk of scandal. He might get through life without being found out but the secret would always be eating at his nerves. He was a homosexual, not just having fun like other boys but dedicated to his own sex. He was weird, sick, a pariah. Becoming an important painter was his only hope. Nobody would care about his sex life then.

He discovered that he could at least act natural in front of his parents with a man he'd made love with. After lunch, Carl proposed a visit to his secret cove and they all went, thus robbing it of its secrecy. Robbie found it odd to see his mother sitting reading where he and Carl had lain only a few hours earlier. Stuart and Carl dropped their trunks at the edge of the water when they swam. Robbie cautiously kept his on and averted his eyes from his father's body. He watched his mother's response to Carl's overpowering charm. He knew that in her case it had nothing to do with sex but she remained brighter and more vivacious with the German than he had ever seen her before. He was glad Carl could put on such a good performance as a ladies' man. When the evening came to an end after dinner, Robbie waited for half an hour to let his parents get settled for the night before he stole off to Carl's bed.

The next morning, their German friend announced that the statue was definitely to be moved that night. They could plan to leave the following night as soon as they had collected it.

"You mean, it'll be lying on the beach all day tomorrow?" Robbie objected. "Isn't that awfully risky?"

"It will be buried under loose sand under a log for a marker. Somebody will stay there out of sight to watch it. They are as anxious for all to go well as you are."

"I think we can leave the plot in Carl's capable hands," Stuart said. "So tomorrow will be our last day? I'd better talk to Angelino."

He told the captain that they'd decided to leave in the next day or two and suggested that he take Rico with him across to Mykonos on one of the tourist boats to stock up on fresh food and ice. They'd taken on fuel at Rhodes and used the engine very little since, so that wasn't a problem. Carl was arranging for them to top up their water tanks from the limited local supply. They would be ready to leave at a moment's notice.

The foursome put together a picnic and made a day of it at Carl's cove. It became an outdoor living room. Helene settled down with her book under the overhanging rock. Robbie sat under a tree with a sketchbook, slightly removed from the others. His mind's eye was crowded with impressions that he'd been eager to get down on paper, rough notes and sketches for future compositions. Stuart had discovered some unusual shells down near the far arm of the little bay and became absorbed in a search for more. Carl was an inexhaustible swimmer.

Helene heard heavy breathing beside her and looked up from her book to see Carl standing over her. He was smiling and water was running in little rivulets down his panting torso. When she found herself comparing his superbly muscled body to Stuart's hard leanness, she hastily looked around. Robbie was within hailing distance. She didn't see Stuart.

"We are alone. Are you very frightened?" he teased.

"Don't be silly," she said, closing the book. He sat down beside her and dexterously drew a cigarette from his case, without getting the others wet, and lighted it with his handsome lighter. Everything he owned was handsome and expensive-looking.

"I will be serious," he said, his eyes narrowed against the smoke. "Have you noticed that I've made a great effort to make friends with Robbie?"

"I've noticed you flirt with him the way you flirt with everybody."

"That's a foolishness Mina Dianopoulou put in your head. Like most men I flirt with women I wish to make love with. You are one of the most beautiful women I have ever known and I think we are meant for each other. I think you feel it, too."

Helene could scarcely believe her ears. This time he'd gone too far. He deserved the full force of her anger. Why was it so difficult to scold him? "Oh really, Carl," she protested, unconsciously finding words that said nothing. "How can you sit there with my son in sight, with Stuart, your friend, about to join us and talk like that? It's incredible."

"Yes, it is incredible," Carl picked her up eagerly. "Stuart

213

is my friend and you and he are good friends, too. That one sees. But you are a woman and friendship is not enough. You and I are not friends."

"And never will be as long as you go on like this," Helene asserted.

"No, we never will be but we can be much more. We can offer each other all the wonderful painful things, the things that make life worth living. I've made friends with Robbie so that no matter what happens he won't be hurt or feel left out. I know how close you are."

"I've never heard such nonsense. You sound as if we were about to run away together."

"Who knows? This may be the last chance we have to talk in private. We must know all the possibilities before I go to St. Tropez. There will be no flirting there. We will be ready to act."

Long unaccustomed to the language of passion, she had an uncontrollable impulse to laugh and felt as if she had been restored to sanity. Her life was complete. She had long since fought her way through passion to peace. Her laughter died comfortably. "You're quite absurd but I suspect attractive men often are. There's Stuart," she added, catching sight of him rounding the farthest point of the little bay.

"It's not absurd for us to want each other. We know it must be."

"You're coming to St. Tropez to visit friends," she said sensibly. She turned to him but found that too much had been said for her to meet his eyes easily, so she looked vaguely over his shoulder. "I hope you won't do anything to spoil it."

"It shall be as you wish, I promise you," he said ambiguously. He expelled a long breath and dropped back flat on the sand. Helene waited. Was he going to leave it at that? She didn't know what to make of herself. She had said all the right things but she didn't feel as if she had settled anything. Not daring to look at him again, she opened her book but could not see the print.

Stuart found them looking natural and at ease. "Am I the only boozer around here?" he demanded. "Shouldn't we have a drink before lunch?" They drank *ouzo* and spread out their picnic and enticed Robbie out from under his tree. "You sure you don't want to change your mind and come with us?" Stuart suggested to Carl when they were eating their simple fare.

"More than ever what I said is true," he replied, lifting his hands in horror. Helene glanced at him and their eyes met briefly. She didn't know what Stuart was referring to but the way Carl had phrased his reply made her feel that it was meant for her in some way.

Wonderful painful things. The grandiloquent words stuck in her mind. There was wonder enough in watching Robbie turn into a stunning man. Was a terrible emptiness awaiting her when his development was complete? Instinct told her that she had nothing to fear. She sensed a passive satisfaction with life in him, no youthful chafing at the bit. He would be content to let life flow around him in its even course. Carl looked as if he could inflict pain, with his powerful body and his golden self-assurance. She could wonder like any woman what satisfactions such physical magnificence might offer. From that to giving herself to him was a huge impossible step. When he came to St. Tropez she would be securely established in her own home, away from this unreal world that played tricks on the imagination.

For the rest of the day Carl treated her as if they had reached some secret understanding. She wanted to slap him. The fact that they didn't have another moment alone together saved her from being put to the test.

"What do you really think of Mum?" Robbie asked Carl when they were lying in each other's arms later that night. "Sometimes you almost convince me that you're trying to get her."

"No, no. We skirmish, as men and women do. Every man must try to conquer a beautiful woman. It's a law of nature. I'm laying the groundwork for the unknown. It doesn't matter if nothing comes of it. She's very beautiful, in the way that you are beautiful. How can I help being intrigued?"

"What in the world could you expect to come of it? You don't think she'd have an affair with you, do you?"

"Would you mind very much if she did?"

"She never would." He spoke out of his deepest convictions. "How could I mind something that I can't even imagine?"

"You may be right. Let's say you are and that something even more extraordinary happened. You said you wished I were your father. Would you like me as a stepfather?"

"You mean—" He was so stunned that for a moment he couldn't think of anything else to say. His mind whirled and bumped to a halt as it framed a thought whose absurdity almost made him laugh. "You mean, you'd take her away from Dad and marry her?"

"It's quite farfetched, I agree. I've never wanted to marry, but with people one must always be prepared for the unexpected."

To his astonishment, despite the wall of incredulity that the suggestion had immediately erected in his mind, Robbie found that it might have appealing consequences. "Wouldn't she have to know about us?" he asked.

"That would remain to be seen. I would certainly insist that she understood and accepted you. I would want your lovers to be part of our life. I think she would want it too, once she realized that you're not like the majority of boys. I would like to save you from a life of secrecy. She will like your not wanting girls."

"I think you're mad." He burst into wild laughter and rolled over and flung his arms around Carl's big body. "I hope you have plenty of money. It's been fun being rich the last year or so. I hated being poor. Don't tell Mum. She thinks I'm a disembodied spirit."

The morning brought assurance that the statue was buried where Carl could find it and Stuart told Angelino that he wanted to sail for France that night. Mr. von Eschenstadt would join the family for an intimate little farewell dinner on board. They would find a secluded anchorage for an evening swim and return before midnight. Angelino could take the crew ashore for supper.

Once these details were settled, the four conspirators felt tension mounting. Although it was unlikely, the statue's disappearance might be discovered at any moment. The prank they had discussed so lightly had acquired a hard-edged reality. They agreed that they might be able to relax if they had a look at the lay of the land and were ready for action. They hadn't taken this wait into account.

The money, part of a hoard of cash Stuart had brought for emergencies, was in Carl's hands. Robbie's eyes were bright with excitement. They all wanted to get on with it.

After a hasty lunch, they motored through rough sea to the southern tip of the island where Carl guided them through a narrow opening into a spacious bay, still and wooded. The water was deep quite close in to shore and Stuart anchored almost within a stone's throw of a log lying on the beach. They all looked at it and at each other, and burst into laughter. Tension eased. The setting felt peaceful and remote. Robbie was sure he could make out the contours of the statue under a light covering of sand. It was going to be even easier than Carl had made it sound.

They lowered the dinghy and dropped a coil of rope into it and their preparations were complete. Carl warned them not to go ashore while it was still light. They swam in the clear pale water. The unfamiliar absence of the crew made the Coslings feel as if the boat belonged to them. As the sun sank, Helene prepared dinner. They had drinks on deck. They were the privileged few, surrounded by luxury and the harmonies of nature, free of the world's strife, except for the undertone of excitement provided by the outrageous act they were about to commit. By nine it was almost dark and dinner was finished.

"So. Our big moment has come," Carl said. He gave Robbie's shoulder a squeeze under cover of the gathering darkness. "What will you say if we find nothing there but the log?"

"Don't even suggest it," Robbie exclaimed. He leaned in against the big body and in an instant discovered what it meant to be bereft. He wouldn't be with Carl tomorrow. How did people survive being abruptly cut off from each other when they had become part of each other's lives?

Carl's laughter boomed. "I'm not such a great fool, eh? Come. We will dig up our treasure."

They pulled the dinghy around alongside and Helene stood at the rail while the three men dropped down into it.

"We'll be right back," Stuart whispered. He realized that there was no need for caution and added in a normal voice, "You better get things cleaned up so we can leave right away."

"Don't let Robbie strain himself carrying that heavy thing," she said.

"Oh, really," Robbie growled. They pushed off and rowed in to the sandy beach. It was dark but not so dark that they had any difficulty seeing what they were doing. The log was a black shape against the white sand. Robbie leaped ashore and sprinted ahead and dropped to his knees to roll it aside. Within seconds, he found a leg and followed it up to the torso, scooping up sand in handfuls. It was as exciting as stripping a lover. Stuart and Carl joined him and the three completed the job together.

Burrowing in the sand, they didn't have to move the statue

217

to secure the rope around the arms and shoulders. They all leaned to the task of dragging it down to the dinghy. It required their combined strength to dislodge it from its shallow grave. Its weight made a furrow on the beach.

In a moment they were sweating profusely and their muscles were beginning to ache. They slipped and staggered across the loose sand and came to a halt with their feet in the water beside the dinghy.

"After this, I will have the right to come look at him whenever I like," Carl said as they were recovering their breath.

"Are you still crazy about souvenir-hunting?" Stuart asked Robbie.

"Maybe we should've practiced on something smaller. How do we get him into the dinghy?"

"One more mighty heave and he will get into the dinghy by himself." Following Carl's instructions, they tugged the statue down beside the dinghy so that it was partly submerged. Carl tipped the boat over on its side and Stuart and Robbie pushed and heaved and splashed each other until the statue was lying in the gunwales. They righted the boat and the statue rolled with a thud into the bottom. "I don't think we'll risk more passengers," Carl said. "I would rather go home in dry clothes. You will tell Helene to look the other way." He stripped and folded his clothes neatly on a seat. Stuart and Robbie were already too wet to care. They heaved and pulled and pushed some more until the dinghy was waterborne and they swam out with it. Helene was standing at the rail waiting for them.

"Throw a towel down to Carl and then withdraw to a ladylike distance," Stuart called up to her. A towel plummeted into the dinghy and she was gone.

They shackled the statue to the pulleys used for the dinghy and climbed the ladder and manned the davit lines, Carl stark naked. They tugged and strained while the tackle creaked ominously, and slowly hoisted the precious cargo up onto the deck.

After that, the dinghy was child's play. They lashed it into place while Carl dried quickly and pulled on his undershorts. They knew that only half the battle was won. The narrow deck was cluttered with nautical gear. They maneuvered their treasure slowly along it, cursing every obstacle. They let it bump gently down the companionway and continued the struggle below. In the master cabin, they wrestled it upright and all fell with it into the locker where Robbie had assured them it would fit. His eye proved accurate. They padded it securely with some old blankets and pushed Stuart's clothes in over it and closed the door. They sank back against the bulwarks, their chests heaving and sweat streaming down their bodies, exhausted but triumphant.

"If anybody wants to take it away from us, they're welcome to try," Stuart said after a moment of silent recuperation.

Carl chuckled. "I think you must buy the boat and exhibit it on board."

"I've already thought of that. Come on, youngster. We better get out of these wet clothes. We could probably all use a shower. Show Carl how everything works in the forward head but take it easy on the water. We're strictly rationed now."

"If Carl doesn't mind, we can economize by taking one together," Robbie suggested, pleased that he could make it sound so natural. At least they would have a chance to say good-bye with their bodies. He came to vivid, sparkling life, fatigue forgotten. "Come on. I'll run up and get your clothes." He pushed Carl out ahead of him. Stuart was aware of the familiarity that had developed between them. The boy had definitely acquired the knack of making friends.

"Tell your mother we expect a double tot of grog for all hands," he called after Robbie's retreating back. He saw the boy's hand lift to the German's arm and experienced a pang of jealousy. Carl was old enough to be his father but he knew how to treat Robbie like a contemporary. Was it too late to re-create their old comradeship on an adult footing? Sharing the adventure tonight was a step toward intimacy. They couldn't steal a statue every day but there might be other opportunities for cementing a loving friendship if he remained on the lookout for them. His son was so—an unexpected word came to him—so endearing. Young, unpretentious, eager for life. He was shocked to realize that it was his first warm effortless response to him as an adult.

Robbie snatched up Carl's clothes from the dinghy and skipped back along the deck to the companionway. He caught sight of his mother in the unlighted cockpit. "We're all coming up for drinks as soon as we get dry," he called over his shoulder as he hurtled below. He burst into his cabin to find Carl just kicking off his shorts. He straightened and turned to him, naked and smiling. "You are very happy, my Robbie. I'm happy for you."

"Happy about the statue, not about anything else." He tugged at his wet clinging clothes and got them off. "I know we have to be quick. Just three minutes with you. That's all I ask." He seized his arm and peered around the door for a quick look aft toward the saloon, then darted across to the shower, crowding Carl in with him. The tiny cubicle forced them into each other's arms and they pressed against each other and kissed. Robbie already had an erection. He could feel Carl's cock going through its immense, thrillingly ponderous transition. He ran the water only long enough for them to get wet. They handed the soap back and forth to each other. Robbie searched Carl's eyes.

"What am I going to do?" he demanded in a hushed voice. "With the others, it was mostly sex and it didn't much matter if I never saw them again. Now it's you and—and everything. I'm your boy."

"Yes. Our lives are joined. I feel it. We'll have many plots together." Carl's eyes had a maddening way of turning cheerfully friendly, as they did now, just when Robbie hoped to discover depths of need in them. Perhaps he was too young for anybody to need him.

"We've got to get out of here," he admitted. He turned on the water and laughed as he felt Carl lift into full erection against him. "There's no room for that in here."

He checked the corridor again and they spilled out of the shower and sprang across to the refuge of the cabin. Robbie locked the door behind them and handed Carl a towel. They stood close to each other and dried themselves quickly, their erections beating lightly against each other. Robbie memorized every detail of the superb body and watched it turn luminously golden as the friction of the towel made all the hairs stand up and catch the light. Carl tossed the towel aside and put his arms around him.

"Let me feel you against me once more, my beautiful boy, and then we will look forward to reunion."

Robbie felt himself being engulfed by the great body and his mouth clung briefly to his lips. "We've been very quick. Nobody can suspect anything. I know how to make you come quickly. I want everything we've ever done together but that most of all."

"Yes, dear heart. You will give me one more moment of great joy." He dropped onto the bunk and sprawled out and toyed with Robbie's hair while he gave his body to the pleasure of his skillful mouth. His mind remained detached. He was taking stock, as a precarious lifetime had accustomed him to do. Even if the summer brought no further developments, he had acquired an asset that he could draw on indefinitely. He caressed Robbie's hair. He had never felt so sure of anybody in his life. Helene remained an enigma though a promising one. The money for the statue figured as a small useful dividend. The fact that he had allowed himself to be more deeply touched emotionally by this boy than the rules permitted counted as a debit; it endowed his climax with a wrenching sense of separation. Time would take care of it.

Robbie sat up and brushed his hair back from his forehead. "Thank God we could have that. I'll save my orgasm for when we're together again."

Carl swung his legs over the side of the bunk and sat beside him and held his erection. "No, no. I will expect you to have found many attractive boys by the time I get there."

The men joined Helene in the dark cockpit more or less simultaneously, so Robbie's moment with Carl went unnoticed. Helene had brandy waiting for them. Stuart poured them generous drinks and they told her about their struggle, turning it into a comic epic and vying for her laughter. She tried to enter into the spirit of their fun but couldn't conquer a feeling of having missed something. It had nothing to do with the statue; that sounded like a thoroughly tiresome chore. It was a sense of incompleteness that pierced her every time Carl's laughter boomed out of the dark. She shouldn't have let the conversation drop when they'd been alone yesterday. She'd assumed that there would be an opportunity to say more. It would soon be too late. In an hour, he'd be gone.

"We better get going," Stuart said, confirming her thought. "It'll be about eleven by the time we pick up our crew. With luck, we should be out of Greek waters by tomorrow night."

Outside the shelter of the bay, the sea was still heavy; the wind hadn't dropped at nightfall as it usually did. They were in for a blow. In the dark, Carl's hand strayed comfortingly over Robbie's shoulders and back. Stuart pulled the wheel over to round the last bluff and headed in toward the pier. The crew was loitering under a lamp waiting for them. He reduced speed.

"Okay, Roberto. Run forward and throw them a line. We won't tie up."

Robbie followed instructions. Angelino caught the line and

221

pulled them in. Rico hugged Robbie as he jumped aboard. Beppo followed.

Farewells were abrupt and brief. Carl took Helene's hand with a gentle pressure and told her that he'd write. He slapped Stuart on the back and gave Robbie's arm a final squeeze and leaped ashore.

"Bon voyage," he called, his hand lifted. In his white clothes, he stood out clear against the night as the boat backed away from the shores where Apollo reigned. Helene sat in the stern, her head turned from him, wondering what more she had wanted to say to him.

The wind blew sharp and favorably from the north. Within minutes, they were scudding along under full sail through a heavily running sea. Stuart looked up at the taut sails and thought of the long days and nights ahead of them. The interesting part of the trip was over. The rest would be drudgery; he hoped Robbie wouldn't be bored. They had made a friend and stolen a statue—and spent quite a lot of money. Carl's projected visit and Robbie's new social responsiveness were promises of a more populated future. Stuart was still no closer to knowing what life as a rich man was going to be like.

Money would have more significance for Robbie than for him. When his school ended next year, he wouldn't have to worry about a job but could devote himself to his painting. Stuart hadn't been convinced that the boy had the discipline and strength of character for an artist's life but he was rapidly revising his opinion. The talent was there; money would free him to make the most of it.

When Angelino and Rico had finished careening around the deck adjusting lines and making everything shipshape, Stuart turned over the wheel to the captain. It was agreed that he and Robbie would each take a regular four-hour watch during the day; the remaining sixteen hours would be divided among the professionals. There was nothing more to discuss until they reached their destination a thousand miles across the sea.

Stuart followed Helene below. Robbie lingered while Rico streamed the log from the stern, taken rather by surprise to realize that the sailor was once more a potential lover. He hadn't given the boy an erotic thought in a month. Would they pick up where they'd left off? If Rico wanted to, he had no reason to object. Carl didn't really want him to be his boy. He had yet to feel needed in a way that would match the enormous need in himself. It was his turn to use Rico as a convenience.

The sailor dropped into the cockpit beside the helm and said a few words to Angelino and teetered across to Robbie and fell into the seat beside him with an arm around him. "We go now, Robbie," he said against his face.

Rico was taking charge of him more openly than before. So be it. If he wanted to play homosexual games, Robbie would teach him to play them more expertly. He found his friend's hard cock and squeezed it and they made a dive for the companionway and tumbled down it. They swayed to the movement of the boat and held each other as they made their way forward to Robbie's cabin. He knew there were no witnesses but the fact that there could be made it a special event; he was going to sleep openly with a lover on home territory.

They stripped hastily and made a rush for the stability of the bunk. As soon as they were in each other's arms, Robbie asserted himself. He forestalled Rico's usual immediate move to take him by performing some sophisticated tricks with his mouth. To his surprise, his partner seemed willing to indulge Robbie's taste for more leisurely lovemaking. Perhaps Rico felt the difference in him and found him more desirable now that he was experienced in offering and taking pleasure. They looked at each other and laughed softly to welcome each other back. Their mouths met and Robbie turned it into their first real kiss. Rico responded eagerly but suddenly broke it off with a little exclamation of displeasure.

"Men don't kiss, Robbie," he admonished him.

"Why not? With your eyes closed you wouldn't know my mouth isn't a girl's. Stop thinking of me as a man. I'm queer. What you said. *Comme ça.* You know that. I wasn't sure before but I know now. If you want to fuck me then do it as if I were a girl. You'll like it more if you stop worrying about my being a boy."

Rico laughed. "You got one plenty big cock for a girl," he said, stroking it.

"It's about time you paid attention to that."

"I get used to it. Boys at home, we play with cocks. I like when it get so big for me. I want you plenty sometimes last two, three weeks. Not many girls there. I sleep with you regular this trip. Hokay?"

"Fine. Will Angelino know?"

"Sure. He gotta know where I am. He know I fuck you."

"He doesn't think there's anything wrong with it?"

"Why wrong? We got no girl. You let that German fella, that Carlo, you let him fuck you?"

"Yes," he admitted, abandoning discretion for the pleasure of speaking openly.

"Sure. He got something you like, I bet. Bigger than Rico. You got one beautiful mouth. That's sure."

"Then kiss me. I'm about to come. You're playing with my cock as if you liked it."

"Sure. I don't mind." He ran his tongue over Robbie's lips and his hand became more purposeful. Robbie opened his mouth to his and their kiss brought them in against each other, writhing with desire.

Rico proved less inhibited than Robbie would have believed possible a few weeks ago, but he understood now the difference between homosexuals and boys who didn't mind having sex together under certain circumstances. The latter had their limits but the fact that they existed made the world seem less hostile.

The world impinged very little on any of them in the nights and days that followed. They were caught up once more in the rhythm of the sea. They ate when they were hungry, slept when they were sleepy, and got gloriously, drunkenly exhausted keeping the boat going. Stuart was vaguely aware that the two boys had worked out some sort of arrangement for sharing Robbie's cabin and it didn't surprise him. Boys liked to stake out their territory like young animals. Helene spent a lot of time in her bunk reading, a superfluous element in a man's world. She was looking forward to home and finding their niche in an environment where they were still almost total strangers. When Carl arrived, she hoped to greet him as a serene and successful hostess, impregnably established in her own beautiful house.

Their progress was marked by geographical phenomena. Everything on the charts turned up miraculously where it belonged. This was Sardinia. That was Corsica. In another day or two it would be St. Tropez. By then, their destination was just another point on the charts. Their reality was the boat and the vagaries of the weather, the daily chores and, for Robbie, the pleasures awaiting him in his bunk. They had already sighted the high dim coast of France on the horizon when Rico joined him in the cabin late one afternoon. He was lying down naked, waiting for him.

"We get there, Robbie." He took his clothes off and stretched out on the bunk. "Tomorrow, this time, we no see each other."

"Don't talk about it. I can't believe it." Robbie kissed him and felt a lump gathering in his throat. His first boy. He was bound to have a special feeling for him, particularly after these last days and nights when they had arrived at something close to a sexual balance. The sailor drew back with a loving smile.

"Is crazy. I want you sometimes like I want girls. Like just for you. For Robbie. Is no wrong, I think. Just crazy."

"I certainly thought it was wrong at first. *Chope et fume.* Remember? I couldn't believe I wanted to do those things. I learned pretty fast, didn't I?"

"Sure. Now you get plenty handsome guys but you remember Rico. Hokay?"

"Always, Rico. Take me so I can't forget."

The next morning passed in a daze of arrival for the Coslings. They couldn't believe that they were really in St. Tropez and that the place looked so exactly the way they had left it. This was home and they had made it. There was the big new hotel planted in Stuart's vineyard. A trick of the landscape suddenly revealed their house sprawled against its hillside, a mirage, a stranger's fantasy. It disappeared from view like a dream behind another outcropping of land. They were getting in close to shore. They passed the little fisherman's port and Stuart's eyes lingered on the handsome house that had once been called *la batellerie.* The close-knit world that had held them and isolated them for a small infinity of time was rapidly disintegrating. They were once more land-based, shaking themselves free from an alien element.

The sails rattled down with finality and they motored into the crowded harbor and found a berth not far from the admiral's yacht. Helene and Stuart were glad to see that it was still there. The midday *apéritif* hour was underway and strollers loitered to watch as they eased in to the quai and made fast. Robbie became aware that a good many eyes were focused on him. He saw two gaudily dressed effeminate young men exchanging remarks while they looked him over. They laughed and gestured to him to join them. Robbie looked hastily away, faced with an unexpected challenge. He was going to have to learn how to behave without giving himself away when surrounded by his own kind. If young men

225

made advances to him, wouldn't his parents begin to suspect that it was because they recognized his susceptibility? He wasn't threatened by hostility but by a too overt acceptance of what he was. He moved restlessly toward the bow to get away from inviting eyes. He'd forgotten how obvious certain types were or perhaps they'd become obvious only now that he knew that he was one of them. He wished he were back in Greece where a manly young boatman could want him without its being considered remarkable.

Helene was the first to spot the admiral. She waved as she saw him, conspicuous in a saffron shirt and royal blue scarf, making his way through the crowd to the foot of their gangplank.

"We're waiting for you," he called expansively. "Come along and have some lunch. All sorts of people wanting to meet you." He came aboard and Robbie returned to the cockpit to be introduced.

"Have a son about your age. Not so good-looking as you by half. A bit odd but not a bad chap. Daresay you'll be wanting to tidy up." He glanced at Robbie's trunks. "You can come as you are. Young people go about stark naked these days. Extraordinary. No hurry, you understand. Don't get around to feeding much before teatime. Can't think why. Deuced unhealthy."

Mrs. Rawls came tripping up the gangplank after him, vibrating with patronizing goodwill and flashing with jewels.

"Now the season can really begin," she cried. "I've only just arrived myself. You don't mean to say you've been all the way to Greece on this adorable little boat! How mad and adventurous! You're still children—beautiful, beautiful children! You must come for a cocktail tomorrow. There are so many people I want you to meet. I've taken a villa. La Pléiade. You know it? And your enchanting place? I understand it's quite the most beautiful house on the coast."

"I should call home and tell them we're here," Stuart said when she was gone. "Everybody else knows."

"What are we going to do about the statue?" Robbie wondered.

"Speak of the devil." Stuart nodded toward the gangplank. The customs inspector was standing at the foot of it. Stuart expected no difficulties but he was pleasantly surprised by the man's complete lack of official zeal when he went to greet him.

"I suppose you're loaded with contraband," he said.

"Of course, we almost sank," Stuart said while his heart skipped a beat.

"Well, don't let me see you taking it off. Send your man around with your papers sometime during the day and I'll fix them up."

"Fine. Come aboard and have a contraband drink."

"Why not, in fact?" The customs inspector came aboard and Stuart had a drink with him. They went ashore together and Stuart returned with Stanley Hilliard at his side.

"Look who I've found," he called as they came aboard. "It's Stanley. American literature's great white hope." Stuart's first thought when they ran into each other was that his expensive clothes looked as if they belonged to him now. He had become a man of substance.

Hilliard stepped gingerly off the gangplank onto the deck. "Is this yours? I heard you'd struck it rich but I didn't know you were *that* rich."

"I'm not. We rented it."

"I see. I was passing through about a week ago and they told me you'd gone to Greece or somewhere. My God, this place has sort of changed, hasn't it? It's one big goddam party. I couldn't get away. And you. I understand you've got the showplace of the whole damn Côte d'Azur. Swimming pools, marble halls, an authentic neo-colossal DeMille production. Is this Robbie? I can't believe it. What a magnificent guy you've turned into. Whatever you've been doing, it agrees with all of you." He kissed Helene's cheek.

"How long has it been? Seven years?" Stuart asked. "What about you? You look as if you've been doing all right yourself. Where've you been?"

"Hollywood. And no cracks. It's a game and it pays the bills. It has nothing to do with writing. It's a whole new thing. When you hold your elbows right and get a good grip with your knees you can make it sit up and do tricks."

"If you like it, what the hell?" Stuart poured drinks.

"I didn't say I liked it. What goddam fools we were in the old days—except you, of course. You and your spinach. I guess you have the right idea, after all. I thought I'd get rich doing what I wanted to do. You just wanted to lie in the lap of Mother Nature and here you are up to your ass in swimming pools."

"What is all this about swimming pools? We don't have a

swimming pool, do we Robbie? Maybe somebody put one in while we were gone '

"They better not. It would ruin everything. Did you call home?"

"Yes. Boldoni and Felix are coming in to get our things off. Everybody sounds fine."

"Did you arrange anything about you-know-what?"

Stuart told Hilliard about the statue. "I think we'd better wait till tonight, the later the better," he told Robbie. "We'll need all the help we can get. How about it, Stanley? Do you want to be an accessory after the fact?"

"If you promise to have champagne and lobster sent into our cell, why not? As a matter of fact, I was going to ask you all to dinner."

"Not tonight. I've promised Boldoni to dine at home. I'll join you after dinner and then you can come out and stay with us."

"We can make you more comfortable than last time," Helene said. She excused herself to dress for the admiral's lunch.

"As a matter of fact; I'm traveling with my secretary," Hilliard said, after she had left.

"I don't think that'll worry anybody," Stuart assured him. "We'll expect her, too."

They agreed to meet at the boat at eleven that night and Hilliard took himself off. "He's right, you know," Stuart said to Robbie, pouring himself more brandy. "You *are* a magnificent looking guy, Roberto. I suppose it would've happened anyway, but the cruise seems to've speeded things up. I thought you might turn out to be sort of an ethereal type but you've turned into a regular body boy overnight. You're going to be a big hit with the girls."

Robbie glowed with pleasure at his father's flattering attention but it also flustered him. Why harp on girls? Would he have to pretend to take an interest in some girl in order to satisfy him? "What's all this Roberto business?" he demanded with an unintentional edge of hostility to compensate for his embarrassment.

Taken aback, Stuart attempted a conciliatory chuckle. "I don't know. Maybe I was pretending to be your Italian boyfriend."

"If you mean Rico, he calls me Robbie like everybody else." Robbie was suddenly close to tears as he felt the moment turning sour. He could do without being told that he was magnificent looking if all his father really wanted was to get in a dig about his "boyfriend." Guilt turned him defensive. "I suppose now you're going to tell me I've been too friendly with him. You started it. You said I should be nice to him."

"Hey, wait a minute, youngster. I wasn't going to say anything of the sort." He looked at his drink and swirled it around in his glass. Was he drunk? He wasn't used to drinking so early in the day. He'd obviously hit on some sensitive spot but he couldn't imagine what he'd said wrong. "I'm delighted to see you making friends, the more the merrier. I used to think you were too standoffish. I expect you'll fall in love in the not too distant future. I was always in love when I wasn't much older than you. It makes life very interesting. Your mother may not think much of the idea—mothers rarely do—but I'll be all for you. Just remember that."

Girls again. Robbie felt threatened by this offer of man-to-man intimacy. He couldn't allow anybody to encroach on his privacy. "I don't intend to fall in love for a long time, if ever," he said coldly. "Right now, all I'm thinking about is getting back to work."

"Well, you've heard about all work and no play. You may not know it yet but your looks are going to get you into lots of hot water. I envy you." He forced his laughter, aware that he was still flirting with trouble. He could see it in the tense dark beauty of the boy's face, in the great darting eyes and the slight tremor of his sensitive mouth. He must be drunk if he expected a seventeen-year-old to emerge from adolescence without any kinks or complexes. He retreated as gracefully as he could with a light tap on Robbie's shoulder. "I promise you one thing. I'll be careful not to pick any fights with you. You're getting too big for me to handle."

Robbie's spirit was soothed by intimations of friendship but he steeled himself against them. "All this talk about love," he growled. His throat was constricted and his eyes smarted. He couldn't be friends with his father. What would he say if he told him that the closest he'd come to understanding the nature of love was with an anonymous naval officer on a changing-room floor?

The admiral was standing in the stern when the Coslings reached the foot of his gangplank. "At last, at last," he cried.

"Party's quite limp without you. Come knock a bit of life into it." They found themselves in the midst of a great many people on the afterdeck. Introductions were haphazard. The only note that emerged clearly was "your house." Everybody seemed to have heard of their house. "I hear," everyone said. "Utterly enchanting, one of the seven wonders." While it was going on, a girl who had introduced herself to him as Anne took Robbie's arm and said breathlessly, "Come along quickly." She led him forward around the cabin to the forward deck. "This is where the children sit. We're terribly careful about not being contaminated by the grown-ups." Robbie followed, displeased by being called a child until he saw that the children included Anne herself, who was certainly over twenty, a long, sleek exquisite boy called Edward, a sturdy young man called John, and a pretty girl called Mellie, who were lounging on cushions under an awning. They weren't naked but might have looked more presentable if they had been. The girls wore one-piece suits that fitted like a second skin, the boys rather droopy trunks of loose-knit jersey that covered them from navel to upper thigh but provided no snug support in the midsection. Genitalia drifted about conspicuously.

"Don't try to understand who we all are," Anne said as she pronounced the others' names. "We're all more or less related by marriage—the admiral's marriages, that is."

She laughed a light pure laugh. Robbie found her charming. She had a delicate face in which bones predominated and her pale brown hair hung down lank and straight, giving her the look of peering through parted curtains. The others grunted amiably at Robbie and relinquished a few cushions for him to sit on. They had drinks in their hands and there was a pitcher of a pale fruity-looking liquid on the deck. Anne poured a drink for Robbie.

"You're the Coslings. I understand you're to be the big event of the season," John said lazily. He waved his glass toward Robbie. "Cheers." He rolled over slightly and ran the tip of his tongue up Mellie's arm from the elbow to the shoulder where he implanted a light popping kiss. When he moved, what appeared to be an erection stuck out jauntily.

"Young love. Isn't it adorable?" Anne commented. "Edward, you're missing it." And then to Robbie, "Edward's the admiral's son and I'm the admiral's daughter. We're half brothers or half sisters or however you want to put it. We used to have the most marvelous sex when we were practically babies. Now he's decided he's a poof. I can't help feeling that I failed somehow."

"Maybe it's just a phase," Edward said comfortably, prone and motionless on a mattress. Robbie assumed it was some sort of joke. They couldn't mean it.

"Tell us about your parents' vices," Anne said, settling into her cushions. "We're terribly keen on parents' vices. That is, they always seem so unimaginative. We keep hoping for something really new and exciting."

"I don't think mine have any," Robbie said, totally out of his depth.

"Perhaps that's better," Anne said. "I mean, for instance, Edward's stepfather smoked opium and shot himself. I mean, if you're going to smoke opium you shouldn't have to shoot yourself. Anyway, Edward found him in the nursery of all places. It's supposed to have given Edward some sort of complex."

"You've got it all wrong, as usual." Edward propped himself up on one elbow and looked at Robbie. "I'm supposed to've got some sort of complex from seeing my mother in bed with the gamekeeper. All very D.H. Lawrence. Is there such a thing as a gamekeeper complex?"

"I think it's a very common one," Robbie said. They found this vastly entertaining and whooped with laughter. Robbie was pleased at having scored in such an unfamiliar atmosphere; his satisfaction was short-lived.

"Which do you prefer?" Anne asked with matter-of-fact interest. "Boys or girls?" Robbie felt his tongue turn into sponge but Edward spared him the necessity of a reply.

"You see what I tell you?" he said. "You push things so. Maybe he hasn't decided yet."

"Well, if we're going to see a lot of each other, which is apparently the parents' intention, it's something we should know, even if it might not affect us personally. He probably thinks I'm an old hag and he's a bit young to be your type, isn't he?"

Edward turned his eyes on Robbie with calm appraisal, leaving no doubt that he was sizing him up as a potential partner. A little shiver of delight ran through Robbie as he realized that the brother and sister weren't joking. He conducted his own appraisal. The older boy was aristocratically good-looking, blond and blue-eyed with high English coloring, but the most striking thing about him was that he looked so nice. Robbie couldn't imagine him doing anything gross or improper. His body was elegantly put together, slim and graceful and delicately articulated; it looked as if it could turn a sexual act into a display of artistry.

"I don't know why you think he's too young for me," Edward concluded, addressing Anne. "I have no prejudice against youth when wedded to beauty. He's extraordinary for such a beardless boy. Such smouldering sensuality. Skin the color of aromatic honey. Look at that throat. What difference does a few years make if we're both prepared to make allowances? I might even be cured of my obsession."

"You see," Anne explained to Robbie without giving the two boys time to make any commitment with their eyes, "Edward is mad about the dancing boy at the Tour Engloutie but Edward isn't *his* type. We're having a terribly fraught summer." Soft giggles emerged from John and Mellie, who were now looking at each other with their noses touching. Anne pushed her hair back from her face impatiently. "Of course, they don't help matters in the least."

"On the contrary," Edward objected. "They're a grim reminder of what even I might've turned into if I hadn't developed more elevated tastes. Can you imagine my behaving like that with my divine dancer?"

Robbie exploded with laughter. Edward looked at him with approval and interest. Having survived his appraisal with high marks, Robbie suspected that he was now going to be pursued in a gentlemanly way. He was faced with the challenge. If Edward publicly proclaimed his inclinations, how friendly could he let himself be with him without publicly compromising himself? How much did the admiral know? How much, whether as a warning or inadvertently, would he pass on to his parents? The atmosphere of freedom he sensed with these contemporaries was intoxicating—the chaste slow-motion love affair that John and Mellie were conducting made his body tingle—but he also sensed its danger. His eyes shied away from Edward's increasingly amused and inviting glances.

He concentrated with difficulty on Anne and heard more about the young dancer who had taken the town by storm. Evidence was accumulating that he was stubbornly addicted to girls. Anne kept refilling their glasses from the pitcher. The fruity drink was intoxicating, too.

Robbie decided that he must be a bit drunk after he found himself in a narrow passage below-decks without quite knowing how he had got there. Edward was at his side, which didn't surprise him. Had their eyes finally exchanged an imperative summons? Had something been said about a pee? He hoped there was more to it than that. Edward's hand was lightly, agreeably on his shoulder and he seemed to know what they were doing. He had been impressed by his length on the mattress but they turned out to be of about equal height. He stopped and opened a door and urged Robbie into a cabin that was so small that after Robbie had backed up against the bunk and Edward had closed the door behind them, their bodies were touching tantalizingly here and there.

"You're absolutely smashing," Edward burst out with engaging schoolboy enthusiasm, his eyes sparkling. "I had to tell you. Your caramel skin—that's closer than honey—your throat of course—every bit of you. I imagine you *are* quite young but you're such a *man* if you know what I mean. And how glamorous to come sailing in from Greece. I'm sure you've just descended from Mount Olympus." His hands moved up Robbie's arms and came to rest on his shoulders. "Oh darling, you *do* like boys, don't you?" he asked almost pleadingly.

"God, yes," Robbie blurted out, throwing discretion to the winds. "I certainly like you."

"Thank heavens. I couldn't bear not knowing. I thought you were holding back. Agony. Shall we linger here a wicked moment or would you rather wait for a whole night of love?"

Robbie wasn't accustomed to courtesy under these circumstances. His rough-and-ready experiences hadn't taught him how to behave with a boy more or less of his own age and background. His erection was straining for release. He was dying to get his hands on Edward's, quite visible in his funny trunks. What were they waiting for? "I thought—" he began hesitantly, letting his body ease in closer to Edward's.

"That I brought you here to make love to you? Of course I did but I don't want to force myself on you."

"Oh no, you couldn't. I want whatever you want." He caressed the exquisite chest encouragingly while Edward deftly removed his trunks and closed his hands around Robbie's rigid sex.

"Oh darling, a lovely long one. I knew it. Perfect for piping a lively tune. I'm green with envy." He dropped down and drew it into his mouth. Robbie cried out and felt as if he had leaped into the air. Somebody wanted him at last as he had wanted all the others. He barely mastered an instantaneous orgasm. Edward relinquished him and rose, peeling off his own trunks as he did so. Robbie was pleased to see that he almost exceeded the norm. Edward moved around with him and dropped onto the bunk and drew him down. At his prompting, they stretched out in a position that was new to Robbie, with their feet at opposite ends of the bunk, so that their mouths were placed where they could easily give each other pleasure. Robbie almost forgot the ecstasy of reciprocation. He wanted to lie back and let waves of bliss wash over him. They moaned and gasped with their mouths full and arrived at simultaneous orgasms. After a quiet moment, Edward sat up, holding Robbie's head in his lap against his rapidly dwindling erection.

"How heavenly. I think boys are so civilized together, don't you?"

"You mean what we just did? Yes." No wonder he'd been longing for somebody to do it. It had been the final revelation; his education was complete. Carl's brief demonstration had been a generous effort to show him what it felt like but desire had been lacking. Edward was the first person to make him feel that satisfying him was his sole concern. He had found his own kind at last. It made all the difference. He moved the side of his face against Edward's soft cock.

"I hope I do it as beautifully as you do," Edward said.

"I can't imagine anybody being better." Robbie began to move his mouth over the subtle perfection of his new friend's body. He sucked and nuzzled the slender joints of his hips, his navel, his nipples and armpits, up his neck to his ears. Their mouths met and their tongues frolicked together. They laughed and drew apart and lay back against the bulwark in each other's arms.

"I'm head over heels with that dancer but so's everybody else. It's really rather common of me. I'd much rather be in love with you. Would you mind, darling?"

Nobody had ever called him "darling." He supposed it was sort of girlish but he loved it. He wondered if he could ever use an endearment with a boy. "What would we do if you were? Nobody ever has been."

"It would be quite tiresome for both of us unless you were in love with me too. That's the trouble with the dancer. Perhaps we'd better stick to sex. That's something you obviously know a great deal about. I've never known anybody so thrilling. It's such a relief to have the first time out of the way. It always reduces me to a quivering jelly. The

234

pounding heart. The heaving chest. Too demolishing. Now we can wallow in the delights of our lovely young bodies."

Robbie giggled. He couldn't imagine this exquisite creature's chest heaving. "You're so silly, darling." He had said the word. If it was girlish, at least he had somebody to share his girlishness with. He felt as if they were drowning together in ineffable sweetness. He held him closer.

"I know I am, but nobody has ever said it so adorably," Edward said.

Robbie drew his lips into his mouth. His cock lengthened into vigorous erection again. He shifted Edward over onto his stomach and sprawled out on top of him and covered his shoulders and back with kisses. He slid down and bit his buttocks. Edward uttered quick moans of pleasure. Robbie flipped him over onto his back and saw that he was nearly erect. His chest actually was heaving slightly. Robbie lifted himself to his knees and bent over him and completed his erection with his hands and mouth.

"You're turning me into a ravening beast, darling. I never dreamed I could function again so quickly." Edward disentangled himself and pulled himself up and knelt in front of him. "Let me see us together. I do want a good look at yours." They put their hands on each other's hips and held them so that their erections lifted side by side. "You see? I'm absolutely *puce* with envy. An imperial scepter. It's divine but do try not to let it grow much more, darling. I can't bear great stallions stampeding over me, can you?" Edward sat back on his heels and Robbie imitated him. They leaned forward with their heads together and stroked each other slowly. "Shall we have a cozy natter about sex? I don't think people talk about it nearly enough—not seriously, that is. The one or two boys I've known with cocks like yours were such aggressive brutes. Do you want to bugger me?"

"No, I'll never want that with anyone."

"I thought you were about to a minute ago. I'd let you, of course. If I fall in love with you I might even want you to, but let's work up to it slowly. Nobody's ever wanted me to bugger them so we don't have to worry about that."

"Why not? I'd love you to."

"Oh no, darling. I couldn't. You're such a man." Edward hitched himself around and sat with his back to the bulwark, his legs spread out in front of him. He drew Robbie to him and opened his mouth for his erection. Robbie exerted gentle pressure and watched it entering while Edward's tongue did thrilling things with it. He was overwhelmed by bliss again.

"Oh God," he gasped. "I love it. I'll do yours in a minute."

Time passed.

They lay together, their hands running idly through each other's hair. Edward's was beguilingly frizzy around the edges. Robbie heaved a deep shuddering sigh of contentment.

"Happy, darling?" Edward murmured.

"Yes, darling."

"My darling."

"Darling. I love us to call each other that." He was a homosexual. Edward was a homosexual. There was nothing loathsome about it. Their acceptance of each other was complete. He was drunk with the sensual awareness that flowed like a soothing current between them. The fruity drink might have something to do with it too. He knew they couldn't stay here much longer but he hadn't the will to make a move. It was his last thought before he slid into a deep sleep.

A familiar drawling voice brought him back to consciousness. The words were blurred and then close to his ear he heard, ". . . so beautiful?" He smiled. He was lying on his back and he had another erection. Edward's hand moved along it and circled its base and lifted it upright. He let it fall with a little slap against his navel.

"My word," a girl's voice said.

Robbie's eyes flew open and he whirled around seeking concealment against Edward's body. Anne was standing beside the bunk. Edward held him and kissed his mouth.

"Have you looked at his beautiful brown bottom?" Anne asked. "I've never seen a boy before with such a beautiful bottom. Perhaps you'd better not look at it now. You really must come out. I told them you were looking at the engine room. It sounds like something that boys would do. I presume we have an engine room."

"We must have. Run along, darling. We won't be a minute. Tell them I'm adjusting a gasket."

Robbie heard her laughter and a door closing. He reared up, shaking his head to clear it. "What's happening? Have I been asleep long?"

"Only about half an hour. It's been heavenly watching you."

"You let Anne see my cock."

236

"Of course, darling. I couldn't deny her such an impressive sight."

"Half an hour! Has everybody noticed we're missing?"

"It doesn't matter. It's quite extraordinary, you know. No matter how many people I tell about myself, nobody really believes me. I don't find it so incredible, do you?"

"I'm beginning to think it's incredible that everybody isn't the same." Robbie laughed, amazed that in this part of the world, even here where he had learned to abhor everything he had discovered in himself, even here an avowed homosexual could be casual and humorous and carefree. What had become of the foul pit of depravity that he had thought awaited him? He fell back into Edward's welcoming arms and their bodies lolled indolently together until passion intervened and they offered each other their mouths.

"What a lovely phase this is, passing or no," Edward sighed while they were waiting for everything to settle down. "I'm so happy we're going through it together. I wonder if I'm a case of retarded development. I don't suppose twenty is advanced senility but I don't feel older than you. Is there much more than a year's difference?"

"Well, actually I'm not eighteen yet."

"Good Lord. So young? That should make me feel wicked but it doesn't somehow. You have such quiet authority. Do you feel very wicked, darling? I doubt it. We'll go to the Tour Engloutie tonight and I'll show you Toni. I'm sure I'll watch him now with frigid indifference but the place is a show in itself. I swoon over the beauties and try not to notice the ghastly camp followers. A bit *too* camp for my tastes but if we're poofsters I suppose we must take the rough with the smooth. You'll be a sensation. Is this a good moment to leap into our knickers, darling, or shall we stay here the rest of our lives?"

"I wouldn't mind." They retrieved their trunks from where they'd fallen and pulled them on. Robbie wished he could match Edward's insouciance at facing the world after such a long suspicious absence. "Does your father know about you?" he asked.

"Oh, yes, the Sea Dog knows but he adheres to the 'passing phase' school. Besides, he's navy, darling. Sodomy is in the grand old seafaring tradition. He'd think I'd taken leave of my senses if he caught me with a cock in my mouth."

"You're the first who's wanted to do it that way with me. I thought nobody ever would. Is it so very unusual?"

"Dear me. How different our experience has been. That's how I found out I was a poof—a lovely boy wanted to pipe a tune on mine and I couldn't wait to make it a duet. I confess I'm depressed by tiddly little ones, but give me one like yours and I become as one possessed, a virtuoso of the cock rampant."

Robbie looked into clever blue eyes and laughed. "You don't know how wonderful this is for me. I don't mean just sex but finding somebody I can really be friends with. Homosexuality is so new to me. I haven't known what to expect. If we're friends, I don't have to worry anymore."

"Please, darling," Edward said, looking suddenly shy and flustered. "Don't make me fall in love with you before I've had lunch. I might not be responsible for my actions. What an adorable boy. I've never thought I had much sex appeal but you're doing wonders for my ego. You were in my arms before I was even sure it was on. Come along, darling. We must."

"I know." They kissed lightly and Edward took his hand and led him out. They mounted to the upper deck and crossed the saloon toward the stern where the party was assembled. As they approached, Robbie was sure that everybody was wondering what the two of them had been doing. The appalling thought struck him that Edward might call him "darling" in public and he let himself be separated from his lover the minute they stepped out onto the crowded after-deck. People had started to eat. Anne appeared at his side and thrust a well-laden plate into his hands.

"Eat, darling," she ordered. "I know sex makes boys hungry. You looked so perfect together. I do hope it's going to be a real affair. Edward's been rather at loose ends lately. Are your parents tiresome about homosexuality?"

Robbie blushed and almost choked and glanced hastily around them. What would she say next? Who would hear her? "They don't know," he muttered.

"Oh dear. Is that a good idea? Edward believes that deception leads to all sorts of dreadful repressions. He feels we must do what we can to enlighten our elders. It's so much more healthy. I must say you looked wonderfully enlightened a little while ago."

Reminded that she had seen his cock, he blushed more hotly. "How did you find us?"

"Where else would you be, darling? Edward thinks casual

sex is immature but from the moment he looked at you he was wild to make love to you. We've talked about you for weeks."

"Really?"

"Of course. Everybody's been talking about the fabulous Coslings."

The fabulous Coslings. Stuart heard the phrase repeatedly. He didn't understand how they had become thus institutionalized, but the fatigue of having been up since dawn and the drinks he had consumed since his arrival made a pleasant blur of everything taking place around him and he handed out rather vague invitations right and left. While he was still taking notice, he had talked to a celebrated writer, two painters, a film star, a prince and his princess, and a cluster of lesser aristocrats. As lunch progressed, they became anonymous if familiar faces, a gallery of nameless new friends.

Helene remained alert and selective with an emphasis on those with residential ties in the area rather than the transients. As she asked questions and exchanged pleasantries, it crossed her mind that Carl would be very much at home in the community that was beginning to take shape.

"We ran into a man called Carl von Eschenstadt in the islands. Have you ever known him?" she asked the admiral, who remained ceremoniously at her side.

"Eh? Von Eschenstadt? Name's familiar. Sounds like a Hun. Bad bit of goods, what?"

"Oh, we didn't think so," Helene protested.

"Dare say I'm thinking of some other chap. These foreign names all sound alike, you know."

She caught a glimpse of Robbie talking to the admiral's fey daughter. She hoped he was making friends with the young people. They would make a pleasant addition to the life she was planning.

The party drew to a natural conclusion. After Robbie had made sure that both his parents had seen him with Anne and other guests, he allowed Edward to reclaim him.

"I can't bear being without you for an instant, darling," the older boy drawled. "That's a very bad sign." They talked some more about the evening. Robbie pointed out that his father was making an event of their first family dinner in the completed house. "Of course, darling, I can't expect to take over your entire life on the very first day. I shall eat my heart out till you come back. Toni isn't on till about midnight. We might pipe a merry tune before or after. Perhaps both. I do

239

hope rather a lot of sex is included in your thoughts of our future happiness, darling."

"I'm thinking of a nonstop duet."

Edward laughed. "You *are* adorable, darling. Now that I've had some lunch, I can tell you quite rationally that I'm halfway to falling in love with you. I'm trying rather desperately not to go further. Tonight might be decisive."

Stuart had arranged for the Rolls to be left for them when Boldoni had come in to take off their luggage. They drove out to the house with lively anticipation while they discussed the party.

"Did you like the admiral's children, darling?" Helene asked Robbie. "I thought Anne quite attractive in an odd original way."

"She's nice but they're all a bit mad. They talk nonsense just to shock people. Edward calls everybody darling." That was the point he had had to make as quickly as possible. His heart seemed to shrink as he adopted a disdainful tone toward the boy who had made him so happy, but he had to protect himself. "Did he call you darling, Dad?" he asked to drive his point home.

"I don't think I talked to him long enough to give him a chance. He seemed rather effete but he has great charm."

"Oh sure, they have plenty of that but I think they're apt to wear thin. You can't take anything they say seriously." He had disposed of the Cumberleighs. He thought of the melting appeal of Edward's eyes and despised himself.

"I'm afraid we'll find a great many people like that here," Helene said, approving his perception. "All fairly superficial. I'm sure you won't be taken in. We'll find the exceptions."

Stuart was sorry to hear the note of aloof superiority creeping back into the boy's voice. He'd hoped he'd been cured of it. "Edward took you on a tour of the boat, didn't he?"

"Yes, a very thorough one. It's quite big."

"Well, that shows he's interested in it. That's something. He's not blasé."

"Oh no, I didn't say that," Robbie agreed, making amends for his disloyalty. He smiled to himself as he added, "He was very enthusiastic about it during our tour."

They fell silent as they approached the last curve in the sweeping drive and sat forward. They rounded it and drove up to the segment of village square. The new plaster, shaded from ochre to soft pink to gray on the various surfaces of the irregular façade, had already weathered slightly and glowed in the late sun. Vines were climbing up it. There were flowers everywhere and the big cork oak they had carefully guarded from the builders cast a lacy shadow on one end of the structure.

Stuart brought the car to a halt and turned off the motor. "So far so good," he said with quiet pride.

"It's lovely," Helene exclaimed incredulously.

The antique wrought-iron gates of the central arch were flung open and people came spilling through, Boldoni and his wife and Felix and Agnès, the handsome new maid. The Coslings were caught up in a tumultuous homecoming. They crowded through flagged passages, jostling each other and all talking at once, past the cloistered courtyard of the guest wing and out to the vast terrace hanging over the sea. They all fell silent abruptly as the proprietors looked around them.

The fountain splashed into a pool of lilies. The rich colors of draperies were visible through the wide French doors of the main house. Red rocks tumbled into the azure sea at the mouth of the cove. The descending colonnade of cypresses joined the beach house to the upper complex. White pigeons strutted on the lush green lawn under the olive trees. Behind, terraces of lemon and orange trees mounted to where "Robbie's Folly" should have been visible.

For a moment, Robbie couldn't find it and then he saw a corner of the small house emerging from the foliage. The last time he'd seen it, it had stood out stark and bare against the hillside. Without knowing why the question had occurred to him, he had wondered then how anybody could come to see him without being observed. The problem now would be to make sure his guests knew how to find him.

"Felix has been at work," Stuart said, breaking the silence. Robbie let out a whoop of joy and went running off down the glade. Pigeons whirled up around his head with a clatter of wings. He found the path he had planned to lead up to the house and leaped up the steps from terrace to terrace, glancing back down as he went to see that he was adequately screened from view all the way. A cypress guarded the door. It was unlocked and Robbie let himself into his private domain.

He stood in a living room about the size of the all-purpose room in the little house he had grown up in. The furniture was simple and serviceable, with a sofa and a few chairs in front of a fireplace. A skylight had been let into the top half of the north end of the wall and adjacent ceiling and the area below it was bare except for a sturdy worktable, waiting for Robbie's easel and brushes and paints. He glanced into the bedroom and his eyes lingered on the double bed he had requested, also without knowing why. Even then he apparently had been thinking of finding someone to share it.

The bathroom and tiny kitchenette, including a refrigerator, completed his house. He went to the end of the living room and stepped out onto the terrace that looked out over the sea. He had to go to the edge of it before he could see down into the main living quarters and the cove below. He could lie naked in the sun in perfect privacy. It was all too good to be believed.

He poked about in closets and cupboards and saw that everything he had sent back from school was here, as were the bags from the boat. He set to work moving in. By the time he had created some order, he had arrived at the realization that no challenges faced him here. This was his refuge; he would stay away from town. Nobody need know who he brought here. He had his work to help him resist temptation. Edward already took it for granted that they would make forays into town together but if the English boy continued to fall in love he would probably be delighted to keep Robbie for himself out here.

It occurred to Robbie that the Cumberleighs' self-proclaimed liberation from their elders was as limiting as secrecy and self-denial. He couldn't be the only one who would be hesitant about public association with Edward's open admission of homosexuality. By saying everything, they made themselves conspicuous. He could indulge himself more freely than they because nobody would be paying any attention. He supposed he had to go back to town for the statue but he wouldn't go to the Tour Engloutie even if he could get away from his father. It sounded like the sort of place that offered nothing but trouble. No matter what Edward said, he wasn't ready to be found out.

Bathed, dressed in cool clean clothes, somewhat rested, the Coslings had Boldoni's gala dinner under the stars. The great terrace was furnished like a living room with groupings of handsome outdoor furniture set about on it. The dining table was set near the edge over the sea. Stuart doubted they would use their impressive reception rooms till winter. Before the meal was half over, Robbie was getting drowsy on wine.

"The statue," he exclaimed to wake himself up. "Do you suppose either of us has the strength to lift it?"

"I hope Hilliard is in good shape. We could let it go till tomorrow. The boat doesn't have to be back for three days. Still, I'd feel better getting it ashore now."

"Me too."

"Look, we don't both have to go in. Stanley's having dinner with friends. We won't have any trouble picking up an extra hand. Even better, I'll take Felix. He has the strength of ten. The statue won't be any secret from him."

"You sure you don't mind?"

"Of course not. It doesn't make any sense for both of us to knock ourselves out." He was disappointed and hurt—he had thought of the statue as a joint venture that they would conclude together—but he was too numb with exhaustion and drink to feel anything very deeply.

"I'm sure Felix could handle it all by himself," Helene said, approving Robbie's withdrawal.

"If you happen to see Anne and Edward, tell them I've collapsed. They wanted to take me to the Tour Engloutie to see some dancer."

"Yes, several people mentioned him," Helene said dismissively. "It doesn't sound like the sort of thing we'd be interested in." She had been shocked by what she'd heard about the Tour Engloutie. She'd caught men eying Robbie during the cruise. She didn't know what men did together nor how widespread such practices were, but she wouldn't allow his beauty to be defiled. He still had a glow of innocence that she hoped he wouldn't lose for a few more years.

"He'd have to be fairly sensational to keep me awake," Robbie said. The subject was closed.

Stuart drove carefully. He wasn't drunk. He was functioning on alcohol. He left Felix in the car and found Hilliard and his girl and they crossed to a café where they found several couples whose names couldn't penetrate the sheath of numbness in which he was encased. The evening crowd was at its height and Stuart had seen lights on *Northern Star,* which meant that the crew was still awake. He resigned himself to waiting till after midnight and ordered a brandy.

"We're going to the Tour Engloutie in a little while, if it's all right with you," Hilliard said. "Have you heard about it?"

"It opened last year. I understand it's properly disreputable."

"They've got a kid dancing there. All the pansies in town go. Next to you, he's the sensation of the season. Pat's crazy for him."

"Nuts," Hilliard's girl said succinctly. She was a smart hard-looking young American. "As any dope can see, he's damn beautiful. He's a nice kid, too. The Lambrechts know him. He's not a pansy."

"You mean you hope he's not," Hilliard said.

"The way you carry on about him, anybody'd think *you* were. I bet Mr. Cosling agrees with me when he sees him."

"You two are coming back with me afterward, aren't you?" Stuart asked.

"Our bags are packed. Nobody'll ask us for a marriage license when we register?"

"Mr. and Mrs. John Doe will do for our circumspect establishment."

All of St. Tropez seemed to be trying to get into the Tour Engloutie. The narrow gangway that led across the rocks to it was so crowded that Stuart's party had to shuffle slowly to the door. Within was a large circular stone-walled room partially open to the sky. The lighting was dim. There was a three-piece band against the wall and a small platform in front of them on which people jigged up and down because lateral movement was out of the question. With the dark and the noise, Stuart had no clear impression of the people around him. They had more drinks and waited.

He felt as if he'd been there all night when the music stopped, people left the floor, the band evoked a flourish, and a man in a white dinner jacket stepped forward and announced, "The sensation of the dance, the great artist for whom you are all waiting: Toni." The room was plunged into darkness and a spotlight flashed on, revealing the dancer.

Stuart's first thought was of the statue. Toni stood with his hands on his hips, his head lifted and turned slightly to one side, poised and relaxed and naked except for a skimpy *cache-sexe*. His body was beautiful but it was his face that held Stuart's attention. His features were neither classic nor pretty in a theatrical way, but oddly pure and distinguished in spite of his youth. Even the golden curls that looked as if they'd been tampered with didn't make him look effeminate. He emanated a godlike pastoral freshness. His exhibiting himself in this way seemed inappropriate but Stuart blamed the audience rather than the boy.

The band burst into a fast blaring Slavic number and the dancer whirled into motion. The dance was preposterous, composed of scraps of classic ballet and bits derived from folk dancing and others that suggested the music hall, but he moved with athletic abandon and a personal style that made the performance arresting. As he watched, Stuart was conscious of a feeling of familiarity. There seemed to be something that eluded him. Did the boy remind him of someone? Of Robbie? No, although they were not unlike in type in spite of the different coloring. The feeling persisted, nagging but not particularly interesting.

As abruptly as it had started, the performance was over. There was a split second of silence and then a storm of applause. The youth stood up to it, breathing heavily. Then he smiled and Stuart knew. It was the smile. He had seen it before. In his semi-drugged condition, doubt, skepticism, incredulity, all were in abeyance. The notion lay in his mind and he stared, deaf to the obscene witticisms being screamed at the boy, to the laughter and the applause. The room was plunged once more into darkness. When the lights came on, the dancer was gone. Stuart leaned over to Hilliard.

"I've got to talk to that kid," he said, feeling an excitement that exhaustion kept out of his voice. "You say you know him?"

"Good God, you too? Stuart, you're a family man. You have a wife and son. Anyway, he's coming to join us. He's a friend of the Lambrechts."

In a few minutes Toni appeared on the other side of the room and started toward them. Men and women caught at him, tried to detain him. He moved slowly through the tables, smiling amiably, disengaging himself gently but firmly from importunate hands. He was wearing a blouselike shirt and tight dark trousers. He reached them finally. Somebody handed him a stool and he sat between Pat and Mrs. Lambrecht, one place removed from Stuart.

At close range, he was more an ordinary good-looking young man. He was heavily tanned and his hair looked less golden. The distinction remained but the godlike quality was canceled by an air of quite mortal good health. Stuart waited until general conversation had been resumed and then, feeling the absurdity of his interest, he leaned back around

Pat and touched the youth on the shoulder. He turned with the smile Stuart had found so familiar but it faded and was replaced by a watchful expression.

"Where are you from?" Stuart asked bluntly. The boy hesitated, as if in the habit of appraising strangers' intentions.

"Are you French?" he asked in his turn.

"No, but I live here. My name's Cosling."

"Oh, yes, of course, I've heard of you." The boy relaxed visibly and the smile reappeared.

"And your name?" Stuart asked impatiently.

"Toni."

"Yes, I know, but your family name."

"I don't use it in the theater. It's Guilloux."

"And where are you from?"

"Brittany, a little village called Guéquamp."

"Is that anywhere near Belcoe?"

"Oh, yes, about twenty kilometers."

"Do you know a family called Sémillon there?"

"Sémillon? Not that I know of. I've never even been to Belcoe. You know it?"

"I used to long ago. There was a girl called Marguerite Sémillon. She's probably married now and called by another name."

"I don't know," the dancer said. "I've never been there." Stuart scarcely heard the other's voice. Belcoe. Marguerite Sémillon. Toni. Toni Guilloux. Was his appearance when he smiled only a racial resemblance? Did Bretons from that part of the coast look alike, as did natives of many remote provinces?

"Your mother and father, they're both still alive?" Stuart struggled on.

"Oh yes, although they're both quite old now. I'm the youngest. It's funny, your knowing Belcoe."

"How old are you?" Stuart persisted.

"Almost twenty-three." A puzzled look crept into the boy's face.

"What's your birthdate?"

"What do you do? Read horoscopes?" Toni asked with a laugh that bordered on insolence. It was the first touch of coarseness Stuart had detected in him and he was reminded of his feeling at the beginning of the dance. It wasn't the boy's fault. How could he avoid being corrupted by such an atmosphere?

246

"I'm interested," Stuart said mildly. "When were you born?"

"The thirteenth of August, one thousand, nine hundred, and fifteen," Toni replied with a laugh. Stuart set himself checking dates but his mind stumbled when he tried to count. August . . . That didn't seem right.

"I'd like to talk to you again some time," he said before he realized that Toni was no longer listening.

"Well, have you found the love of your life?" Hilliard asked.

"He comes from a village near a place where I once spent a summer. He reminded me of someone I knew there."

"That so? As a matter of fact, I was thinking he looks a little like you. He has the same kind of nose, poor fellow."

They stayed on long enough to give Toni time to finish the drink they had ordered for him and then they all left together. Once outside, the Lambrechts announced their intention of going to bed.

"What are you going to do?" Stuart asked Toni. "You're finished there for the night?"

"Once an evening is quite enough," Toni said emphatically.

"You don't like it?"

"Not much. I only do it to pay for my vacation. Not that I would have to pay for it, if you follow me, but I'm no gigolo."

Stuart forgave him for thinking he had to say it. "Why don't you come with us? We need all the muscle we can find." He explained about the statue and asked Toni to come out to the house for a drink after they had loaded it into the car. Toni brightened.

"I'd like to see your place. Of course I've been to some of the grandest villas on the coast, but they say yours is unusual."

"Well, you'll see for yourself," Stuart said. Since they had spoken French, he explained to Hilliard and his girl what had been arranged. He went to the car and nudged Felix, who sprang into action from a dead sleep.

As they boarded *Northern Star* Stuart spoke loudly so that if the crew awoke they wouldn't bother to come out. When he opened the locker, Hilliard whistled.

"Did you steal it or kill it?" Swaddled in blankets, stained with greasy water, it looked like the victim of some terrible calamity.

The four men wrestled with it and after a struggle managed

to get it up onto the afterdeck. There they trussed it in ropes and eased it slowly down the gangplank. At last it was installed in the back seat of the Rolls. Passersby stared.

"Thank God you came along," Stuart said to Toni. "I don't think we could've managed without you."

"I don't think you could. As a rule I shouldn't do heavy work like that because of my dancing. I've got to be careful not to strain a muscle."

"Well, that's it. Let's go. Do you remember the road, Stan?" Hilliard assured him that he did and they went off to get their car while Stuart and Toni climbed into the Rolls, with Felix in the back to watch over the statue.

"How did you happen to get this dancing job?" Stuart asked as they started out of town.

"Oh, I've been going to classes in dancing and dramatics in Paris and the man who runs the place knew the man who owns this joint and they arranged it." He spoke slangy Parisian French.

"Have you always wanted to work in the theater?"

"Not exactly. It's a long story. I went to Paris to find a job and ended up as a waiter. Then I met René Barteau. D'you know him? He's quite well known in the theater. He thought I had talent and arranged for me to take these classes and he's helped me get small parts. I've been promised a part in a film in the autumn."

A commonplace story, Stuart concluded, possibly blameless, possibly not. "What do you think of those people who come to see you?" he said pointedly.

"*Les pédés?* They make me shit. They don't fool around with me." The answer satisfied Stuart. The boy could have evaded the question but he had spoken with conviction.

"What made you decide to leave home?" Stuart asked.

"Well, you know Brittany. Who wants to live there the rest of their lives? Besides, we didn't even live in the village. My family are peasants. All they think about is their crops and the animals. I liked school. I read a lot. I guess it gave me ideas." Stuart recognized himself in reverse. He seemed a nice simple kid, with the touch of imagination that had drawn him to the big city. His son.

"It's too bad you have to work here if you don't like it."

"Oh, well, it could be worse. I'm having a big success." He couldn't make Stuart out. So far, he had betrayed none of the signs Toni had grown quick to detect, but this sounded as if it might be an opening. Was he going to offer to keep him? He had learned in Paris that he could expect just about anybody to try to go to bed with him. This had its advantages professionally but hadn't much affected the moral principles that had been bred in him.

He had never gone to bed with a woman unless he was attracted to her, and never for money. In the case of the few men it had happened with, vital interests had usually been involved. He couldn't see that it did him much harm. He always hated his partners after it was over but he didn't often like them much before it began, either. As soon as he was well enough established he would get married and people would stop bothering him. He liked this man and wanted to see his house. He had heard people talking about it since he'd arrived and he was looking forward to mentioning casually that he had been there, but it wasn't important enough for him to go to bed with him. The fact that the American couple was following them was reassuring. He turned and looked back.

"I think your friends are behind us," he said.

Stuart decided to leave the statue in the car till morning. Felix took charge of the Hilliard luggage as soon as the other car pulled in behind the Rolls. They all got out and gathered in the village square.

"You've built a goddam town," Hilliard exclaimed.

"I'm planning for villagers to come out and perform a jolly dance but I haven't bought them yet." Stuart swayed slightly and put a hand on Toni's shoulder for support. He felt bone and muscle under the loose shirt. His son. "I think I'm finally getting pissed." He led the way to the guest wing so as not to arouse the whole household. "The rest of it's over there," he said with a wave of his hand. Vistas of sea could be glimpsed through arched openings. "I'll give you a tour in the morning." He went along the colonnaded passage, opening doors and switching on lights.

The rooms were furnished with handsome old Provençal pieces and fabrics in cool colors and white. There were vases of flowers everywhere. Stuart went to a centrally located bar cupboard and threw open the doors.

"Now in theory, there's liquor and ice in here," he said, "but since I've just got here I don't know much more about it than you do." He found everything where he expected it to be while the others wandered about exclaiming with admiration.

He put out drinks and told Pat to take her pick of the bedrooms. He sank into a chaise longue in the courtyard and decided that he would never be able to move again. Toni stood nearby. The drive in the dark had been a break in continuity and Stuart looked at him with fresh eyes. He seemed to have shed all resemblance to the exotic dancer he'd seen perform. He looked like a very handsome well-built country boy wearing rather eccentric clothes. The shadowy light toned down the golden curls. Stuart remembered that he was supposed to take him back to town.

"Oh yes. Are you anxious to get back to town?" he asked. "Would you mind spending the night out here?"

"You mean in one of these rooms?"

"Sure. Don't you like them?"

"Of course. That would be fine," the boy replied, smiling in the way Stuart found so appealing. "I thought I'd go back with your friends. I didn't understand they were staying."

"Fine." He'd have another son staying under his roof. "Tomorrow you'll meet my wife and boy. Robbie's a few years younger than you but I hope you'll like each other. I really must leave you all and go to bed. I'm dead."

Robbie saw him while he was having a late-morning swim. He glanced toward shore and was stunned to see a naked youth descending the steps to the beach. Golden curls glinted in the sun. In his haste to get to him, Robbie gulped water and almost sank before he burrowed strongly into the sea. He stood when the water was thigh-high and pushed his way in as the young stranger approached the edge of the rippling sea. He was a vision; Robbie couldn't believe he was real. He wasn't quite naked but nothing concealed the athletic glory of his body, the powerful thighs and calves, narrow hips, lithe torso, and light, graceful shoulders. The scrap of cloth around his loins barely contained the private glory. His face was a mask, a drawing composed of a few deft strokes—big eyes set out close to the surface of his cheeks, a straight nose, a bold ripe mouth, a strong jaw. A few squiggles for the crown of golden curls and it was done.

"Good morning," Robbie called in French. He freed himself from the pull of the sea and quickly crossed the last few yards of beach that separated them.

"You must be Robbie," the vision said. A fervent wish that Robbie were a girl accompanied Toni's first close look at him. He was more beautiful than his most recent girl. Since he was obviously, conspicuously a boy, the desire that had sprung up in him died, leaving a residue of unaccustomed affection. He felt instantly protective of him. "I helped with the statue last night. Your father asked me out for a drink and then suggested I stay. Oh, I'm sorry. My name's Toni." They shook hands.

Of course, Robbie thought. It had to be. He was the dancer from the Tour Engloutie. No wonder everybody was mad about him. When he spoke, the mask assumed all the depth and complexity of a handsome young man's face, a seductive crease at the corner of his mouth, the hint of a dimple, something faintly asymmetrical about the eyes. A face of potent appeal. "I wish I'd known you were here. You could've stayed with me." Robbie blurted it out, wondering if he could make any impression on a vision.

"If I had, maybe you'd've lent me something to wear," Toni said, as if he would have been glad to stay with him. "I had nothing to swim in except this thing I wear under my dance trunks. I do an act without much on."

"I've heard about your act. They say you're sensational." Robbie permitted himself a closer look at the garment in question. It sat so low on his hips that it just covered the base of his cock. He noticed that his pubic hair was cut in an unnaturally straight line along the edge of the cloth. He tore his eyes away from the engrossing spectacle. "We can swim naked here but not if my mother or anybody's around. Would you like me to give you something? Why don't you come up to my house? I'd like to show it to you anyway."

"You have your own house here?"

"Yes, that's what I meant about staying with me. There's room for a friend."

"You and your father are being very nice to me. Thanks for saying you've heard I'm sensational." He smiled enchantingly, a smile of pure pleasure. He spoke rapid Parisian French, chopping off the ends of his words. *Sensationnel* became *sensas*. Robbie decided to drop the drawl he had adopted from Edward the day before and become a Parisian. "This *place* is sensational, what I've seen of it."

"Come on. I'll show you more." He resisted the temptation to touch him as he headed him back up the steps. His heart was pounding. With any luck, he was going to see the talk of the town naked.

"I couldn't figure out why your father was interested in

me," Toni said. "He made a big point about where and when I was born, as if he knew something about me. I think he was a little drunk."

Robbie laughed. "I'll bet he was. We had a big day. I was supposed to go see you last night but I was too tired."

"You didn't miss much. I'm not really a dancer. I want to be an actor."

"Everybody says you're amazing."

"I guess it's a pretty good act but I'll be glad when it's over. I have to shave everywhere." He lifted an arm to reveal an immaculate armpit. He passed a hand across his lower abdomen. "Even here. My hair isn't really this color either. I'm pretty blond but it's been curled and touched up. I feel sort of silly."

"You don't look silly. It's beautiful."

"Thanks. Your father said he hoped we'd like each other. I guess we're going to." For a devastating moment, he put a hand on Robbie's shoulder.

Robbie dropped behind as they started up the path to his house. The little G-string left Toni's buttocks bare. They were taut and smoothly rounded and looked as firmly sculptured as marble. Robbie was reminded of the statue. He wanted to stroke them as he had the statue's. "Here we are," he said as they turned at a clump of laurel. He moved up beside him and screwed up his courage to give him a pat on the back as he ushered him in. His hand tingled with the contact.

Toni moved into the living room with the assured air of a performer making an entrance and looked around him. His first guest. Robbie's mind tumbled about trying to remember if he had any experience to guide him in this situation. How had he let the others know that he wanted to make love with them? Toni turned and looked at him with a light of friendly envy shining in his big green eyes.

"Well, this is pretty marvelous. You have it all to yourself?"

"Yes, I'm an only child. You see, I want to be a painter." He nodded at the easel he had set up under the skylight. "This was going to be my studio but it sort of grew into a whole house."

Toni's eyes moved to the open door of the kitchenette. "You can even cook here."

"I could if I wanted to."

"All you need is a girl. Do you have one?"

"Oh no," Robbie objected facetiously. He wasn't going to

make the mistake he'd made with Rico and let Toni think he needed help getting a girl. "I wouldn't want a girl here. She might get ideas about staying."

Toni laughed. "You're pretty smart for a kid. How old are you? About twenty?"

"Not quite. How did you happen to help my father with the statue?"

"He was with people I know, friends of the people who're staying here."

Robbie hovered near him, hoping to pick up some signal of sexual interest from him. He didn't. The conversation wasn't leading anywhere. "I'll get you the trunks." He hurried off to the bedroom.

Toni wandered to the end of the room to admire the terrace and the vast seascape beyond. A fabulous place. He continued to be puzzled by the episode—the father's special interest in him, the air of expectancy in the beautiful boy. There could be an obvious explanation for that, but he was tired of suspecting everybody of being a pederast (*un pédé* in his truncated vocabulary) and Robbie wasn't his idea of one. He was too boyish and guileless. He wanted to relax and act natural for a change even though he found it puzzling to feel such immediate affection for the kid. His life didn't have much room for disinterested friendship.

"Here. These will probably fit," Robbie said, returning with a pair of his trunks. His brief absence had given him time to resign himself to being sexually uninteresting to the dancer. Anne was convinced that he was exclusively for girls. At least Toni seemed to like him and he was determined not to do anything to displease him. He was going to prove to himself that he could be a homosexual without committing any social outrages.

Toni took the trunks and held them up for a brief inspection. "Sure. They'll fit. We're built alike. You're a little taller and I'm probably a bit heavier but otherwise we're practically the same."

"I wish I thought my body was as beautiful as yours."

"If mine's beautiful, yours is, too. I don't think much about guys' bodies being beautiful. I'm too busy looking at girls." He laughed amiably. "It's probably different for artists."

"Maybe. You can find beauty anywhere. Like the statue. It's a man but it's beautiful."

"I didn't see it. It was all wrapped up in blankets." Toni's hand moved down over one hip. Robbie saw that the G-string was fastened by a little hook at the side. Toni gave it a twist and the bit of cloth fell away. Robbie's heart pounded up into his throat. His eyes flew to their goal. They gathered an impression of compact vigor that made him clench his fists to keep his hands under control. The balls were tucked up snugly between his thighs and almost concealed by the hang of the ample phallic cylinder. It was unquestionably, discouragingly inert.

The clipped and shaped pubic curls gave it startling prominence so that it swelled into enormous erection in Robbie's imagination. "I'll bet your fans would give anything to see you like this," he said, lifting his eyes.

Toni responded with his enchanting smile. "A pretty girl can have a look for nothing. As for the *pédés*, they'll have a long wait. You're my friend. We don't have to stand on ceremony."

Robbie turned away, breathless with his effort at self-control. Toni hadn't suspected anything. He would never let him find out, even if he had to turn himself into a different person. The most sought-after boy on the coast was his friend. "Come on and have a swim," he said, hitting the right note of comradely masculinity.

Stuart woke up feeling as if life had taken a momentous turn. He lay for a moment with his eyes closed, piecing together the events of the previous day. Of course. He had found a son. That was momentous enough. He had always suspected that he had another son. A brother for Robbie. He had yet to find out if he liked the youth but he was bound to like his own son. When had he been born? August. 1915? His mind came to a stop before a mathematical impossibility. Only a few months off but try telling that to a pregnant girl.

Maybe he'd misunderstood in that noisy place. Maybe dates had been juggled to legitimize him. Except that Toni had never heard of the Sémillons. That tore a fairly big hole in his theory. He could shore it up by assuming all sorts of intricate plotting but what would be the motive? Rested, his mind clear, he knew that only intensive investigation could prove anything. Yet the sensation of having found a son was so stimulating that he decided pretending was almost as good as knowing. Nothing need prevent him from taking an interest in the boy and offering him a second home. He opened his eyes and saw that Helene's bed was empty. He looked at his watch. It was almost noon. The window was shuttered but through it he could see the gleam of sun on the sea.

When he came out onto the terrace he saw Robbie below on the edge of the water. As he looked, Toni rose from the sea and came splashing up beside him. The two stood together with their heads bent, looking at something Robbie held in his hand. Stuart didn't move, gazing down at them with a mixture of pride and excitement. There were like two sides of a medal. Robbie was all poetry and spirit, with his dark brooding eyes and his sensitive mouth. His splendidly developing body seemed almost to belong to somebody else. Toni was all physical, with the vigorous beauty of nature, a patrician athlete-warrior. From this distance they looked about the same age. As he watched them, he heard steps behind him and Helene's voice.

"Well, lazy one, what finally got you out of bed?" She followed the direction of his gaze. "He's absolutely superb. What a pair they make. What's he doing here? Where did you find him?"

"Have you met him? Have you talked to him? He's the dancer at that new place in town."

"I've been busy all morning in the kitchen going over everything with Boldoni. Felix said we had an extra houseguest. I just saw him down there with Robbie."

It couldn't have worked out better. Stuart was delighted that the two boys had met without the inhibiting presence of elders. "You know the Marguerite story. He comes from the same neighborhood. Last night I was drunk enough to decide that he was my long-lost son. I'm not so sure this morning but I don't guess it really matters. If it's all right with you, I think I'll ask him to stay."

"You can ask all of St. Tropez, if you like," she said with a laugh. "Boldoni's taken over completely. He thinks he's back in the hotel business. I've never seen a happier man in my life."

"I knew that would work out. Did you tell them people are coming for drinks? We better have something to feed them in case I said lunch. I'm a bit vague. I'm not even sure who I asked. The admiral's crowd and a few others, I think. We shall see. How about a swim to give us courage?"

"I'd like one. I'll run put a suit on."

Helene met Toni. It was quickly apparent that Robbie was fascinated by him and she opened her heart to him. She wanted to hear more about Stuart's notion that they were half brothers.

Stanley and Pat wandered down full of praise for the beds and the breakfast. Stuart regretted having asked them to stay. He wanted to get the feel of just the four of them together. His new family. "Oh, did you see the statue?" he asked Robbie.

"No. Toni said you brought it out. Where is it?"

"We left it in the car. I guess it's still there."

"Come on, Toni. Help me get it out to the terrace."

"Ask Felix to help you," Stuart said. "Toni's not supposed to do that sort of work."

"Oh, that's what they tell you in class but I can't be bothered."

"Okay. I'll come hold my end. I haven't ruptured anything yet." The three of them went off together.

They struggled through the last stage of the statue's journey and unwrapped it and stood it at the head of the stairs leading down to the beach. It beckoned toward the sea.

"You're right," Toni said to Robbie as they stood around it admiring it. "It *is* beautiful."

"Wait till we get a pedestal for it. It should be up three or four feet higher so that it dominates the whole place. Don't you agree?"

"Yes. You could put a sign on it saying 'This way to the beach.'" They all laughed together. Stuart had had time to see, from the way the boys worked together, from the constant references they made to each other, that they'd already made friends. It was all he'd been waiting for. "I'd like to talk to you for a minute, Toni. Shall we go to your room?"

Toni's suspicions of the night before stirred again as they left Robbie with the statue. It was unlikely that his host would take him off in front of his own son if he intended to make a pass at him but stranger things had happened to him. He was glad he'd changed into Robbie's trunks; he was asking for trouble wearing the little thing he'd had on earlier. Sober and in the bright light of day, Cosling was a very good-looking man with an amazingly trim body for his age, but Toni couldn't imagine allowing him to make love to him, no matter what he was prepared to offer in return. Something was in the air. The speculative glances the older man kept giving him were getting on his nerves.

They crossed the inner courtyard to the room where Toni

had spent the night. The bed had been made and his clothes put away. Stuart closed the door. "When did you say you were born?" he asked without any preliminaries.

They were going to go through that again. "August 13, 1915."

"That's what I thought. And you've never heard of a family called Sémillon?"

"No."

"Okay. Never mind." Stuart approached him, looking into his green eyes. They stood facing each other near the end of the bed. He liked the boy's steadfast gaze. The fresh purity of his good looks was striking, almost masklike in its lack of hidden depths. He could find no trace of resemblance today to Robbie or himself; only the radiant smile supported his suspicions of last night. He wasn't smiling now. He looked watchful, guarded, even faintly hostile. Stuart smiled reassuringly. "Do you like it here?"

"Of course. It's the most beautiful place I've ever seen."

"I'm glad you think so. You must be wondering why I keep harping on when you were born. I'll explain. This is going to sound a bit mad but last night I thought you might be my son."

"Your *what*?"

"Yes, I know. It sounds like something in a play. The fact is, it's possible. You'd have to've been born five or six months sooner but otherwise it fits. You see, I was in love with a girl I mentioned last night, Marguerite Sémillon. It was just before the Great War. She thought she was pregnant. I was all ready to marry her but our various parents intervened."

"You were in love with her?"

"As only a boy of seventeen can be. Just about Robbie's age. You might wonder why I left her but it wasn't just the parents. It was the war. I had no choice but I've always wondered if I had a son your age somewhere in Brittany."

"I'll be damned." The watchful look faded from Toni's eyes and the radiant smile lighted up his face. No wonder this man had behaved strangely with him. He wanted a son, not a lover. It was impossible, but he was as intrigued by the idea as his host seemed to be. "But look, my parents' name is Guilloux," he pointed out. "My mother's name is Ernestine. We don't know any Sémillons."

"Exactly. The only thing is, when you smile you look very much like Marguerite. I noticed it immediately last night. It's easy to make up a likely story. Say Marguerite wasn't married

257

off quickly but was sent away somewhere to have a baby. The Guilloux agreed to take it for one reason or another. The later birthdate could have been fixed to throw me off the scent if I'd ever come back to inquire. It's not too farfetched. I'm enjoying pretending to be your father. Wouldn't you like to pretend to be my son?"

Toni's smile had become a permanent delight. He laughed. "I have a sister who was almost fifteen when I was born. She's always talked about how huge my mother was when she was carrying me. Do you suppose she went around with a pillow under her dress until it was time for me to be born?"

Stuart laughed with him. "All right. Stay a Guilloux if you want to but I still have plans for you. Let's sit down. Wait. We mustn't get the cushions wet. I'll get towels."

While Stuart did so Toni had time to assess this odd development. Now that suspicions had been allayed, he found that he liked the man who wanted to be his father. There was something youthfully responsive and generous about him; he wasn't grasping or self-centered the way people seemed to get as they grew older. He'd liked the way he'd thrown himself into the chore of getting the statue home instead of letting others do the work. He couldn't think of him as his father—he had a father and a family and loved them—but he wouldn't mind being treated like a rich man's son. Stuart returned with two towels and dropped them into chairs.

"Did you say Robbie is only seventeen?" Toni asked as they sat.

"Yes."

"The little rascal. He let me think he was twenty." His smile continued to dazzle.

"Don't tell him I let out the awful truth."

"There's something funny about him. I mean, the way I feel about him. I took to him right away, almost as if he were my brother. Do you think people have some instinct for recognizing blood ties? That might mean more than the way I smile."

"If they do and you really are my son, you should feel it with me."

"Maybe I do. Enough for pretending, anyway. Does Robbie know about this, about the girl and everything?"

"No. Why don't you tell him? If I do, he might think I'm trying to make some big point about it. I don't think I always handle him right." Stuart hitched his chair closer and put a purely paternal hand on his knee. "What I've been wanting to suggest is that you stay with us for the summer."

Toni more or less expected it. Faced with a decision, he hesitated. He had become a local star overnight and he liked the attention he was getting, or at least some of it. He had broken free from his family. Did he want another one? He would undoubtedly meet all the important people here, but only as a member of the Cosling party. You had to be a loner to get ahead. The strange world he had so recently entered imposed certain conditions and he had quickly gathered that one of them was that he should remain free to be pursued.

"I don't know," he said perplexedly. "Of course, I love it here but how would I get in and out to work?"

"That shouldn't be a big problem. I imagine there'll be a lot of coming and going between here and town. You have to be in about eleven? We could probably arrange to take you but I'd prefer you to be free to come and go as you please."

"That would be better," Toni agreed. He wondered if he was going to be offered an automobile. He had been offered automobiles before, but not by anyone like Stuart.

"I was going to get a motorbike for Felix. Would that do? You and he could work out the times when you need it. Can you ride one?"

"Oh sure. We have one on the farm." Toni was having a lesson in tact. Stuart was making it easy for him to accept without feeling that he was getting too deeply obligated.

"How much longer are you going to be appearing in that place?" He glanced at the golden head. In the daylight, he was pretty sure it wasn't natural. He suppressed a little twinge of distaste at adopting a son with dyed hair and removed his hand from his knee.

"I'm booked until the end of July but they're already talking about an extension if business goes on being so good."

"You must be pleased to be such a success even if you don't like the work. I don't suppose you'd consider giving it up. I'd pay you whatever you're getting there of course, so you wouldn't lose anything."

"Ah no. It's not the money. You'd laugh if I told you how little I get. It's my career."

Stuart supposed that it was impossible to talk about a theater career without sounding a bit pompous. He remembered the hint of insolence last night, but there was none of that now. He was simply making it clear that he was his own man. Stuart liked him for it and didn't mind waiting to be thanked for offering him a home. He sat poised and assured, enviable in his youth and physical splendor, accepting as his due anything that came his way. Stuart had a feeling that he might be in the presence of a star. "I certainly don't want to interfere with your career. On the contrary, I'd like to find ways of helping you but we'll probably have plenty of time to talk about that. Don't let's get sidetracked. Let's decide whether or not you want to move out here."

"There's another thing. I don't know about Robbie, but I have girls. Would there be any difficulty about that?"

"You mean, you'd want them to stay here? I don't think I want to run a bawdy house. Does that sound old-fashioned?"

"Of course not. I wouldn't expect them to stay, any more than I would at home, but you know how it is. If you get caught up with a girl you don't think much about anything else. I wouldn't want to be tied down socially."

"I understand. I expect it to happen with Robbie any day now. Have you seen his house?" He thought of the way Robbie had sort of teamed up with Rico and hoped he'd feel the same way about Toni. "Maybe you'd like to stay up there with him. You'd be even more independent. Of course, we'd have to ask him. If I'm not mistaken, there's only one bed up there but we could put in another."

"I've shared beds with my brothers all my life. That doesn't matter. He might not want me around all the time."

"Well, I'll leave that up to you two. I don't expect to fill all these rooms. You can keep this one if you want. Is it settled?"

"I appreciate your suggesting it. I really do but—well, I know everything's very informal down here and so forth, but you don't know me at all. You know I'm probably not your son. I don't quite see—"

"Why I want you to stay?" Stuart interrupted. "Forget about being my son. Let me try to explain. You see, we lived here for a long time very simply—probably more simply than you've ever lived." He looked around the handsomely appointed room. "All this luxury is still very new to us. I suppose I want to share it, bring it alive. I've always been sorry that Robbie's an only child. I'm sure he'll love having you here even if you're not brothers. You give me a new interest in life. If that sounds sort of pathetic, you've got to remember that I'm not used to being rich. When I first came here, all I cared about was my freedom. I worked for it and fought for it and in ways that I didn't expect or want, I got more of it than I'd asked for. I've got to find out what to do with it."

"I imagine this is the most extraordinary conversation I'll have in my entire life," Toni said as if he were just beginning to take it in.

Stuart smiled at him thoughtfully. "I'm not thinking only of this summer. We'll talk more about it when we know each other better but I think my wife and I will want to spend some time in Paris in the future. Robbie probably will too when he's finished school. If I take an apartment, it could be yours most of the time. You'd be doing us a favor by taking care of it. I promise you one thing: I'll never spoil you with money. I believe in people making their own way. The only reason I mentioned quitting your job is that I don't think much of that place where you're working. I guess that's show business. You must know what you're getting into. I'm sure you can handle it. Is your hair dyed?"

"Yes. It's not really this curly, either."

"It must be a nuisance keeping it like that. I have a hunch you're going places. It'll be exciting to watch. I think Robbie's going to make his mark too. Maybe I'll become a patron of the arts." Toni's smile flooded him with sweet funny memories.

"Well then. If you'll lend me a car, I'll go in this afternoon and get my things." There was no reason to hold out any longer. He hadn't jumped at the invitation; he'd made sure that his wishes would be respected. They both stood. "I don't know how to thank you, Mr.—what am I supposed to call you?"

"Well, certainly not Papa." They both laughed. "What *have* you been calling me? I haven't noticed."

"Monsieur."

"That won't do. What's wrong with Stuart?"

"Very well, thank you very much, Stuart." He gave the name a fine French flourish.

Stuart gripped his shoulders and gave him a little shake. "We can thank each other. I think it's going to be good for all of us."

Robbie lingered with the statue, cleaning and polishing it and making a careful study of proportions to be sure he got the pedestal right in relation to the surrounding landscape. He lay on the lawn looking up at it and made calculations with his eyes. Toni found him there.

"Are you worshiping Apollo?" he asked, smiling in the way that made Robbie's heart stop. He leaped to his feet.

"Oh, I do. What did he want to talk to you about?"

"Guess. I'm going to stay here all summer."

"No. Oh Toni, how marvelous. It's what I've been thinking about all along. I was afraid you wouldn't listen if I suggested it."

"I had to make sure I'd be on my own. You know. I have to see people and make contacts now that I have the chance. I found out why he's been asking me all those questions. Are you ready for a surprise? He thinks we might be brothers—half brothers."

"What are you talking about?"

"It's only an idea." Toni told Robbie the sketchy little story, looking at Robbie's mouth as he did so. He found it very seductive, with the slight fullness of the upper lip, a reaction left over from his initial fleeting thought of him as a girl. If he were a girl, he would've kissed it by now. Brothers kissed. Maybe he would yet. "You see, he's just making a wild guess. He knows that but he says he likes to pretend."

"Yes, I suppose he does. Well, I'm not pretending. I think it's true. I feel it. Don't you?"

"In a certain way. It's funny. I mentioned it to your father. I feel almost the way I do about my favorite brother, Pierrot. He's a good deal older. You're my baby brother." Their eyes met and Toni slipped an arm around Robbie's shoulders and gave him a gentle hug. Robbie took a deep calming breath. Life with Toni was going to be full of hazards and pitfalls but if he managed to avoid any hideous *faux pas*, all his problems were solved. He would never be lonely with Toni here. He would devote himself to his work and try not to think about sex. Being brothers would permit them to take small liberties with each other, an embrace, even a kiss. That would be enough. Perhaps someday he would be able to tell him about himself. It was something a brother should understand and be tolerant about.

"Not such a baby," he said, drawing away with an attempt at brotherly bravado. "I'm bigger than you are. I also happen to have a house of my own where I *might* let you stay. Did you talk about that?"

"He said it was up to you."

"You see? Your baby brother is a very important person. Would you like to be with me?"

Toni looked into smiling dark eyes and was struck by the depths of raw emotion in them. It was something he should learn how to do as an actor—to smile and look tragic at the same time. He must remember that. Robbie was dangerously sensitive. "He said I'd be more independent up there with you. What do you think? We won't get in each other's way?"

"You're older. You can tell me if I do anything you don't like. There's only one bed but it's a double. Is that all right?"

"He said we could have another but I don't care so long as you wash regularly."

"I'm as clean as a whistle." They laughed and their eyes told each other that they were going to have a good time together. Toni realized that Stuart had given him much more than a beautiful place to live. He was having a fresh taste of the wholesome life he had abandoned more than two years ago. He was again with people who could be kind to each other without waiting to see what they could get out of it. He was amazed at what a relief it was.

"You know, the theater is pretty tough," he said, looking from Robbie to the statue and deciding that Robbie was more beautiful. "Everybody's out for himself. People don't let themselves like each other. Oh, girls, of course, but that's different. It's about time I found a friend."

Robbie found it extraordinary that a boy with the world at his feet could be looking for a friend. Thanks to his father, he was going to be it. He hadn't felt so grateful to him for years. "Everybody thinks—" He broke off self-consciously as his father appeared in shirt and slacks.

"I'm ready for whatever guests land on us. You two needn't change. If anybody wants to swim, show them the beach house. Have you been talking things over?"

"Toni says he'd like to move in with me," Robbie said, careful not to sound overenthusiastic.

"Fine. I told him it was up to you. You must admit I've picked out a pretty special brother for you."

"He'll be all right if he doesn't think being older gives him the right to boss me around." He checked an impulse to thank him. He didn't want his father to think he had some particular reason for wanting him here. Let him take full responsibility for the invitation.

Activity quickened around them. A vast awning had been unfurled over part of the terrace. A white-jacketed Felix was busy at a drinks table under it. Agnes bustled. Boldoni emerged briefly in full chef's regalia to cast an eye on another long table where food was being set out. Helene crossed the terrace looking grandly beautiful in a simple summer dress.

"You boys are going to stay as you are?" She looked from one to the other with admiration. "You're both stunning."

"Toni's staying here now," Robbie interjected. "Did you know? He doesn't have to dress like a guest."

"Your father said he was going to ask him." She turned to Toni. "So you've accepted? I'm so pleased. You and Robbie will have such fun together." She gave him a welcoming maternal kiss on the cheek and felt immediately that he wasn't indifferent to women. It amused and flattered her. Life had an added zest when sex was acknowledged, however distantly. She need no longer fear or deny it.

Minutes later, the terrace was swarming with guests. Stuart was pleased to find that he recognized most of them. There were the prince and princess who instantly became Hilda and Alex, the famous French playwright, the film star, the film director. The heir apparent to a Scandinavian throne accompanied by a famous French beauty had been brought by somebody. Wives were standard equipment. Stuart found that he had selected his guests with more attention to their permanent local ties than he had realized. They all had houses nearby, some on lease, some recently built, a few remodeled old farm houses purchased for a song when the tourists had first begun to take notice of the place. None of them, it appeared, could compare to this one. The house. The house. The fabulous house that belonged to the fabulous Coslings. Everyone was agog. Of course, it was pointed out, the Coslings had owned the whole peninsula so they'd had the pick of the choice sites. A French woman publisher who, Stuart assumed, had been with the admiral the day before turned out to be the owner of what had once been a sail loft. It had been known in the old days as *la batellerie*, she told him.

Toni watched the guests arrive and was satisfied that he'd made a wise decision. The theater people were at the top of their field. He had met some of them casually but now he could cultivate them on a footing of equality. Word had already spread somehow that he was a member of the family. He was no longer just a flash celebrity but an established resident of St. Tropez. He was introduced to a very pretty model from one of the big Paris couture houses. They agreed that they made an attractive couple if the director was looking for new faces. She was bright and ambitious. They began to have fun together.

Drink flowed. People sampled the hors d'oeuvres and exclaimed over their excellence. The admiral and his party were the last to arrive. Robbie was glad to see that Toni looked thoroughly occupied with a pretty girl as he geared himself to Edward's audacious conversational style. Their eyes met and Edward's charming face lighted up as he came ambling over looking very elegant in a white shirt and loose scarf and white flannels. Robbie moved to meet him. He saw Edward's eyes widen as he caught sight of Toni. They stopped in front of each other and Edward put his hands on Robbie's elbows and held him.

"Darling Robbie. Don't say a word until I tell you I adore you. It's happened. I fought it all last night but I'm a prisoner of my unnatural passion. Now tell all. Where did you find him? I knew there was some explanation for your not appearing last night. You *are* a wicked darling. I'm not only *bouche-bée* but consumed by *jalousie.*"

Robbie laughed while his cock stretched and hardened. "You needn't be. There's no hope for either of us. My father brought him. I wanted to come see you but I couldn't keep my eyes open. He's going to be staying here from now on."

"Here? With you? I'll go slit my wrists. It runs in the family."

"Please don't. I've seen him naked. There wasn't a quiver."

"Is it enormous?"

"How could I tell if he's not interested in me? It looked as if it might be."

"My word. Naked. I couldn't've kept my hands off it even though you've cured me of him. I've fallen in love with you, darling. This time it's real. I wanted you to be the first to know." Edward's eyes moved over him and his face was suddenly grave. "I've never wanted anybody so much in my life. Will we have a little duet later?"

"God, yes. I'm ready now. If you talk to him, be careful not to say anything that'll give him ideas about us. I don't want him to know about me. He wouldn't like it."

"The agony of being a persecuted minority. I'll try to behave, darling."

The party pursued its successful course. More substantial food appeared and was consumed with cries of gluttonous pleasure. Boldoni hadn't lost his touch. Toni took his model down for a swim and was followed by others including Anne and Edward. Robbie discovered that one of the guests was a well-known painter and conversed with him and his wife for some time. People came and went in groups as Helene conducted tours of the house.

Robbie was talking to his mother when Toni reappeared wearing his tight pants and loose blouselike shirt. He put a hand on Robbie's shoulder and offered him his enchanting smile.

"I'm going to town to pack," he explained. "Michèle has a car. She's taking me. I'll be back by six."

Robbie moved closer to him with a hand on his waist to detain him. "I've heard people talking about Mrs. Rawls' party tonight. Are we going?" he asked his mother.

"Oh, I know her," Toni said. "She invited me several days ago. Is it tonight? I meant to check."

"In that case, we all might as well go," Helene said. "If we don't, she'll just go on inviting us until we do."

Robbie absently allowed his hand to become caressing. He caught himself and hastily turned the caress into a little pat and let go. "Okay. I'll be waiting to help you move in." He watched the graceful swing of Toni's body as he left. Helene saw that his eyes were bewitched when he turned back to her and gave her a kiss.

"He's fascinating," she said. "He's remarkably unspoiled. He's crazy about you. He says he wants to be your friend."

"I have no objection." He squeezed her hand and hurried away to look for Edward. The coast was clear to launch their affair. Planning to do it in what was practically Toni's bed didn't seem quite right but he would need plenty of sex with Edward if he expected to forget about sex with Toni. He found the admiral's party strewn out along the beach, sitting and lying about as if they were there for the day. Edward sat up lazily and reached for Robbie's hand and pulled him down beside Anne.

"How sweet of you to come see us, darling. Have you noticed how well behaved I've been? I haven't clung to you like a limpet. Just being able to look at you from time to time made my cup runneth over."

Robbie glanced around to make sure nobody but Anne was within earshot. "I'm thinking about music. Do you want to come see my house?"

"I long to. Come on, darling," he added to Anne.

"But—"

"She knows what we're going to do, darling."

"Haven't you grasped what a blessing in disguise I am?" she asked Robbie. "If people think I'm with you, they won't suspect you of indulging your boyish fancies."

"But you *will* be with us. Then what?"

"If you have a whole house, there must be a corner where I won't be in anybody's way."

Robbie realized that it made sense. He could carry it a step further and ask her to pretend to be his girl for official purposes. They all stood and shook sand off and left. Edward paused to admire the statue. Anne was right. They made an innocent trio as they wandered on down the glade toward Robbie's house.

"Last night was quite fatal," Edward said when they reached the cover of the terraced citrus groves. He draped himself lightly around Robbie as they climbed. "If you'd been with me, I might've kept my head. Alone, I was at the mercy of my mad desire. I think that's what makes people fall in love—being deprived of their loved one. I imagine if you're with someone all the time you might fall in love without even noticing it. Anne can tell you how I suffered."

"He looked quite haggard by bedtime," she said from ahead of them.

Robbie kissed the side of his face. They hugged each other and laughed. Robbie couldn't help wishing that this was Toni, but Edward's physical elegance had an appeal of its own.

"Well, this *is* a little bit of all right," Anne commented when they entered the living room. "What a lucky child. Is there a bedroom? Of course. And you even have a terrace. That's where I'll be." She effaced herself with sisterly tact.

They moved in against each other and kissed until Edward drew back with glazed and spellbound eyes. "Oh darling," he whispered gravely. "I do love you."

Robbie's heart swelled with gratitude. He was old enough to be loved at last. Edward cared about him more than anybody else in the world. He found it rather awesome. He touched his lips with his fingertips and smiled hesitantly and led him to the bedroom and closed the door. Minutes passed in a slow-motion rediscovery of each other before they thought of removing their trunks.

"Oh darling, don't let's come for hours," Edward said. "It's too heavenly."

The room gave them scope for invention. Edward worshiped his cock with a fervor that he recognized as equal to his own. Nature intervened when they could no longer contain themselves and they lay on the floor in each other's arms, gazing at each other incredulously.

"That may not have been entirely civilized but it was utter bliss," Edward murmured. "Your brown body is magic, darling."

"Whatever it is, you make it that way."

"What're we doing down here?"

"I don't know. It just happened. It's lovely and cool." They burst out laughing.

Edward sprawled on his back with his arms flung out. "How I wish this were ours. I can't bear to miss a single minute of life with you. Are you frightened of war? I am. This may be the most perfect moment of my life. I've not only had glorious sex with a boy I love with all my heart but I'm also off that blasted boat. That's paradise enough." He sat up and tossed his hair back from his forehead. Robbie pulled himself up against his back, kissing it as he cuddled in against it, and held him close. Their mouths met for a long indolent kiss. Robbie could feel how happy he made him. It was amazing being loved. Just by being here he satisfied all Edward's deepest desires. Life's mysteries were being slowly revealed to him. "Dear Lord, just *feel* you," Edward said when their mouths parted. He ran his hands over Robbie's dark chest and shoulders. "You *are* a man. I'm sure there's some mistake about our ages. You *must* be older than I am. My lord and master."

"I hope I fall in love with you. I don't know what it's like yet. I can't be really grown up until I do. Something's happening to me. There seems to be more of me for feeling things. Your saying you're in love with me makes me feel an awful lot for you."

"I'll say it constantly, darling. I *am* in love with you. You have a lovely way of letting me know you want me. It's about to get hard again. You're divinely insatiable but shouldn't we go? The parents will be wanting to leave." They picked themselves up off the floor and moved in against each other and kissed again standing up while Edward's hand encouraged Robbie's nascent erection. "Have you been invited to a party by that dreadful Rawls woman?" Edward asked with his lips moving against Robbie's.

"Yes. We're going. Toni too."

"Then the evening won't be a total loss. Do you think we'll be able to let go of each other, darling?"

"I suppose we should."

Anne's voice called from the other side of the door, "We ought to go soon, darlings."

"Come in," Edward called back, smiling into Robbie's eyes.

"Wait," Robbie cried. He broke away and looked around frantically for his trunks. Edward moved in against him once more.

"It's all right, darling. Hide against me. I'm so happy that I want to share it with her."

Anne entered. "There you are," she said as if she'd just run into them on the street. "Are you having a lovely time?"

"We were," Edward said. "We're just trying to disentangle ourselves from each other."

"You don't look as if you're having much success. Why aren't you in bed?"

"We don't need anything so commonplace as a bed." Edward's erection was lifting against Robbie's. Their hands began to move secretly on each other.

"Well, then. Come along," she said sensibly.

Robbie liked her even under these trying circumstances. He realized that Toni gave him an excuse to make a point about reticence without sounding childishly concerned about his parents. "Now that Toni's here, you're not going to tell everybody I'm a poof, are you?" he asked. "He doesn't approve."

"I was afraid of that, darling."

"I wish you wouldn't say it about Edward, either."

"You do rather overdo it, darling," Edward agreed.

"Everybody knows and it happens to be one of the most interesting things about you, but if you want people to think you're as dreary as everybody else I won't say another word. If you're not making love, why go on standing there? The parents will be waiting."

"Actually, we're making mad love even if you can't see it. We'll be with you in five minutes. There, be a lamb and close the door after you."

Robbie remained dutifully with his parents until the last guests had departed. He left them discussing the party to return to his house to wait for Toni. Relaxed and sexually satisfied, he was more confident of being able to deal with the miracle of having his adopted brother as a room-mate. He couldn't be in love with Edward if Toni filled his mind with impossible dreams, but he had a lover to count on for a regular sex life. Their desire was so simple to satisfy that it could happen almost anywhere, at any time, even at parties. Anne would be there to cover up for them. Tomorrow he would go to work.

He unpacked paints and brushes and laid them out on the worktable. He had half a dozen virgin canvases, sized and ready to go. He clamped one on the easel. He had been evolving some advanced and intricate techniques under the guidance of M. Monneret, the art teacher at school, and he was eager to find out what his eyes had learned in the last two months. His thoughts lingered briefly on his teacher. Maurice? Possibly. He understood things now that had meant nothing to him last winter. Actually, Maurice was rather like a grown-up Edward. He smiled to himself as he peeled off his trunks and went to the bathroom to shower.

He was wearing a dressing gown when there was a flurry outside the door and Toni and Felix appeared carrying bags. He saw only Toni. Toni's smile overturned whatever equilibrium he had achieved with Edward. "Here I am," the dancer said, making a little gesture around the room.

"Wonderful. I hope there's room for all your things."

"You know. Actors. We're peacocks. It isn't as bad as it looks. We don't have to open that bag. It's city clothes. Only this one's for here. It's hot." He pulled his shirt off over his head and advanced to Robbie and put a hand on his shoulder. "You're not sorry you let me come?"

Robbie took a deep tremulous breath and hoped for the pounding of his heart to subside. He was here, no fantasy figure but a slightly sweaty, flesh-and-blood young athlete who was going to live with him. "Of course I'm not sorry. I've been waiting to help you unpack."

"Thanks. Shall we take everything to the bedroom and sort it out there?"

"I've got this one." Robbie grabbed a bag, eager to get him moved in so that he could begin to take his presence for granted; he had to stop trembling whenever he approached. They spread clothes out on the bed and Robbie took charge of putting them away. Toni watched him admiringly. He seemed so competent and well organized for a kid his age. It was at odds with the other side he sensed in him, the dark intensity that impressed, even awed him. There was a fire in him that he supposed might be artistic temperament. He sometimes worried that it was something he lacked. He still felt very much like the ordinary normal country boy he had started out being. Michèle had made him forget that he'd wanted to kiss Robbie's mouth but he still felt curiously possessive and protective of him.

"Isn't Michèle a knockout?" he asked as Robbie cleared the last things off the bed. "I think I'm going to get her."

"I'll bet you get everybody you want." Robbie kept his head in the closet and wondered if it sounded as if he were offering himself.

"I've been doing pretty well recently. What about you? Have you had lots of girls?"

Robbie hoped that Toni wouldn't be as tiresome about girls as Rico. He shifted clothes around in the closet and shrugged. "Not really." He thought of Anne and experimented with the truth. "I've been naked with one or two."

"And they wouldn't let you go very far? I know. Nice girls your age are pretty careful. If it weren't for older women, I don't know what we'd do for sex. You mean you're a virgin?"

"Does having your cock sucked count?"

Toni laughed. "Sure. You're only slightly a virgin."

Robbie felt that he'd skirted the subject neatly. He closed the closet door. "I've got to come see your act," he said.

"Oh no. Definitely not. Not that dance. I'd feel foolish." He went to Robbie and held him by the lapels of his dressing gown. "I don't want you to go to a place like that."

Robbie was increasingly aware of how free Toni was with physical intimacies. He wondered how long he'd be able to ignore them. Standing so close together was almost like an embrace. "The Tour Engloutie? What's wrong with it?" he asked into his eyes.

"Haven't you heard? The *pédés* are making it their head-quarters. If you don't know, so much the better. You're just at the age when somebody might try to take advantage of you."

Robbie wished sex were a forbidden subject as it had been when he was growing up. He was afraid of saying something damning at any minute. "Has it got something to do with age?"

"Well, to do with being defenseless and inexperienced. You're so open with people. You are with me. If I was inclined that way, I might get the wrong impression."

Robbie was very aware of the hands on his chest. Was it possible for Toni to want him without knowing it? "I want to make any impression you want me to make," he said with cautious ambiguity.

"You have. You know that." Toni dropped his hands and kicked off his espadrilles. "I know you're all right but you've got the kind of looks that drives them crazy."

"It seems you do, too. I've *got* to see you perform," Robbie insisted.

"Not there. Promise. I don't want to be responsible for your going to places like that." His tight trousers and brief triangular undershorts joined the espadrilles on the floor. He stood devastatingly, unself-consciously naked in front of his young friend. "You must tell me what to do about laundry. I need a shower. Come on and talk to me." He put a hand on his shoulder and headed for the bathroom.

Robbie struggled to keep his eyes on his face but a random uncontrollable glance told him that his cock remained irreproachably inert. He shoved his hands into the pockets of his dressing gown to make sure that his at least remained out of sight. He was going to have to get used to staying more or less erect all summer.

As the small house party gathered on the terrace for Mrs. Rawls' party, Robbie told his parents about Toni's prohibition. He wasn't sure they knew what homosexuality was but he knew they'd approve of Toni's strict views about the places he frequented. "I wanted to go see Toni tonight," he said, "but he doesn't think I should go there."

Stuart looked at his young guest with grateful respect. "Good for you. I'm not much at putting my foot down but it struck me as no place for kids. Not because of your performance. Because of the crowd."

"You should see some of the places in Hollywood," Pat said. "They're taking over the world."

"Along with Hitler?" Stuart suggested. "I've heard some funny things about him."

"If only they were true," Hilliard said. "We could make it cream puffs at ten paces and finish him off."

It was a subject that clearly embarrassed them all and it was quickly dropped. Robbie was cast into outer darkness.

He had a consoling ten minutes with Edward behind some shrubbery at Mrs. Rawls' rented villa. The party was much like the Coslings' lunch, only bigger. Toni devoted himself to Michèle and a group of film people. As soon as he left for his performance, Robbie was ready to go and was glad when his elders took him home. He immediately withdrew to his house wondering how late Toni would be.

He got ready for bed but when he lay down, thoughts of Toni proved too potent to make him an acceptable bedmate. What if Toni discovered him with an erection? He wore no pajamas during the summer and he hadn't seen any among Toni's things. Going to bed naked together suddenly became an insuperable problem. Why hadn't he thought of this sooner?

He rose and put on his dressing gown and went out to the living room and stretched out on the sofa with a book. If Toni came in soon he would stay here until his friend was asleep. He read for half an hour, his heart thudding anxiously whenever he thought of Toni. What was he doing? His performance was over by now. Would he really come home or would he go off with that girl? There was a great craving emptiness somewhere in him when he thought of the couple together. He had to come home. All his things were here. The book slipped from his hands and he slept.

He was awakened by a voice and laughter and hands moving on him. He smiled and his eyes fluttered open. Toni was perched on the sofa beside him with nothing on. Robbie's dressing gown had fallen open, leaving all the front of him exposed. As Robbie's eyes focused, Toni gave his erection a tug and laughed.

"It's a big one, little brother. Are you dreaming of your lady love?"

Robbie struggled up and tried to twist away from him but he was too late. "Oh Toni. No," he cried and fell back and was gripped by orgasm. His ejaculation spattered his forehead and cheeks and chest. He covered his flaming face with his hands and uttered a groan of shame.

"At your service." Toni chuckled and Robbie felt him rise. "You were having a wet dream. You better go wipe yourself off and come to bed." Robbie parted his hands slightly and looked at him. He was standing over him casually, looking down at him, his cock still virtuously quiescent. Robbie hadn't damned himself in his eyes; it had been a natural phenomenon. He scrambled to his feet, holding himself so as not to drip, and hurried to the bathroom.

He awoke the next morning feeling more deeply contented than he had known it was possible to be. He lay for long minutes without moving and gazed at the naked sleeping figure beside him. Toni was on his side, his back turned, the sheet around his waist. By moving his foot cautiously, Robbie was able to pull it down farther so that he could see his buttocks. He was entranced by the agile grace and power of the peacefully unconscious body. He registered every detail with growing love and desire—the endearing disarray of the curls on the pillow, the strong slender neck, the smooth tanned skin, the muscles of his back and shoulders, the ridges of his spine and the small hollow at the base of it where he longed to put his mouth. This extraordinary creature who radiated glamour even in his sleep had seen him with a hard-on, had held it and thought that a dream had given him an orgasm. Toni was incapable of suspecting him of illicit desires. Toni had the power to make him what he wanted him to be.

When he'd soaked up all the contentment he could absorb, he slipped soundlessly out of bed and grabbed a pair of shorts from the closet and went to the bathroom to start the day. A thermos of coffee and hot milk had been left for them in the kitchenette and he drank some while he opened tubes of paint and studied color balances. He was moving away from the figurative and he had learned that this new approach required much more concentrated and rigorous control of form than anything he had done before. He could become so engrossed that he lost all sense of time. He put one of his Greek sketches on the table in front of him and laid an undercoat on the canvas in blocks of strong color and waited with bated breath to see what was going to happen. Something always did, usually more or less what he expected but there were often surprises. It was the ability to deal with them that made art. He knew that he was finally launched on original work.

He had no idea how long he'd been at it when he became aware of the bedroom door opening. He glanced up. Toni was poised invitingly naked in the doorway, one hand on the jamb, the other on his hip. His erection seemed to stretch halfway across the room. Robbie fumbled with his brush and dropped it. When his eyes were once more capable of accurate observation, he saw that it was about the same size as his own.

Toni laughed. "I'm like you last night. My brothers and I used to be like this all the time. There's something sort of ridiculous-looking about a guy with a hard-on but it feels good."

"You've got a big one, too," Robbie said through lips that felt parched. If he repeated things that Toni had said he couldn't get into too much trouble.

"Like yours. I told you we're built alike. Mine's bigger than my five real brothers. They used to make me show it off every morning to see if it had grown. My debut as a performer." He laughed again and glided into the room with an eccentric dance step and disappeared into the kitchenette. "Did you say I'd find breakfast in here?" he called back.

"Yes, in the blue thermos. There's fresh bread, too, and butter in the fridge if you want it." Passing on this prosaic information helped Robbie get a grip on himself. He retrieved the brush and wiped up spattered paint, thinking of his Greek brothers. They had made him feel like one of them. Toni was his brother. Maybe brothers were permitted special liberties. It was the only explanation of what seemed like Toni's constant provocations. If they were intended in the way Robbie wished they were, they would have made love by now. The image of the sinuously gliding body and the careless swing of his erection continued to rock his mind. His shorts were too loose to confine developments. His concentration was shattered; his mind was crowded with phallic forms. He put his hands in his pockets and followed Toni to the kitchenette. He was standing in the middle of it drinking his coffee. His cock had dwindled to its usual proportions. He looked at Robbie over the rim of his cup with smiling eyes.

"I'm staying out of your way," he said. "I'll pull myself together in the bathroom and then go for a swim. Was I all right in bed? I didn't kick you or pull the sheet off or anything?"

"Not that I know of. I slept."

"Me, too. It's almost noon."

"Really? I was up at nine."

Toni set down his cup and moved to Robbie and put an arm around his bare shoulders and walked him into the living room. "Can I see what you've been doing or don't you like people to look?"

"I don't mind, but you won't be able to make head or tail of it yet."

"Then I'll wait. But hurry up and do something you can show me. I'm dying to see your work. I'll bet it's exciting."

"I'll bet yours is, too."

"Oh that." His laughter was charmingly self-deprecating.

"You saw what they'd really like to see at the Tour Engloutie. That's all it amounts to, really. I just prance around while everybody wishes I'd take everything off." He turned Robbie to face him and put his hands on his shoulders and looked him over. "With a body like yours, you could do as well. I had a good look at you before I woke you up last night."

Since looking was permitted, Robbie took a long look at the soft plump curve of the cock that was almost touching him. It bore no resemblance to the taut soaring shaft that had been thrust toward him only minutes ago. Not a quiver disturbed its inertia. His pockets enabled Robbie's hand to retain firm control of his own. He lifted his eyes and looked into the untroubled purity of Toni's face. "I'm amazed you let me see you with a hard-on. I was pretty embarrassed last night."

"Don't be silly. Brothers don't pay any attention to those things. All guys are hard when they wake up."

"I'm like that quite often. I don't know why." He hoped that would explain anything that might happen in the future.

Toni smiled and gave his chin a pat. "You'll get a girl soon. She'll take care of it." He turned him around to face his easel and gave him a little push. "Go back to work. I'll go wash up." Toni smiled to himself as he went to the bathroom. He hoped he hadn't shocked the kid. Showing off his erection wasn't his speciality but he felt something pent-up and explosive in Robbie that might be released in horseplay. His shame last night over a perfectly ordinary occurrence had verged on hysteria. There was always the danger of a highly emotional boy getting a crush on an older friend. Toni wanted to defuse any stray sexual currents that might be generated between them. Affection guided him; he wished they really were brothers.

Robbie studied his morning's work. He'd made a good start but he hadn't the will to go on with it now. He had to be with Toni. He got himself into the discreet confinement of a pair of swimming trunks and was cleaning his brushes when Toni emerged from the bathroom looking scrubbed, combed, and radiant, also wearing trunks.

"I'll go along," he said, approaching Robbie's worktable. "Are you coming soon?"

"I'll come with you. When I'm just starting something, I don't like to work too long at a stretch. I get all involved and can't see what I'm doing."

"You're lucky having something you can do on your own. Nobody can tell you what you're supposed to do."

"That part's good but it takes so much time. I don't want it to get in the way of doing things with you."

"Don't worry. I'm here now, little brother. We'll do lots of things together. I hope you don't get sick of me."

"I probably will in about ten years." He wiped his hands and tossed the rag aside and dared initiate the contact that Toni seemed to take for granted. He ran a hand over his shoulders and gripped his neck. "Let's go." He felt as if his whole being were being jolted into some new alignment. All of life flowed from Toni. Being allowed to touch him and feel him against himself was as necessary as air. He had somehow escaped sex for the moment; he was wholly integrated into the very substance of his friend. The contentment he had felt a little earlier was undercut by a vast dread of losing him.

They swam. The Hilliard couple joined them, followed by Stuart. Helene drifted down in a slightly old-fashioned bathing costume with a little skirt. They all had drinks from the bar in the beach house. No guests were expected. The party that night was to be at Madame Joffrey's remodeled house on the old fisherman's port. Toni said that Michèle might stop by later to pick him up for a swim.

"If it's really a swim you want, there's no need for Michèle to take you anywhere," Stuart pointed out when he had a moment alone with Toni at the edge of the sea. "There's even a reasonable amount of privacy down here in the evening. Those things close." He indicated the louvered shutters that pulled across the wide opening of the beach house sitting room. It was furnished with comfortable outdoor things and a daybed. Dressing rooms for men and women were on either side. "Actually, you'd be quite comfortable down here if you want a house of your own. I keep forgetting it's here."

"I'm fine with Robbie."

"Good. You're getting settled in? Felix is bringing the motorbike out this afternoon. I hope it's understood that you can ask whoever you like here during the day. In the evening I suppose we better coordinate our activities for the sake of the help, but you're free to have people for dinner, even if we're going out. Just let me know."

"You think of everything. You're truly astonishing."

Stuart put a hand on his shoulder. "I think we make a very handsome family, if you'll forgive me for including myself.

277

Stanley and Pat will be gone in a few days and then there'll just be the four of us for a while. I'm looking forward to that."

"Am I included in the party tonight?"

"Of course. Why wouldn't you be?"

"Madame Joffrey is a very important woman. She wouldn't ordinarily ask anybody like me. Did you mention me?"

"Not by name. She asked me how many we'd be and I said we were four and two houseguests."

"You *are* a good guy. I'll bet she'll be surprised to see me."

"What is this? Does she have something against you?"

"Not personally as far as I know. Some people don't invite entertainers in cheap nightclubs to their houses. She's one of them."

"I see. In that case, you'd be doing me a favor if you tell her you're my son. She's frightfully impressed by my father. I'd love her to think that his grandson is an entertainer in a cheap nightclub." They looked at each other and chuckled with mutual understanding.

"I like you, Stuart. I may yet call you Papa."

They had an informal lunch and Robbie returned to work in a blaze of creative dedication. Contentment had once again become a deep singing rapture that he felt all through him, from toes to fingertips. What was happening to him? How could a virtual stranger alter all of life? He tried to remember what he'd been like before Toni had come. He was possessed by smiling green eyes. His life was Toni's.

He was immersed in his work when Toni unexpectedly joined him a little later. "Didn't Michèle come?" he asked, not letting himself abandon his work.

"No. I'm sort of glad she didn't. It's so wonderful feeling I've got a home for a change. I've got to write and let people know where I am. If I'm not in the way, I just want to sit around your house and enjoy it."

"Our house."

"Is it? Okay, little brother. Our house."

Shocks and tremors passed through Robbie when he glanced up from time to time to see Toni wandering around the place, from the bedroom to the terrace to the bathroom and back, sometimes in a dressing gown, sometimes with a towel around his waist, once with nothing on at all, making himself at home. It was a glorious distraction, adding an extra excitement to his work.

When he had put his brushes away for the night, they both dressed in white dinner jackets. Robbie had acquired his at school in the spring and it was already getting tight around the shoulders. They admired each other playfully and were in high good humor when they joined the others.

The party took place on a giant roof garden and revealed a more formal aspect of local social life. The women, few of them in the first bloom of youth, were glitteringly chic and the men had a distinguished air. Stuart recognized several important political figures. There were editors and journalists and a famous member of the *Académie Française*. Michèle wasn't there and Robbie stayed close to Toni's side, where he wished to remain for the rest of his life. When he caught sight of Edward, he reluctantly responded to the appeal of his eyes.

"I hoped you'd be here," he said, joining him beside a small tree. He regretted that he was only being polite.

"I find the atmosphere rather rarefied, don't you, darling? Shouldn't we sneak off to the yacht for a little down-to-earth music?"

"Later, maybe." He looked into Edward's nice eyes and saw a glow that he supposed was love in them. He wanted him but knew he couldn't let anybody but Toni touch him. How could he tell him without hurting him? "Actually, I can't, darling," he began with difficulty. "I shouldn't even call you that. He wouldn't like it. Something's happened. Well, nothing really, not like you might think. I don't suppose it ever will. I think he'd hate me if he knew but I can't help it. I've got to keep myself sort of pure for him. Do you understand?"

Edward's eyes grew wistful. "It sounds awfully as if you've fallen in love with him, darling."

"I suppose I have. I've never felt like this about anybody before. I want you. I honestly do, but I just couldn't. Is that crazy?"

"It breaks my heart but I understand, darling. If you're so sure nothing can happen with him, maybe you'll get over it and want me back. I'll be waiting."

"You're sweet. I've loved it. I won't make love with anybody else. I promise you that."

"My poor virginal darling. I can't say I envy you. Haven't I heard something about dinner at your house tomorrow? We'll still want to see each other, won't we?"

"Of course. I never know anything about our social life. I

279

hope you're right about dinner. Why don't you and Anne come for the day? I've started work again but the sea's still there."

"We'll see. I have one thing to thank you for, darling. There's no reason for me to stay at this depressing party any longer. I think I'll take Anne for a little pub crawl. I won't promise to be as virginal as you."

The flippant note told Robbie that, despite his declarations of love, Edward didn't need him. Toni certainly never would. Could the craving that had been kindled in him on a changing-room floor ever be satisfied in his love of men?

He returned to Toni's side wondering if he'd regret having renounced the safety valve of sex. It wasn't going to make living with Toni any easier but he'd had no choice. He couldn't imagine having pleasure in anybody else's arms. Was it always like this when you were in love? Did it cut you off from everybody else? He hadn't realized that it was happening until he'd seen Edward. What else was he going to learn about love?

He learned a great deal in the next few hours. He learned that he didn't care where he was so long as Toni was there. He didn't find the party depressing. He ate some superb food. He talked to overpoweringly elegant ladies, always more or less within touching distance of his friend. When it was time for Toni to leave for his performance, he stood beside Robbie and held his arm. His eyes were full of green mischief. "This has been a very interesting evening," he said. "I've met some people who could be helpful. I may be late. You know what I said about older women."

Robbie was left smiling into a void. He couldn't speak. He didn't know who any of these people were. Edward and Anne were gone. He had to get home. He had to be where Toni belonged. He looked around for his mother and saw her surrounded by men. She caught his eye as he approached and turned to him. "I want to go home," he said, finding that he had to pronounce the words with great care. "Can I take the car? You'll be with Mr. Hilliard, won't you? Can't you get home with him?"

"Of course, darling. Are you all right? You haven't been drinking, have you?"

"Of course not. Only a few glasses of wine."

"I'm not sure the same is true of your father. He has the keys. Tell him I said you could go. I'm afraid this hasn't been much of a party for you but I can't tell you how many people

280

have said that you're the most fascinating young man they've ever met."

"Thanks. Tell me more in the morning. I feel sort of funny."

"We're all still tired, darling. Drive carefully. We won't be long."

Robbie drove slowly, feeling unreal and bereft. He thought he'd said goodnight to his hostess but wasn't sure and didn't much care. What difference did anything make if Toni weren't with him? He could go through the motions of living but nothing had any meaning. The only reality that directed him was the need to be where Toni would expect to find him.

As soon as he got to his house, he threw his clothes off and pitched himself down on the bed and pressed himself into the mattress on the side where Toni had slept last night. He buried his face in his pillow and opened his mouth for kisses. He felt his body against his, his arms holding him. Their twin erections thrust up hard against each other. Toni's was in him, filling and possessing him. He flung himself over onto his back and shouted and sobbed with his orgasm.

He staggered up and dragged himself to the bathroom and washed and hung his clothes up. If he kept busy, time would pass and Toni would be here. He went through Toni's clothes, trying things on, fitting his cock snugly into trousers where Toni's had been and watching it swell. They could wear each other's clothes. They were brothers. They belonged together. Where was he now?

He'd expected Toni to do things on his own. He had his job and girls and contacts to make to further his career. He had known it and happily accepted it this morning. What was the matter with him now? He was sure Edward had never gone through anything like this over him. He reasoned himself into some degree of calm and lay down hoping for sleep, choosing the middle of the bed so that Toni would have to move him in order to get in. He dozed fitfully but started up, reaching for Toni, his body wracked with emptiness and longing. He sat motionless for minutes at a time, listening for his footsteps. Was this being in love? It was a nightmare. He didn't think he could survive it much longer without losing his mind.

As the hours passed, dread settled over him like a pall. His heart pounded erratically so that he had trouble breathing. There was a sick hollow in the pit of his stomach. Something might have happened to Toni. What if he weren't here in the morning? How would they find him? He couldn't get through a search for him without breaking down. Everybody would guess what was the matter with him. Toni was all right. He had to be all right. He'd said he might be late.

The dark had begun to pale when he heard the door open and close. He almost shouted with relief. Toni was back. He was here. His heart hammered exultantly. He heard footsteps in the next room. They approached, light and assured. He entered the bedroom. Robbie could see his pale form moving and altering shape as he took his clothes off. He choked back ecstatic laughter while he pretended to be asleep. He hadn't known it was possible to rocket from one emotional extreme to another so quickly. Rapture flowed through him again and soothed his nerves and untied his knotted muscles. He felt him getting into bed. He twitched and muttered as if in his sleep and let Toni's hand shift him into a different position. A hand remained on his shoulder as Robbie plunged into a deep dreamless sleep.

His happiness the next day was shot through with anxiety about the evening that would inevitably follow. Was he going to have to suffer through a nightly agony? If he tried to subdue his passionate response to Toni during the day perhaps the shock of being without him at night would be less intense. He decided to adopt a more guarded manner and not let him dominate his thoughts. He managed when he was working but it took two to make it work the rest of the time. Toni was always near, always offering him the enchantment of his smile, always touching him lovingly. It was a torment of bliss.

Edward had been right about dinner. The admiral's family was expected along with Madame Joffrey and Mrs. Rawls. Toni wandered around naked while they prepared for an informal evening. Sooner or later, Robbie supposed, he was going to wonder why his roommate was always so modestly covered and why his hands were almost always in his pockets.

"That woman I met last night," Toni said, pulling a pair of his brief triangular underpants out of a drawer and handing them mysteriously to Robbie. "Her husband is one of the producers of that film I might be in in the autumn. She thinks she can fix something with the director."

"How wonderful. You'll be a star in no time."

"I can always dream. She doesn't think it's good for me to be working at the Tour. She says I'm apt to get a reputation as a *pédé*. She thought I might be until she found out otherwise." He laughed and ruffled Robbie's hair. "You were sleeping peacefully but it was almost daylight when I got home. The point is, if the film really comes through in the next few weeks, I could refuse to extend my contract. I'd have all of August off."

"You mean you'd stay here but you wouldn't be working?"

"That's the idea. Thanks to your father, I could afford a real holiday." He saw Robbie's face light up with an almost unearthly radiance. Once, a girl had looked at him like that after he'd made love to her. He was deeply touched. He moved closer and put an arm around him. "We could have some fun together without worrying about getting to the show on time. Would you like that, little brother? I know our father would."

"I'm speechless. That's the best news ever." Only a few more weeks and then at least he'd know that Toni didn't *have* to go off every night.

"Well, keep all your fingers crossed. It all depends on the film. It's not the greatest part in the world but it's a start."

"I know you'll get it. I'm sure your lady friend will insist. Are you going to see her tonight?"

"No, her husband's coming down for the weekend. She's going to handle it through the director in Paris. I know him. I think he likes me."

"Of course he does. Who doesn't? You're all set." He looked at the underpants he was holding. "What am I supposed to do with these?"

"I thought you should try them. Your cock's awfully big for those shorts your wear. I noticed it last night. Everything shows."

Robbie blushed and giggled in his amazement that a normal boy would notice such things. He had to go into the bathroom to get himself into the brief garment.

The dinner for fourteen was agreeably relaxed. Edward was languidly successful in concealing any heartbreak he might be feeling. Toni charmed Mme. Joffrey and Mrs. Rawls made a great fuss over Robbie. Toni left for work saying that he'd probably be right back. Robbie was left with a fixed smile and vacant eyes. The party ended as abruptly as if all the lights had been turned out. He groped in the dark for something to reply to a question he hadn't heard. Why hadn't he suggested going with him? He couldn't have, of course. It would have been rude and might have made people wonder. If only he could tell everybody that his life depended on Toni, that he loved him with all his body and soul. Love was what life was all about. They weren't doing anything wrong. He might make more sense about it if he could share the wonder of it with the world. He was in love. He knew it now.

It was after midnight and he was wondering if Toni had finished his performance when the party broke up. He went on smiling until the guests were gone. He sat with the remaining quartet of elders and heard them talking without knowing what they were saying. He was counting the minutes. The performance was surely over now. Toni was taking off his makeup and washing. He was getting into his clothes. Beautiful people crowded around him vying for his attention. He ignored them, pushing his way out, thinking only of getting home.

Robbie slowed down his scenario. There was a particularly beautiful girl. Toni paused to talk to her and find out who she was. Perhaps he'd make a date to see her tomorrow. Robbie halted the action to allow plenty of time for this.

He heard his father and Mr. Hilliard laughing. He looked up at the star-bright sky. He poured himself a glass of wine. There. Toni had finished his business with the girl. He was out and headed for the motorbike. In another fifteen minutes he would be home. He edged around in his chair to face the archway where he would make his appearance. What if he didn't? Would he be able to handle his disappointment without everybody seeing that he was going through a crisis? Toni was there.

Again, he swung from gathering despair to almost uncontainable euphoria in an instant. He didn't shout or leap up as he had felt he was bound to do. He sat quietly and smiled into Toni's eyes as he approached with his light graceful step. His golden head threw off reflections from the candlelight on the table.

"Salutations, everybody," he said. He was greeted warmly and pulled a chair over beside Robbie and put a hand on his shoulder as he sat. Stuart asked him if he wanted something to eat. "It seems ridiculous after that magnificent dinner but performing always makes me hungry. All actors are the same."

Robbie was immediately on his feet. "I'll get you something. What do you want?"

"Not a lot. Do you suppose there're any of those fabulous jellied eggs left over from lunch? I'd love a couple of those."

When Robbie returned with a tray, Toni was alone.

"Where is everybody?" he asked, putting down the copious meal he'd gathered from the refrigerator.

"They said to say goodnight. They want an early night. Thanks, little brother. You're spoiling me. It's so damn nice here. I really love coming home."

"I love your being here." He hitched his chair close and watched him spooning up the rich mixture of poached eggs and goose liver and wine jelly. Toni's hands fascinated Robbie. They were blunt-fingered and powerful-looking, as if he could knock a man down with one blow.

"I saw Michèle tonight. Do you know what she said? She said to tell you that if you were ten years older she'd try to marry you. She thinks you're the sexiest guy she's ever seen."

"She must be crazy. Hasn't she looked at you?"

"Well, I wondered about that myself." Toni laughed. "I know what she means. Your ass, for one thing. I don't know if girls pay any attention to guys' asses but there's something about yours that makes you want to touch it."

Robbie was suddenly struck dumb. They seemed to be skating on very thin ice. What was he supposed to say now? "You better not," he said, hoping to hit the right note of man-to-man jocularity.

"I don't know. I might give it a pat some time just to make sure it feels as good as it looks. I asked Michèle to come to lunch tomorrow. I'll bet you could get her if you tried."

"What about you?"

"Oh, I'm still trying but I'm willing to let the poor girl have her choice. I have Mme. de Mornay to console me." He scraped up the last of the eggs and buttered a piece of bread and drank some wine and attacked the beef filet and potato salad that Robbie had found. "You know, your idea of a little light supper is a revelation. Everything's so good. Maybe we should get married. I'll never find a girl who'll feed me like this."

"Maybe you should marry Boldoni."

Toni laughed. "That's a possibility but you're much prettier. No, I'll marry you and keep Boldoni as our cook. You don't mind waiting up for me like this?"

"God, no. I love it. Actually, I waited quite late last night."

"You shouldn't have. I warned you I might be late. Mado de Mornay is a very sexy lady. Did you hear what Mme. Joffrey said tonight? She thinks I might be right for the lead in a play that's opening in one of her theaters later in the fall.

She wouldn't've noticed me if I weren't staying here. I happen to know she likes girls, thank heavens, so I don't have to worry about that. She's not my idea of something I'd like to find between my sheets."

Robbie's faint hopes were dashed by these sophisticated references to a world he would never know. Toni was beyond his reach; jokes about getting married and touching his behind meant nothing. He watched the strong jaws working as he chewed the last of the beef and longed to stroke the hollows of his cheeks and trace with his fingers the firm voluptuous curve of his lips. Serving him food was an act of worship. "It sounds as if the theater has a lot to do with sex," he said.

"It gets on my nerves at times. That's why I said I envy you your painting. I could never make love to a woman I didn't want but you get into situations that are pretty tricky sometimes. With somebody like Mado, I'm all in favor. I can have my fun and maybe get a chance at a job at the same time, but it's just a matter of luck. Mado wasn't interested in my brilliant talent until she made sure I could give her what she wanted in bed."

"I'll stick to painting."

Toni laughed and poured wine for both of them, then put his arm around Robbie and moved in close against him. "That's why I feel so good with you. It's so nice and simple for a change. We can love each other without trying to take advantage of each other. Do you love me, little brother?"

"Yes. God, yes," he said, trying to keep the fervor out of his voice. How long could he go on with this masquerade? Toni held him as if he were about to make love to him, but there was nothing erotic in the embrace, only sweetness and affection.

"Good. Shall we have a swim before bed?"

"Sure. I— Shall I get our trunks?"

"Why bother? We don't need anything at night."

"No. I just—I guess I don't feel like it." He couldn't be naked with Toni unless they were lovers. He wouldn't be able to get ready for bed, let alone get into it, without Toni seeing what he wanted. It was folly to suppose that he could go on like this day after day for weeks on end. His body would betray him. He struggled for control. He mustn't let Toni know. He began to tremble. There was a knot in his throat.

"Hey, what's the matter? Aren't you feeling well?" Toni shifted around so that he could look at him. He felt Robbie's body begin to shake. He had been contentedly eating and hadn't been aware of any tension in the air. There was a wild glitter in Robbie's eyes and his face was rigid with some sort of anguish. His trembling became more pronounced. "My God, Robbie. Are you sick?"

"No. It's nothing. Let me—"

Toni gripped his arms and pulled him around to look into his eyes. "Tell me. I've been chattering about myself and haven't been paying attention. What're you so upset about?" Robbie's eyes darted about desperately as if he were looking for salvation. His mouth opened but no words came out. He gasped and uttered a cry and flung himself against Toni, burying his face against his shoulder. He was sobbing and trembling violently. Toni held him firmly and tried to identify his distress. He couldn't remember witnessing anything quite like it. "Now listen, just relax," he said soothingly. "It's all right, whatever it is. Tell me."

"No. Oh no, Toni. Please," Robbie wailed.

"Please what?"

"Don't you know?"

"No. How can I?" Something about the way Robbie's hands clung to him alerted him. He drew back hastily and held him at arm's length and stared into his tear-streaked face. "You're not— Are you trying to say— Oh, for God's sake. You're not a *pédé*, are you?"

"Yes," Robbie cried, choking out the words. "I can't help it. I swore I'd never let you find out. Oh God. I'm so in love with you."

Toni let go of Robbie and watched with distaste as he collapsed against the table, his head in his arms, his shoulders heaving. "Oh, shit," he muttered and rose and strode off down the glade.

Thoughts of killing himself fluttered through Robbie's mind while his body was wracked by sobs. What was there left to live for? Toni would despise him. Why had he supposed he could live happily as one of the damned? He had no hope of love. He was doomed.

His sobs slowly subsided as grief and shame were extinguished by fear, fear of being found by somebody in this state, fear of what Toni might do. Would he leave? Would he tell his parents why he was leaving? He would have to face him again and beg him not to. He'd promise to do anything he wanted if he'd stay. They could agree on some reason for his moving down into one of the guest rooms. They wouldn't be friends anymore so nothing mattered. He would renounce his love. If he couldn't bear living without him—last night had proved that he couldn't—he would have to face that too. He raised his head and found a glass of wine in front of him and gulped it down. A final sob escaped him like a hiccough and he shuddered. He had to be prepared to see contempt in Toni's eyes. Fear chilled him as he dragged himself to his feet.

Toni undressed, wondering how he should handle the kid. He could clear out and go on about his business but life had been charged with exciting new promise in the last couple of days. Being here had made a big difference. More important, he was afraid that Robbie's delicate emotional balance might tilt him into despair if he walked out on him. He didn't want to precipitate a great drama. Stuart had been good to him. There were better ways to repay him than to drive his son into a nervous breakdown. The simplest solution would be to take Robbie to bed and let it happen, but he was almost sure that he wouldn't be able to do anything. Not with Robbie. It would be a denial of the deep protective affection he felt for him.

How had he been able to function with the others, whom he hadn't even liked? He'd been drinking, for one thing. Drink dulled his mind to what his body was doing. He'd seen some bottles in the kitchenette. He finished putting his clothes away and went in and found some brandy and gave himself a generous slug. Now that his initial distaste and disappointment were passing, what he really wanted was to stay and help Robbie through it, even demonstrate to him that he was mistaken about himself. It was so easy to get sexually confused at that age. It all depended on what his experience had been. Possibly some remark of that silly ass Edward had given him the idea that a normal crush was a great homosexual passion. If he could straighten him out, he would have accomplished something good for both father and son.

He wandered around the room, drinking his drink. Should he go down and get him? He didn't think Robbie would leap into the sea and swim off to eternity but he was awfully highly strung. He might do something crazy. He wanted to give him some time alone to calm down, but if he didn't come soon he'd go find him. He heard somebody slowly dragging his feet up the path.

He started to make a dash for the bedroom to get his dressing gown but decided to stay as he was. He was still convinced that physical familiarity was the best antidote for sexual stirrings. He stood facing the door. Robbie entered. He looked distraught but under control. His glance took in Toni and moved hastily away as he advanced hesitantly into the room. "You're not leaving?" he asked in a dead voice.

"You don't want me to, do you? We've got to do something about this."

Robbie looked at him and his eyes darted away again, seared by the splendor of the naked body. He stopped beside his worktable and put a hand out for support, his heart hammering at Toni's approach. His throat knotted and his eyes swam with tears of relief. "You don't loathe me?" he asked with difficulty.

"Of course not. I'd hate it if you were really queer but I don't think you know yet. You haven't tried anything with me."

"How could I? I knew you didn't want it."

"That doesn't stop most *pédés*." He stood close to Robbie. "Why don't you go wash your face and get undressed and we'll talk?"

"You don't mind being naked with me? You're not afraid I'll do something awful?"

Toni took his hands and put them on his cock. "There. It's just a cock. It's so like yours that it can't even have the interest of novelty."

Robbie's heart stopped. His hands felt numb. He was holding the core of Toni's splendor. He gazed at it for an incredulous moment and looked up. "Oh, Toni," he murmured. "Oh, my God. You're so wonderful."

Toni was moved by the yearning in the dark ardent eyes. He touched his cheek tenderly. "Go on. Get ready for bed. I want to talk to you."

He went. Toni sat on the edge of the table and drank and hoped he was handling this right. Short of leaving, he couldn't see any alternative. There was no point being rough with him. That would just lead to hysteria. They would find out together why he thought he was queer and go on from there. He couldn't believe anybody would *want* to be queer if there was anything to be done about it.

Robbie emerged from the bedroom with his hands in his dressing-gown pockets. Toni drained his glass and put it down and stood. "I'm naked. You can be too," he said, going to him.

"But I'm—I—"

"You've got a hard on? We've seen each other like that." Robbie removed his hands from his pockets and his erection swung out between them. Toni put a hand on it. Robbie's whole body gave a little leap. Toni smiled reassuringly. "You don't have to be shy with me. That's probably part of the whole trouble."

"You don't understand," Robbie protested breathlessly. "The other night—I wasn't dreaming. I came because you touched me."

"We'll have to fix it so that I can't make you come." He took the dressing gown and put his arm around his waist and headed him back toward the bedroom. "Come on. We're going to bed. The way things are, I can do what I've been wanting to do." He dropped his arm and ran a hand over his buttocks. "Yes. Just what I thought. It's fantastic, like that statue."

Robbie was breathing deeply, trying to stave off a climax. He didn't understand what was happening but everything that Toni did was more exciting than making love. He glanced down and saw that Toni's cock remained soberingly inert. He was just being kind and friendly. They reached the bed and Toni gave his behind another caress and they dropped down and stretched out together under the sheet. Toni propped himself on an elbow and put his hand on Robbie's chest and looked down at him with eyes full of solicitude. Robbie put a hand over Toni's and pressed it against his heart.

"It's a shame, really," Toni said, "that loving somebody is so different from wanting to make love. I want to kiss your mouth. The first time I saw you, I wished you were a girl so I could." He lowered his head and their lips touched. It was a gentle, passionless kiss but it sent tremors of delight racing through Robbie's body. He didn't dare wonder what he might do next. "How many times has it happened?" Toni demanded.

"You mean how many boys? Ten, I think, in the last two months. No. Nine. None before."

"I see. It's gone further than I thought. Edward?"

"Yes, but not anymore. I told him last night I wouldn't because of you. I've never been in love before. I didn't know what it was like."

"What *is* it like, little brother? I'm not sure I've ever been."

"It's everything. It's knowing that there's only one person in the world who matters. I didn't know until yesterday and

290

I've been half insane ever since when you weren't with me. I worship everything about you, even your girls. I'd do anything for you. I don't care if I never see anybody else." He felt his sublime substance against him, the hand on his chest, the other that was beginning to move through his hair, the flaccid sex pressed against his hip. Could he think of anything to say that would arouse it? "You don't want me but I know I'll never be any happier than I am right now. A little while ago, I thought of killing myself but I never will as long as you're alive. I'll always want to be somewhere you can find me if you need me. I'll always hope you might love me the way I love you."

"I can't, so what're we going to do now?" He kicked off the sheet and moved his hand from Robbie's chest down to his erection and held it. "I want to find out how to make it stop getting hard for me."

"The way you touch me—haven't you ever done it with boys?"

"A few—when I was drunk and with somebody who wanted it very badly, and it was late and cold outside and I was in a comfortable place I didn't want to leave. Once, I almost thought I wanted it too, but it's never been good." He didn't see any need to tell about the few other times when he'd done it for professional advancement. It sounded too much like whoring.

"What did you do?" Robbie asked, hardly daring to breathe.

"Nothing. I just lay there and let them suck my cock."

"Let me," Robbie whispered. "Oh God, please. That's all I want."

"I didn't want to see them again afterward," he warned sharply.

Robbie's eyes contracted with pain. "Would you feel that way about me?"

"I don't know. Maybe not, but don't you understand? I love you. I don't want to see you doing a thing like that."

"Does it disgust you?"

"For a boy to do it? Of course."

"We're naked together. You're holding me. You're doing things with my cock that're about to make me come. I thought only homosexuals would do that."

"I wish nobody had ever heard of homosexuality. I can do things with you that I wouldn't do with anybody else. Once everybody starts talking about homosexuality, I can't even kiss you without being queer. Those nine boys. You probably wouldn't've thought of wanting them if you hadn't heard that things like that happen; and if you *had* wanted them you wouldn't've thought that it made you a queer. I don't suppose one more will make much difference. Go on. Do it if you want, but you've got to promise you won't do it with anybody else."

Robbie's eyes widened and his heart began to go through its complicated changes of pace. "That's easy. I told you. Nobody exists but you. Do you mean it?"

Whatever Robbie was, Toni knew that this was no ordinary crush. His great eyes blazed with an intensity of passion that caused a flutter in the pit of his stomach. "I'm trying to do what's right for you. It doesn't do anything for me but you can try." He dropped back and lay out flat.

Robbie uttered a strangled exultant cry and in a fever of adoration moved his mouth over the smooth resplendent body that had been offered him. He darted his tongue along the thrilling concavities alongside Toni's pelvis and felt his friend's cock beginning to stir at last. His heart was pounding as his mouth reached it and moved over its soft velvet length. His lips parted and drew it in and took possession of it. His heart was going to burst from his chest. He worshiped the god in Toni. The flesh in his mouth was alive, lengthening, swelling, stretching his jaws. It claimed him and took possession of his mouth with a long rigid thrust. Toni made little murmuring sounds. Robbie moaned with ecstasy. His offering to the god was pleasing. He was in deep communion with all the beauty in life.

If he kept his eyes closed, Toni thought, it could be a girl, except that Robbie did it more excitingly than anybody ever had before. He made his desire startlingly vivid. Toni didn't know if this was proof of a perverted nature or simply the effect he had on Robbie. In either case, there was no doubt that he craved the cock in his mouth. His cock. His orgasm was quick and agreeable.

Robbie was transported onto a new level of bliss as he swallowed the precious fluid and felt his own orgasm gathering to an overwhelming climax. He flung himself back with a groan. He was aware of quick movement beside him and of lips on him. His orgasm exploded into Toni's mouth. When he could see again, Toni was sitting hugging one knee, his back turned to him. His shoulders rose and fell and grew still. Had it really happened? Robbie went spinning off into the clouds and returned with a shock of apprehension. Why didn't Toni say anything? The silence was becoming frightening.

"Did you do that with the others?" he asked faintly.

"No," Toni replied in a neutral voice.

"Did you hate it?"

"Not exactly. It was strange. I knew it wouldn't kill me. Girls like it but I'm not a girl. I won't do it again."

"You didn't have to."

"No. Kids pledge eternal friendship with their blood. I suppose that's what I was doing."

"Oh God, I love you so. I don't care if we never do anything again. I just want to be with you."

"Don't be silly. You'll go on wanting sex. Until we get you over this, you won't have it with anybody but me."

"There couldn't be anybody else."

"But it's so unnatural," Toni burst out. He dropped back and lay beside Robbie. "Don't you feel it? Look at our bodies." He moved a hand roughly over Robbie's chest. "There's nothing here for me to play with and make love to." He moved his hand down to his shrinking erection. "Here, this just gets in the way. There's no way for me to take you."

Robbie looked into the green eyes and saw no remorse or shame or hostility for what they'd done, only concern and perplexity. Nothing was going to stop them from being friends. They could talk about anything. "There is a way," he said carefully.

"Sure, but I don't want to think about it. We may not be brothers but we're friends. I don't want us to be disgusted with each other. How did this start? What happened the first time?" Robbie told him about Rico. Toni listened, shaking his head impatiently from time to time. "I could kill the bastard. He's probably found out that if he can't get a girl he'd rather have a boy than masturbate, but look what he's done to you. You wanted sex, naturally, and you discover that you can have it with a boy and away you go with eight more. I guess we have to count me. Nine more."

"Have you always thought about girls? I mean, when you masturbated or had a hard on or something, did you always wish you had a girl?"

"Of course."

"I never have. I tried to but it always turned out to be a man."

293

"It's probably because you grew up alone. You didn't have any brothers or kids to play with. Kids are always curious about each other's bodies. They show off their cocks and jerk off together and all that. I used to fool around with one of my brothers. It probably happens to a lot of boys but they get over it. You never had that so it's probably just happening to you now. You'll get over it too, but it's dangerous because you're too old for it. It's apt to become a part of your grown-up life."

"What about boys like Edward? He's had girls but he'd rather have a boy."

"He's a *pédé*. They exist, of course, but they're different. There's something wrong with them. I can always spot them. I knew about Edward right away. You're not like that."

"I'm not sure. I'm glad you don't think there's anything wrong with me."

"There isn't. You can fool around with me the way my brother and I did. We didn't do what we just did, but we might have if we'd thought of it. We did some pretty crazy things. You'll get bored with it. I know you will. Then you'll be ready for real sex."

"You mean with a girl?"

"Well, isn't that what sex is all about—a man and a woman? You don't pay enough attention to girls. I've noticed. I don't mean trying to get them but just making friends with them. They're nice. When you find one you like you'll want to touch her, and if she likes to touch you, you'll soon want a lot more. It's natural. You've probably noticed how much I like to touch you, and with girls it's even more so. Maybe I do it too much but that's the way I grew up. We were always hugging and kissing and keeping each other warm in bed at night and everything. You never touch me. It doesn't seem natural."

"I've been afraid you'd guess. Every time I touch you I get a hard on."

"That's part of being alone. If you touched me all the time, you wouldn't. A guy can stay hard only just so long." He gathered himself together and scrambled up on Robbie and lay out on top of him. He slipped an arm under his head and tilted it up to him. He put his mouth on his and darted his tongue between his lips. He rolled away and lay on his back, laughing. Robbie was gasping. His chest was heaving. His revived erection lay on his belly. Toni reached for it and lifted it and let it drop. "I'll bet in another week or two, I won't be able to make it get like that even if I want to. I hope you'll still let me kiss your mouth every now and then. It's so beautiful. Are we ready to go to sleep? I'll hold your cock. That should give you sweet dreams."

"It'll be the most fabulous night of my life. You don't know what I've been through. I've been so terrified for you to know. I don't understand how you can be so wonderful to me."

"We're brothers. I won't be much of a lover but I'll do what I can to make you happy so long as I'm the only one. If I ever find out you've had the eleventh, I'll leave. Don't forget that."

"There'll never be another with you here. I promise." They looked into each other's eyes and their heads moved to each other and they kissed lightly. Robbie turned out the light and they rolled in close against each other and Toni put his hand where he'd promised it would be. Robbie took a deep shuddering breath and his eyes brimmed with tears of happiness. Deep incredulous contentment washed through him and he slept.

In the solitary peace and clarity of morning, he slowly digested the fact that Toni simply didn't believe that he was different from other boys; he was only suffering from a slight indisposition that Toni was going to cure. Since the cure included free access to Toni's body, he resolved to do his best to give the impression that little by little it was having an effect. Maybe it would have. When he thought of how pleased Toni would be, he hoped it would.

He went to work with an exhilarating new freedom of concentration. Nothing could distract him. He was the luckiest boy in the world. He was in love and he had declared his love and hadn't been punished. His beloved lay only yards away, sprawled out in their shared bed as he had left him, in the full flower of his morning vigor. It added a new dimension to his work. For the first time, he was working not only with his mind and senses but with an overflowing heart. He didn't know how love could affect painting but it was bound to show somehow.

It showed when the two were together in public. Toni grew more lavish with his physical endearments, apparently to remind Robbie that if he needed a man in his life, he was it. Toni straightened Robbie's hair, adjusted his clothes when a collar needed smoothing or a jacket wasn't settled properly on his shoulders. He held his hand when he wanted to draw him aside for a private word and put an arm around him when they were standing together talking to others. Robbie quickly relaxed into easy reciprocation. Toni was so conspicuously engaged in his heterosexual pursuits that nobody thought it was anything more than charming. The rumor had spread that they were long-lost brothers and people found it natural that they should want to establish a warm contact with each other. Toni had been right about one thing: Robbie stopped getting an erection every time they touched.

Helene, glowing with pleasure at seeing them so sweetly happy together, was at the same time troubled by a new awareness of Robbie as a sexual presence. Intuition told her that they couldn't be so free with each other in public without carrying it further in private. They were bound to kiss and caress and fondle each other. She was profoundly shocked when she caught herself wishing that she could see them naked in bed together. She didn't find it surprising that Robbie, with his sensitivity and refined instincts, should form an emotional attachment with a boy rather than a girl. There was a vast difference between that and the ghastly world that was apparently on display where Toni performed.

Robbie and Toni's lovemaking remained on the level of the night of their first shared orgasms although there were moments when Robbie still hoped that it might go further. He discovered that Toni responded sensually to water; he always got an erection when they swam naked together and it was easy to arouse him in the shower. Toni maintained that they looked ridiculous that way whereas to Robbie the dancer's graceful priapic body was the epitome of beauty but they agreed that it felt awfully good and they didn't always carry it to the usual conclusion. Just having erections together was an exquisitely tormenting thrill for Robbie, so he exercised restraint for Toni's sake. Toni admitted that his mouth was marvelous but he was waiting for him to get over wanting to demonstrate its capacity to give pleasure.

"You see?" he said one day when they were naked in the kitchenette sipping cold wine before dressing for dinner. "You don't get a hard on anymore just because I'm around. I told you that's the way it would be."

"Maybe you were right," Robbie said, suppressing a giggle. He loved him so and he was so silly. He was tempted to put a hand on him anywhere and let him see what happened. "Does it mean there's a girl looming on the horizon?"

"Don't laugh. She'll be along any day now."

Robbie was grateful that he hadn't volunteered to pick one out for him. He never stopped being grateful to him for one thing or another. He was grateful to him for his life. Toni had even learned how to ease the pain of the nightly separations that often stretched into the early hours of the morning; he promised that if he found him asleep when he came home late, he would wake him with a kiss, not the usual quick peck they frequently exchanged but a real long deep kiss of the kind that could give Robbie an orgasm. After the first night it happened Robbie almost hoped that he'd be late all the time. He was able to go to sleep with a smile on his lips looking forward to the ecstasy of waking up with Toni's open mouth on his, of his dangerous-looking hands moving with infinite gentleness over his body, touching the places where it thrilled him most, culminating in a feathery caress of his erection that always made him come instantly into the towel Toni had waiting for him. These moments always followed hours of great sexual activity for Toni, so Robbie expected his ecstasy to be solitary, but Toni's tenderness and solicitude made his heart almost burst with love.

The Coslings decided to give their first large-scale party on Bastille Day, the fourteenth of July, a decision reached by what had become known as the Committee of Four now that Hilliard and his girl were gone. It developed into a party to celebrate Toni's first film engagement. The day before (the thirteenth, henceforth his lucky day) he heard from his agent that the contract had finally been drawn up and awaited only Toni's signature.

"You're very proud of him, aren't you, dearest?" Helene said when Robbie went rushing down to the main house with the news before Toni had finished his breakfast.

"God, yes. Aren't you?" He and his mother had always been demonstrative but he realized that he'd drawn back from her in the last few months while he'd been finding more passionate embraces. He threw his arms around her and hugged her and remembered the comfort he'd always found in her bosom.

"Of course," she said with brief uncertain laughter. She was startled by the change she felt in his body. A rich eroticism seemed to emanate from his pores. The way he held her (even her!) crackled with sensual electricity. He had undergone some profound emotional experience that had altered him completely. It wasn't difficult to guess its source. She put her hands on his chest to assure herself that this was the child who had been with her always. "It's a big day for all of us but you're his special friend. You're probably even more pleased for him than he is for himself."

"Maybe. He doesn't take himself very seriously. That's one of the amazing things about him." He wondered if she knew that he was in love. They had always been so close that it wouldn't surprise him. He'd like her to know if she didn't have to know that sex was involved in it. Love flooded him and overflowed to include the world. He hugged her again and kissed her. "You see what it means? He can quit at the end of the month. He'll be with us for the rest of the summer without having to go off every evening."

"I think he may still want to go off in the evening, dearest," Helene said with an indulgent little smile.

"Oh sure. That." Robbie laughed. "But not *every* evening."

His skin had a lovely texture. She stroked his chest lightly and in spite of herself the image recurred of him lying naked with Toni in bed. What a beautiful sight it would be. She must stop thinking about it. He was radiantly happy. She didn't want to know more. She slipped out of his unnerving embrace. "You must tell him that the party is now officially for him."

"That's sweet. He'll be pleased." He moved to her side and put an arm around her waist as she started across the terrace. She was carrying a pair of garden shears. Toni was right; it was good to touch and hold people, to feel close to them and show that you loved them. "Isn't it funny? We're going to have a movie star in the family."

"It's very exciting, dearest. I must say, your father can still astonish me. Who else would have picked out a son in a bar?"

"Do you think he really is my brother?"

"Of course not, but it's an intriguing idea. I keep thinking what fun it would've been for you if we'd found him sooner. Do you remember how we used to choose the flowers for our funny little house? Felix will be furious with me but I'm going to gather a bouquet."

"Okay. I'll go tell Toni about the party."

That evening, he helped Toni go through his cosmetic routine of tinting and curling his hair, shaving his armpits, trimming his pubic hair. "There," Toni said when they were finished. "That's the last time I'll do that. I may be looking a bit shaggy by the end of the month but the hell with it."

The simple marble pedestal Robbie had designed had arrived a few days earlier and the statue was mounted on it, presiding serenely over the steps down to the cove. Stuart had hired a boat for the party and had it filled with fireworks. When the glittering company had assembled, when a flood of drink and an avalanche of Boldoni's inspired culinary creations had been consumed, a spectacular pyrotechnic display took place at the mouth of the cove, accompanied by gasps and cheers. Stuart was afraid that he might've overdone it—anything that followed risked being an anticlimax—but the big hit of the evening was a surprise even to him.

People swarmed over the terraces and down around the beach house. Stuart was about to say something to the heir apparent when the clear tinkling notes of a mechanical piano came from the direction of the house, bearing a message of absurd heartbreaking gaiety. After a frozen moment, Stuart muttered some excuse to His Highness and strode toward the house. Near the elaborate buffet stood a screen which Stuart had supposed served some function in connection with the meal. From behind it, the music swelled. He hurried over to it and peered behind. There was the old piano, Boldoni leaning on the crank in his chef's cap and long white apron. Tears burned in back of Stuart's eyes and his throat tightened.

"I bought it back while you were away," Boldoni explained. "I remembered you used to like it." Stuart put out his hand and squeezed his well-fleshed shoulder.

"Old friend," he said, not looking at him. His eyes were fixed on ghosts, on Helene, tense and racked with love for him; on Odette, all laughter and innocent sensuality; on wide-eyed funny little Robbie, just turning into a person. He retained the smell and feel of those evenings under the moon on the dusty vine-covered terrace with the scrubbed boisterous men from the quai and their hearty women—so many memories came tumbling out of the battered clattering old box. Was it only eight years ago? Stuart looked at Boldoni with a wistful smile.

"It was a wonderful idea. I'm glad we've got it," he said.

To the guests, ignorant of the piano's origin, it was a bit of deliberate originality.

"How too divinely clever," exclaimed some and, "Isn't it

299

mad," said others. Everybody began to dance. The small band Stuart had hired proved superfluous. Everybody clamored for more of the spirited old tunes churned out by the piano.

People danced, people swam, people continued to eat and drink. Helene was courted by a dozen men and thought it the best party she had ever been to. She found the strains of the mechanical piano infinitely more charming in this gorgeous setting than among the noisy crowd at Boldoni's. The party didn't even begin to break up until dawn. By then, the fireworks had been forgotten but the piano went clattering gaily on.

It was a world of parties, yachting parties, beach parties, cocktail parties, dinner parties. If there'd been any theater, there doubtless would have been after-theater parties. They were dancing on the edge of a volcano. A cliché, but Stuart felt it strongly. There were scare headlines every other day but people discussed Hitler's troop movements as if they were moves in a chess game, interesting but of no consequence to everyday living. After Czechoslovakia and Austria, would Poland be next? The "inevitable" war was taking so long to get started that he understood the tendency to dance. His memory of the other war, his war, was that it had burst upon the world like a bolt from the blue. Everybody was suddenly fighting for survival. Now, there had been so much time to prepare that it seemed reasonable to believe that all the necessary precautions had been taken. France had its impregnable Maginot Line. England had the Channel. The States didn't even enter into it. Hitler might want a war but how was he going to fight it? That was the general consensus of opinion. Stuart, who had come only slowly to believe in war's inevitability, now felt its imminence in his bones. Perhaps it was wishful thinking. He had an uneasy conviction that the evil embodied in Hitler, if unchecked, would end by being more devastating than any war. It wasn't a popular view. There were plenty of pro-Nazis around. The volcano.

The Coslings were invited everywhere but as they settled in they became more selective. Robbie and Toni ruled out lunch parties, the latter because lunch came too soon after his late breakfast. Stuart and Helene were acquiring a small circle of real friends, including Jane Cumberleigh, the admiral's fourth wife, and Hilda and Alex, the Middle European princelings, but Stuart still had a sense of living through an interlude in his life, much as he had during the cruise. He told himself regularly that he must cut down on his drinking but it didn't seem particularly important. They would while away the summer, but then what? It was difficult to come to grips with the future with the threat of war hanging over them. The Committee of Four spoke often of Paris and it was more or less understood that they would have a reunion there during Robbie's Christmas holiday and look around for an apartment.

Stuart observed, with amused detachment, that Helene was enjoying the attentions of attractive men more than she ever had in the past. There were plenty of attractive women who acted as if they wouldn't mind some attention from him but he felt no inclination for flirtations. Was that side of life permanently closed for him? He thought so. The years of devotion to hard work had killed his taste for sexual distractions. He was much more interested in the part he could play in Robbie and Toni's futures. Toni was a major addition to their life. Stuart was well pleased with himself on that score.

In many subtle ways, Helene made a point of treating Toni and Robbie as a couple. The more she watched them, the more she preferred that Toni absorb the shock of Robbie's nascent sexuality than some silly susceptible girl.

Robbie became quickly aware that Helene arranged their days so that he and Toni would always be together. It bound him to her more powerfully than anything in the past. She knew, or suspected, and was offering him her blessing. He showered her with endearments as generously as Toni did him.

Robbie had no trouble denying himself an eleventh man. Whatever went on on the port didn't penetrate the world they frequented. It was redolent of sex but only of the most conventional sort. Affairs vied with troop movements as a favored topic of conversation. Only Mrs. Rawls provided a touch of the perverse. She always had attractive young men staying with her.

"You're a very cruel boy," she accused Robbie one evening with a flirtatious tilt of her head. "Don't you know you're breaking all my poor friends' hearts? They think I keep you away from them."

"But, Mrs. Rawls—"

"Now, now. Won't you even give an old lady some small pleasure and call me Flip?"

He smiled in an attempt at his worldly manner but he still dreaded anybody making assumptions about him. "I'd like to call you Flip but you mustn't embarrass me. I may not be as sophisticated as I should be but I don't like what you said about your friends."

"Good heavens. I'm sorry. I'm the soul of discretion. I find it so natural for attractive boys to be attracted to each other that it never occurred to me I'd offend you."

He avoided her young friends although there were a few he stole second and third glances at and whose eyes promised uninhibited sex. He belonged to Toni. Their lovemaking might never amount to much but it was more precious to him than he would've believed possible. They belonged to each other, despite Toni's girls.

The month was drawing to a close when a note arrived from Carl von Eschenstadt announcing his imminent arrival. He was traveling by boat to Marseilles and would be here in a matter of days. Helene read it while she was having breakfast in bed and tossed it over to Stuart.

"Good," he said as he glanced through it. "Those guest rooms are growing cobwebs."

When he had withdrawn to the bathroom, she rose and carried the note to her dressing table where she sat and read its impersonal phrases again. She tucked it behind some bottles and smiled at herself in the mirror. He would have to outdo himself to hold his own now, she thought.

Robbie heard the news with intense excitement and a touch of apprehension. He had done his best to follow Carl's advice. He had fallen in love with a boy roughly his age. It wasn't his fault if Toni hadn't fallen in love with him. Would Carl think he was silly to pin all his hopes and dreams on a boy who liked girls?

He remembered the almost hypnotic power Carl exercised over him, but perhaps that had been because they had met so early in his discovery of himself. He'd been awfully young two months ago. Even so, despite his total dedication to Toni, he knew it would require an enormous effort of will to refuse if Carl wanted him. Need he refuse? Carl wouldn't be the eleventh man. He had been the eighth, to be exact. Toni was trying to prove that he wouldn't go on wanting new boys. Maybe he wouldn't. He hadn't for a month. Looking speculatively at Flip Rawls' friends wasn't the same as wanting them. At least he would be able to talk about everything with Carl.

Toni's engagement at the Tour Engloutie had only four more days to go. Robbie begged to be allowed to come see his performance but Toni was adamant. He didn't want Robbie to see him in that atmosphere. He warned him that he would be out a lot until his final appearance. Mado de Mornay was staying over for it and then was off for Italy. She had plans for their last few days.

His hair was beginning to grow out into its natural color but it wasn't different enough to look odd. It had coppery rather than golden tones but was still very blond. Robbie loved watching the transformation; it made him feel that he was getting to know more of the real Toni. He had so little hair under his arms that Robbie wondered why he'd bothered to shave it. As for the pubic part, it was turning into a lovely froth of blond curls.

On one of the evenings Toni was engaged with Mado, the Coslings had been invited to dinner by a poet famous primarily for his friendship with Picasso. Picasso was there. Robbie was speechless with awe. When he was introduced to the great man, somebody said something about his being a painter, too. Robbie wanted to drop through the floor.

"No, no," the master said with robust laughter. "He's too beautiful to do anything. He must just sit and let us all eat him up with our eyes." His own black bullet eyes looked as if they could shoot him dead.

Robbie remained so overwhelmed by the commanding presence that it wasn't until dinner was half over that he became fully aware that he had acquired a dark admirer. The evening was an informal affair with a buffet meal and tables set up in a garden where the guests could eat it. Robbie had somehow become part of a quartet made up of two young women and a trim, handsome man in his thirties, Latin in type and slightly reminiscent of his childhood hero Valentino, although Robbie had gathered that he was an American called Jeff. His eyes were dark and seductive. Without paying much attention, Robbie let his own eyes grow flirtatious as the glances he intercepted became more explicit and provocative. A knee pressed against his under the table finally captured his full attention and told him how far the flirtation had gone.

Alert at last, with a burgeoning erection, he saw that Jeff was the most exquisitely groomed man he'd ever seen and made him think of silly words he'd never used like "suave" and "svelte." His shapely hands had gleaming manicured nails and every hair of his dark head looked as if it had received individual attention. His brows were perfectly shaped arches and his lips were red and lush. Something about him seemed to offer rare and exotic sexual thrills. Robbie suddenly felt cheated by the lack of development in his sex life.

He exerted insinuating pressure with his own knee and promptly reprimanded himself and broke the contact. Their eyes met briefly and Robbie immediately re-established it, which committed him more deeply. He forced himself to think of Toni, getting a grip on himself and making a definite break by moving his chair back from the table. He launched into a rather forced discussion of Picasso with the woman on his left, remembering that Jeff had introduced him to his wife. She was here. He was married. What did Jeff hope to accomplish by making a pass at him?

Robbie was ashamed for having responded but it helped him rally his virtue. What would Toni think of him if he knew what he'd been doing? He'd probably leave. In a few days, he wouldn't even have his work to keep him here. That was the end of it. He wasn't going to betray everything that was most precious to him.

As soon as the meal was finished, he broke away from his group and mingled with the other guests. Whenever he saw Jeff getting close, he drifted on. In order to avoid the risk of further contact, when it was time to leave, he slipped away with his parents without saying goodnight to him.

He had felt the surrender in himself and had barely avoided disaster. Nobody had ever made him feel needed, not even Edward. He had recognized something in Jeff that forced him to confront his need to be needed. Safely back in his house, he subdued the hunger that had been stirred in him by imagining Toni everywhere, naked and godlike. He had his return to look forward to. By tomorrow, he would have forgotten Jeff.

At lunch the next day, Stuart told his family that he'd had a call from their host of the night before. "Paul wants to bring Picasso and his crowd over some time this afternoon. Actually, I suggested it last night to that American associate of his, Jeff Benjamin, but he thought Mr. P. was going to Antibes today."

"Jeff Benjamin?" Robbie asked with a small shiver of guilt.

304

"Yes. Weren't you sitting with him at dinner last night? He has something to do with the master's American interests. His wife's attractive but she got rather pissed. Wouldn't it be sort of exciting to let Picasso see your work?"

"My God. No," Robbie cried. "I'd die. There's nothing finished anyway."

Toni took his hand and pressed it encouragingly. "Don't be silly. He's a painter. He can see what you're doing whether it's finished or not. You've got to get used to showing. Why not start at the top with Picasso as your first public?"

"Will you be there to catch me if I faint?" They all laughed.

"Not if he isn't here before four. I'd hate to miss him but I have a date."

Robbie tried to go back to work after lunch but he was too nervous to concentrate. He lined up the three canvases he'd been working on. One of them was almost finished, the other two in varying stages of progress. He supposed Toni was right. A painter might not like them but he could see what Robbie was driving at and how he was going about it. A good hour's work was probably all that was needed for the nearly finished one but he didn't dare touch it for fear of making a false move. He had too much on his mind. Would Jeff be part of the "crowd"?

Toni joined him for half an hour to dress for his date. He gave him a peck on the cheek as he was leaving. "I'll bet he's impressed. Watch him closely and remember everything he says. I want to hear all about it tomorrow. I probably won't see you till dawn. Sleep tight."

He wasn't going to have Toni to protect him. He was on his own. He pottered about at his worktable for an hour and began to wonder if they were really coming. His rational side hoped they wouldn't. It would be too nerve-wracking and wouldn't accomplish anything, anyway. Picasso couldn't make him a better painter and he was determined to ignore the other. Agnes appeared to say that his mother had sent word that M. Picasso had arrived.

Robbie quickly changed into swimming trunks and combed his hair and went down to see what fate had in store for him. Jeff was there, looking suavely, urbanely, impeccably handsome in the daylight. His casual summer clothes neutralized his body. Robbie wished he could see some saving blemish, like a lot of hair on his back and shoulders or a tiny cock. Their eyes met and Robbie knew that Jeff had come for him.

The squat massive figure of the master was surrounded by an entourage that included several strikingly handsome women and a beautiful young boy. Robbie recognized one of the women as Jeff's wife. Stuart was handing out drinks, assisted by Felix.

Robbie watched Picasso taking in everything around him. His eyes didn't dart but moved deliberately from one focal point to another, piercing everything that came within their range. He kept up a running commentary to anybody who happened to be listening, breaking into laughter easily. He moved briskly around the terrace, drawing his entourage with him, comparing the place to some other property, to the other's detriment. His eyes settled on Robbie and ran him through.

"Ah, the young painter," he greeted him. "One doesn't expect a painter to be so beautiful. Don't you agree, Raoul? Notice the hands. Remarkable. They don't belong to him. Perhaps they're the painter. Where do you work, young man?"

"I'll show you if it wouldn't be a bore for you. You don't have to look at my work. I don't have much anyway."

"One picture. Show me one picture that's been painted with spirit and I'll be satisfied."

Robbie sought Jeff's eyes once more and found them waiting attentively for his. He was thrilled by the need he saw in them but he remained determined not to give in to it. He turned and led the group across the glade and up the steps to his house. They all crowded in and stood near the easel. Picasso took a few steps into the room and looked around.

"You have this for your work at your age? You're a very fortunate young man." He turned to the pictures. Robbie had left the almost completed one on the easel. The other two were propped on the table beside it. Everybody moved in close around the master while his eyes tore the canvas on the easel to ribbons. He picked up one of the others. He handled it deftly, not touching the painted surface.

Robbie took a step back to give him room and came up against Jeff. Waiting fingertips strayed over the back of his naked thighs. He was immediately aroused. He let a hand creep around behind him and encountered hard flesh. He moved his hand over it and gripped it. His curiosity was satisfied. He knew now what he had decided to deny himself; it felt like a great deal. Fingers climbed up under the leg of his trunks and caressed the cleft between his buttocks. His heart pounded. To have Picasso holding his work while he held a hard cock was a lot to absorb all at once. The great man turned to him.

"You're very beautiful, young man. If you work hard, you may also be a painter. Continue."

The group seemed to exhale a collective breath of relief and everybody started to talk at once. If they were talking about Robbie, he didn't hear them. Tears stung his eyes. Picasso had told him he might be a painter. He wanted to throw his arms around the stocky figure and smother him with gratitude. He turned instinctively to Jeff and saw a glint of conquest harden in his eyes, coupled with humor as if he were amused to find him so easy to get. Robbie had indulged himself more than he should have only because he was sure he couldn't be had. What about the wife? Where could it happen? Certainly not here in Toni's house. Jeff joined his wife in a general exodus.

Robbie closed the door on the last of the visitors and fell onto the sofa and sat with his legs stretched out in front of him, his feet on the floor. He dropped his head onto the backrest and closed his eyes and waited to calm down. He was bursting with pride and self-confidence. You may be a painter. Continue. He wished that he either hadn't let Jeff distract him in his moment of triumph or that Toni's cure were working more quickly. He didn't want an eleventh man; he wanted only to experience again the passion of need he had known on a changing-room floor. Could a girl make him feel it?

He sat up and stretched hugely and let his body go slack. It had been a grueling ordeal. He hoped that everybody had gone. He was dying to tell his mother all about his showing and repeat the master's words.

He gave a hitch to his trunks and hurried out and went springing down through the terraces. There was nobody out around the house. He went to the statue and looked down at the beach. There was a scattering of people there, all wearing swimming things. He didn't see Picasso or others of his party but he saw Jeff. He too was in trunks. He was talking to Hilda. Robbie started down, reassembling his resistance.

As he approached, he could see that he wasn't going to be saved by blemishes. Like his head, Jeff's body was a luxury product, as polished and gleaming and groomed as a racehorse. It wasn't muscular but smoothly knit with a voluptuously fluid line. He could see no excess flesh anywhere on it yet it made a richly opulent impression. He had a heavy gold chain around his neck. Robbie had never seen a man wearing a necklace; it accented the opulence. His hand knew the feel of the bulge contained in his trunks.

Jeff looked up as he crossed the sand toward his mother and their eyes met once more. Jeff's took masterful possession of him; as far as he was concerned, Robbie was his. Robbie tore his eyes away and spotted Jeff's wife farther along the beach talking to one of their neighbors called George Petit. He saw that everybody had drinks as if they were going to stay awhile. Why did a married man get started on a thing like this? It was maddening. He wished Jeff would take his wife and go.

He dropped down beside his mother. She greeted him with a cry of delight. "Oh darling. It's been so exciting," she exclaimed. "M. Picasso was very impressed. I heard him talking to the others. He said to me, 'Your son may be one of the elect. See that he works.' Aren't you thrilled?"

"I'll say." He bubbled with proud laughter. "Do you remember how we used to sit on the beach while I made messes with watercolors? You should've kept those things. We could send them to the Louvre."

"Don't be silly, dearest. Of course I kept them. Every one."

"Did you know I was a genius even then? What a clever lady." They put their arms out to each other and kissed and sat back laughing.

"Now that you're a distinguished painter, I suppose I'll have to stop asking you to run errands. Would you mind terribly running up and telling Boldoni we'll be eleven for dinner? The Petits and Jeff and Betty Benjamin are staying."

Robbie tried not to let anything show in his face. He made his smile brighter. "When Picasso told you to make me work, I'm sure he didn't mean helping around the house. Okay. Just this once." He kissed her again and hugged her and stood.

He was careful not to let his eyes stray to Jeff as he left. The siege was going to last all evening. He found everybody in the kitchen excited about the great man's visit. He had to tell them all about it. Boldoni went off to his quarters and returned with a small smudged framed portrait of himself. Robbie had signed it in the corner.

"It was done by one of my distinguished clients," Boldoni said solemnly.

They all laughed and passed the little watercolor around and praised Robbie's childish effort. He was touched that Boldoni had kept it. He left them all gathered around it and was headed back for the steps down to the beach when he caught sight of Jeff standing uncertainly in the archway leading to the drive. He was carrying clothes over an arm. Jeff made it impossible to avoid him by calling Robbie's name. Robbie's muscles tensed as he reminded himself of all that was at stake with Toni and renewed his vow. He couldn't help the flutter of excitement in the pit of his stomach. He turned and made a little show of seeing Jeff for the first time and went over to him.

"You're a hard guy to corner," Jeff said with the glint of conquest in his eye. "You ran out on me last night. Why?"

Robbie started to pretend that he didn't know what he was talking about but realized that his having felt his cock made it difficult to assume an air of innocence. "What did you expect? I was with my parents."

"It's probably just as well. I wasn't organized. Your mother said she thought you were up here somewhere. She said to ask you to show me a room where I can change."

Jeff obviously thought he was organized now. Robbie resented his assuming that he had won. Feeling his cock wasn't the same as making love to him. "You could have done that down there," he pointed out, preparing to turn him down.

"So it seems, but I told your mother I wanted to soak in a tub. Some nerve. My wife's gone back to the hotel. She'll be at least an hour fixing herself up. We're all set. Your mother said I could wear what I came in."

"I see. Well, come on." He started for the inner court with Jeff at his side. He couldn't refuse to show him a room. He was momentarily trapped but he would find a chance to escape.

"This is a stunning place," his companion said. "The port's pretty wild, isn't it? A boy with your looks must have quite a time here."

"I don't go out much. I mean, we mostly go to people's houses."

"Luckily for me. I've been waiting to tell you that you've got the sexiest ass I've ever seen in my life."

"You're sexy all over," he said. He could acknowledge what was going on without giving in. "You know I think that. The trouble is—"

"We understand each other beautifully. We won't have any trouble."

"Yes, but you see—"

"I see, all right. You want my cock. It's very flattering with a kid half my age."

"I'm very attracted to you. I admit it. It's just that there's somebody else. I don't—"

"Denying yourself at your age? That's a bit premature, isn't it?"

"I'm not sure. These are the rooms. They're all about the same. You might as well take this one." He opened a door and stood back. Jeff gripped his arm firmly and pushed him through. He moved him out of the way and closed the door and locked it and stood in front of it, barring the exit. Robbie was sure he hadn't wanted it but here he was. A scuffle in the courtyard would have been ridiculous. Jeff's eyes were intent and purposeful.

"We're in luck. I don't think anybody saw us. Well, do we or don't we?"

Robbie attempted a last stand but his will had crumbled. He was here. It was exciting. "I shouldn't. I—"

"That was a rhetorical question," Jeff said sharply. "Take that thing off. I want to see you with a hard on." He tossed the clothes and the toilet case he was carrying onto the bed.

Robbie felt the compulsion of their shared hunger. Only a man who was determined to have him could stir him to a complete awareness of himself. There was so much in him that nobody had yet touched. He was trembling with excitement and had some difficulty disentangling his erection from his trunks while Jeff watched. He straightened and stood naked in front of him. Jeff took a long look.

"That's quite a cock," he said. "You're an anatomical masterpiece." He hooked his thumbs into his trunks and peeled them off. His erection swung out toward Robbie. Robbie stared. It was just enough bigger than his own to inspire awe of its phallic majesty. He couldn't ignore its command. He dropped down and ran his tongue along it and watched it lift majestically. He opened his mouth for it and offered it his obeisance.

"You really know how to suck cock," Jeff murmured after a

moment. He gripped his hair and made several slow deep thrusts. "Do you want me to come like this?"

Robbie shook his hands off and released him and sprang up. "No. Take my sexy ass. Your cock gives me goose bumps. I want it inside me." They reached for each other and their mouths opened for a wrenching, writhing kiss. Jeff's luxurious body was more powerful than it looked. They broke apart, breathing heavily.

"We don't want to wreck the bed," Jeff said. He grabbed his toilet case and they hurried each other into the bathroom while he unsnapped it and took out a tube. They sank down onto the bath mat, grappling with each other. Their coupling was athletic and unrestrained. Robbie cried out once, "Oh God, it's good," as he was filled and possessed once more. Need incited need. He battled to release his darkest yearnings. His craving to deliver himself completely was deeper and more imperative than he'd realized. He didn't see how he could go without it again for so long.

When it was over they lay panting on the floor together until Jeff withdrew slowly and leaped up and went to the shower. Robbie struggled up and washed himself on the bidet. He was drying himself when the shower curtain was pushed back and Jeff reappeared, as sleek and glistening as a seal. Robbie looked at the handsome stranger, incredulous that their bodies had been joined in passionate possession and surrender. With his hair in disarray, he looked more vulnerable, younger, less unattainably worldly. He didn't know why he'd thought he could resist him. Jeff looked at him with unsatisfied lust in his eyes.

"That was the best ever," he said. "You're sensational."

"Do you want it again?" Robbie asked, approaching and handing him a towel.

"That goes without saying. My wife drinks, God bless her. We'll manage." He began to dry himself slowly, eying Robbie's body.

"If you like boys, why're you married?"

"One doesn't necessarily exclude the other. She's rich, for one thing. I can hardly marry a rich boy, worse luck. Look at me. I've fallen for a boy who's young enough to be my son. What would I do if I *weren't* married?"

"How old do you think I am?"

"No more than twenty? Having children at fifteen is unusual but it's possible. Last night, I told myself to go slow but I knew I was going to have you. All the organization was worth it."

"Organization?"

"Why do you think we're here? I made the big boss change his plans so I could come here with him. I gave my wife the idea that she wanted to go back to the hotel. I let your mother think I was a bit pushy by asking for a room. I knew I'd find you waiting somewhere."

"That was an accident. I didn't want it to happen."

"Of course you did. You still do. Are you thinking about the famous Toni? I've heard. Isn't it good in the hay?"

"Not really. He likes girls. I'm in love with him."

"I could make you forget him. If we were in New York, I'd take you on permanently." They dropped their towels over the side of the tub and moved in against each other, their hands roaming to re-create the ecstasy they had offered each other. Their tongues played together. Their cocks stirred and lengthened. It was turning into something more important than Robbie had bargained for. A man wanted him; love had blinded him to how much he needed it. He wanted to give himself in some unimaginable way so that there wasn't any part of himself that hadn't been possessed. Jeff drew back and lifted his hands to his face and caressed it with his fingertips.

"You're incredibly beautiful. I guess we can risk another half hour. What does a wife do if she finds her husband in bed with a boy? Probably screams her head off and then laughs at him for the rest of his life. Will anybody wonder where you are?"

"They'll think I've gone back to the house. Your wife doesn't know about you?"

"Nothing specific. We'll try to keep it that way." He pulled a fresh towel from the rack and picked up the tube of lubricant. "We might as well go to bed. Your mother will think I had a nap and never allow me in the house again." He put an arm around him and led him back to the bedroom. "Your work's good, you know. The big boss wouldn't've said so if he hadn't meant it. When you get around to showing, you'll get in touch with me and we'll do business together."

"That won't be for a long time. You'll have forgotten me by then."

"I might forget a painter but I'm not likely to forget the sexiest boy I've ever known." He pulled the cover off the bed and spread out the towel and they lay in each other's arms, their erections hard against each other again. "I'm going to give your cock some of the attention it deserves." He began to move his mouth down over him.

"I want you to fuck me again."

"That, too. If you were mine, I'd suck you off at least twenty times a day and fuck you as often as I could get it up."

"Are you as crazy about sucking cock as I am?"

Jeff held Robbie's upright and kissed it. "I'll show you."

Robbie whimpered ecstatically. "I'm going to come," he gasped. Jeff nodded and applied lubricant to him while he received his ejaculation. Their bodies slid around and fitted in against each other intricately and thrillingly and Jeff entered him. "Oh God, yes. Take me," Robbie cried.

"Is my cock good, honey?"

"Sublime. Oh yes. Take me with it. Let me give myself to your big cock. I'd like it there all night."

"We'll see what we can do about that."

Robbie slipped back to his house to change for dinner. He didn't encounter anybody but he wasn't particularly worried about that; nobody would suspect what had happened. Thinking of Toni, he was sad and ashamed that he had been able to forget him for so long. It was more regret than guilt. Toni didn't want him. He wanted him to have girls. Robbie knew that his needs were too deeply fixed in him to change. Whether Toni believed it or not, he was a homosexual. He needed a man to love him, or at least to make love to him. Nothing had happened with Jeff that could equal the happiness of one minute with Toni but the passion they could generate together was electrifying. The only way he could atone for his broken promise was to refuse Jeff later, but he would be ready for the twelfth man. There would always be another until he found out everything he could know about himself.

Jeff's wife returned for cocktails. After dinner, everybody wandered around the terrace drinking brandy and talking in shifting combinations. Jeff found a moment for a private exchange with Robbie.

"My cock's very ready for you," he said. "Betty's riding high. A few more brandies and a sleeping pill should do the trick. I'll forget my toilet case in the room and come back for it. Wait around for me. I'll allow time for the others to go. Hilda and Alex are about to call it a night."

"No, we mustn't," Robbie protested in an undertone. "I've thought about it. It's too dangerous. What if somebody saw you!"

Jeff's smile remained confident and possessive. "You're in experienced hands. I won't do anything to compromise us. I have to protect myself too, you know. Just follow my lead and don't worry." He was perched on the balustrade and shifted his legs to reveal the long thick ridge of his cock. "Think of that in you."

It looked even bigger than it actually was. Robbie admitted to himself that if they were locked in a room he wouldn't be able to keep his hands off it. For the sake of everything that was most sacred and precious to him, he had to make sure that they weren't locked in a room again. What if Toni came home unexpectedly? "Please. Try to understand," he said earnestly. "I told you I shouldn't. I'd never forgive myself if I let it happen again. I've promised Toni. I can't explain it. Please believe me."

"We shall see. I'm not going to beg." His conqueror's eyes looked undaunted.

"Thanks. I'm sorry." Robbie felt as if he had taken a step toward redeeming himself. He was able to deny desire, if somewhat belatedly. He hoped Jeff understood that he'd been turned down.

They mingled again with the others and the guests soon began to make their departures. Betty was unsteady on her feet and clung to Jeff for support. As they moved toward the archway, Robbie was struck by inspiration.

"Didn't you have a toilet case with you?" he asked Jeff.

"So I did. What a clever boy."

"Did you leave it in the room? I'll run get it." Virtue sharpened the wits. He knew from the anger he caught in Jeff's eyes that he had still been planning to come back for him. He avoided looking at him when he returned with the case and politely performed his duties as a junior host. When they were all gone, he said a hasty goodnight to his parents and hurried back to his house. Their house. Toni's house. Being in it helped him to think his way back into the person Toni wanted him to be.

He was going through a difficult period but his beloved friend was helping him over it. Any day now he would fall for a girl. The innocent physical play Toni permitted them was enough to satisfy his still undirected sexuality. He didn't really want to feel Jeff's body against his again. He went over Picasso's memorable words. He was a painter. That was the main thing.

The day had exhausted him. His body was eased by Jeff's possession of it. He had resisted temptation finally. He slept.

He was awakened by movement in the bed. Consciousness returned with a rush of contentment as he reached out to Toni. His hands encountered the body he had denied himself and his heart stopped. He tried to scramble away but Jeff was on him, pinning him down. A lamp snapped on. Robbie blinked in the sudden light. All his body responded to the naked body on top of him, even while he fought him off. Jeff looked down at him and laughed. Fingers delved between his buttocks and applied lubricant. Robbie twisted his hips and thrashed about, trying to free himself.

"No. Oh God, no. Not here," he cried.

"We mustn't desecrate the chaste matrimonial sheets? I like it here." He bent Robbie's arm behind him and got a painful grip on it and lifted him so that he was sprawled out on his back with his head against Jeff's abdomen. He wanted to hide the evidence of his desire but pain forced him to lie still and expose it. Jeff's erection prodded the side of his face. "There, you little cocksucker. God, what a body. A big young cock wanting me. Okay. I'll take your beautiful ass." He exerted additional pressure on Robbie's arm and flipped him over onto his stomach and straddled him. "There. Lift up. Put it in you. Don't you wish yours was as big? In you, dammit."

"No. I beg of you. You're raping me. Oh God. Please. Not here."

"It's exciting, isn't it? He might walk in any minute. This may teach you not to play games with older men. Beautiful boys drive us wild. Come on. It's not rape if you want it. Struggle, damn you."

"I can't." Robbie was overcome by tears. "Do it. Oh God, do it. Quickly. Don't let him find us." Robbie surrendered to his need while his body was shaken by sobs. It didn't matter if he found them. He couldn't go on pretending with him.

He continued to weep quietly long after Jeff was gone. He was vile. All queers were vile. How could he hope for anybody decent to care for him? Everything that he cherished in himself and found beautiful was an illusion. He was nothing but a cocksucker. He had defiled Toni's house, his bed, his trust. He forced himself to get up and change the sheets but he didn't think he would ever be able to lie with him in peace again.

When Toni finally slipped into bed beside him, he couldn't bring himself to welcome him but grunted in simulated sleep and rolled away from him.

Toni grinned as he settled back to sleep. He was curing his young friend of his obsession with him. Girls would be next.

To his amazement, Robbie was able to face Toni the next day as if nothing had happened. Something had stretched and relaxed in him so that he no longer felt a need to prove himself. There was nothing left to prove. He was what he was. Toni would eventually find out. His love remained intact, tempered by the deepening awareness that an impossible change would have to take place in both of them before it could offer any real rewards.

Toni gave his final performance two days later and Robbie was faced with a month of their being together more constantly than before. Would he be able to preserve Toni's illusions that long? He was eager for Carl's imminent arrival; he needed guidance. There was a phone call from Marseilles and then Carl was there, blonder, more bronzed, more radiant than ever. He looked at them all and seemed to say, "So. I have arrived. Now life can begin." His youthful high spirits were infectious. Within an hour, Toni felt as if the family had acquired another member.

Carl had arrived before lunch and was given a tour of the house. He was stunned by it and said so with flattering enthusiasm. Stuart had made no secret of having made a considerable fortune in real estate but Carl hadn't been prepared for anything like this. It was a small principality. He noted its privacy and its strategic location at the entrance to the bay. It was a find; he was already enlarging his plans for the future.

"Come on, Toni, we've got to show him *our* house," Robbie exclaimed.

The three of them climbed up together. "Don't let me look at your pictures," he said to Robbie. "I am seeing too much at once. Later, I will come and we will look at them and I will be able to really see them." He noted the double bed. He saw the way Robbie looked at his friend. He had subjected Toni to close scrutiny. The godlike serenity of his good looks would be a magnet to men inclined that way but he found no trace in him of the availability that he had always detected in equivocal male beauties. Robbie was in love with him. How far did Toni's indulgence go? The circumstances of his being here,

316

which had been explained, intrigued him. It confirmed the emptiness he had sensed in Stuart's life. He sorted out the explosive elements in the situation and saw how easy it would be to precipitate a crisis. Something to keep in mind.

When Robbie rose from the lunch table to go back to work, Carl got up too. "May I come with you? I want to see what you're doing and then I'll leave you in peace."

"Come on, but don't forget I'm a genius. You're supposed to stand in front of the canvas in hushed amazement." He looked at Toni and pledged himself to him with his eyes before facing the unpredictable hazards of being alone with Carl.

"Now you must tell me everything," Carl said as they started up through the terraces. "You're in love."

"You can tell?"

"Of course."

"Can everybody?"

"Only those who are looking for it, I think. He's so deeply and openly fond of you that it appears very innocent. I would never have guessed that he's your lover."

"He isn't. Not really." Robbie was still explaining his peculiar relationship with Toni when they reached the house. They stood facing each other beside his worktable.

"So. You're in love but you are not having a love affair," Carl summed up. "How long do you think that can go on?"

"I don't know. As long as he'll let it. Did you expect us to be lovers again?"

Carl drew him close and kissed him on the mouth. He felt the control he still exercised over the boy and was satisfied. He gripped his shoulders firmly and drew back. "You don't want us to be while you're in love with Toni, do you?"

"I know I shouldn't. I wouldn't dream of it if things were different. Can I come to you if I get desperate? It's hard to do without something I need so much."

"You two must stop playing games with each other. You must tell him that you're not going to want girls, that you want only him."

"But it's not just that he isn't like that. He hates anybody who is."

"Nonsense, my dear. He doesn't hate you. Seduce him. You already have, I think. He's not a homosexual but anybody is capable of homosexual love at least once in their life. I will talk to him about you."

"I knew I needed you here," he said with grateful affection. Carl was the one known, stable element in his life. Only he could help him break the stalemate of his passion.

Carl kissed him again, briefly and lightly this time. "We're allies. We will always be able to count on each other. Now I wish to be shown a work of genius."

Robbie laughed. "Well, a *budding* genius." Two canvases were finished now and he had made great progress on the third and started a fourth. He propped them all up around the easel and waited uneasily while Carl looked. His work was growing too important for him not to care what people thought of it. Carl was really looking at it.

"I have been looking at paintings all my life," he said finally, "and I still don't trust my own judgment. I see here great strength, an almost frightening intensity of expression. It's so dense, Robbie. I will have to look again and again. It is foolish to say that I *like* these things. They excite and fascinate me and make me want to see what you will do next."

"That's good enough for a budding genius." He laughed with proud relief. He was apparently doing something that people connected with. Toni refused to comment on the grounds that he knew nothing about art but he often watched Robbie at work and hugged him and nodded with mute approval. Robbie had asked his mother to wait until he had at least three things finished but he couldn't expect her to be objective. Carl counted. "Now you know everything about me," he said.

"And very fortunate I am, my dear young friend. I'll leave you to your fascinating work. Till later."

Carl's success continued that evening with the friends who had been invited for drinks to welcome him. Rather crossly, Helene restored him to the head of her list of attractive men. He easily outshone all the others. She watched him charm Hilda and Jane Cumberleigh and several others, and noted with approval that his charm wasn't as superficial as the old Greek lady had suggested at their first meeting. He charmed them because he liked them. He charmed her because he liked her more.

He turned to her constantly for her opinion and didn't leave her side for long. Perhaps because she had recovered her social ease and was no longer flustered by men's attentions, she felt far less impregnable than she had in Greece. When she felt his attention straying, she made an effort to hold it. She was very aware of the splendid body under the immaculate white clothes. Lending herself to the usual give-and-take between the sexes risked leading her too far. When their eyes met and held for a second too long, her heart gave a warning flutter of desire. She told herself that after he had been with them a few days, she would get used to him and recover her sangfroid. He made no attempt to disguise the fact that he was still determined to have her. She must find a way to enjoy him without encouraging him too much.

Only the admiral struck a sour note. "I say, that's the chap I told you about," he said to Stuart, drawing him aside.

"Told me about?" Stuart repeated.

"Yes, wasn't it you? Perhaps it was your good wife. Don't like to speak about it, but I rather think I ought, you know. Dirty bit of goods, von Eschenstadt. Knew him years ago in Cairo. Ran off with a chap's wife and afterward bled him white. Blackmail, that's what it amounted to. No saint myself, but one must draw a line."

"Don't you think it might have been a misunderstanding?" Stuart suggested uncomfortably. "People often get these stories garbled."

"Quite so, but I knew the chap. Whole thing took place right under my nose. Awkward running into him here."

"Well, yes, it is," Stuart agreed. It was awkward to hear such a story about somebody who had become a friend. Should he speak to Carl about it? None of their new friends were saints but this was the life their money had bought them and Helene was enjoying herself. The season would be over soon. It had brought them Toni. He was worth all the rest. "Do you feel you have to cut him or anything of that sort?" Stuart asked.

"A little late in the day for anything drastic," the admiral admitted. "I shall simply give him a wide berth. Thought I should explain."

"Yes, of course. I'm glad you did," Stuart said, relieved that there weren't going to be any scenes.

He and Carl were returning to the terrace after seeing off the last of the guests when Carl referred to the story himself. "He is a real character, your admiral, no?" he said easily. "Did he tell you what a scoundrel I am?"

"He told me a story."

"It is not the most admirable episode of my career," Carl said with a candid smile. "I was still young enough to believe that love excuses everything. The lady felt she had a right to certain sums of money from her husband. I agreed to get

319

them for her. Of course, everybody thought it was for myself and I felt very heroic sacrificing my good name for a beautiful woman. Shortly after the lady had her money, she left me."

Stuart laughed. He had known it would turn out to be something of the sort. He would set the admiral straight.

During dinner and the evening that followed, the five of them achieved a harmony that was peculiarly their own. Carl was the ringleader in providing boisterous fun and the others played off him, dazzling each other with the pleasure they found in each other's company. Toni was profiting from his freedom by integrating himself fully into family life. His Mado was gone. Robbie suspected that there had been jealous scenes with Michèle; she had faded from the picture. He was between girls. He seemed to be in no hurry to find a new one. He'd told the Coslings that it was such a relief not to be making his nightly appearances that he didn't care if he didn't leave the place for the rest of the summer.

"Shall we give another great party for Carl?" Helene asked as dinner was drawing to a close. "The first one was the talk of the town. We'll have to think of something sensational if we expect to outdo ourselves."

"Please. Spare me," Carl protested. "Whenever people talk about giving a sensational party it always turns out to be fancy dress. I can never decide what I want to be."

"We could make it fancy un-dress," she suggested. "These two in nothing but loincloths the way Toni did his act—that would give people something lovely to look at. But we're half naked most of the time anyway. I hear there's a beach right out at the end they call Tahiti where people wear nothing at all. We'll have to be more original than that."

They went on tossing fanciful ideas about. Stuart watched her slightly aloof grandeur dropping from her like discarded veils. She'd probably had an extra glass or two of wine. Her eyes sparkled. She was almost girlish. Robbie felt it when he left the table with her. She hooked her hand under his arm and pressed herself against him. He looked down at her and smiled and caught an almost flirtatious look in her eyes. Things were changing between them. He had felt it vaguely for the last few weeks but tonight it was so pronounced that it was impossible to overlook. The mother-son demarkation was getting blurred; they were becoming more aware of each other as people. He was beginning to think of her as a contemporary. The way she held him now gave him an odd little thrill that was almost sexual. It startled him. Was it possible that she was leading him to girls? He realized how comforting it would be if he could feel like this with a girl. No more deception. No more hidden lust. No more fear of discovery. He couldn't seriously hope for it but he supposed it might be a faint possibility.

"Aren't you pleased he's here?" she asked so pointedly that he wondered if she'd guessed about Carl, too. "Toni likes him, doesn't he?"

"Oh yes. He says he's like another brother." Carl and Toni were still at table, finishing their wine. He wondered if Carl was talking about him. What could he possibly say? Carl would know how to handle it.

The two youths left their elders still drinking companionably at midnight. "I love being on vacation," Toni said on their way up to the house. "No more asses to kiss until I'm back in Paris. Don't let me get silly about some girl, little brother. I want to be with you for the rest of the summer." Robbie held his hand in silent happiness until they had closed their door behind them. "Shall we have some wine to put us to sleep?"

Robbie followed him to the kitchenette and watched him open a chilled bottle and fill two glasses. He moved in close to him to take his. Toni ran his fingers through his hair and held his neck. Robbie put a hand on his shoulder and looked into his great tranquil green eyes. His curls had smoothed out into waves. He looked more down-to-earth and ordinary, more farmboy than sylvan god. Robbie found the new natural Toni less glamorous and utterly endearing.

"I talked to Carl about you," Toni said, looking at him thoughtfully. "Did you tell him anything about us?"

"I told him I'm in love with you and that you don't want me to be a *pédé*."

"You've been to bed with him?"

"Yes. He was one of the nine or ten or whatever it is."

"I thought so. It puzzles me. Why would he want you when he obviously wants women? I guess some men can make their own rules. He seems to think I should enjoy you while I've got you. Why does he think I'd enjoy it? That's what I don't understand."

Robbie took a long swallow of his wine and hoped he knew how to take advantage of what Carl had tried to do for him. "Because you say you love me. He doesn't think I should pretend that you're curing me," he said slowly. "He accepts the fact that I'm queer. He made love to me as if—well, as if I were a girl, so I guess he knows. At times, when I feel you're never going to want me, I start thinking about others. I don't want to but I can't help it."

"Other men?"

"Yes."

"But there haven't been any others since I've been here, have there?"

"Yes. One. He came with Pic—"

"You filthy little pig," Toni cried. "I warned you I'd go if that happened." He struck him hard across the face with the flat of his hand. Robbie's ears were still ringing from the blow when his glass was snatched from him and Toni's arms were around him and he was kissing him where he'd hit him. "No. Please. Oh God. I'm sorry, little brother. I didn't hurt you, did I?" He continued to murmur incoherently until Robbie kissed him in return. He held him close. "There. I love you so much that I almost wish I *were* queer. We belong together, I know that. I don't know what's happening to me. I get so wildly jealous. I can't stand thinking of Carl having you, or Edward or anybody else. I won't *let* anybody else have you. Come to bed, little brother." Toni picked up the glasses and the bottle and gave him a little push toward the door. Robbie's heart was beating with reckless elation. Something had happened. He'd made Toni jealous. Perhaps he'd seduced him.

Toni put down the wine on the bedside table and quickly pulled off his clothes and turned to Robbie with an erection. Robbie stared at it, thrilled and amazed. Except in the sea, he had never had an erection with him without some preliminary stimulation. Toni saw the direction of his eyes.

"Yes, I want you with it," he asserted vehemently. "I want to make you belong to me but I don't know how. Everything would be wonderful but we can't change our bodies. I won't suck your cock. I wish you didn't want to suck mine. There's nothing about your body I want." He approached as Robbie removed the last of his clothes. "I like to look at it and touch it. I want *you*. I don't see what I can do about it."

"Take me the way I want you to," Robbie begged. "It won't be disgusting. Why don't you take me?"

"Because you're not a girl." It burst out like an accusation. "I won't treat you like one or let you act like one." He turned and flung back the bedclothes and pushed Robbie down. He fell beside him and gathered him into his arms. When their mouths met, Toni's was hungrily passionate in a way it had

322

never been before. Robbie responded with all the love and passion that was in him. Their bodies writhed urgently against each other. Their kiss deepened and endured. Toni slid up on top of him and worked his hips in simulated copulation. Robbie could feel the need in him at last and all of him opened out to meet it. He moved his body and thrust it up to blend with Toni's. Their erections clashed and strained against each other and their breath grew labored. They were one and together and loved each other.

Their mouths broke apart with simultaneous cries and they shouted together while their bodies leaped and thrashed about with their orgasms. They remained as they were, Toni lying on Robbie, while their breathing subsided.

"There," Toni said finally. He lifted his head and looked into Robbie's eyes and was stirred by the love that glowed in them. "Is that enough for you, little brother? That's the only way two guys can make love without turning into perverts. Cocksuckers. Sodomites. We've got to stick to the way our bodies are made. Do you feel how much I want you now? Is that enough to make you belong to me?"

"Oh God, yes. If we can have that, I don't need anything else. Nobody else will ever have me."

"No. We'll pretend we're shipwrecked on a desert island. If we were, we'd be doing things like that soon enough. I don't want you to suck my cock anymore. Is that something you think you need?"

"No. I want to make love to you everywhere but I won't there if you don't want me to. You said you liked it."

"I do but I hate for *you* to like it. Girls do. I want us to love each other like men. You're not some special third sex. Everybody has some female in him, you maybe more than most, but you're a man. I love you as a man. If that's queer, I can't help it."

"You'll still want girls."

"Naturally, but they can wait. I just want you for a little while. Do you understand? I'll be your lover always if you don't make me feel like a pervert. I feel so good with you."

"Oh God, Toni. You don't know. When you say things like that I feel as if I've got everything I could ever want in life." His eyes filled with ecstatic tears.

"It's true." He kissed him and rolled away from him and lay on his back. "We better wash up. What a mess. That's part of it, I suppose—our sperm all mixed up together. I wish it were possible for two guys to fuck a girl at the same time.

323

That's what I'd really like—you and me in the same girl. What an idea. Come on before I get hard again."

Carl and Helene had their first time alone together the next morning on the beach. Stuart had gone into town on some errand and the boys had not yet appeared. She and the German were stretched out side by side on deck chairs wearing swimming things. Helene was alert and slightly on edge, wondering if he would take this opportunity to renew the declarations he had made in Greece. Keeping her eyes off his body required a much greater effort than she remembered; he was a magnificent physical specimen. The sun gave her an excuse to keep her eyes closed.

"You know why I have come here," he said after a brief silence.

"Because we invited you, I should think," she said lightly while her heart began to beat uncomfortably.

"I wouldn't have needed an invitation. I would have come. Life was intolerable without you."

She uttered a peal of laughter and all her slightly jangled nerves smoothed out. She didn't have to fence with him; she could take him or leave him. She would leave him of course, except that it didn't have to be as simple as that. If life was intolerable without her, she could relax in the pleasure of his company without having to be constantly on her toes to please him. If she wasn't trying to please him, she would be less conscious of them as male and female. "Really, Carl," she protested mildly, "what do you expect to gain by saying things like that? Where does it lead?"

"Into my arms, of course." His smile was youthful but assured.

"I should think you've already been here long enough to see how impossible it is to conduct an illicit affair. We're all together all the time. Nobody has any privacy except Robbie up in his little house. One would have to be awfully rash and determined to even consider it. I'm afraid we're both too old to be either."

"I'm not proposing an affair. I'm proposing a life. I would settle for no less."

She laughed again. He was making it easier and easier for her. She let her eyes roam over his handsome body. An affair with him might be tempting under favorable circumstances; what he was suggesting was too farfetched to require comment. "No wonder you're still a happy-go-lucky bachelor if you always insist on your affairs lasting a lifetime."

324

"I've bided my time. I have always known I would find the right woman before I was forty. I've let it go till the last minute, perhaps, but I am no longer in a hurry." He sat back and admired her heroic beauty. He had never known a beautiful woman to successfully renounce passion. She was at the height of her ripe maturity, waiting to be plucked. He had no intention of forcing it but would give her a week or two, or perhaps more, to come to him. When her passion had been reawakened, she would fall as completely under his control as Robbie.

"You mustn't blame me when you discover you've been brought here by an illusion," she said complacently after another brief silence. "I warned you my life was made. It shouldn't take you more than a day or two to see it for yourself."

"So? This place is a beautiful shell. I've seen that already. Robbie is the only life here. Robbie and Toni."

"Congratulations. I didn't think you were capable of saying an unflattering word to a woman. Are they having a love affair?"

"There is much love between them. I don't know how far they go in expressing it. Toni isn't a homosexual."

"Good heavens, of course not. Do you think we'd have him here if he were? I wasn't suggesting anything vile. I meant a platonic love affair of the sort boys have at that age."

He listened carefully to her choice of words. It didn't suit him yet to pursue the subject; there were other aspects of this situation he could exploit to propel her into his arms. He sat forward and looked at her. "Robbie has developed extraordinarily in the two months since I've seen him. His physical attraction is quite mesmerizing."

"Yes. I might not have put it quite that way but I've noticed it too."

"Of course. You're falling in love with him. I have come in time to save you from that."

She stared at him for a paralyzed instant. Her hands flew to her ears as if she could block his words. Blood rushed to her cheeks. Why did she think she could relax with him? He was the devil incarnate. Her mouth dropped open and she shook her head dazedly. "You're evil," she said barely above a whisper. "How could you dare say such a thing to me?" He looked coolly self-confident. A little smile played around his finely modeled lips.

"Come, come," he said. "Do you think it so terrible

because you know it's true? I'm sure it happens quite often and is sternly repressed. It would be the greatest calamity that could befall you. All your hoarded passion would wither and die. You would lose forever your chance for a full life. I won't let it happen to you."

"You must be mad," she said, recovering her voice and slowly stemming the flood of her horror. "If you mean I'm becoming aware of him physically, how could it be otherwise? I'm sure most mothers are thrown off balance by suddenly facing a young man, after living for years with a child. In Robbie's case, a strikingly attractive young man, as you've just pointed out. To call it falling in love is sheer madness. I don't think I'll ever forgive you for it."

"You will, my dear, when you come to realize what I've helped you escape."

"Really, Carl. I don't want to continue this conversation." She gathered up her book and the other odds and ends she had with her and rose. He noticed that her hands were trembling slightly. He admired her elegant carriage as she left. He had planted the seeds. He would nurture them to a fine flowering. He was resigned to the fact that it was impossible to get along in the world without, however inadvertently, trampling on others, but for once he didn't think anybody was going to get seriously hurt. Even Stuart might end by thanking him.

Helene felt anything but thankful to Carl. He had set up a train of thought that seemed to have no end. She couldn't deny that she had felt odd stirrings recently in Robbie's presence. She had dreamed of seeing him naked in all his thrilling young virility. He was part of her. It was natural to want to know her own creation. The thought of any real physical intimacy with him repelled her. She wouldn't dream of allowing him to see her naked. How could anybody say she was falling in love with him?

When she returned to the beach before lunch, Robbie and Toni had joined Carl. As beautifully developed physiques, there was little to choose between them except for a sort of raw power that was distinctively Carl's. Youth endowed Toni and Robbie with a special shining grace. Since Toni had stopped working, there had been small differences in the way they treated each other that were growing more pronounced. Their constant touching was filled with hidden caresses. When he looked at Robbie, Toni eyes were filled with gloating tenderness.

She observed them closely now. Robbie was practicing handstands under Toni's tutelage. Toni placed his hand very near Robbie's crotch as he supported his legs in the air. His hand moved and they laughed as Robbie dropped down and sprang to his feet. Boys could touch each other there without thinking anything of it. She didn't need Carl to tell her that Toni wasn't a homosexual. He hadn't said it about Robbie, as if there were no need to state the obvious. The boys sparred playfully with each other and jostled each other into the sea. She felt not the slightest trace of jealousy. A woman falling in love with either of them would be automatically jealous of their happiness with each other.

She turned to her tormentor and resumed her seat beside him. She must face up to him once and for all. If he had talked about her falling in love with Robbie in order to make her question everything she had been and everything she had become, he had succeeded. She had sacrificed passion for peace and contentment. Was her life the poorer for it? He had yet to convince her that it was but she hadn't wondered for years.

"Has Stuart come back?" he asked unexpectedly, lying out with his eyes closed.

"Yes. He's going over some bills in his study. Did you want to see him?"

"No, no. I have been wondering about privacy. He has been gone most of the morning. Do you know where he's been?"

"As much as I need to know. This house has to be kept running. Are you suggesting that he's been with a girl?" She said it witheringly but was reminded that that was where he *had* been once upon a time when he went off on errands.

"I'm suggesting that people who have been together for many years don't usually check up on each other every minute of the day and night. If you think of your days, I'm sure you would find many hours when neither of you has the slightest idea what the other is doing."

"So you're thinking of a clandestine affair after all."

"No, no, but we must have each other sooner or later so that we will know where we wish to go from there. I'm accustomed to a nap in the afternoon in hot climates. I will be waiting. Half an hour can alter a whole life."

She looked at his body again and at his handsome face in repose. With his lively eyes closed, it was curiously peaceful. She allowed herself to imagine being held in his powerful arms and her heart accelerated. She took a quick breath and shook her head to dispel the thought.

"I'm afraid I'll have to avoid any private conversation with you," she said, resuming her grandest manner. "I decided to ignore what you said about Robbie. Now this. You have the effrontery to suggest that I'd come sneaking to your room like some common trollop."

He opened his eyes and looked at her and winked. He threw his head back with full-throated laughter and sprang up and went racing down into the sea after the two boys.

She was left seething with frustrated indignation. It didn't matter what she said to him or how she treated him. Everything bounced off his self-confident air of knowing her better than she knew herself. She could at least retain enough poise and dignity to let him make all the moves in whatever game he thought they were playing.

He had arrived in a racy little convertible that he'd bought in Marseilles. Several times when they went out in the evening she rode with him. It would have been easy for him to take the wrong turning, to stop on a deserted road, to make love to her, not in a real sense but enough to break down her guard. He was always a model of gentlemanly deportment. They always arrived at their destination just ahead, or on the heels, of the others. In spite of herself, she wished increasingly that he would do something that she could come to grips with. Did he really think she was going to fling herself on him?

When he'd been there a week, he announced to the assembled family that he'd decided to rent a house of his own. There was a chorus of protests.

"We're losing our customers," Stuart commented. "We'd better fire the staff."

"I can't live with you for the rest of my life, my friend. I like it here. I haven't settled anywhere for quite a long time. A year or so here should be most agreeable. Who knows? It might become permanent."

"Well, it'll be one more house where we'll be invited to parties," Robbie said. "Do you know where it'll be?"

"Somebody told me last night of a farmhouse that is just remodeled. Not on the sea but close. Furnished, of course. I am not so domesticated that I want to start buying curtains. That may come." Carl glanced at Helene.

She remained silent. She saw the move as his answer to the

problem of privacy and it alarmed her. Did he know that she would come to him once the danger of discovery had been removed? He had been right about their days. There were many hours when Stuart wouldn't notice her absence and there were many easy explanations to offer him if he did. She caught herself thinking about Robbie. What if Robbie, with his quick perception, felt a change in her relationship with Carl? Was there something unnatural about not wanting her son to suspect her of an involvement with another man? Must she force herself to give in to Carl in order to prove that her feelings for Robbie were purely maternal?

Carl's decision continued to trouble her and nag at her nerves for the rest of the day. She awoke the next morning with it still on her mind. She and Stuart had breakfast in bed as usual. Could he help her? Perhaps she could lead him to take some stand that would eliminate Carl. The old grateful feeling of utter dependence on him revived in her.

"I'm not sure I'm pleased about Carl moving quite so firmly into our lives," she said experimentally. "I mean, taking a house and so forth. Don't you think he's rather rushing it?"

He looked at her over the top of the morning paper. "I don't see that it makes much difference what we think. The whole peninsula is open to the public. We have only ourselves to blame."

"Yes, but you might be able to discourage him. You could point out the drawbacks. It's awfully quiet here during the winter. Perhaps he doesn't know how beastly the weather can get. You could make it clear that we're planning to spend some time in Paris. It's a bit odd his deciding to settle in so quickly."

"Is it?" He put the paper aside, astonished. He'd thought she was as pleased as everybody else to have him here. He heard an incomprehensible note of anxiety in her voice and gave her his full attention. "I have the impression that that's the sort of life he's led—moving in wherever it strikes his fancy. He has friends here and there along the coast. People take to the life here very easily. Why not Carl?"

"I'm simply not sure we want to make such a friend of him. Jane Cumberleigh told me a story that I haven't wanted to repeat. It—"

"About blackmail in Egypt? The admiral told me and Carl told me about it himself. There's not much to it."

"Perhaps not, but that's not the only thing. Alex asked me

not to say anything, but he thinks the statue is a fake. Something about the marble. He seems to know a lot about such things."

"A fake what? It's a statue. Carl told us himself that it's probably a Hellenistic copy. I can't see what the statue has to do with him."

"He arranged it all. You handed over quite a large sum of money. Maybe nobody cared whether we took it." Faced with slightly amused indifference, she felt increasingly cornered. In the old days he would have taken charge by now, explaining to her what she was trying to say. Couldn't he understand that she felt threatened or had they both reached the point of not caring what the other did? She tried again. "The point is, where does he get his money?"

"Where does anybody get their money, old dear? Where does Alex get his? For quite a small community, there's an amazing number of people with no visible means of support. Carl fits in very nicely."

"You can say what you like but there's one bothersome little thing after another. I just don't feel we can trust him."

He pushed his tray aside. Something was wrong; it didn't hang together. He'd seen how much she enjoyed herself in his company. If she was getting bored with him, why make a point about trusting him? It would be easy to start seeing less of him once he was out of the house. He felt a sudden hard kick of jealousy in the pit of his stomach. Unlike the little flutters of jealousy he'd felt in Greece, it carried the dread weight of certainty. She was making a case of him. It was unlike her unless he had really got under her skin. Perhaps she had already committed herself in some way and was trying to back out.

He pulled himself out of bed and went to the low table in front of the window to get a cigarette. He lighted it and puffed on it, taking time to compose himself. He turned back to her. "I'm ready to believe that he might be a dubious character, but what do you expect us to do about it in a practical way?"

"I leave that up to you. Men know how to deal with each other." He was wearing a white toweling robe that made him look very tan and added bulk to his spare frame. His physical charm was undiminished. He hadn't lost the weather-beaten look he had acquired in the vineyards but it didn't detract from his distinction. He looked like the gentleman farmer he had been, fit and capable. She wanted him to take command as he had in the past. He would have been eloquent in defense or condemnation of their guest and would have somehow made the situation manageable. She realized how much of their life had been built on his words. Whatever she had hoped for this morning wasn't going to happen. Everything in him seemed dimmed. She had failed to ignite him. "You might at least persuade him to postpone his decision about the house. Tell him you'd be offended if he refuses our hospitality so abruptly."

He was puzzled. Was it possible that she had succumbed so completely that she couldn't bear to think of him under a separate roof? He watched her realign her forces and close herself to him. She had expected something more of him but he couldn't intervene. Freedom had always been the basis of their relationship, to the point of not providing it with a legal seal. Even if there had been no Odette in his past, she had the right to find in another man whatever she needed. Jealousy afflicted him like a sickness, making his throat and chest and limbs ache. "That seems an odd approach to a man we can't trust," he said, steeling himself to present the smooth surface of ordinary intercourse. "I should think the sooner he's out of the house the better."

"Suit yourself," she said as if she were already thinking of something else. She felt totally alone. He hadn't picked up her plea for help. Should she have waited till later when he would've recovered from his usual hangover? If things came to a visible crisis with Carl, he would probably have a few extra drinks and ignore it. She would have to save them single-handedly.

He watched, despite his determination to give her her head. By the end of the day, he was convinced that he had lost her, if not permanently, at least for as long as it took for whatever it was with Carl to run its course. Although he couldn't imagine how they'd managed it, numerous small signs suggested that they were already lovers—the way they sat together with easy familiarity, the smiles and looks of complicity they exchanged, Carl's masterful domination of her. They never touched, even when they thought they were unobserved, which might be significant. People who were merely fond of each other, without any sexual undertones, found constant ways of expressing it, in the way Robbie and Toni did. Above all, Helene's manner was so completely at odds with her behavior this morning that he could only believe that she had been motivated by guilt.

331

He wished he could find out something about Carl that would discredit him and send him running. For all anybody knew, he might be a Nazi. He invented a satisfying fantasy in which the French intelligence authorities came and took him away for espionage. Why not? There were probably things going on here that the Germans would like to know about.

Carl was undoubtedly an adventurer. Was he also a fortune hunter? Did his ambition go beyond a pleasant affair? Did he know what a catch she was? Because of their marital status, or non-status, he had invested everything equally in both their names. Helene could walk out tomorrow without the nuisance of signing a single paper. Apart, they might not be able to live so comfortably in the States, for instance, but here they were both rich.

Carl leased his house and reported that he would be able to move into it in another week or so. He undertook to widen their social horizon. After a few phone calls, he arranged for them all to be invited by Maxine Elliot to a party in Cannes. Stuart remembered her name as that of a great American beauty who had had a career on the stage and who had retired to England where she had become the familiar of royalty before the war. He was surprised to hear that she was still alive.

"Very much alive," Carl assured him. "Quite a fat little lady but still beautiful in the face."

Toni pointed out that the date conflicted with a party some of his film friends were giving locally, a party to which he'd already arranged to take Robbie. In the way that constantly endeared him to Robbie, Carl backed them up.

"Yes, yes, stay here for your party," he urged them. "The other will be very grand, for older people, not much fun for you boys."

Stuart was aware of being pushed aside even in the life of the family and was outraged by Helene in a way he had never had cause to be before. Why did she allow it? He could persuade himself that she needed a flirtation, an affair, whatever it was, at this peak period of her life, but she should have the sensitivity and consideration to make sure that it didn't encroach on his basic rights. He would stand aside for her but he wasn't going to stand aside for Carl to take over the household. It was time for Carl to get out; he wondered how much longer he could put up with him.

Once more he went over the argument that he'd been

having with himself, starting with his own transgression with Odette. Helene's beauty was still unblemished but it couldn't last indefinitely. After forty-five, no woman could hope to retain the bloom that most men looked for in a casual love affair. This might be her last chance to renew herself at the passionate source of life before they settled down for the long haul of middle age and the horrors that followed it. He could imagine trotting out the same justifications for himself if he suddenly fell for a pretty girl. What was good enough for him should be applicable to her. He would forgive her when it was over if she didn't humiliate him while it was going on. She hadn't had a clue about Odette until he had chosen to tell her.

Dates fell into place. Carl was going to take possession of his house the day after the party in Cannes. By then, August would be more than half over and the summer would be on the wane. The Coslings' plan to give a party for Carl somehow became an end-of-season affair, more a farewell party for Toni and Robbie. Having a party given for them seemed to Robbie like a public consecration of their love. He couldn't see beyond it to an actual parting. Life without Toni was unimaginable; something would happen at the last minute that would permit them to stay together. Perhaps Carl would help him make a case for giving up school and going to study in Paris instead.

"I'm going to miss Toni. I love watching them together," Helene said. She was sitting on the beach with Carl in the late afternoon on the eve of the Cannes expedition. Robbie had just come down from work to join his friend for a swim. They were the one bright happy note in her increasingly tormented life. Stuart had chosen to withdraw completely. He drank steadily most days and was spending a lot of time indoors, claiming that he had business to take care of. Her time was running out. When Carl moved day after tomorrow she would learn how deep his grip on her was. She hoped that his being gone would free her and that she would slowly return to an even keel, but the thought of him alone in a nearby house, waiting, continued to be unnerving.

"They are beautiful young animals," Carl said as they emerged from the sea adjusting their trunks. He had no intention of leaving without jolting her into making some positive move toward him. It was time to play his trump card. "To see Robbie head over heels in love is a joy, although it should also make me a bit jealous."

333

"You would call it being in love?"

"Most definitely. I thought we agreed about that."

"I said something about platonic love. I don't see how anybody can be in love without its becoming—" Her voice trailed off. She was touching on something that had drifted through her mind as an amorphous thought but that she hardly dared put into words.

"Without its becoming physical? That, too. What I said about Toni is true, but a quite normal man can have pleasure with a boy. I'm sure they have found ways of satisfying each other that aren't offensive to him. With Robbie it is quite different. You are surely aware that he is a lover of men."

Her breath caught on a gasp. "Is he?" She sounded more bewildered than outraged. He glanced at her and saw that her lovely face looked thoughtful but not dismayed.

"Of course. Do you mind?" he asked.

"Mind? How could I help minding? It would be a terrible tragedy. I don't believe it's true." She minded because she knew she should mind, but her thoughts had strayed close enough to the possibility to have prepared her to accept it. Somewhere deep within her, she welcomed it. She could dismiss the threat of girls forever.

"I can assure you it's quite true," he said. "I had intended to tell you sooner or later. He offered himself to me in Greece. We have been lovers." He sat back calmly without looking at her and felt the bombshell rock her.

"You're a monster." Her voice came out with a strange forced rasp. She wanted to scream. She wanted to leap up and fly from him. He leaned forward and held her with his eyes.

"Am I? Is it monstrous for me to have wanted him when you, his mother, want him also? I knew from the beginning that I would have you both. He is beautiful in the same way that you are beautiful. It is impossible to want one of you without wanting the other. Boys have played little part in my life, but he gave himself to me unsparingly and it was glorious. I will provide the physical link that you crave with your son."

She cringed from him, staring into his hypnotic eyes. Her mind was filled with an image of Robbie's graceful young body bending to his implacable will. She saw a perverse beauty in it but she wanted to destroy it with her own reality. She wanted to replace Robbie's body with her own. The control of years crumbled under his probing gaze. She raged with desire. She remembered her mad husband and the searing lust that Stuart had been able to unleash in her and her body began to tremble. She wanted to tear Carl's trunks off. She wanted him to take her here on the beach. She wanted Robbie as a witness. She was appalled by herself and alive. "Please," she begged in a hushed voice. She was aware of the boys coming closer. "No more now. I'll come to you on Thursday."

"Of course. That is why I am here. That is understood."

"Stuart knows nothing about Robbie, does he?" she added in an urgent undertone.

"No, no. It would be a great misfortune if he did."

Carl had arranged for them to dress for the party after the drive to Cannes, where friends had offered the use of their villa. Stuart was to take Jane and the admiral, who already knew Maxine Elliot. To allow for the more than two-hour drive, they were ready to leave in the middle of the afternoon.

"See that somebody puts these things in the car, will you, dearest?" Helene said, giving herself a few last-minute touches at her dressing table. They had packed their evening clothes and toilet articles in a small suitcase.

"Sure," Stuart said. He left her and went in search of Felix. He encountered the boys, who had come to see them off. Carl appeared. Robbie and Toni stood holding each other in a loose embrace, arms around shoulders, hands on hips, leaning against each other. Stuart had seen them stand like this dozens of times but today it bothered him. Robbie was absently toying with the hair on the back of Toni's neck. Weren't they beginning to overdo this sort of public intimacy? He must warn Toni that it might look odd to others.

They chatted about their respective evenings until Helene joined them. They told each other that they might meet in the early hours of the morning and then the trio of elders was off, Helene in Carl's car.

They had almost reached town when Stuart realized that he didn't have the suitcase with him. He honked and Carl pulled over and Stuart stopped beside the little car. "Do you have our clothes?" he called to Helene.

"You said you'd take care of it," she replied with a little frown of impatience.

"Never mind. You two go ahead. If the Cumberleighs don't keep me waiting, I'll be only ten minutes behind you. I have the address." They waved and Stuart backed up and turned around.

He found the suitcase where they'd left it and had started back to the car when he heard a cry from below. He recognized Robbie's voice. The cry struck him as odd, like panic or ecstasy. He dropped the bag and went to a tree near the steps where he could look down at the beach without being seen. The two heads, blond and brunette, were bobbing in the sea quite close to shore. They moved in toward each other. Neither appeared to be in any kind of difficulty that would explain the cry. As he watched, a wave broke behind them and tumbled them over and cast them up on the beach on their backs. They were both naked. They both had erections. They rolled lazily over to each other and their mouths met. Their bodies moved against each other. They broke apart and scrambled up and, covering themselves with their hands, ran in a crouch toward the beach house and disappeared from view.

Stuart stood rooted to the spot. For a moment, he thought he was going to be sick. He had never seen two men kiss. He gagged and swallowed his nausea. He had an impulse to go down and tear them apart, give Toni a good beating and throw him out. He thought of Robbie's age and let it pass. He was finally able to move and turned and went to the drinks table. He poured himself a slug of brandy and swallowed it and held the empty glass while he stared sightlessly at bottles and his mind grappled with what he'd seen.

He had seen two young men with erections. He had seen them kiss. He had seen their bodies move lasciviously against each other. One of them was Robbie. He hurled the glass against the wall. It shattered with a cheerful tinkle. Rage boiled up in him. What were they doing now? He wanted to mutilate Toni's beautiful face. That damned vicious— He thought again of Robbie's youth. Enough damage had been done. He didn't want to add to it. Perhaps by tomorrow he would have got himself sufficiently under control to deal with it reasonably. The brandy was already dulling his rage. He made a rush for the suitcase and hurried to the car.

Another quick brandy on the admiral's yacht made it possible for him to smile and chat sociably. Negotiating the perilous curves of the Esterel was a disagreeably sobering chore and anger and anguish once more stirred in him. The scene on the beach had acquired the blurred edges of a dream but it hadn't been a dream. He had witnessed it. He thought of all the times in the last few weeks that he had seen them reach for each other, hold each other, lean in against each other. They had dared carry on under his very nose. Everybody knew that such things happened with schoolboys but Toni wasn't a schoolboy; he was a symbol of what the place had become, a haven for every corrupt and depraved taste. Who was responsible? He had admitted the hordes of serpents into his paradise. It was up to him to limit the damage.

He wondered about Edward. Did the sensible woman at his side know things about her stepson that would be helpful in dealing with Robbie? It might be a comfort to talk to Jane, but how could he admit to anybody that his son was a moral and social leper? Besides, Robbie was too young to be discussed in such terms. There was time to save him.

More brandy awaited him at their destination. By the time they had all changed and arrived at the party, Stuart was insulated against further shock. He took in the spectacular setting from an alcoholic distance. The "château" was wedged into the rocks between railroad and sea. Vast terraces descended to a swimming pool hanging precariously at the edge of a cliff. A chute of water connected it to the sea below. Stuart decided that he would slide down it before the evening was over.

He dutifully paid respects to his hostess, a fat imperious little lady with astonishingly beautiful eyes. He wandered aimlessly among the rich and famous, beaming at anybody who met his eye, wondering why he was here. He beamed at the portly figure of Winston Churchill, acknowledging a kindred spirit; he too had seen all his hopes and plans go awry.

"Barry's son, eh?" the failed statesman growled after Stuart had introduced himself. "I shouldn't think that would be much fun. Sorry about Ben. I miss him. You have any objections to being a lord someday?"

"A lord? Why me? I'm an American."

"An American like me. American mothers. Makes us tough. Barry's pushing for a peerage. He's not satisfied with Ben's baronetcy."

"You mean one of those lifetime things?"

"The old rascal's not satisfied with that, either. Wants the real thing. Dare say he'll get it once the war's on. Useful to us."

"There's going to be a war?"

"Next week. Next month. If not, I see little hope for the future of civilization, do you? Who's that Hun you have with you?"

"We're with him, really. He brought us. He's a friend of Miss Elliot."

"That so? Something fishy there. Rings a bell. Must ask the old girl."

They drifted apart as Stuart looked around for another drink. There was plenty fishy about Carl. Carl. Robbie. The world was falling apart around him but this wasn't the time to think about that. He would face a few facts tomorrow. Take a stand. Tonight was for dancing on the edge of the volcano. Had to watch his feet.

He was still on them, although he was developing a tendency to bump into things, when he found himself making an effort to focus on Hilliard. He leaned forward, peering, and put a hand on his old friend's shoulder. "Is that you, Stanley? Are you still here? I thought you'd left."

"We've had a little spin around Italy. Wonderful party, isn't it? Quite an impressive guest list."

"Not bad, as pansies and whores and international has-beens go. We have quite a nice selection of those at our end of the coast. Are you coming to stay with us again, Stanley?" He was having difficulty forming his words. Better take it easy on the drink, he warned himself.

"Not this time, worse luck. Time to head for home. It's been the best summer I've had for years. When I'm back at the factory, I'll be thinking of you. You knew the answer all along and stuck to it."

"You really think so, Stanley? You're a bigger fool than I thought you were."

"Thanks, old man. Nice of you to say so. What seems to be the trouble?"

"Trouble? How could there be any trouble? I was talking to a fellow a little while ago who thinks we need a war to save civilization. Are you aware of the civilizing effects of war, Stanley?"

"Take it easy, fellow, take it easy. Had a bit to drink, haven't you?"

"Yes, I've had a bit to drink. Isn't that the answer you were speaking of? Or did you mean a life of luxury and ease?" His voice rose as his mind drifted back to vanished dreams. He

338

was launched; words slowly led to other words. "That was an accident, you know. Remember the spinach? I'm the fellow who wanted to dig his feet in the good earth and grow like a tree. And you're the fellow who wanted to write a good book. Remember? What happened? That's a good question and I'll try to answer it for you. Take myself, for instance. I thought there was more to life than making money. I wanted to be free to live the kind of life that seemed good to me. That meant being on the land and growing things. There's nothing wrong with that, is there, Stanley? It's a free country. Except that it isn't. There's no such thing as freedom. It's just something somebody put in a book and I believed it. I bet everybody here believes it, too. The sacred right of the individual to achieve his own destiny. Look at them. What are they doing with their sacred right? Creating havoc. Havoc, Stanley. You think I've got the answer and I don't know a goddam thing."

There was a sudden lull in the festive din and Stuart talked in a loud voice into silence. People exchanged amused glances and began to listen. Helene heard him and started toward him.

"I can't see you have much to complain about," Hilliard said as music filled the void again.

"Hollywood's dulled the old perceptions, my boy. You just see pictures. Lovely wife. Why, here's the lady in person. Fine, upstanding son. Beautiful place. Seems to me you used to be more acute in the old days. There's all the material here for an ugly little story and you miss it all."

"You're drunk," Helene said calmly. "Why don't we go before you make a spectacle of yourself."

"All part of the entertainment, my dear. Little lecture on truth. Having a good time, Carl? You don't realize what a good friend I am to you. She wanted me to forbid you the house. Said you were a Nazi spy or something, but I stuck up for you."

"That's enough, Stuart," Helene said tensely, keeping her voice low. "Stop this or go."

"No, no, nothing like telling the truth to liven up a party. I'm the leaven in the dough. I was just explaining to Stanley here that our beautiful façade conceals all the rubble of three wasted and ruined lives. He's going to put it in a film."

Helene's eyes widened for a moment as she caught a glimpse of the horror of Stuart's total indifference. This was

339

the final betrayal. This was a repudiation of all that she had clung to. She turned from him abruptly. "Take me away from here," she murmured as she swept past Carl.

Stuart watched her retreating back. He wanted to run after her. He wanted to call out to her. He didn't see Carl walking at her side. For a ghastly moment, he felt as if something irreparable had broken in him. His glass slipped from his hand and rolled in the grass. Hilliard picked it up.

"You might as well have another drink," he said.

Stuart continued to stare after her. Perfect freedom. She was free to go. He was free to stay. Robbie was free to roll around on the beach with his boyfriend. Why not? As he stared at the spot where she had disappeared into the house, he felt a great emptiness opening up within him. It was all emptiness—all of life was emptiness. He felt a sort of cataclysmic relief at knowing that there was nothing to hope for, and out of the night's immensity a breath of knowledge touched him: without bonds, there is no freedom. . . . He heard a girl's voice at his side.

"I'm not used to being out without the children," it said.

He turned and found Anne looking up at him through her lank hair. "I didn't know you were here," he said.

"A gentleman insisted. I've decided to find out what the grown-ups are like. I've decided to start with you."

Stuart looked at her dimly for a moment. "I think you've made a poor choice," he said, taking the replenished glass Hilliard held out to him.

Helene sat huddled well over on her side of the seat, unable to look at the man who was driving. Now that there seemed to be no hope of postponing the inevitable, she felt doomed. Stuart had condemned her with his eyes, had almost willed her to give herself to Carl. Their ruined lives. Was he punishing her for all the years she had sublimated her passion for him in her devotion to Robbie? She had a sudden sense of having been manipulated by him always, as if their life together had been a sort of play, conceived, written, and directed by him; he probably already knew how the last act ended.

"He may be following us," she said dully.

"It is unlikely. How can he drive? The Cumberleighs will take care of him. Everybody saw how drunk he was getting. Dolly Parkinson spoke to Jane about possibly spending the night."

"How could he behave so disgracefully? Doesn't he see what he's doing?"

"You mustn't judge him harshly. Something is seriously wrong. I saw it as soon as he arrived this afternoon. He wasn't drinking in his usual way, quietly and steadily. He seemed driven, almost obsessed by something. I can't help wondering if it has something to do with Robbie and Toni."

"You think he's guessed?"

"What else could it be? He was all right when he went back for the bag. They have been behaving very openly with each other recently. If it must all come out, I will do my best to make it easy for the boy."

Helene was touched and warmed by the tenderness in his voice when he spoke of Robbie. Driving over with him this afternoon had given her a taste of what it would be like to be really with him. He had been full of hearty high spirits, charmingly attentive to her but without the insistent undercurrent of sexuality that had so unnerved her. He had made her feel young and desirable and aware of the possibility of an easy relaxed physical rapport of a sort she had never known, as if, as he said, they were meant for each other. Stuart's forcing the issue had plunged her once more into conflict. She instinctively resisted the inevitable where passion was concerned. Just because they were going back to the house alone together didn't mean that she was going to give herself to him. "I won't allow him to hurt Robbie," she said, clinging to what she knew and trusted. "Stuart's never understood him. He's an artist. He's always responded to beauty. Whatever he might feel for a man, it would always be more spiritual than grossly sexual. Stuart wouldn't understand that."

"We shall see. Everything is coming to a head. I've been preparing for it. We must think of ourselves now. And Robbie too, of course. I will take care of you both."

"I don't understand any of this," she protested, lifting her head and allowing herself to ease in closer to him.

"Must we both understand? You have lived too cautiously and emptied your life of everything but your growing passion for Robbie. When I have rid you of that, I will open your eyes once more to all that you have missed. You see, I do not say I will make you happy. Happiness you must find for yourself."

"I *am* happy. Nobody can take that away from me, not even Stuart."

"Not even somebody who might take Robbie from you?

Oh my dear, don't you see the appalling danger that's facing you? I will save you from it."

"Please, Carl, you confuse me so." Passion? Danger? Why did he go on insisting on it?

"Only for a little longer," he assured her. "We're almost there." He dropped a hand from the wheel and held hers. "There. Put your head on my shoulder. We will be like little children, leaning against each other to keep the darkness at bay."

She did as he suggested and felt his powerful body moving against her as he guided the car. She no longer felt threatened by him, no longer felt compelled to resist him. He had the confident strength of knowing what he wanted and would show her what she wanted. She had followed Stuart long enough in his pursuit of some truth that always eluded him. He would allow nothing to be simple, nothing easy. She had found no dark corners in Carl, no hidden depths, only his direct masculine drive for possession of her. If it was inevitable, it had the simple inevitability of human appetite.

"Are we to be in love with each other?" she asked quietly, testing him.

"Oh my dear, I don't know what that is. I'm a man. You are a beautiful desirable woman. That is enough. The rest is words."

"Yes, perhaps so." So many words. Stuart had been dinning words at her since the beginning of time. She didn't want to hear any more. If he could publicly proclaim the ruin of their lives, she could act. She lifted her head and looked down the path of light projected by the headlights, realizing that she didn't care if he knew that she was being unfaithful to him. Let Carl handle it in any way he chose.

When they drew to a halt in front of the house, there were no other cars in the drive. "The boys aren't home yet," she said.

"It is still quite early." He reached across to open her door for her. "The night is filled with parties and we are alone."

"Yes." Her heart accelerated as she felt his breath against her cheek, his arms brushing against her, the fresh clean smell of him filling her nostrils. Was he going to kiss her at last? He drew back and let himself out and came around to her side to accompany her into the house. He stopped when they reached the cloistered court of the guest wing and turned to her and drew her into his arms, a big man capable of making

342

her feel almost frail. His mouth on hers was demanding and possessive. He had held Robbie like this. He knew the feel of Robbie's beautiful body against his. She was holding her son's lover. He released her with a flash of his big white teeth.

"Go and get ready for bed," he commanded. "I'll wait for you here."

She moved in a trance to obey him, unable to grasp the reality of what she was doing. In an hour, her body would have been joined to Carl's, a life would have ended and another born. Or would it be simply a sexual act leading to nothing? If so, she would have lost everything. Except Robbie. They would have shared a man; her soul trembled at the thought. She undressed and washed and scented herself and combed her hair. She felt quite detached from her surroundings but moved with precision. She put on a dressing gown and was ready. For what? She still couldn't convince herself that she was doing something so commonplace as going to bed with a man. Her sense of her own inviolability was offended.

Her heart began to race again when she knocked on his door. He opened it and stood before her casually, unself-consciously naked. Reality engulfed her with a giddy rush of sensual impressions. In the soft artificial light, his powerful bronzed body looked startlingly young. Desire clawed at the pit of her stomach. He reached out and opened her dressing gown and she saw his sex lengthen and lift into a prodigy of virility. Her breath caught. Surely Robbie would be shocked by such a display of raw lust. His fingers moved lightly on her.

"Your breasts are like a young girl's. How lovely." His smile didn't gloat at his triumph over her but made it a shared triumph. "I have never before waited so long for a woman. It makes it more thrilling than it has ever been."

She abandoned herself to his skilled worship of her body, wondering if he brought such ardor to his lovemaking with a boy. Had he and Robbie aroused each other to such a pitch of erotic tension? An image of Robbie's body writhing ecstatically under him, like hers, kept interposing itself between them. She uttered a cry to banish it as he finally made his enormous entry into her. . . .

Habit woke Robbie at the usual hour, but he remembered how late they'd been up and slid in closer to Toni and held his erection and waited to drift back to sleep. He could miss a morning's work. He wanted to prolong the feeling he had had all night of having been totally absorbed into Toni's life. Going to the party practically as Toni's date had been only the beginning of the evening's wonders. Their special relationship had been acknowledged in the way Toni's friends had welcomed him. Toni had flirted with several girls without making him feel excluded. The night had ended with their taking one of the most attractive girls out to a deserted beach where they had all stripped and swum naked together. He and Toni had fooled around in their usual way and Toni had encouraged the amorous play that Robbie habitually tried to keep in check. It seemed to drive the girl wild with desire. She joined in. Robbie hadn't dreamed that girls could be so uninhibited in their enjoyment of boys' bodies. She had teased his cock until he had almost felt as if he wanted her. Before he knew it was going to happen, she had maneuvered his entry into her and he immediately felt shamefully imprisoned in her mysterious interior. His body felt defiled as it never had before. He could find nothing in his nature to prompt him to satisfy her desires and his orgasm was a physiological function, without pleasure. Afterward, the vicarious thrill of watching Toni's practiced possession of the girl had been one of the memorable moments of his life.

It had been daylight when they drove her back to her hotel. She had given Toni another erection in the car and taken care of it with her adventurous mouth. Girls really did do it. He wasn't even sure of her name. Ginette? Anyway, he knew what it felt like to perform the act that he was supposed to like. He slept again.

It was after noon when they finally emerged and found the place deserted. "I guess we're not the only ones who slept late," Toni said as they paused at the head of the steps looking down at the empty cove. "I wonder why only Carl's car was there when we got in. Maybe our parents stayed for the night."

Robbie's heart always gave a little joyful leap when Toni underlined their bond. Our parents. Robbie put his arm around him and hugged him, more in love with him than ever after last night. They could be together always now, even if it meant having a girl from time to time. "I'll go find out what's going on," he said, releasing his beloved friend.

When he came out from his visit with the staff, he saw that Toni had gone on down to the beach and he rejoined him there. "They say Dad hasn't come home yet. Carl and Mum

344

were here but went out a couple of hours ago. I guess she's helping him get settled in his new place."

"Well, then, we can strip for action. It's too bad we didn't bring Nenette home with us." He laughed into Robbie's eyes as they peeled off their trunks and made a dash for the sea.

They swam and pulled their trunks on again and went up for a light lunch in the shade on the great terrace. Robbie wished that they could live like this forever, without the distraction of others. Toni reached across the table while they were having coffee and held his hands.

"I was so proud of you last night. This morning. You know now how much you can please girls. Are you going to work this afternoon?"

Robbie stroked the hands that held his. "Don't you want to come up to the house for a little while? I can do anything that a girl can do." He dared say it because he had functioned at dawn to Toni's satisfaction. He had won immunity from his loved one's disapproval.

"No, no. No more of that. We're entering a new era. Before you know it, you'll be running off with girls on your own."

"You should see my cock. I promise you I'm not thinking about girls."

Toni laughed and lifted a hand and caressed his cheek briefly. "You're incorrigible. Wait till next year. I think we'll laugh a great deal about all this. That's good. In another year, you'll be very much a man and I'll no longer wish sometimes that you were a girl. Go on. Get to work."

"Okay. I always do whatever you tell me to do."

"Not always," Toni reminded him.

Robbie blushed. "Nothing like that will ever happen again."

Toni returned to the cove and stretched out naked on a towel, sunning his back. He dozed. Movement near him aroused him and he quickly lifted his head. Stuart was standing over him, looking down at him. His eyes were cold. He looked sick.

"Put something on," he ordered and turned away. Toni leaped up, wrapping the towel around himself, and followed Stuart into the shade of the overhanging beach-house roof. "I can't take much sun today. Actually, I've never felt so shocked and appalled in my life. Where's Robbie?"

Toni was alarmed by Stuart's manner. He felt a seething

hostility in him but couldn't believe that it was directed at him. "At work, as usual," he said, steeling himself for bad news.

"Have you seen Helene?"

"The people in the house told Robbie that she and Carl went off somewhere this morning. They didn't come back for lunch. We haven't seen them."

"Good." He let himself down slowly into a wicker chair. "There's no need to waste time in discussion. I want you to go immediately."

"Go? Where?"

"Anywhere you choose. Get out of this house." Stuart saw Toni's face settle into an expressionless mask of beauty but his eyes remained direct and untroubled. He pulled up a chair and sat without being invited.

"I don't understand," he said quietly.

"Does that matter? It's my house." The affection that had been growing in him for this youth had died the instant he had seen Robbie in his arms. He had to summon all the patience and understanding that was in him for his son; Toni had no claim on his sympathy. His sense of fair play impelled him to add a few words of explanation. "I came back after I said good-bye to you yesterday afternoon. I forgot my bag. I saw you and Robbie down here."

"You did? We came down for a swim. We often do. Whatever you saw, I'm sure you misunderstood." Had he seen them holding hands? Hugging each other?

"Are you so sunk in depravity that you don't remember what you did?"

"I don't remember anything in particular. We were— Oh." His eyes dropped. Stuart saw a flush creeping up under his tan. Toni desperately rallied his defenses. It was bad but he had to save Robbie. "We got knocked down by a wave and fell around on top of each other. Is that what you saw? I was afraid it might look peculiar, being naked and so forth. I wasn't thinking of you but I warned Robbie that we should be more careful. I still say it wasn't what you think."

"Is your getting an erection with a boy open to a variety of interpretations?"

"Yes. I always get a hard-on when I swim naked. I don't know why." He knew that he was engaged in a battle for Robbie's future, perhaps even for his sanity. He mustn't fail him. "Robbie's enough of a kid still to find it fascinating. I've told him it doesn't mean anything."

"And you kiss him to convince him of how meaningless it is?"

"Yes, I kiss him sometimes," he announced angrily, warning himself not to get carried away by his indignation at the injustice of the attack. "I'm not a *pédé*. I like girls. We play around like kids. Just after I arrived, he told me he was in love with me. It's not unusual for boys his age to be mixed up about sex. I've been getting him over it."

"So you admit you've made love with him." Stuart wondered why he went on with it. He'd seen what he had seen. There was nothing to talk about.

"Not in any real sense," Toni continued more carefully, determined to make him understand. "I love him. He's beautiful. It's natural for people who love each other to want to touch each other. We haven't hidden it. I haven't allowed anything—well, you know—any of the things that homosexuals do together. How could I? I'm not a homosexual."

"You're making a pretty fine distinction. Physical intimacy is physical intimacy."

"All right. There's been lots of that. You know your own furniture. You've known from the beginning that we were in the same bed. I love it. I always slept with my brothers. Robbie grew up alone. Can't you imagine what that might've done to him? When boys are finding out about sex, they often play around together until they've satisfied their curiosity, and then they start thinking about girls. Robbie didn't have any of that. He's still a sexual adolescent. I've been careful not to make any mystery of my body so he wouldn't get obsessed by it."

"You've simply introduced him to practices that could easily turn him into a homosexual."

"I refuse to speak for Robbie. You can talk to him. He'll tell you whatever he wants you to know. I don't think he'd mind my saying that I didn't teach him anything he didn't know already. Why should doing what all boys do at one stage or another turn anybody into a homosexual?"

"I find your views on sex a bit special. Whatever you think all boys do, I can assure you I didn't do them. I was an only child too. I'm not going to have Robbie corrupted by your strangely tolerant attitude. This conversation isn't getting us anywhere. I've decided you have to go."

"But haven't you listened to what I'm saying? You've got to think of Robbie. You're forcing an issue he isn't ready to face yet. I don't know whether I should tell you private things but

347

I arranged it last night so he could have his first girl. I think he liked it. Once that's happened a few more times, he'll get over this idea that he's queer."

"He thinks he's queer?" Stuart seized on the word as if it were an admission of guilt.

"Only because he thinks he's in love with me," Toni said hastily. He had to weigh every word. He mustn't let Stuart think he had a case of perversion on his hands. If he took a strong line with Robbie, he would push him irrevocably over the brink where he was now hovering. He went on as eloquently as he could, pleading for caution. "Please let me handle this. I care so much about him that I'm willing to beg you to let me stay. I'm glad to have this chance to talk about it. He needs me. He's given me his complete trust. He's taken me as a model. You must know you can trust me. You've been good to me. You've treated me like a son, like Robbie's brother. Do you think I'd take advantage of that? I hate homosexuality. I love Robbie. I don't want him to go that way any more than you do."

Stuart looked at him, impressed in spite of himself with the changes he saw in him. He remembered his insolent little swagger when they had first spoken to each other. He was handling a conversation that must be embarrassing for him with dignity and good feeling. With his natural, uncurled fair hair, his whole person exuded a fresh wholesomeness that was in shocking contrast to the scene Stuart had witnessed. That he could so successfully conceal what was at best a streak of depravity made him seem sinister. Robbie was soft enough without being indulged in an incipient vice. The thought of Toni showing him how to fuck a girl wasn't particularly savory. Stern discipline was called for, not moral laxity. If it involved forcing an issue, he was in the mood to do so. He had sat back long enough. When he had dealt with Robbie, it would be Helene's turn. He might be uncertain about his role in life but he could at least restore order in his family. He felt a pang of loss when he thought of his plans for Toni but he wasn't going to be swayed by this persuasive youth. "It sounds as if you're the one who's in love and you just want to continue your dirty little affair in comfort," he said brutally.

Toni winced as if Stuart had spat at him. "I can't believe you feel that way about me but I'll take it, for Robbie's sake. Please listen to me. I hope Robbie doesn't have to know about this talk. If you want me to go, please give me a few more days. Robbie mustn't know you've thrown me out. I warn you. He'll hate you for it. He cares about you and respects you and it may destroy him. I'll get somebody to send me a wire from Paris saying I've got to get back for the film. I'd like a few more weeks with him, but never mind. You may be right. It may be time for me to go. I've never felt like this about a boy—a man—and it may be getting too big for me to handle. Treat him gently. He's bursting with love and can be hurt so easily. Will you give me a day or two so my going won't be a tragedy for him?"

"No. I know how to deal with my son. I want you out of here in an hour. Felix will take you wherever you want to go." He felt as if he were coming to grips with a challenge again, a feeling he had missed since he had sold off the land. Once more, he had a goal clearly before him; he would devote himself to Robbie's well-being. He felt revived and invigorated, no longer oppressed by last night's hangover and last night's guilts. He pulled a wad of francs out of his pocket and dropped it on the table beside him. "There. That should make up for anything you lost by giving up your act." Getting rid of Toni so decisively made him feel less hostile toward him.

Toni glanced at the money. It looked like more than he'd ever seen at once in his life. He stood abruptly and hitched up his towel. "You don't have to pay me off. Will you at least back me up if I tell him I've had a phone call and have to leave immediately?"

"No. I want him to know why you're leaving. He has to learn that there's a limit to what decent people will accept. You can tell him I'm waiting here for him. I want to talk to him."

Toni clenched his fists and forced himself to relax them. He was breathing heavily and took a deep breath to steady himself. "I hope you don't regret this. I mean that with all my heart."

"Take the money."

"No. All I want from you is for you to think about what I've said. I don't suppose you will until it's too late." He turned and gathered up his trunks thoughtfully and slowly mounted the steps.

Robbie turned distractedly from his easel as Toni entered their house. "I've hit a tough patch," he said, returning his attention to the canvas.

Toni stopped a few feet from him. "My poor dearest little

349

brother," he said, close to tears; tears of humiliation left over from his interview with Stuart, tears of sorrow for what this was going to do to Robbie. "We've both hit a tough patch."

It took a few seconds for the words to penetrate Robbie's concentration and then he slowly lowered his brush and turned. Anxiety sprang up into his eyes as he saw the gravity of Toni's expression. "What is it? What's the matter?"

"Your father saw us on the beach yesterday afternoon."

Robbie's eyes widened with alarm. "Saw us? Saw what?"

"Saw us kiss and our erections."

Robbie's mouth dropped open and a hand flew up to cover it. His eyes had a wild, hunted look. He shook his head and dropped his hand. "What did you say? Did you tell him he was mistaken?"

"How could I? He knew what he'd seen. I didn't tell him much. I told him that he didn't understand, that we'd fooled around in a childish sort of way because you're a bit mixed up about sex like most kids are. I told him you had your first girl last night and that that was probably the end of it as far as your thinking you were in love with me and all that. That's about all. I begged him to leave us alone and let us work it out together. He threw me out."

A tremor shivered through Robbie's body and he grew very still as if he were balancing something on his head. "What do you mean? Threw you out of where?"

"Here. He gave me an hour to get out of the house." He saw Robbie's face begin to disintegrate and he stepped in close to him and gripped his arms. "I lied to him. I told him I didn't want you to be a homosexual. I don't care what you are. If you have to be a homosexual to love me the way you do, all right. Nobody else ever has. I almost fell in love with you while I was talking about you. I don't know. Maybe I did. Maybe I fell in love with you when you had that girl, seeing that I hadn't prevented you from being a man. The way he spoke to me, he made me feel I'd been wrong to be so careful with you. He probably thinks we've done everything already, anyway. I can want you now because I feel as if the man in you belongs to me. I want to make it true with our bodies so that we're part of each other. I want to give you everything you want."

"Oh yes. Oh God, yes, Toni. Please. Take me. I've longed for it so." He was out of his clothes in seconds and Toni's towel was gone. They flung themselves on each other. Their cocks pressed up hard against each other. Toni's mouth was passionately urgent on his.

Their hands tried to grasp the essence of each other. Robbie's head swam with bliss and incredulity. Toni wanted him as much as he wanted Toni. He had never believed it could happen. He didn't trust his legs to hold him upright. They broke apart with their chests heaving. Robbie almost burst into tears at the glowing wonder in Toni's face as he looked at him with intense green eyes.

"Go get whatever you use," he said in an odd hushed voice as he moved them toward the bedroom.

Robbie ran ahead to the bathroom and found the lubricant that Jeff had left and applied it hastily. He snatched up a towel and hurried back to the bedroom just as Toni was throwing back the bedclothes. He threw the towel out on the bed and crouched down in front of him and looked with awe at the taut lift of the erection he was preparing for himself. He scrambled up onto the towel and sprawled out across the bed on his stomach. His breath was choked in his chest by the pounding of his heart.

Toni dropped down over him and lifted his hips to him and entered him. Robbie shouted with triumph as Toni slid deep into him, bringing him instantly to climax. He felt as if his limbs were being shaken loose from his torso by the rapture of his orgasm.

Toni moved in him slowly, asserting his right to him and savoring his possession of him. Robbie moved to his rhythm, giving himself to the need and desire he felt in him. He could feel his glorious body all through him, taking him, making them one. It could never be like this with anybody else.

"Oh God, let it always be you," he prayed through scarcely moving lips.

"Yes, I'm taking your beautiful bottom at last. I feel as if I belong here."

"Oh yes. Please do. Only you."

Toni's drive gradually accelerated and his body seemed to vibrate with mounting tension. Robbie's erection revived and pushed up against his belly with the excitement of approaching ecstasy. They both cried out and called to each other. Robbie's body was agitated by a frenzy of participation. He wanted to make it the most memorable sexual experience of Toni's life. He wanted to make him need him always.

Every move Toni made—his hands gripping him every-

351

where to hold his body to him, the hard lean pressure of his thighs as he straddled him, the indomitable thrust of his cock—was an additional act of conquest and Robbie dissolved into a delirium of surrender. The release was shattering; spasms flung Toni's body about on top of him, they moaned and laughed and bit each other and were finally still. Robbie felt as if he had had another orgasm but his persistent erection was lodged uncomfortably against his belly and told him that he hadn't.

Toni suddenly pulled away from him and leaped up. Robbie gasped at the emptiness he left in him. Some essential part of him had been torn from him. He pulled himself up and followed him to the shower. Toni made room for him but didn't look into his face. His eyes were on his erection. He ran a soapy hand over it and held it under the stream of water and dropped down and drew it into his mouth. Robbie's body was wrenched by a great convulsion that almost knocked him off his feet.

"Oh God," he cried. "Toni. I'm coming."

Toni held his cock in his mouth until it began to subside and then stood and looked at him. There were signs of strain in the set of his mouth and in the intent green eyes. "I don't know what's happening to me. If that's wrong, it's a wrong I can share with you. If we're supposed to feel guilty about it, we can share that too. I want to force myself to like everything you do. It doesn't even seem like sex. It's different. It's something that exists only between you and me."

Robbie laid his hands on Toni's chest. "After this, you can't go. If you did, I'd have to go with you."

"That seems to be the way we're headed. Listen. You've got to go talk to him. He's waiting for you. You don't have to admit anything. I didn't give him much to go on, just that we love each other. I said that we've never really made love together. That was true at the time. Just kid stuff. Tell him that living with a friend for the first time made you wonder about things you'd never thought about before. Tell him that you're getting it straightened out now and that there's no problem. Something like that. Tell him about the girl. For God's sake, don't give him the idea that you think you might be a homosexual."

"No. He mustn't find out about me. I couldn't stand it."

They left the shower and dried themselves. Robbie went back to the easel and retrieved his shorts. Toni followed him.

352

Adequately dressed, he turned to Toni and held him and kissed him gently. "I love you with all my life," he said. "What're you going to do?"

"Let's see what he says. I can't talk to him. I don't think he really believed anything I said. You've got to convince him that I was telling the truth. Don't break down, whatever he says. I feel as if we were getting married finally. Everything depends on you. You've got to convince him that you're in control of yourself and know what you're doing."

"I do. I've given myself to you for always."

They kissed lightly again. Tears gathered in Toni's eyes once more as he watched Robbie go. What were they getting into? He had betrayed himself and Stuart. He had committed the acts that were repugnant to both of them. He had betrayed Robbie, too, by letting him think it meant more than was possible. He went to the bedroom and pulled out his empty suitcase and began taking things out of drawers. He was so nearly in love with Robbie that it frightened him. It couldn't last. He couldn't, even if he wanted to, realign all his sexual urges. No boy, not even Robbie, could offer him the satisfaction he found with girls. He might fall all the way in love with him for a day or two but then he would begin to resent him for getting such an unnatural hold on him. Why prolong it? He didn't think Stuart would relent. He began to move more rapidly and with decision.

Talking about going away together was childish nonsense. What would he do with Robbie in Paris? He couldn't go around with a beautiful boy at his side. People would begin to laugh at him. It would be disastrous for his career. Aside from the small matter of money. He doubted if Stuart would subsidize Robbie for a life with a male lover.

Better go. Go quickly. With luck, he might get away before Robbie came back. He had at least given his little brother what he had wanted most; for a moment, their bodies had belonged to each other. Robbie knew that he loved him more than either of them had expected. The boy would have the memory to comfort him until he found somebody else.

He hurried into the bathroom and gathered up his toilet articles. He pulled out the bag full of city clothes that he'd never unpacked. He could manage the bags on foot; he didn't want to alert Robbie to his departure by asking for help. He dressed and went out to Robbie's worktable and picked up a pencil. It had been an extraordinary summer, full of promise and revelation. Later, perhaps, when there'd been time for adjustments, they'd all get together again. His tears spilled over as he scrawled a note on a sheet of drawing paper. . . .

Robbie found his father sitting under the roof of the beach house with a bundle of money and a drink on the table beside him. He came to a halt in front of him. Stuart looked up at him, detecting an aura of exaltation about him, incendiary and defiant. He warned himself to cool the boy down before he said anything to provoke him.

"Hello, youngster," he said amiably. "It seems we have some things to talk about."

"You can't send him away," Robbie asserted, keeping his distance.

"Come sit down and let me try to explain why he *has* to go."

"Before you say anything else, I want you to know that I love him more than anybody else in the world."

"I see." Stuart nodded encouragingly. "That's a pretty sweeping statement but I respect your feelings. The only trouble is, you haven't had much time to find out what people are like. You must agree that somebody who's lived a good deal more than twice as long as you have has had more chance to test his judgment. Would you accept that?"

"I guess so." Robbie was thrown off balance by his father's conciliating manner. Toni had prepared him for an attack. He was carried back to his childhood when he had talked to a figure of final authority about everything. He wished it could be like that again. He approached slowly and sat in a chair near Stuart, facing him. "What do you have against Toni?"

Stuart congratulated himself for having won the first point. He felt more relaxed. "I don't deny that your perceptions may be much sharper than mine but there's still the question of experience to test them. You know how much I've tried to like Toni, *have* liked him. I've pretended that he was my son. Unfortunately, there seems to be a serious flaw, a failure to recognize the clear line between right and wrong. Nobody can be allowed to molest minors of either sex. It's against the law."

"Molest? Who's molested anybody?"

"I saw you together yesterday. We mustn't forget that. I don't see why people can't talk about sex. It's a pretty basic fact of life. Everybody knows about it. Of course, there're certain things one wants to keep private, but in a general way

354

I think it's a reasonable subject of conversation. Do you feel like telling me what's been going on with Toni?"

"If you saw us yesterday, you know just about everything that's happened so far. I like him to kiss me and he doesn't mind every now and then. Usually just on the forehead. He's been with girls all summer. You know that. When we're in bed he lets me hold him. Things like that. He laughs at me. He says he used to do things like that with his brothers. He says I'll get it out of my system and forget about it."

"Do you think you will?"

"I don't know." He lowered his head and looked at his feet. He longed to tell all of it. Denying the glory of what had just happened risked diminishing it. If he told the truth, was there any hope that his father wouldn't condemn him? He was being very gentle and reasonable. Studying the articulation of his feet, he wondered if he could explain it all away as part of being an artist. He looked up and added with conviction, "I'll never forget anything that's happened with him. I love him."

"Nobody wants you to forget a friend. Let's find out more about this. He's made a point with me about the things all boys do. I've been trying to remember what I was like at your age. I never did any of those things. I don't remember anybody wanting to do them with me. Maybe I wasn't attractive enough to inspire a romantic passion in my classmates. You're a beauty so maybe you'll have a problem. Have many boys been after you? At school, for instance?"

"No. Nothing ever happened at school. I've never seen anything going on around me."

"Good. I thought Toni's attitude might be a bit special. So as I understand it, you've lived up till now without being troubled by abnormal desires."

"Almost." He couldn't let him think that Toni had introduced him to sex.

"Almost not abnormal?"

"Almost till now."

"You mean, something's happened since school that's made you uncertain about yourself?"

"Rico. You wanted me to make friends with him. I did. He wanted me to have sex with him. I was horrified. I didn't know such things were possible. He made me do things that I never dreamed anybody would want to do but he was my friend and I wanted to please him. I found out how ignorant I

355

was. He'd had lots of girls and didn't think there was anything strange about what we were doing. After a while, it began to seem all right."

"But, Robbie, don't you see the danger you're facing? You said I know everything that's happened *so far*. Maybe it was a slip of the tongue but I think it might be significant. One thing leads to another. You've seen the queer men here. Do you want to be like them?"

"No."

"Thank heavens for that. I wouldn't let you be even if we had to move somewhere else."

"They're not always like that. Do you remember those three brothers who took me out that night in Poros? Two of them were married but they all wanted me. The Greeks don't think it's abnormal. They make it seem perfectly natural. There were others everywhere we stopped. It began to make a connection with things I'd dreamed about when I was little."

"Such as?"

"I can't say exactly. It's very vague. Mum always made me feel that sex was beneath me, so I thought it was. I never let myself think about it consciously."

"I'm sure she couldn't have meant that. She'd undoubtedly like to think of you as being sort of refined and fastidious about sex but she certainly doesn't think it's beneath you."

"It's not. I know that now."

"I'm beginning to understand this a little better. Up till a couple of months ago, you've had a very solitary life. It worried me. I always hoped you'd bring friends home from school. Now all of a sudden people are paying attention to you, even wanting you physically. It's enough to make you lose your head. I'm more than ever convinced that my first instinct was right. Toni isn't good for you at this stage. There's something ambivalent about him. Believe me, grown men don't generally kiss boys on the mouth and have erections with them. He may like girls but he's still capable of taking advantage of latent susceptibilities in you. He's probably right about one thing—all boys probably are violently attracted to a friend at one time or another. I remember when I was very young I had a crush on an older boy. If he'd been like Toni, it might've led to something that could've scarred me for life. This is a very delicate and dangerous period in your development. You've got to be very conscious of anything that feeds whatever little ambiguities may be in you. Conscious of it and reject it. You should try to get your mind off sex. That may be difficult in a place like this where you can practically smell it in the air but, even here, the sort of girl you'd like probably wouldn't be ready for a real affair. That's a problem for most boys unless they're ready and willing to settle for whores."

"Toni says it isn't sex with us. It's something different and special between us. We were with a girl last night. He's wanted to arrange it ever since he's been here."

"Yes, well, it was probably good for you but I don't like his having to arrange it, as if it were a sort of extension to whatever he wants with you. Still, I can't compare my experience with yours. I started having sex when I was very young. There was nothing fastidious about it. I fancied chambermaids when I was thirteen. You haven't had a chance to know many chambermaids. When I was about your age, I fell madly in love with the girl I thought might be Toni's mother. I wanted to marry her. It was ridiculous but it didn't seem so at the time. My mother very sensibly put an end to it but she needn't have bothered. The war came along that summer and it would've ended anyway."

"If something like that happened to me would you do what your mother did?"

"I hope I wouldn't use her high-handed methods. She went behind my back and paid people off. I wouldn't do anything like that but I'd certainly oppose you in every way I could. It's axiomatic that youth needs guidance. It takes time to know what you want in life."

Robbie scented victory. It was impossible, after the way he had spoken, that his father would do anything so high-handed as forbidding Toni to stay. He had remembered Toni's warning and hadn't said too much—just enough so that he could speak more openly if later other problems arose. It was wonderful having a man-to-man talk with his father. The dark cloud of homosexuality was dispelled for the moment. He felt accepted. He wanted to end the conversation so that he could get back to Toni but he was careful not to appear rushed. "Well, I doubt if I'll want to get married for the next year or two, if ever. It would interfere with my work."

"Exactly. You have your work to keep your thoughts occupied, but I still think you need a bit of guidance about homosexuality. You mustn't let yourself think of it as being normal or natural. It can be dangerous to be overtolerant. Unless you were living in Greece, what they think of it is a dead issue. It's part of their heritage, but the ancient Greeks were in many ways a primitive people. Even so, when Plato talks about a man's desire for a boy he makes a very strong case for sublimating it into something purely spiritual, so it wasn't all that accepted even then. I'm shocked by what you say happened on the trip. If I understand correctly, you let yourself be defiled and degraded. Weren't you disgusted with yourself?"

"I was terrified at times. I wondered what was going to become of me. Then you brought Toni and it was all right. With him here, I don't care if I never have sex again. I've promised him I won't with anybody else."

Stuart shifted impatiently in his chair. "With anybody else? With anybody period, any male. That's what you've got to promise yourself. Without him, it'll be much easier to establish some sort of discipline for yourself."

Robbie felt that the outcome was still open. *You don't have to admit anything.* He had to resist the luxury of being honest with his father and trying to win his approval. "All right. Toni told me earlier, before you came back, that from now on he expects me to stick to girls. He called it a new era. I told him I'd do anything he wanted me to do. Does that satisfy you?"

"No, it doesn't, Robbie. You've got to tear this tendency in yourself right out by the roots, before it gets a grip on you. Even if I let Toni move down to a guest room so that you wouldn't be sharing the same bed, you'd be constantly reminded of what existed between you. No. A new era. It's the only thing that makes sense for you. Why do you think I care whether or not you're queer? Because I love you, that's why. As long as I have some control over you, I'm not going to let you ruin your life. That's final. Toni's going today."

"You don't think it's high-handed to send away the one person in the world I care about?"

"No, I don't. I invited him here. I can withdraw the invitation. I'm simply exercising my right to have who I like in my house."

Robbie's shoulders slowly rose. His head sank between them. His face was contorted with an effort at control as a sob was torn from him. "I love him so," he gasped brokenly.

"Stop it, Robbie," Stuart rebuked him harshly. "You're my son, not my daughter. You're talking about a man."

Toni's voice was in Robbie's ears. *Convince him that you're in control of yourself and know what you're doing.* He made another supreme effort and lifted his head and threw it back defiantly and met his father's eyes. He breathed deeply until he had conquered tears. "Yes, a man," he said. "What about freedom and being in touch with nature and living a natural life—all the things you've always talked about? I'm a human being. There's nothing unnatural about that. Whatever I am, I guess you and Mother had a lot to do with it. Why can't I be free to love whoever I like?"

"I may have talked a lot of nonsense, Robbie, but I've never claimed the freedom to defy the laws of basic human decency. Whatever we've made of you, you have a will of your own. I expect you to exert it to resist whatever streak of perversion you may have in you."

"That's what you call it. Not everybody agrees with you." If Toni was being turned out, why go on pretending? He had nothing more to lose. Maybe his father's decision would be shaken if he could make him understand that it was too late to talk about resisting his most basic needs. "I'm not going to go on lying to you. I *am* queer," he said quietly while a great surge of pride leaped up in him at daring to declare himself. His heart was beating rapidly but he was no longer afraid of his father. Words came out in a rush. "I wasn't disgusted with myself. Only sometimes at first when it was so new to me. I've done things I wouldn't do again but I've had beautiful moments with boys who wanted me and loved me and made me feel that I'd never be lonely again. Do you understand? I've done everything because I had to, like breathing. When we got back here, I found Edward waiting for me. I made love with Jeff Benjamin. It's the only time I broke my promise to Toni but that was because I'd given up hope of anything with him. I've done everything I could to seduce him and, thanks to you, maybe I've succeeded. What he told you was true but it isn't anymore. You made him realize that he wants me and loves me the way I love him. Decency for me is being faithful to the love that's in me. I intend to be. You don't know anything about love. You want everything to be nice and polite and pleasant. You're afraid of feeling. It's not even enough for Mother. Why do you think Carl is here? He understands. You don't know what love is."

Stuart felt as if he were sinking under a succession of blows. The extent of his failure stretched out limitlessly before him. Helene. Robbie. The life he had planned for all of them. He rallied the force to speak. He had to save his son. He drained his glass and rose to replenish it and returned to his chair. "All right, Robbie. You've had your say. I'd think we'd both better calm down and think things over."

"Does Toni stay?" Robbie demanded.

"There's no question about that. If he has any decency in him, he'll be gone by now."

"If he goes, I'll go with him."

"You're really asking me to be high-handed. You'll do exactly as I tell you. You're not of age. What about your mother? Do you have no regard for her feelings, either?"

"She won't let him go," Robbie said.

"Do you mean to say you'd be willing for her to know?"

"She knows I'm in love with him. I don't have to tell her." There had been such a depth of understanding in her treatment of them both recently that he was sure it was true. He could count on her, just as he could count on Carl.

"Very well. You force me to speak to her. But that won't change anything as far as Toni is concerned." Won't it? Stuart wondered. He no longer knew what he could expect of Helene. He picked up the wad of bills and tossed them to Robbie. "I just wanted to make it clear exactly how matters stand. I could dictate to you but I won't. I'll let you choose. If you're going, you'll find that useful. It's about five hundred dollars. Tell Toni it's my contribution to your honeymoon. I won't give you more. If you have the guts to go and he has the guts to take you, I might have to revise my opinion about everything you've said to me." It was a gamble he didn't expect to lose, but better to lose than resort to his mother's methods.

Looking at the money in his hand, Robbie couldn't believe that this was happening. His father had tricked him somehow. All his thoughts had been directed toward keeping Toni here. Even though they'd mentioned it, would Toni really take him to Paris? His passionate declaration of love had been so recent and unexpected that Robbie hadn't digested it yet. Toni was in love with him at last. That made anything possible. He looked at his father across the yawning chasm created by the revelations he had made about himself. His scalp crawled. He couldn't go on sitting here with him. He would never be able to face him again.

He pulled himself to his feet and made a little gesture with the money. "Thanks," he said.

Stuart played the understanding father to the end, not believing for a moment that Robbie would go. "You can come back whenever you like. Keep in touch. I'll come to Paris if you want me."

Robbie turned from him and started the climb back to his

house with dragging feet. He had done everything that Toni had told him not to do. Toni had counted on him to handle his father diplomatically so that he could stay. He mustn't let him feel that he was being forced to share his disgrace. He would make their going away together sound like an adventure, a trial period, so that Toni wouldn't feel that he was getting too involved. The money would pay for a place to live for months. Perhaps he could start selling his pictures. He couldn't be a burden to Toni. Maybe his life was really beginning.

By the time he reached the house, he had coaxed himself into something like hope. Toni had taken him as if he really needed him. They were going to live together. Why did he find it so difficult to believe? He entered to an unnatural silence. "Toni?" he said experimentally. His glance fell on a note on his worktable and he forced himself to it while his whole body became a knot of pain. There were only a few words: "Much as I'd like to marry you, it's against the law. Let's start laughing about it now. I love my little brother."

He made a dash for the bedroom door and flung open the closet. There were gaps in the ranks of clothes. He turned and stumbled forward a few steps.

"Toni," he screamed, and fell headlong and began to beat the floor with his fists.

Carl found him an hour later. He was lying on his back staring vacantly at the ceiling. Carl crouched over him and gathered him into his arms and stretched him out on the bed. "I've seen your father. He's too drunk to make very good sense. He says he's sent Toni away. Did he find out about you?"

"I've told him everything. Almost everything. Not about you." A wail started in Robbie's throat and rose and broke and he was wracked by sobs. Carl held his naked shoulders. Robbie tore at buttons and pushed his shorts down over his hips. "Take me, Carl," he gasped. "Fuck me. Make me know who I am again."

Carl finished undressing him and rose and stripped and saw the lubricant on the bedside table where Robbie had left it. He lay down beside the boy and took him in his arms again. A shudder ran through Robbie's body and his sobs subsided. "I will take you home with me. Your mother is waiting for us. You mustn't think about anything now."

"Take me. I want a thousand men. Love doesn't mean anything. I want to be wanted." He moved over Carl's robust body with unrestrained lust and made a wanton display of his erotic skills. Only sensual innovation could obliterate the nightmare of Toni's absence. Carl anticipated his needs and drove him until he was satiated and listless. He could feel the boy giving himself completely into his hands, turning to him for the smallest decision including what clothes to wear. Robbie couldn't bear to look at the depleted closet and drawers. His will was suspended by grief and loss.

"Do I have to see Dad?" he asked with a shadow of apprehension.

"No, no. He is probably still down at the beach house, very drunk. We can all talk some other time." Carl carried a small bag with a few of Robbie's things and led his stunned charge down through the citrus grove and hustled him into the car without encountering anybody.

"Did you say Mother's waiting for us?" he managed to ask when they were moving.

"Yes. She will be with us. We'll all be together now."

"Will my father allow it?"

"I told him but I don't think he understood. He laughed rather foolishly. We must talk when he's sober."

Robbie's distraught mind couldn't quite grasp what Carl was talking about. It was inconceivable that the family could be broken up, but Toni had been a part of it and he was gone. He couldn't face his father again. Existence as he knew it had been framed in immutable relationships. They were all gone. Even his mother was gone. Carl had taken her. His mind fragmented and ceased to function rationally. He couldn't relate to anything around him. They were driving through vineyards into a setting sun. He didn't know who he was. He was aware of a smart modern villa and then he was in what looked like a well-appointed hotel bedroom. Carl handed him a glass and a pill. The glass contained something alcoholic and he washed the pill down with it.

"Get undressed." Carl pulled the covers back from the bed. "You must sleep now. Everything will be better when you've had some rest."

"Will you sleep with me?"

"Perhaps. I will be here. Don't worry."

When he was naked Robbie began to shiver slightly, and Carl led him to the bed and pulled the light covers over him. He wasn't sure who Carl was. He was tired. He needed a rest.

He woke up in the dark and didn't know where he was. He reached out for Toni but he wasn't there. He had to be nearby. They had gone somewhere together. He pulled himself out of bed. His body felt heavy and he was unsteady on his feet. He stumbled around in the dark. He ran into something and began to weep, whimpering with his helplessness. His eyes slowly adjusted to the dark. He could make out the shapes of furniture and a stretch of wall with a door in it. He found it and opened it. There was a hall with a staircase at the end of it. In the other direction, quite close to him on the other side of the hall, light showed under another door. He heard the murmur of voices. Toni? He still couldn't remember where he was; it was all unfamiliar.

He crossed the hall, heedless of his nakedness, and tried the door where the light was. It was locked. He pounded on it and began to sob. Everybody was shutting him out. Everybody had deserted him. The door opened and Carl stood in it, wearing a light blue dressing gown. Carl, not Toni. Carl had brought him here. He hurled himself against the big man and took his mouth with sobbing kisses. Over his shoulder he saw a woman lying on the bed, her head propped on a pillow, the sheet stretched across the top of her breasts. Her shoulders were bare. It was his mother except that it wasn't his mother. It was a younger, desirable-looking woman who resembled his mother. Why wasn't Carl sharing her with him, as Toni had wanted to share with him? He felt his erection lift between the folds of Carl's dressing gown to meet hard flesh. He tore open the front of Carl's dressing gown and swiveled his hips up against him.

"We're lovers," he cried in a choked voice. "Show her that we're lovers."

"She knows, my poor dearest boy." Carl let his robe slip from him and grappled him into the room, closer to the bed. "There are no secrets between us."

Robbie fell back before his advance and for a moment stood alone and isolated, displaying himself to the woman. Carl stepped in against him and their bodies were briefly tangled together. Robbie exerted all his strength and pushed him aside.

"What are you doing here?" he shouted wildly. "I won't allow it. I'm yours. You have no right to be here. She belongs to me. She's always belonged to me. I have nobody else left." He backed away and collided with the bed and toppled over and lay across her. Arms held him. Soft hands soothed him. Only the sheet separated them. He felt it slipping away and they were joined in their nakedness. He felt the warmth and comfort he had always felt against her body. He was reclaiming her. She belonged to him again. A hand stroked his erection and guided it. Their bodies were shaken by sobs. Their tears intermingled. Horror beat about his head like the wings of birds as he moved his hips and drove his orgasm into her. They screamed into each other's faces and Robbie rolled away and lay gasping on his back. Carl pulled him to his feet and lifted him in his arms and carried him back to his room.

Robbie awoke in broad daylight. As his mind cleared, it was gripped by horror. A chill shriveled his toes and crept up his legs. It had happened in his mind. If his mother had offered him the comfort of her bed, his drugged and overwrought imagination must have turned it into something it hadn't been. He remembered Edward and Anne talking lightly of their parents' vices. Hadn't they referred to somebody who was having an affair with a son or a daughter? The casual conversation had stayed with him until his feverish imagination had cloaked it with reality. He felt the ineffable gentleness of a hand stroking his erection. It had happened.

As his mind edged closer to assimilating the monstrous fact, part of him continued to recoil from it with horror while he also became aware of a still core of peace in him. He felt complete and free in a way he never had before. His mother knew why he would never want a girl. She had somehow explained with her body his aversion to what was considered normal and had atoned for diverting him from common human experience. She knew all of him and accepted him as he was and had delivered him to his passion for men.

He was fully awake but incapable of leaving the shelter of the bed, not knowing how to face the others. What awaited him outside? The door opened and Carl entered carrying a tray. Robbie sat up.

"You are awake?" Carl brought his usual light breakfast and settled it on his lap. He looked fresh and alert and masterful. "It's a beautiful day. We've had a note from your father. He has gone away. He says he will not be back until after you have returned to school."

"School?" Robbie made a derisive little sound in his throat.

"Of course. You must go back to school. It is most important."

"I don't feel much like a schoolboy this morning." If part of him had hoped that his father would restore order to the chaos that had engulfed them, he knew that he couldn't expect it. His father was capable of making a stand for

364

whatever he believed in but something gentle and ineffectual in him made him withdraw from the havoc he had the power to create. He had made his stand about Toni but had undermined it by giving him the means to go with him. He had offered him freedom but hadn't accepted the truth.

"You mustn't brood about what happened last night," Carl said, standing at the foot of the bed. He was wearing shorts and an open shirt and was very handsome. "It was necessary for all of us. Do you want us to try to find Toni? I don't know exactly what happened but isn't it possible he is still here somewhere?"

"I suppose so but it wouldn't do any good." He had tried to give all of himself to Toni but when love was within their grasp, Toni had rejected it. It was the only explanation for his departure before knowing the outcome of his talk with his father. If he couldn't find love with somebody as good and tender and upright as Toni, it was unlikely that his nature would permit him to find it with anybody. "No. Toni doesn't want me. If nobody's there, I might as well go home. Tell Mother I'm all right. I want to see her but not quite yet. Tonight, or tomorrow. Tell her I'm beginning to understand. I want to go find Edward. I think he'll stay with me as long as we're both still here. Anne too, probably."

"Good." Carl nodded with satisfaction. Everything was working out according to plan. He had them both in his power. There would be a great scandal. Everybody would gossip and speculate about what had happened to the Coslings. Everybody would know about his part in it and would find an easy explanation for why he was here. He also controlled a comfortable fortune. He had discussed Helene's financial situation with her. There was plenty of time to establish himself securely before war overtook them. Stuart would eliminate himself. "Your mother's car is here. We don't need it. We'll be on the other side of the house. You can slip away whenever you're ready. You know we'll always welcome your friends."

"Of course. Where are we?"

"Not far from your house. You'll see as soon as you go out. We'll be waiting for you, my dearest boy."

As soon as Carl had closed the door behind him, Robbie pushed the tray aside and threw back the covers and looked down at his heavily tanned body. He could be justly proud of it. He caressed himself and quickly gave himself an erection. Bigger than the norm. Big enough to get all the lovers he wanted. He had to fill the terrible void Toni had left. There was no further need for restraint. His mind was filled with beautiful boys and sturdy cocks ready to take him. Edward would be his guide to the night life here; they would debauch themselves together. He would give himself to all the men who wanted him. He suspected that he would have to sink to whatever depths his appetites carried him before he found the stability and decency he had mentioned to his father. He thought of school and getting back to his art teacher. Maurice would be impressed by his summer's work. Perhaps Maurice would save him.

STUART

Stuart saw the letter as soon as he entered the room. It was on top of the small pile of mail placed as usual on the table in front of the fireplace, beside the brandy and the bottle of soda. He went slowly over to it and picked it up and stood with his back to the fire. His hand trembled slightly as he tore it open. It was the first word he'd had from Helene since just after war had finally been declared.

He read through it quickly and then looked up and stared straight ahead of him, not seeing the room, or the terrace or the sea framed in the enormous glass doors. It's going to be another nice day, he thought. Then he looked at the letter and read through it again.

5 February 40

Dear Stuart,

When you read further you will understand how difficult it is for me to write this. I am writing not for my sake but for Robbie's.

I am at present in the military prison at Toulon. There is no need for me to tell you how I got here—the maliciousness of neighbors. It seems I am to be tried for "communication with the enemy" because of some letters I wrote to Carl. If it weren't for Robbie, I would almost find it funny. If you have some impulse to help me I must ask you not to.

You must think only of Robbie. He has been in Paris since the war started although Maurice had to join his regiment immediately. We talked about having Christmas together but travel is very difficult. Then this happened a few weeks ago. I have written begging him to stay where he is since there seems to be no danger of this war turning into anything serious. Thank heavens the States is staying out.

His address is 18 rue de la Faisanderie, care of Delannoy. I'm sure he would meet you halfway if you would only get over your impossible attitude toward what you consider his abnormality. I don't know how long I will be kept here. I know you will always be generous with money but with the world so uncertain I would feel happier if I knew you were in closer touch with him, otherwise I would not have written. I hope you are well.

Helene

Stuart placed the sheet of ruled paper carefully on the table and looked at the brandy. Would it help to have a drink? No. He could go for days at a time without drinking. But what did it mean? Helene in prison? It must be some sort of military formality. His first vision of a cell and a cot and bars was undoubtedly exaggerated. In a case like this, they would put her in a hospital wing or something of the sort. Strange how after only a few months of war one could take such things for granted. He was prepared to be taken away any day and held until it was decided that he was a harmless nonbelligerent. It happened all the time.

He rang a bell beside the marble mantelpiece and sank into a big armchair in front of the fire and put his hand over his eyes. He heard footsteps approaching and looked up.

"Oh, Agnes, is Mlle. Cumberleigh up yet?" he asked the maid. Felix was gone, caught in the mobilization.

"Yes, I've taken her her breakfast. She said she was going to write letters until it was warm enough to go out."

"Tell her I'd like to see her, would you? And tell Boldoni I won't be here for lunch." He sank back in his chair and looked up at the ceiling. With his chin lifted his face showed little sign of age, but the last couple of years of hard drinking were taking their toll. He was putting on weight. His muscles had softened and he was no longer capable of prolonged physical effort.

He heard the door open and he looked up as Anne entered, her slight body enveloped in a silk dressing gown that looked too big for her. She pushed the sleeves up to her elbows and crossed her arms on her chest as she walked over to him and stood in front of the fire. She wore her hair more becomingly now, brushed back from her forehead, and her bony face had acquired an ascetic beauty.

368

"We can let the fire go out," she said. "It's going to be another lovely day."

Stuart looked at her and pointed at the letter lying on the table. Her eyes lingered on his face for a moment and then she picked up the letter and read. He watched her from his semi-reclining position. Her face was expressionless. There was an extraordinary firmness in it. The line of her chin was straight and strong and her full mouth closed firmly.

"What does *she* consider his abnormality?" she said. She finished and put the letter down where she had found it. "Dear God, why did everything seem so funny once upon a time?" she said in a flat voice. She turned and sat in the armchair opposite Stuart with one leg folded under her and cupped her chin in her hands and gazed into the fire. "It isn't just Edward being killed. We probably would've thought that was funny—dying for king and country." She looked at Stuart with wide level eyes. "Helene being put in prison should be a real howler. I suppose you're going to her."

"Yes," Stuart said.

"I suppose it wouldn't do any good to tell you you're insane."

"No," he replied, not taking his eyes off her.

"All right. It'll only take me a minute to pull on some clothes."

"You don't have to go."

"I know, but I wouldn't pass up a trip to Toulon. All those sailors." Her laugh hadn't changed. It came clear, pure, and sudden as she rose and, with a swipe at her hair, went off toward her room.

Her being here was an accident. She had come wandering back to St. Tropez just before Christmas because she had been caught in France by the war and could think of nowhere else to go. There was nothing to take her back to England. When Stuart ran into her on the port, her news was that the admiral had dropped dead a year or so earlier, shortly after the Cumberleighs sailed away at the time of the Munich scare, and that Edward had been killed in a training accident in an airplane. Stuart had hardly known her in the old days, but under the special circumstances of the war she seemed like a real friend and he felt obliged to offer her shelter. It had turned out very well.

He looked around the enormous room with its soft rich old

fabrics, turquoise and eggshell white, pale citron-yellow and deep rose, its highly polished wood, its great vases of multicolored tulips. She had brought life back to it. He could look at Helene's ivory-inlaid chess table with the superb ivory and gold figures without wanting to smash it. The figures stood in the positions of a game he and Anne had abandoned the day before. He rose and picked up the rest of his mail and flipped through it. It was a comfort to know that Anne would be with him during what promised to be a disagreeable day.

He left the fire and crossed the carpet and the marble floor beyond to one of the big doors and stepped out onto the terrace. His steps were a trifle heavy but youthfulness still clung to him. His hair was still thick and the gray in it wouldn't show until it had gone completely white and his skin, in spite of premature sagging, was a good color. He took a breath of the crisp air and turned his face to the sun with his eyes closed.

Anne returned to find him so. She paused for a moment to admire him. With his eyes closed and his head tilted back he looked vulnerable. She liked that look; it opened up to her areas of personality that had never existed in the admiral's conventionally unconventional world. Indeed, everything about the Coslings seemed to be on a larger scale; they had the grandeur of figures in classic tragedy so that she couldn't imagine uttering to Stuart the words she had rehearsed so often in her mind. She advanced toward him with her firm smile.

"You'd better take a sweater in case we're late," she said. He was wearing slacks and a jacket and an open shirt. He looked down at her and took her arm.

"Thank God you're here," he said.

When they reached Toulon in Stuart's new sporty little Matford, he drove directly to the navy prison. He left Anne in the car with an abstracted wave and went in to begin his inquiries. They took time. He waited. As he was passed from one brusque uncommunicative official to another, his anxiety increased. What had Helene done? And how could she suppose, no matter what had taken place in the past, that he would sit back and do nothing? He was at last granted an interview by the assistant director of the prison.

"I don't quite understand your position in this affair, monsieur," he said angrily as he shuffled through the papers on his desk.

"I've just heard from my wife that she's been arrested. I want to know what it's all about and I want to see her." Stuart spoke with the patience that comes with repetition.

"Your wife?" The man put his finger on a sheet of paper and read, "Helene de Chassart, born June etcetera, daughter of etcetera, widow." He pronounced the word emphatically and looked up.

"Oh, well, that's nothing, we—"

"I don't pretend to understand you foreigners," he interrupted. He looked again at the sheet of paper. "Mother of Robert Cosling. He is your son?"

"He is."

"It is nothing that you aren't married to the woman you call your wife? It is nothing that you have an illegitimate son? It is nothing that this woman is in intimate correspondence with a subject of an enemy power?"

"Of that I know nothing. That's what—"

"You call this woman your wife and yet you know nothing of a relationship she has maintained publicly in the region for a year prior to the outbreak of hostilities?"

"Just a minute," Stuart broke in. "In the first place, that isn't what I said. In the second place, you will stop calling my wife 'this woman.' My private affairs are not your concern. My wife and I had a friend called Carl von Eschenstadt. It seems to me quite normal that she should write to him."

"You're an obliging husband, monsieur," the official said, and Stuart flushed hotly. He clenched his fists and made an effort to control himself.

"That, after all, is my business," he said evenly. "I'd appreciate knowing why my wife has been arrested."

The man's manner suddenly broke its stern official bounds. "She has corresponded with the enemy via a neutral country, Switzerland," he cried. "For a year and a half we have been interested in this man's activities in the region. What is he doing here? He leaves one month before the outbreak of war. She writes. We intercept the letters. Letters of passion, she maintains. But how do we know what they might conceal?"

Letters of passion. Stuart winced and took a deep breath. "And if they're simply what she says they are?" he asked.

"A crime for which she will be tried and imprisoned. If we find that she has communicated information, it will be much worse."

Stuart felt physically ill. He swallowed several times and

straightened in his chair. Helene imprisoned like a criminal? He would get in touch with someone. It would be arranged. "I'd like to see her," he said.

"Ah, that's absolutely out of the question."

"But I insist. You have no right to hold her incommunicado."

"Regulations permit her to see her lawyer on appointed days and members of her immediate family."

"Very well. Do you mean this isn't the right day?"

"I keep telling you. You have no status."

"I'm the father of her son."

"Yes, yes, there is that." The official pulled at his lower lip and looked at the documents before him. He finally burst out angrily, "Very well. You may see her. Today. But only in my presence, you understand? You must not embrace her or take her hand. If you do, I'll be obliged to hold you, too." He glanced at his watch. "It's too late now. You must come back after lunch. I'll try to arrange it."

Stuart returned to the car and settled in behind the wheel without a word to Anne. She looked at him anxiously but forced herself to wait until he was ready to speak. They drove along the port until they came to a sidewalk restaurant.

"We might as well have something to eat," Stuart said. They sat in the sun, a rare treat in early February. In the distance, the sea sparkled. Stuart could think only of Helene shut up somewhere in that gloomy pile of masonry. They ordered and then, sensing a slight lifting of his spirits, Anne risked a question.

"Did you see her?"

"No, I've got to go back after lunch. It looks serious."

"How long has it been since you've seen her?" she asked, looking at him bravely, although she didn't like to hear him talk of Helene. Helene was the barrier, Helene made it impossible for her to speak.

"How long? I don't know. September of '38, wasn't it? About a year and a half, I suppose."

Time meant little to him. Drink had mercifully blurred the past. He knew there had been a disastrous party and that Helene had been gone the next day. He knew that he had cleared out and had been gone for a month, visiting specialists in Switzerland and Germany about Robbie's misfortune. These interviews hadn't led to much. So much depended, he was told, on the degree to which the subject would be ready to cooperate. Stuart knew that Robbie couldn't be counted on to cooperate at all.

He returned to find Helene intransigent. He didn't want to remember that period. She was even more impenetrably armed against him than she had been after Robbie's childhood illness. He could find no part of her that he could reach. Even Carl seemed to have no great hold over her, which puzzled but reassured him. It was a phase; she was making some final effort to discover and rally all her independent resources. When she had acquired confidence, she was bound to turn to him again within the limits of whatever new alignment she was seeking. He couldn't believe that their life had been a total lie, that his quest for truth and freedom had been less than honorable, no matter how faltering it had been at times.

Her ripe beauty had subtly altered, had acquired mystery and a perverse eroticism that he had never felt in her before. He found it very uncomfortable to be with her when nothing that she was becoming or had ever been was directed toward him. Robbie was safely back in school. Stuart hated the house for having misled him even briefly into believing that it might be a substitute for everything that the property had represented to him in the beginning. It contained nothing but reminders of their failures with each other.

He had gone away again, with no purpose or destination in mind. He had wandered from England to Canada, for a pointless visit with his father who had been assured that he would soon be a lord, to New York and back. When he returned, Helene was gone; she and Carl had rented a house in a village farther along the coast. He drank, marking time until she came back to him. Their paths never crossed.

"Poor Stuart," Anne said. He sat looking out toward the sea, not touching the food in front of him. "I'm sure it's wrong your taking it so hard. Do you think you'll get her back by being chivalrous and forgiving? I like it, but do you think she will?"

Stuart leaned forward and put his elbows on the table. "I don't suppose so," he said. "At least, she'll pretend not to. I don't expect to be thanked."

"But you want her back, don't you?" She spoke with a disciplined lack of emotion, punishing herself for past triviality. Stuart found it impossible to feel sorry for himself with her. She was brutally childlike and wise.

"I don't think it really matters to me anymore," he said. "I

373

don't think you can get people back, in that way. But you can't let them go, either. I'm not being chivalrous. I'm doing this for my own sake. You know as well as I do that I couldn't do anything else."

"I suppose not. And yet it's very odd." She studied the small fried fish speared on her fork. "You're doing it for your sake. And she'll refuse any help for her sake. I don't know what that means but it makes me feel lonely."

"It means that the world is lonely unless you know how to break through."

"Break through?"

"Yes, you can break through with love. I haven't found out yet what you do when love fails."

Stuart returned to the prison at the appointed hour and was again received by the assistant director. He nodded curtly when Stuart entered and picked up the telephone.

"*Ça va. On attend,*" he said into it, and returned to a perusal of the papers in front of him. The silence was oppressive. Stuart shifted in his chair. It creaked deafeningly. He held himself motionless. There was a knock on the door and it opened simultaneously. Helene stood in the doorway. Her eyes swept over him and came to rest on the window in the opposite wall.

"I don't wish to see this gentleman," she said.

"Bring her in, bring her in," the man behind the desk said angrily. "We're not here to cater to the wishes of the prisoners."

A guard appeared at her elbow and led her into the room. She was wearing a dress that had been made to be worn with a belt. Without one, the dress hung on Helene like a sack, giving her a slatternly look. Stuart rose, keeping his eyes on her face. That was all right. She had altered very little. There was a new fullness under her chin and a slightly haggard look around the eyes, but her hair was rich and dark and she was beautiful.

"You don't have to talk to me if you don't want to," he said. He was glad he could speak English to her. Even if they could be understood, it gave him the feeling of speaking to her privately. "I wanted to tell you that I'll do anything I can for Robbie."

"You could have written," she said, without looking at him.

"I thought perhaps you'd want to talk over—that is, do you think I ought to go to Paris to see him?"

She lifted her clasped hands in front of her. It tried all her control to speak of the boy.

"If you could see him without fighting, I think you should."

"It is permitted you seat yourself," the prison official said in English. The guard had withdrawn. Helene sat down but Stuart remained standing beside his chair.

"Good, I'll go," he said. And then, because he wanted to talk to her and knew that she had always liked to talk about Robbie, he went on, "How's he been? Has he been painting?"

"Oh, yes." She looked at him impulsively and quickly averted her eyes. "He's made tremendous progress. That's why he's in Paris. He's working with Beauchamps. I'd thought of joining him when—" Her voice broke off abruptly and she concentrated on the picture of Stuart her brief glance had imprinted on her mind. How could he look so old? How could he look so broken and defenseless? She had actually feared his coming, feared his trying to take charge of her with his old slightly aloof kindliness. The glimpse she'd had of him had allayed her fears.

"Listen," he said gently. "I know you don't want to ask me to help you. But I'm going to whether you like it or not. If there's anything you can tell me about this thing, I wish you would."

"There's nothing much to tell," she said, unable to control the impulse to speak of it. "I wrote Carl, naturally. He left me a Swiss address where he said he would always be reached. These people are trying to turn me into a spy. Nothing can possibly come of it."

"But it seems that writing in itself is some sort of war crime."

"I have a good lawyer. There's nothing else to be done." She tried to put confidence into her voice. She would not have him feeling sorry for her.

"That's not true. Influence is all that counts in things like this," he said with distaste. "If you hadn't kept your French passport, they couldn't do a thing. That's my fault. Even if I have to use my father, I'll get you out of this." His voice was the voice she knew and she forced herself to look at him to dispel the effect it had on her.

"I've told you, I don't want your help. I'll tell my lawyer to refuse to cooperate with any steps you take."

It cost her a terrible effort to reject his offer. The thought of going back to the cell, of having to submit to the rough indifference of her jailers made any help seem like the gift of life itself, but she had to head him off. The decision she had made had been her own; its consequences must be her own, too. She was reasonably certain that her present predicament had been brought about by the denunciation of another woman, a woman who had long played an important part in Carl's life and of whose existence she had learned only after she had left Stuart. If he got involved in the case, he might learn of her existence, too. If for no other reason, she had to stop him. There were many things about her life with Carl he mustn't know. And yet there was little about it she regretted. Only by accepting his help now would it all be turned into a tragic error. She had to get through this alone.

"I promise you, I'll hate you if you do anything about it." She saw him bow his head and she struggled against the pity and tenderness that surged up in her; she struggled against the need she felt for somebody to turn to.

"I don't see really how that would change anything," he said musingly. She could still hurt him more than he would have believed possible. "I've got to the point where I'd almost prefer hate to nothing. But I haven't got to the point where I can see you here and wash my hands of it. I'm sorry you're against it but, after all, your pride, or your conscience or whatever it is, should be satisfied by having refused. I think it's very brave of you."

"Leave me alone," Helene screamed, so that the official jumped and Stuart reached instinctively for the support of the chair.

"Yes, of course I will," he said with his eyes lowered in the silence that followed. "And don't worry about Robbie. I'll see he's taken care of. Of course, with the war and everything, you'd both probably be better off in the States. Perhaps when you get out, you'd consider going back." He turned to the official. "I think that's all we have to say to each other. Thank you very much."

The official, who had been staring glumly at nothing, pressed a button on his desk and the guard entered. He advanced to Helene and touched her on the shoulder. She rose, her dress hanging grotesquely around her, and started toward the door. Stuart took a step forward.

"Helene," he said. She stopped with her back to him but he realized that if he tried to say another word he wouldn't be able to hold back his tears. And what was there to say? She belonged to Carl, or to herself. He turned abruptly to the wall and his mouth opened in a spasm of silent agony. When he turned back she was gone.

He stayed long enough to ask about conditions at the prison and to learn that he could deposit money to an account which Helene could draw on for small comforts. He also obtained the name and address of her lawyer.

When they were home again, Anne urged him to have a drink. He looked so tired.

"No, I don't think so," he said. "I don't need it anymore. At least, it doesn't do any good anymore. I'm afraid I'm not an alcoholic by nature." They wandered around the place while Stuart pulled a weed here, trimmed back a branch there, but the sun had lost its strength and they soon retreated to the living room.

"I better get off to Paris in the morning," he said when they were settled in front of the open fire.

"I'll go with you."

"No, not this time, Anne. If you really want to be helpful, you'll stay here and wait for me. It'll be a comfort to know you're here to come back to." He sighed and looked at her. "It's not much of a life for you, is it?"

She sat with her legs tucked under her and she looked small and young in the high-backed armchair.

"It's a funny time," she said. "Nothing seems to lead to anything. Do you really think the war's going to last long?"

"I don't see what's to stop it. Russia and the States will get into it eventually, I should think. One of these days, I'm going to have to do something about it."

"Oh, but you're—"

"Too old? Carl and I are almost exactly the same age and he's apparently valiantly serving the fatherland. I'd have done something before now only I was still a little groggy when it started and then you came along and I wanted to make sure that Helene and Robbie would be all right."

"I keep trying to think what makes you seem so old-fashioned," Anne said. "I guess it must be because you seem to care. Everybody I know would have got married again or had quantities of dazzling mistresses, or taken dope or something. Of course, you *did* drink, but you don't seem to have put your heart into it."

"All the more reason I should go get myself killed. There doesn't seem to be much else left for me to do." Anne's firm mouth closed more firmly and she looked away. Had he hurt her? She surely couldn't expect him to pretend that she had given him a new purpose in life. He was profoundly grateful to her but his gratitude was tempered by his conviction that there was little left in him worth saving. He rose and leaned against the back of her chair and put his hand on her shoulder.

"I think maybe we'd better have that drink after all."

He drove to Paris alone the next day and took rooms at the Ritz. He immediately sent for a tailor and offered a stiff premium to have several suits made for him overnight. He intended to play to the hilt his role as the rich and influential son of a rich and powerful father. He knew there was no point in asking for direct aid from his father. He had sneered at Stuart's domestic difficulties when he had seen him more than a year ago.

"We Coslings do badly with our women," he had said. "You, though, have had the good sense not to get tied up legally." Stuart was glad now that he had stopped off to see the disagreeable old man. It permitted him to give the impression that they maintained a normal father-son relationship. He was the heir of an English milord.

His game almost worked. Expensively groomed and handsomely tailored, he cut a fine figure. The Cosling name carried even more weight in wartime than in peace. After an initial contact with his father's French lawyers, Stuart had no trouble gaining admittance to ministerial antechambers. For several days he had high hopes.

"You and I know that anybody connected with the Coslings is above reproach," the dignitaries he interviewed said in substance. "But there is this tiresome matter of public opinion."

For Helene's sake, he was ready to make the most of the distasteful fact of privilege, but in the end it failed him. "It would change everything if she were your wife," an underminister explained. "As your wife she wouldn't be a French citizen. As it is, think what the press would make of it. Government corruption. The mistress of a highly connected person. Espionage. National security. We simply cannot afford any scandal. Couldn't you marry the lady in question? We could manage it secretly perhaps and after that it would be easy."

Of course, there was no hope of persuading Helene to accept such a solution. He could do no more.

It hadn't been all wasted. His efforts had assured Helene of special attention. He had been practically guaranteed that she would be tried by sympathetic judges who would deal with her lightly. Of course, if they'd been married— The knife was being turned in the wound.

He waited to get in touch with Robbie until he knew what success he was going to have. He wrote him a note now and asked him to call. He telephoned Anne, too, and found that it helped enormously to listen to her hard young voice. When Robbie phoned the next day, they arranged to dine together at the Ritz that evening. Stuart could draw no conclusions from the boy's manner on the phone except that he didn't sound actively hostile.

Robbie hung up in a quandary. There was no point in seeing his father unless it might help his mother in some way. He no longer dreaded facing him; he just didn't think they would ever have anything to say to each other. He had survived the worst period of his life without his father's or anybody else's guidance, and had found that he wasn't totally without character. His father's disapproval had become irrelevant.

The few weeks he had spent with Edward after the collapse of his parents' life, those few weeks leading up to his last year at school, had cured him of his hunger for promiscuous sex. He had done the rounds of the bars for the first time, and under Edward's disapproving eyes had gathered together groups of attractive young men and taken them home and given himself to anybody who wanted him. Group sex. Exhibitionistic sex. Voyeuristic sex. He had learned the limits of purely physical satisfaction. When his head count (cock count?) passed fifty he stopped keeping track. He was no longer interested. He wished that Edward could fill the strange terrible emptiness that he felt in himself but they couldn't quite connect. Anyway, they were about to be separated by the normal course of events.

School meant Maurice. When he was once more seeing him daily, he wondered why he had pinned all his hopes on him. He was everything Robbie remembered him to be— attractive, reserved but charming, quietly humorous—but never by the slightest glance or word or gesture did he betray any hint that he might be romantically or sexually interested in Robbie or any other boy. The only thing that Robbie had to go on was that in his middle thirties he was still a bachelor, one of only two bachelors among the teachers.

The only classmate he had felt close to was gone so there

was nothing to distract him from his preoccupation with Maurice. A handsome new boy looked at him with suspect interest but he had chosen celibacy until he had arrived at some resolution with Maurice.

As was usual among the masters and the senior students, some small social life developed between the art teacher and his favorite pupil. They took a few trips along the coast to museums and exhibitions. Maurice proposed dinner in town on a couple of Saturday nights. Robbie pressed himself against him, let his hands stray as intimately as he dared, tried to engage his eyes flirtatiously, but if Maurice was aware of it, he made no sign of responding. Despite all the evidence to the contrary, some irrational conviction persisted in Robbie that his elder was playing a game with both of them.

There was a moment of panic during the fall when there was talk of the school being closed by a threatened general mobilization, but an elderly British statesman returned from Munich announcing "peace in our time" and life resumed. Christmas approached. Robbie began to get desperate. He had heard from his mother that his father had returned and gone away again. He didn't feel emotionally stable enough to face her and her companion in the dangerous confinement of Carl's rented house. The situation was too explosive; anything might happen. The prospect so unnerved him that he began to wake up sobbing in the night. His personal life needed some direction. Only Maurice could provide it.

He knew that he wasn't in love in the blind headlong way he had been with Toni but he thought that if they were lovers something deeper, surer, more rewarding would come of it. He had admired Maurice's trim fit body on the tennis court. Although his manner and personality denied his sexuality, Robbie found him intensely desirable. The thought of arousing him from his rather British diffidence thrilled him. He wanted to find peace in the tranquil enclosure of Maurice's arms. More immediately, he was desperate for somewhere to go for the Christmas holiday.

None of his wiles succeeded. He even showed him, among others of his recent drawings, a full-length sketch of himself, naked, in which he had subtly emphasized his partially erect sex without exaggerating its dimensions despite the temptation to do so. Maurice barely glanced at it and reproved him for wasting his time on such literal figurative work.

He seized on what he thought of as a final attempt at seduction when Maurice told him he was going away for the weekend. The master had a collection of very expensive art books that he never allowed out of his apartment. Robbie asked him if he would leave his key with him while he was gone. He improvised a project for which the books would be useful references. Maurice hesitated.

"I suppose there'd be no harm if you don't let any of the other boys know. I don't want them to think I'm playing favorites."

Once Maurice was gone, Robbie hurried into town and had a copy of the key made. The next step was simply to get into Maurice's bed as soon as Maurice was in it. If that didn't work, he would know that there was nothing to hope for. At worst, Maurice could have him expelled, but he thought it more likely that he would be given a severe lecture and be made to promise to mend his ways.

As Sunday evening approached, when he was due to return Maurice's key, Robbie's nerve began to falter. Would he be able to go through with it? Circumstances turned out to be in his favor; Maurice was late and in a hurry and collected his key amid the usual bustle before dinner. Knowing he was back, Robbie had to fight the temptation to go to him that night, but for some reason he had settled on Monday night, when the routine of school would have resumed, and he decided to stick to his original plan for luck.

By Monday night, he was nearly frantic with anxiety and anticipation. His whole future was at stake. He worked himself up into an agony of indecision while he waited for it to be late enough for Maurice to be asleep. Should he give the whole thing up? Even if Maurice didn't have him expelled, he might withdraw the friendly interest he had taken in him and his work. He didn't know how he had thought of such an outrageous scheme. Duplicating the key. Creeping naked into his bed. Maurice would think he'd gone mad. Perhaps he should try to forget it and settle for the handsome new boy, whose advances were becoming increasingly bold. Robbie had had an occasion to observe that he had a very impressive cock. They were rare. None of the boys he'd picked up in St. Tropez had exceeded the norm.

If he had allowed himself some relief from his self-imposed celibacy, he wouldn't be goaded into pacing the corridors in his dressing gown now, breaking the rules, pretending to go to the toilet, waiting for midnight. Maurice was two flights of stairs above him, in an apartment on the top floor of the building where Robbie shared a cubicle with two classmates.

He could be with him in less than a minute. Feeling him so close, he knew that he was doomed to carrying out this final bid for his heart's desire.

Nothing happened the way he had expected. To begin with, Maurice was awake. Robbie had oiled the lock and he entered soundlessly except for the click of the door closing. He had learned the lay of the land. Maurice's bedroom was straight ahead of him, more a curtained alcove than a room. Robbie paused to let his eyes adjust to the darkness. A voice broke the silence.

"Who's there? Is that you, Robbie?"

Robbie's heart leaped into his throat. He stood transfixed while his mind seized on the fact that Maurice had expected him. Surely that meant that Maurice wanted him. "Yes, sir," he gasped.

"Stay where you are." A light switched on. He heard movement in the alcove and then Maurice appeared tying a dressing gown around himself. He looked very young with his hair ruffled and the dressing gown clinging to his trim athletic body. He looked as if he were naked under it. He stopped on the other side of the room and faced Robbie. "Did you do something to the lock so you could get in?"

"Not exactly, sir. I had the key copied."

The sides of Maurice's mouth twitched. "I should've thought of that. Did you meet anybody coming up here?"

"No, sir."

"What about your roommates?"

"Sound asleep, sir. Anyway, I told them I wasn't feeling well and might go to the infirmary."

"I see. You've thought of everything. Good. Now you'd better tell me what you're doing here. I might have an idea but I think if you do things like this you should be prepared to offer an explanation."

"Yes, sir." Robbie began to tremble all over but his eyes didn't flinch from Maurice's level gaze. "I want you, sir."

Maurice looked at the floor and nodded briefly. He turned away and went to his desk and sat and adjusted some papers. He remained with his back partly turned to Robbie. "Can you explain just how you mean that?"

"In every way, sir. I thought you'd be asleep. I was going to get into bed with you."

Maurice uttered a harsh impatient sound and swung around in his chair. His dressing gown fell away from his

382

handsome, firmly muscled chest. "Have I ever given you the slightest sign that you could have what you wanted?"

"No, sir."

"You're sure? Not a word, a touch, something in my eyes?"

"Nothing, sir."

"Then how can you have the temerity to come here with this insane idea in your mind?"

"I don't know." Tears stung Robbie's eyes. He pressed trembling hands to them and dropped his arms back to his sides. "It's something I feel when we're together. I feel as if I belonged with you, as if we belonged to each other. Maybe I've just imagined it."

"Even if you haven't—" Maurice started up and sank back into his chair and pulled his dressing gown around him. "My poor Robbie. You're so young. Don't you understand that at your age these infatuations happen? As we grow older, we learn how unimportant they are. I think you'd better go to bed. In the morning, we'll have forgotten all about it."

"No, sir. I don't believe you. This isn't unimportant for either of us. If you really wanted me to go, I'd feel so ashamed by now that I wouldn't be able to stay."

Maurice's expression hardened and he suddenly looked older. "Don't you understand that I'm trying to be kind?"

"It's not very kind to tell me to go when I'm baring my soul to you." He could finally move. He advanced into the room and pulled open his dressing gown and dropped it and stood just out of Maurice's reach. His erection slowly lifted between them. "I'm baring all of myself. I'm not ashamed. I'm yours. I want you to take me."

Maurice's eyes flickered over him but otherwise he made no move. His control was unshakable. "Have you thought what would happen if we were found like this together?" he asked.

"Yes, sir. There'd be a frightful scandal."

"It would be the end of school for you and the end of my career. Is a few minutes' pleasure in bed worth that?"

Robbie choked with relief and uttered a strange sound like a sob. He was saved. Maurice wasn't going to reject him. "You admit it would be a pleasure? Why should anybody find us? Are you expecting somebody?" He summoned up his last reserves of courage and took another step forward and dropped to his knees. He pushed Maurice's legs apart and found the erection he was sure would be waiting for him.

Even in the tensions of the moment, he was able to observe that it surpassed the norm. He bent over it and drew it into his mouth and moved his hands up over Maurice's body, pushing his dressing gown out of the way until he was totally exposed to him. He ran his fingers along the scattering of hair that defined his pectoral muscles. He felt as if his heart were melting in the joyful heat of learning the feel of him. Maurice shrugged off the dressing gown and gripped the sides of his head and lifted it away from him. He moved forward to the edge of the chair and pulled him into him so that their erections touched. They were naked together at last. Robbie shuddered with ecstasy. "Oh God, I've wanted it so," he moaned.

"How can I know what this means to you?" Maurice said with a hint of bewilderment in his voice. His eyes were altered beyond recognition, full of tenderness and desire. "Is it just sex? I'm in love with you. Does it sound ridiculous to you? I've been in love with you for months. I suppose you've felt it even though I've done everything I could to conceal it. You're a beautiful boy. I'm a mature man. Do you have any idea what I'm talking about?"

"I don't know. Do you mean I'm too young to know the difference between love and sex? Try me." His voice grew husky with the wonder of being loved. "I want you to take me. I'll be yours. I understand that."

"Do you know anything about homosexuality? I don't mean boys playing with each other. I mean the deep love that men can have for each other."

"I'm a homosexual. I hoped you were too. I've been in love with a man before. I want us to love each other."

"If there's any doubt in your mind about what you're saying, you'll be leading me into a very great sin."

"Unless you think making love is a sin, you shouldn't worry. I know what I need. You can't corrupt me. I've done everything. If you don't take me, I'll have to wait for somebody else I can give myself to. I can't imagine it being anybody but you."

Maurice rose, drawing Robbie up with him. They held each other lightly, their eyes meeting almost at a level; Maurice was a little taller. Robbie glanced down and saw that his erection wasn't quite as big as Maurice's, nor was his body as muscular. He had chosen well. Maurice was his master in every way. With all his guards discarded, his sexuality had become vivid and compelling. A little smile played around his lips.

"My dearest Robbie," he said in his gentle cultivated voice. "I'm quite worn out with resisting you. Bless you for bringing it to an end. What now? Is any of this possible? I'm holding the beautiful body you drew me a picture of. You didn't do your cock justice. I feel rather as if all my fantasies had finally broken my grip on reality."

They made love with an abandon that Robbie was proud to have stirred from the depths of Maurice's reserve. When they had washed and returned to bed, Robbie found the peace he had longed for in Maurice's arms. They talked, laying the foundation for what Robbie already thought of as their life together. They talked about the great difference in their ages. "Haven't you ever wanted a son, sir?" Robbie asked and they both burst into laughter. "I'm sorry. It's a habit I'll have to get over. Darling Maurice. Just think. You can make me what you want me to be. I'll be your obedient son and your passionate lover. It sounds like an ideal combination."

"I'm so terribly in love with you, my dearest. I'm not sure I'll be capable of much paternal authority."

"I belong to you. You can do anything with me. You've come into me and taken possession of me. I'm yours. I love you, Maurice."

They talked about Robbie's sexual experiences and Maurice's, and about fidelity. "It shouldn't be a problem at your age," Maurice said. "Youth has ideals and faith in the future. It's only as we grow older that we grow careless and self-absorbed. We begin to feel the passage of time and every opportunity missed seems to diminish life irrevocably. The fact of infidelity, the fact of holding another body is unimportant. I assume we'll have enough consideration for each other never to do anything that the other might find out about. It's the admission of a failure to love truly and wholly that does the damage. Perhaps you have to be unfaithful at least once to learn that."

They talked about the future. "I'll have to leave here when you do," Maurice said. "I've violated my most sacred oath. I swore that I would never lay a hand on one of my students. It wasn't difficult until last spring when I fell in love with your work. I've been obsessed by the fear of seeing you leave school without ever having you and knowing you and making love to all the beauty I see and feel in you. It was like knowing my life was coming to an end. We must be very careful while we're still here. I don't want us to leave under a cloud. Fortunately, I don't have to stay to make my living, but I owe it to the school and to myself to make an honorable departure."

"What can we do for the Christmas holidays?"

"I'll have to think. Nobody must know about it if we go somewhere together. We have many plans to make. My life from now on will be yours, my Robbie."

As far as Robbie was concerned, the foundations they laid that night had remained unshaken. At the end of term, Maurice took him to a beautiful small family château in the Loire valley. He discovered that Maurice was very well off. Robbie had never felt so cherished and worshiped, except perhaps by his mother. Maurice devoted himself to anticipating his every wish. His sexual appetites were as voracious as Robbie's; they spent a great deal of time naked in front of roaring fires. All their interests were shared. Robbie found to his surprise that despite his caution at school, Maurice frequented an undisguisedly homosexual circle, writers, musicians, theater people, a painter or two, who came from Paris for lunch or dinner. Maurice displayed Robbie proudly; they were treated like a newly married couple. It was the beginning of ten months of growing harmony that was brought abruptly to an end by the war.

Robbie longed for Maurice to be here to help him through the meeting with his father. Even after four or five months, he was just beginning to learn to do without Maurice. He would ask Raoul to go with him this evening, although he knew Maurice wouldn't approve. Maurice made allowances for his father's lack of understanding and thought Robbie should try to find an opportunity to arrive at a reconciliation. Maurice didn't know how impossible it was to get anywhere with his father, especially when he'd been drinking. The thought of his drinking decided him; Raoul would be a comfortable buffer against conflict. Maurice had arranged for him to stay with Raoul before he was called up. Robbie thought of him as his maiden aunt.

Stuart spent the hour before Robbie was due trying to prepare himself psychologically for their reunion. They had last met the previous summer, when Robbie had stopped for the night with Maurice Monneret, on their way to join Helene and Carl. Stuart hadn't known how to behave with them. Nothing in his experience had prepared him to deal with an openly homosexual couple. It was something to be swept out of sight, hidden in dark corners, but there was nothing furtive about this pair, nor was there any suggestion of depravity in their behavior.

Their making a kind of normalcy of their perversion made it additionally shocking to Stuart, a parody of human decency. If Robbie would recognize his sickness and ask for help, he would offer him guidance and sympathy and understanding. What could he offer a boy who placidly accepted his role as another man's wife?

He didn't know what Helene expected him to do for Robbie, except to assure him that he would provide all the money he needed. If he was working well, there was no point in his going anywhere else. He wanted to make him feel that he would always be welcome at home should the world situation change, he wanted him to know that he was taking an active interest in his mother's case, he intended to urge him to spend some part of the summer at St. Tropez if Helene were not yet free. Further than that, he was at a loss. Perhaps an evening alone with the boy would enable him to see him with fresh eyes, not as his own creation whose progress he had watched since infancy with love and hope but as an important talent in his own right whose sex life needn't concern him.

Robbie arrived with a friend. Stuart was barely able to be civil as Robbie introduced the stranger as Raoul Bertot, a large good-looking young man who on second glance appeared not so young. His dark hair shone so glossily, his skin was so well cared for that he almost achieved the freshness of youth.

"I told Robbie you might want to see him alone," he said, taking Stuart's hand with smooth self-confidence, "but he assured me that you would want to meet me and I welcomed the opportunity."

Since, as arranged, Robbie had come directly to Stuart's suite there was nothing to do but invite them in. It turned out that Robbie's address was in fact Bertot's and he was a friend of Maurice. He held some diplomatic post at the Belgian Embassy. Stuart told himself that he was going to have to learn to take it for granted that any male he met with Robbie might be his lover. Perhaps Maurice had chosen Bertot as a replacement to keep the boy out of trouble. The nature of their relationship was suggested by the way Robbie drew back and let the older man take the lead in the conversation. Robbie's eyes remained alert and penetrating but seemed to have lost some of their fire; he had a slightly languid air, like a woman who is accustomed to male attentions. Stuart thought he detected a growing effeminacy in the way he used his hands but admitted to himself that this might be because he was looking for giveaway characteristics. It was the first time he had seen him without a trace of a tan and the beard that showed under his pale skin was unexpected.

Whatever else might be said about him, he was a man and he was his son; this fact still held an element of wonder for Stuart. He was still beautiful rather than handsome but Stuart reminded himself that despite his mature manner, he was not yet quite nineteen. There was still time for his features to set into firm masculine lines. He was beautifully dressed in a tweed suit and a heavy silk shirt. He was obviously well taken care of. There was nothing Stuart could offer him.

"Robbie's been terribly upset about this thing with his mother," Bertot explained after Stuart had ordered drinks and they had seated themselves in the little gilt-and-satin armchairs of his elegant sitting room. "I persuaded him not to go down there. I thought she must know what was best."

"Oh, you know about—" Stuart began uncomfortably.

"He knows everything," Robbie said with a faint note of defiance that he immediately told himself to guard against. His father didn't look as if he'd been drinking and he felt only the rather ineffectual gentleness in him. He was sorry for having brought Raoul.

"Of course, the thing's absurd," Bertot said. He spoke as a disinterested observer, which Stuart supposed might have something to do with his being a diplomat. "As absurd as to say that Carl was a spy. We know all about Carl von Eschenstadt. Of course when he went back to Germany, because of his connections and because he knew all of Europe so well, he fell into an important post in intelligence, just as he's always fallen into everything he's ever done. The best reason I know for thinking the Germans might win is because Carl's gone home. He's the last person in the world to choose the losing side."

"You know Carl?" Stuart asked.

"Yes, of course. Now, what have you been able to accomplish? Robbie's very anxious to know what can be done."

Stuart looked at Robbie, who was apparently content to leave everything in the hands of his spokesman. He uncrossed his legs and crossed them again. The elegant little chair creaked. Looking at Robbie all the while, he told of his activities of the past few days. When he was finished, Robbie looked across him at Bertot.

"What do you think?" he asked.

"I think, under the circumstances, your father has done everything that could be hoped for," Bertot said authoritatively. Stuart felt as if he weren't there. "There's nothing more to be done but wait and try to keep it moving." There was a knock on the door and the waiter entered with the drinks.

"Just leave them over there," Stuart ordered, indicating a table against the wall. The waiter was young and Stuart caught Bertot's eyes running over him from head to foot. He felt a tightening in his stomach and he rose quickly and stood between them as he tipped the man and hastily dispatched him.

"You're staying for dinner?" he said with a neutral voice as he gave Bertot a glass.

"That's very kind of you. Perhaps you'd like an evening alone with Robbie."

"Of course not," Robbie interjected. "We haven't got anything private to discuss."

Stuart rapped his knuckles down lightly on the back of a chair and took a few steps around the room to get control of himself. He stopped in front of Robbie, his back to the other.

"No, of course not," he said easily. "Actually, dinner isn't a very good idea for me. I want to get off early in the morning and I still have a lot to do. I don't think there's anything else of importance we have to talk about. I must tell you frankly that everything I've done here has been against your mother's wishes."

He paused, conscious of the man behind him, and then forced himself on. "She didn't want me involved because she doesn't want me to touch her life in any way. Whatever I've done, I've done because I felt I had to. I'm telling you this so you'll believe me when I say that she *did* approve of my getting in touch with you. You needn't feel that you're betraying her by accepting whatever help I can offer you. I'm not talking about money, of course. I'll send you whatever money you need, but nobody knows how this war is going to turn out. I think you'd be much better off in the States when your mother is freed. Meanwhile, if they start bombing Paris, for instance, you should certainly come home. I want you to feel it *is* your home. Let's forget about everything that's happened in the past. You're almost of age. I can't tell you how to live your life and as long as your mother and I are separated and you choose to live with her, it's none of my business anyway. Don't worry about my trying to interfere with you. That's all. The way things are today, we can't come to any final decisions. The future will have to take care of itself. For your mother's sake, let's try—"

Robbie lifted his great dark eyes and for a moment they looked at each other. Stuart turned away. "Let's just try to keep going," he muttered thickly. Without seeing him, he held out his hand to Bertot. "Monsieur. Finish your drinks. Glad to have met you. I've got to make some phone calls." He passed around the back of Robbie's chair and touched his shoulder lightly as he passed. "You'll hear from me soon. Keep in touch." He managed to get to the bedroom door and close it behind him. For a moment, he thought he was going to fall. He lurched forward to a chair and fell into it and his mouth stretched open in a silent cry of despair.

He was glad to be home again with Anne. The world seemed clean and decent within the gates of his house. He got in touch with Helene's lawyer, who turned out to be a reasonable man. He was glad for whatever help his client was offered and he agreed to follow up the contacts Stuart had made without mentioning it to her. Stuart wrote to Robbie and Robbie replied. He had no definite plans for the summer but he would certainly be down sometime or other. And a postscript: "Do you ever go to the films? Did you know that Toni is Anthony Beaupré?" It was the only personal note in the letter but it made Stuart feel that perhaps communication might someday be re-established between them.

Spring came on. The war seemed quite unreal. Everybody agreed that it was, in fact, a *drôle de guerre*. He and Anne went out a little and saw something of the stragglers left behind from the old days. It wasn't much of a life but Stuart felt that he was at least keeping afloat.

And then the world fell apart. Something called the "Blitz." Dunkerque. The abandonment of Paris. The defeat of France. As the scope of the catastrophe became evident, Stuart tried frantically to get in touch with Robbie and finally decided he would have to go find him even though it was folly to go anywhere during the upheaval. Then a single line arrived: "Don't worry about me. I'm waiting for Carl." In the midst of it all, Boldoni somehow procured two automatic pistols and insisted that Stuart keep one of them within reach.

"Those dirty Bosches," he exclaimed fiercely, brandishing his own pistol. "God knows what might happen now."

In the profound silence that seemed to follow the uproar of collapse, the feeble voice of the Maréchal was heard in the land and Stuart began to hope that for Helene at least the disaster might have a favorable outcome. Only then did he hear that she had been tried and condemned to three years' imprisonment just before the French Armistice. The lawyer's letter had somehow gone astray. He looked at it for a long time, the carelessly typed words announcing the end of a life. How could Helene survive three years? She would come out, if she came out at all, broken and old and finished. For what? For writing letters to a man she loved. Stuart didn't believe in divine retribution but if he had he would have cursed his God. Helene didn't deserve this. It wasn't her fault that she had ceased to love him. She had had the courage to break the habits of a lifetime when a new love had called to her. Of course, if they had been married— The price that was being exacted for their offense to society was cruelly heavy.

He took the letter down to the beach where Anne was waiting for him. He handed it to her and sat down beside her, remaining wrapped up in his long beach robe. Since his body had begun to go to pieces, he had grown excessively modest. She read the letter and handed it back to him.

"If Carl's coming back, I shouldn't think that sentence would mean much." She lay on her back supporting herself by her elbows and threw her head back to the sun. She beat the sand lightly with her palms. "He'll have her out in no time."

"I suppose I'd better go through the motions with Vichy just in case." He had forgotten Carl. That was probably why Robbie was waiting for him. He felt somewhat cheered.

"Oh, let it go. Stop being a martyr," she said with an impatient toss of her head. "And take some of your wrappings off. You look ridiculous."

"I look ridiculous in any case," he said with a smile, but did as he was told.

"You're getting a pot," she said, eying it. "Most men do. Women too, for that matter. I can't wait to have one." She puffed her stomach out and her laughter was strong and clear.

Stuart looked down at the creases around his middle. He didn't like softness and he had allowed himself to go soft. Too much money. Looking down at himself, he remembered how wary he had been of money and he wondered why he had ever thought any good would come of it. He rolled over onto his stomach and looked at the girl beside him.

"You know, Annie, now that things have settled down a bit, we've got to do something about you."

She shot a sidelong glance at him. "Oh dear, are you going to try to send me away again?" He had thought she ought to leave a month ago but the rapidity of events had put it out of the question.

"You know, you won't be allowed to stay here indefinitely. Granted you're a girl, you're English, you know."

"What about you?" She too rolled over onto her stomach and propped her chin in her hand.

"I'm not English but I doubt if Americans will be welcome much longer. I've got to hang on as long as possible to see that Helene and Robbie are all right, but there's nothing to keep you here."

"Really? And where do you suggest I go?"

"Back to England, I should think."

"Whatever for?"

"Safety. The Germans might arrive tomorrow. Besides, what sort of life is this for you?"

"What sort of a life is it anywhere for anybody?" She turned herself over onto her back again and lay flat. She knew she was going to speak at last and she wondered if it was only the momentousness of recent events that made her feel she had so grown in stature that she could breach his almost saintly isolation. There was a moment's silence and then she said, "I say, Stuart, I think you're old enough to know. I'm in love with you."

Stuart made squiggles in the sand with his fingers, waiting for her words to make some sense to him. His first impulse was to tell her it wasn't possible since there was nothing left of him to be in love with. Was it a joke? She lay very straight with her arms at her sides, as if she were laid out in a morgue. Her eyes were closed.

"Don't lie there like that. It's depressing." He realized he was catching a manner from her. "And don't say things like that without looking at me. I don't know what you mean."

"I don't want to look at you. I might blubber. Worse, I might laugh. I'm tired of laughing. I don't want to laugh any more."

"Well, say something. I don't know what you're talking about."

"You don't know what being in love means?" She lifted her hands and brushed them together and folded them on her breast.

"I don't know what *you* mean. Is this one of your famous complexes? A father complex in this case, I presume."

"A Stuart complex. Just a great big unmanageable Stuart complex."

He heaved himself around to a sitting position and looked out at the sea. There was a lump in his throat. It had been so long since anybody had spoken his name in just that way. "You mean, if I let you, you'd be willing to stay here with me indefinitely?" he asked incredulously. It was no good to tell her that he wasn't worth loving. The fact that she did, or thought she did, made it untrue.

"Isn't it mad?" She laughed but broke it off. "I will *not* laugh. It's not funny. It's hell and it's wonderful and that's the way I want it to be. Go on, tell me how impossible it is. I suppose you'll feel you have to say it. And after that I'll tell you something."

"All right. It's impossible. Now tell me." Stuart had been struggling against an impulse to take her hand, to do anything to express his gratitude for her. But tenderness would be as wrong for her as laughter. He sat cross-legged like a buddha and waited.

"I've found what makes life worth living," she said in her flat even voice. "Lots of people tell you it's love so I suppose it shouldn't come as a surprise to me. Except that I didn't believe it. I grew up with people who seemed to be living for love and it was a mess. It's only since I've been here with you that I've understood what love is. People say love but they mean sex or using people to have their own way. The admiral was like that. He had to have wives to worship him. When they saw through him, he got new ones. As for sex, I'd seen enough of that by the time I was fifteen. And I don't mean I don't care whether I go to bed with you, because I do desperately. But just with you, and not with anybody else in the whole wide world, and nothing you can say will change it. I'm terribly happy right now. I know I may be terribly unhappy by tomorrow and I'm ready."

The struggle within Stuart was intensified. He wanted to hold her against him and find peace. Happiness for her. Peace for him. She offered devotion and hope for the future and peace and it wasn't enough. She couldn't grant him absolution.

"Annie, Annie," he said brokenly, facing away from her, "everything you've seen here should warn you that love isn't enough."

"Isn't it? Then what is? Why does it seem enough to me now?" Did he really believe what he was saying? She sensed in him a waiting, a delicate balance, like an avalanche held in check by a single stone.

"I think—" He groped for a truth that seemed to hover almost within his grasp. "Love is only the beginning. It's not the end. It's enough only for the moment it takes to acknowledge it. If you deny it, you have nothing. If you accept it—well, it's a beginning. The chances are it will fail you, but that's a risk you've got to take to live at all. It should carry you on to a greater truth, something more complete. That's where I've stopped. Religion? I believe the world is bigger than myself and that's a religious thought, but I don't believe in a life hereafter. I believe the answer is here, in this world. I don't know. I don't know."

He leaned back and stretched out on his side, looking down at her. Her eyes flickered open when he said no more, and closed again. "What are you going to do with me?" she asked.

"I'm going to send you home, Annie." His throat ached with the words. "I don't know what I'll do when you're gone. You're all that's left."

"Then let me stay," she interrupted, a new note of urgency in her voice.

"Wait, dear, listen," he said gently. "You think your happiness is with me. I could tell myself that if I can make you happy at least one of us would be better off, but it isn't as simple as that. You can't offer me happiness. Nobody can. So I haven't the right to attempt to offer it to you. Love can't be unselfish." He stopped, astonished at what he was saying but drawn on by his glimpse of truth. "Love must be demanding. Otherwise it's charity. It's the demanding that makes the connection. I used to be proud of being undemanding. Freedom. My theme song. I don't know what I was thinking of. There isn't anything in the world worth having that doesn't involve a surrender of freedom. You can't have convictions, ideals, beliefs of any sort without becoming to some extent a prisoner of them. Love is the ultimate prison. That's what I would never recognize. I'd like to be the prisoner now of the people I love but nobody wants me anymore. Except you, Annie. You'd start making demands I couldn't fulfill even if I wanted to. This is something you've got to know, my dear, and accept as one of life's cruelties. Forget me."

He lay back and they remained side by side, their eyes closed, listening to the beating of their hearts and the wash of the sea on the sand and high above them the faint turning of the sky.

"I feel clean," Anne said at last. "I feel as if something had burned out of me. It hurts." Stuart fumbled beside him for her hand and held it. They were silent again for a long moment.

"Did you know Edward was in love with Robbie?" she asked abruptly. She lifted her hand and placed it palm upward across her eyes. Stuart wondered at this unexpected turn in her thoughts as she went on, "I hope you don't mind my talking about it. You see, I was a little bit in love with Edward myself, so I like to talk about him to you. For a little while, when you first went away, he thought it might turn into something important, with Robbie. Poor darling. Everything would've been so much worse if it had. He said that Robbie was really looking for a father but they say that about everybody these days. Am I looking for a father? I doubt it. I've always been rather against fathers. We were all very much against you."

Instinctively trying to ease her hurt, she had retreated back across the years, so that momentarily Stuart became once again the enemy, the unsympathetic parent bent on repression. Not understanding, he said, "I'm sorry. I just can't think of love as having anything to do with Edward and Robbie."

"Oh, why can't you just relax and accept life?" she cried. She sat forward and angrily brushed sand off herself. "People are all different but sometimes they can make each other happy. But no, you've got to turn it all upside down and drain all the—the— You're cold and inhuman."

He looked at her agitated back with longing and regret. "I didn't use to be. I suppose you get that way when nothing seems to matter anymore. I'll never be able to believe that what Robbie calls love matters but it goes much further than that. We're all such masters of self-deception. At dreadful moments, I think I almost understand the communists. We're filled with such nonsense about the individual. All it amounts to is the individual's right to subjugate other individuals for pleasure and profit. Considering where that's got us, there's much to be said for relegating the individual to a back seat in favor of collective welfare."

"You've given up more completely than I thought you had," she said sharply without turning to him. "I don't think you've ever stopped to consider what a terrible thing you did to Robbie when you sent Toni away. Was that in the name of collective welfare? Something appalling happened afterward. Robbie could never talk about it but I know it had to do with the three of them—Carl and Helene and Robbie. You know of course that Carl was Robbie's lover as well as Helene's."

"No." He lay still, waiting for the shock waves to pass. He felt them more acutely than he thought he could feel anything. He finally risked speech. "Knowing that everything I'd lived for culminated in that, you can still believe that there's something in me to love? I suppose that's why you told me—to rouse me from the dead. You've got to learn that just because you're in love with someone, he won't necessarily fall in love with you." He said it to hurt her. It was the first act of real self-abnegation he had ever performed. She sat for another moment and then stood.

"Good. Thank you. I think that makes things clear enough. I'll arrange to go right away."

He knew anger would help her. In silence he watched her walk firmly down to the water's edge and slide in.

After a few telephone calls after lunch, she found out that the complicated process of her repatriation could most easily be arranged through the consular authorities in Marseilles. Stuart wanted to take her there but he didn't want to soften her anger against him and when she refused he didn't insist. He made sure she was adequately supplied with funds and let her hire a car. She avoided him the rest of the day.

The next morning, just before her car was due, she came out to the terrace where he was waiting for her. She was wearing a light summer dress and looked as if she were just running into town on an errand. She stood straight and still in the doorway and looked at him. "I wanted to go away being angry but it wouldn't be true." She laughed and gave a swipe at her hair and then looked at him gravely. "Being angry is no better than laughing." She paused and made a little motion with her hands, which hung at her sides. "Will you kiss me?"

"I hoped you'd let me," he said. He walked slowly over to her, keeping his eyes on hers, and took her in his arms. She lifted her arms and put them around his neck. She felt incredibly small and frail. He kissed her tenderly and then she buried her face against his chest.

"Oh, God, are you going to be all right? " she whispered.

"Yes, of course," he said, stroking her hair. "Are you?"

"Would you've made me go anyway if I hadn't said anything?"

"Of course. I told you it was the only thing to do."

"Stuart," she whispered, and looked up at him. Her eyes were dry, her mouth firm. "Will you kiss me once more?" He did so and they clung to each other for a moment. Then they broke apart and took a few aimless steps away from each other.

The rest was all hurried and anticlimactic. There was her luggage to brought out. There were Agnes and the Boldonis to say good-bye to. The car arrived. Before he knew it, she was gone. . . .

That summer Boldoni had a stroke. He was sure he was going to die and he wanted to die in his own house and Stuart had no choice but to let him go. With only Agnes to serve him, he shut up most of the house for the duration.

The pinch of war began to be felt. Certain foodstuffs grew scarce. Coal would certainly be scarce that winter. Stuart found an old man in the neighborhood to help him plant some of the upper terraces in vegetables and he began clearing trees in the wood along the drive. It was slow going and the exercise, instead of slimming him down, had the opposite effect. He put on weight steadily. In addition to the familiar chores, Helene's case kept him busy. That was slow going, too. The Vichy government was in the process of organization. The lawyer was confident that not too much time would pass before her trial was reviewed and the sentence reversed, but he reported that the prison regime had been hard on her. Meanwhile, Stuart received another uncommunicative note from Robbie saying that he was well and that Carl was doing what he could to arrange Helene's liberation. In spite of Stuart's loathing for the German, the news was encouraging. He could come to no decision about his own future until Helene was free.

Then, on a hot September morning as the vintage was approaching, Robbie telephoned. He wanted to know if Stuart had meant what he'd said about the house being his home.

"I can't talk. I just want to make sure I can come there no matter what."

Stuart felt a twinge of alarm. "Are you all right? Are you in—"

"Is Boldoni there?" Robbie interrupted.

"No, he's not here anymore. He's been sick. There's only Agnes now. Not very luxurious."

"Good. Will you send her away?"

"Look, what is all this?"

"I just want to know. If you'd rather, I won't come."

"Of course not. This place is as much yours as it is mine. Of course I'll send her away."

"Good. Then we'll be there in about an hour. Is that all right?"

"Sure. But who's—?" Before he had a chance to ask who "we" was, Robbie had hung up. Troubled and perplexed, he told Agnes he was going away for a while and offered to drive her to her family in town. He hurried her off and hurried out again. He hadn't been back long before he heard a car in the drive and nervously went to meet his son. Carl was with him, looking if possible more buoyant, more self-assured, more radiant than ever. He sprang out of the little black car and greeted Stuart enthusiastically.

"At last, old friend, after all these months. It seems a long time," he exclaimed, advancing with outstretched arms. "Who would have thought I would be returning with a victorious army, eh?"

Stuart watched stolidly as Carl approached. Should he hit him? Should he simply turn his back on him and order him off the place? Perhaps he was here for Helene's case. He had promised Robbie that his welcome would be unconditional. For their sakes he must make one more supreme effort at self-control. To shake hands was out of the question. He nodded and turned as the German reached him and took Robbie's hand and patted him on the shoulder.

"It's good to see you," he said. "Come in. There's so much to talk about."

"Nobody's here?" Robbie asked quickly.

"No. But why all the secrecy? What's the matter?"

"But *Carl*," Robbie said, his eyes widening with surprise. "Don't you understand? He's not supposed to be here."

In his confusion, Stuart had forgotten. In his white shirt and shorts, Carl fitted so naturally into the setting that he had forgotten that his presence in Unoccupied France was illegal, subject to severe penalties. Out of the corner of his eyes, he

398

saw Carl put a finger to his lips and then he heard him laugh with boyish playfulness.

"Behold M. Sernas, wine merchant," he said, with a bow to Stuart's back.

"I see," Stuart said thoughtfully. He took Robbie's arm and led him through the gates toward the house.

"So beautiful. So beautiful," Carl cried ecstatically behind them as they came within view of the Apollo. He stopped and cried out, "Ah so, this is what I've been waiting to see."

"Would you excuse us a minute?" Stuart said over his shoulder. So long as he didn't look at him, Stuart could just manage to address him. "I want to speak to Robbie."

"Yes, of course. I must unpack the car."

Stuart and Robbie continued on across the terrace and into the living room. Stuart gestured at a chair and sat down himself. Alone, he was able to look at Robbie for the first time. He was tanned and healthy-looking but there was another change since he'd seen him in Paris. He studied him an instant and realized that his hair was shorter than it had been before. It gave him a manly, clean-cut look. Stuart smiled his approval.

"Well, tell me everything," he demanded. "He's here to help your mother?"

"Mother's out. Didn't you know? Day before yesterday."

Stuart jerked forward in his chair. "Oh, thank God. How wonderful." He sat back with a sigh and looked out across the terrace. He felt as if he he been freed, too. "Is she all right? I haven't heard a thing. The mail's uncertain these days."

"Yes, she's fine," Robbie said. "Of course, it wasn't easy. She's lost a lot of weight. It makes her look older."

"And he arranged it?"

"He did what he could. He had influence but the pardon had to come from Vichy."

"I see, but then—" Stuart hesitated, puzzled. "I'm very pleased to see you, but why did he come? You can understand it's not very pleasant for me to see him. Isn't it dangerous for him to be here where he's known?"

Robbie moved around uncomfortably in his chair. "That's why I asked you if Boldoni was here. Carl can't stay at hotels. The risk's too great. He has some things he has to do along the coast."

Stuart stared at the boy. He had accepted Carl for Helene's sake, but since that reason was no longer valid wasn't he free to act as he chose? "People aren't allowed to violate the Armistice for personal reasons, no matter how important they are," he said. "You mean he's here on some secret mission?"

"Yes, as a matter of fact, he is." Since the Paris visit, Robbie felt confident of being able to handle his father. Seeing him now, heavy and unkempt in old slacks and sandals, he felt more sure of himself than ever. Something remained, a sort of atavistic filial response that he combatted by saying more than good sense suggested.

"And after he's finished, he's going to pick up your mother and take her back to Paris?" Stuart asked, still attempting to stave off the moment when his anger would pass beyond control.

"Well, no," Robbie said, rubbing his index finger against the palm of his other hand. "You see, well—time passes. Things change. Carl hasn't played a big part in Mother's life for some time. It's only natural that Carl—"

"You mean he's had enough of her?" Stuart broke out. His hands made a convulsive movement on the arms of the chair but he warned himself that he mustn't give way. "What's she going to do?"

"We've taken a house for her outside Toulon."

"We?" he asked distantly.

Robbie colored and his mouth worked before he answered. "Mother and me. Of course, you wouldn't understand. Mother's known all along that she wasn't the only person in Carl's life. He's not the sort to go in for domesticity and all that. He's too alive. Even with me—" Robbie's flush deepened and he leaned back and brushed his hair back several times.

Stuart looked at the floor and then lifted his eyes and let them travel slowly around the room, seeing nothing. There was too much to comprehend all at once. Helene had been freed. Carl was here to carry out a mission on behalf of the enemy. He was no longer interested in Helene. Helene had known all along. *Even with me*—Robbie's liaison with Carl was still active. "I think you must be insane," he said at last. "It's the best I can think of you."

"Now, just a minute—"

"No, it's all right," he said quietly. "I have nothing to say. This is your home. You're not twenty-one but you're getting there. You're your own master. All understood. But will you

400

simply tell me this? How does Carl dare to come here? The situation *is* unusual. I think even you'll admit that. I'll overlook whatever you're suggesting as far as you and he are concerned. But he did go off with my wife. And he has good reason to know that I have no sympathy for the government he represents. Why does he come here?"

"Because I told him to," Robbie said. He felt embarrassed and guilty, but not for his father's sake. His father was a cipher. One had only to look at him to see that he was half gone on drink. He was bloated and unwieldy. His fumbling attempts at fair-mindedness would prevent him from taking a strong stand. He was spent and ineffectual. "I knew I could trust you when you told me this was home. This is just the sort of place Carl needs as a base. I told him you'd make no objection if I wanted him to use it."

"In brief, if I understand you correctly, you're working for the enemy." Stuart folded his arms and looked up at the ceiling.

"What do you mean?" Robbie protested defensively. "Whose enemy? The Germans have won the war. They're perfectly willing for the French to run their own country so long as they cooperate."

"I see. Well, how long is our friend to honor us with his presence?"

"Three or four days this time. We have to be back in Paris within a week."

"And your mother?"

"I tell you, she has a house outside Toulon." Robbie's voice began to break. "She's aged. She needs rest and special care. I'll be coming down again from time to time."

"Splendid. Now let's see." Stuart withdrew his eyes from the ceiling and looked at Robbie vacantly. "Where'll we put you? I'm afraid the house isn't running quite as you remember it."

"I thought we'd take my house," Robbie said.

"It's all under wraps. Almost everything's been put away." Stuart looked at him thoughtfully and Robbie pushed at his hair. "Your hair looks better that way," Stuart said, nodding at him. Robbie smiled in acknowledgment. "Yes, your house," Stuart agreed. "That's the best idea. You can camp out somehow."

"What about meals? Shall we have lunch here?"

"I think not. You can get whatever you want from the

kitchen and take it over there. You haven't forgotten how to cook?"

"No, indeed," Robbie said with another smile. He wondered if his father had already had a lot to drink this morning. There was something definitely odd about his eyes. Robbie stood up. "Well, I'll go along and help Carl with the things. Will you be around?"

"I'll be around. Come for a drink before dinner if you like. But not Carl, if you don't mind. And don't feel you have to."

"I'll see. It's wonderful to be here again." He hurried out, eager to escape the accusation he felt in his father's manner. It was only a pale reflection of what he knew Maurice would make him feel.

Carl had burst into his life once more when he was alone and frightened by the cataclysm that had been taking place around him. Raoul had been ordered to follow the government in its flight from Paris. He didn't know where Maurice was. As far as he could learn, he had crossed over to England with remnants of the French army after Dunkerque. Carl offered familiar protection in his hour of need. Maurice would have understood that. Maurice knew all about Carl. Fidelity ranked high on Maurice's scale of values but he had made it clear before he went away that he didn't expect his young mate to live a monkish life. Dignity and self-control were his watchwords. So long as Robbie didn't debase himself, he would be forgiven. He wasn't sure whether consorting with the enemy, as Maurice too would consider Carl, counted as debasing himself. Carl had made him feel safe again in the ominously moribund occupied city. He seemed to know everybody of importance who was left and all the important new arrivals.

Maurice would be glad to know that somebody was looking after him but Robbie knew there was more to it than that. In Carl's company, he underwent a personality change that would have shocked Maurice; he became a stereotype homosexual because that was what Carl thought he had become. Carl didn't understand him any better than his father. He felt as trapped in falsity by one as by the other. Only Maurice could restore him to himself. He assumed that Carl's duties would take him away quickly, as happened with everybody, and was startled by his suggestion that they take a trip into Unoccupied France together. He wanted to refuse but something from the past made it impossible. He prayed that

Maurice would never find out about it. If everything went smoothly there was no reason why he should.

Stuart sat for what seemed like a long time after Robbie had left, presumably thinking, but when he came to with a start from some sort of reverie, he found that his mind was blank. He knew that he had to turn Carl over to the military authorities but that wasn't thought. It was a simple duty. Why? Had he always done his duty as the world saw it? That was something to think about but he wondered if it mattered. Nothing he did to Carl would restore Helene or Robbie to him. There was a war on. He knew which side he was on. Carl was the enemy. Thought wasn't required. It was an automatic reflex: Destroy the enemy.

He wasn't sure that Robbie was the enemy—yet. Could he report Carl without implicating Robbie? He could turn friendly, try to lure the German into town alone for a drink and set a trap for him. How deeply was Robbie involved in their mission? Was the nature of their work such that it would be known immediately that Carl had an accomplice? He could of course kill the man with his bare hands if there were no other way.

He found himself pacing the big room and stopped in front of the glass doors that were open to the warm September morning. He looked out. These stones, these trees, this glimpse of sea and sky were all that was left that he could call his. That and whatever beliefs remained within him that made him a man. What do I believe? he wondered. I believe, he said to himself and stopped. It was as complete an answer as most men could give to the question but he wasn't satisfied. He wished he had been born with blind instincts so that when he was wronged he could strike back. He wished he had an instinct to kill.

What would it be like? He tried to imagine it. Did you steal up on your victim while he slept and stick a knife into him? The moment between selecting the vital point and performing the act would be one he would find impossible to bridge. If you had a gun—he had a gun, he remembered, and it was a reproach to him. Damn Boldoni for insisting he take the thing. Well, could you take a gun and walk up to a man and pull the trigger?

He heard voices calling down the glade and he retreated into the room, his mind at last operating as he tried to settle on the best method of dealing with Carl. The authorities were undependable these days. Robbie might be involved. He hadn't much choice. . . .

Robbie and Carl threw open windows and pulled covers off furniture. A look at the bedroom revealed that the mattress had been removed so that the sofa in the living room offered the only sleeping accommodations.

"You think he doesn't mind too much my being here?" Carl asked as Robbie started to unpack his bag.

"Oh, he minds, but he'll work it all out in his head. He always does. It probably has something to do with the wrong he's done me." Robbie spoke flippantly and ended with a caricature of outraged innocence. Carl laughed and approached him.

"Wicked boy," he said, patting Robbie's cheek. "You deserve a reward, eh?" He dropped his hand to the boy's buttocks and gave them a squeeze.

"Thank you, kind sir," Robbie said, and laughed, too. "What do you want for lunch? I'm allowed to take anything I can find in the kitchen." Carl smiled into his eyes as the boy leaned against him with his hand on his shoulder.

"You're beginning to like Paris again, now that my countrymen have taken over, eh? I hope it won't go to your head."

"To my head, indeed." Robbie despised the person he turned into with Carl. They both roared with laughter. . . .

Stuart spent a strange afternoon during which time seemed to slow to an eternity and an invisible curtain seemed to have dropped between him and the world around him. When he handled objects he couldn't feel them. He noticed it when he went to get the gun. It seemed without substance as he checked its mechanism to make sure it was ready for use. He hid it behind some books on his night table and then went out to his car and drove into town and drew out a large sum of money from the bank, all the while feeling that the car, the bank, the bundle of bills that were delivered to him were not there.

Something else wasn't there. His freedom was gone. He felt as if he had been delivered of a great burden. He doubted if he would ever be free again. Whatever happened, whether real bars closed around him or he was confined by the figurative bars of the mind, he would be a prisoner of his act.

When he returned to the house, the little black car was gone and he made a slow tour of the whole place, aware that it was a tour of farewell but feeling nothing. He made careful note of all the things there were to do, figs to be picked, zinnias cleared out, orange trees pruned. He returned to the house and wrote letters. He wrote to his business manager in New York explaining that he was going to try to get to England to offer his services and that until further notice all income was to be paid to Helene. He left a blank for her address and made a mental note to get it from Robbie. He wrote a similar letter to Paris. He wrote a note to Agnes telling her that he was leaving, instructing her to arrange for the disposal of the pigeons and outlining a general program for the maintenance of the house.

Then he just sat, staring at his desk top. As the afternoon wore away, he was suddenly seized by an attack of nerves and he sprang into activity to quiet himself. He packed a bag, he went out to the kitchen and made himself a sandwich, he took a shower, perhaps his last for some time. Nothing helped. He remained taut with apprehension. Would he be able to manage it? Would his nerve fail him at the last moment? Would Robbie give him trouble?

He returned to the living room and made himself a stiff drink. And then, because he knew that alcohol couldn't alter his resolve, he had another and another until he was slightly drunk. He became sleepy and went unsteadily to the bedroom and got the gun and carried it back and stuck it under the pillows on the sofa. Then he stretched out with his head over it and went to sleep.

Robbie came in not long afterward and saw the bottle beside his father's sleeping form. He shrugged his shoulders and went on to his house to report to Carl that Stuart had passed out.

Stuart awoke slowly in the dark. Before he was half awake the consciousness of what he had to do was upon him. His head ached and his stomach felt hollow. He groped for the bottle and took a drink out of it and then he pulled the gun out from under the pillows and rose fumblingly and started toward the door. He stumbled against some furniture and steadied himself and completed the perilous journey across the marble-paved floor.

At the door, he steadied himself once more and looked out at the terrace and the moonlight and the cypresses. The fountain tinkled silver in the pool. At the head of the steps, as if returning from a midnight plunge, the white limbs of Apollo glowed. He was indifferent to the spell of the moonlight and the night's fragrance and the murmur of the sea. Beyond the olive trees he had seen a light shining from Robbie's house.

He moved in a company of ghosts, ghosts of things, ghosts of people. There was an act to be accomplished. Would it give meaning to everything, or would there never be a meaning, never an end in sight? He carried the gun at his side as he moved heavily toward the house beyond the olive trees.

He stopped once and stood still in an attitude of intent listening. Somewhere in his mind he heard the ghostly tinkling of the mechanical piano and he lifted his head defiantly. You stars, you worlds, whirling through eons of time into dark infinity, what is the significance of a man? What secrets do you withhold out there in your immensity? Where does the pattern begin and end?

He lowered his head slowly and looked around him. His mind played with memory, retreating back across time, back to the beginning when he had stood here with Helene and said, "And you see, we'll put the house here," drawing lines in the dust with a stick. He lifted the automatic and looked at it disinterestedly. It glinted sharply in the moonlight. He let his hand drop to his side and looked up at the light. He felt that he was on the verge of a discovery that had been withheld from him all his life, the basis of a greater faith than any he had known. He would know in a moment. He must first commit his act of war.

He started again toward the light. The uncertainty had gone out of his body. His sandals slapped against the steps as he mounted them and he made no effort to silence them. He was prepared for them to come out and greet him. It would be easier if they did. He heard voices and a burst of laughter and he edged his hand back against his leg so that they wouldn't see what he was carrying. He reached the open door and they were before him. Robbie was standing naked in the door of the kitchenette, laughing. Carl was sitting on the edge of the sofa with his trousers unbuttoned as if he were about to take them off. He turned, a smile on his lips, as Stuart appeared in the door.

Looking into his eyes, Stuart calmly lifted the gun and pulled the trigger three times. Carl rose slowly from the sofa but his face was gone and he crashed forward onto the floor, his trousers tangled around his knees. Stuart had the impression that it had all taken place in utter silence. He turned to

Robbie. The boy's eyes, wide and staring, were on Carl. He turned and began to vomit onto the floor of the kitchenette. Stuart put the gun into his pocket and leaned against the door, looking into the night.

He had done it. He felt nothing at all, neither remorse, nor the satisfaction of revenge, nor horror. His mind was clear. His head no longer ached. He felt as if he had acquired an extra lucidity. His thoughts turned to his next moves. He intended to spend the night with Boldoni. He would get off first thing in the morning and drive to the Spanish border. Once across it, he would be safe, but whether he should cross it openly or by the underground system he had heard of depended on whether or not his crime would be detected. He had to hide the body. That was going to be unpleasant. Would Robbie report him? Robbie was the unknown element in the situation.

As he thought of the immediate future he realized that for the first time since his legacy had permitted him to give up his job, he was acting under the stress of necessity. The choice was no longer his. At least, not if he wanted to save his own skin. He had recognized that this would be so this afternoon but he hadn't known what it would feel like. It felt fine. He sensed a whole world of comradeship waiting to receive him. He had joined the ranks. He had killed the enemy and earned a place in the mainstream of the common struggle.

Man's desires were too untrustworthy to be dignified by perfect freedom. Individual right? Individual freedom? The emphasis was all wrong. Common rights. Common freedom. Love was the beginning, not the end. Only through order could the true freedom of the spirit be achieved.

He had rejected his uniqueness and gained proportion. He knew now that what mattered was not just himself but himself as part of a human community, and he saw too that it mattered most of all how that community was constituted. The romantic cries, "Love," and means, "I am all." True wisdom replies, "I am all and you are all; this is the basic contradiction that must be resolved."

He was aware of silence. The sound of Robbie's retching had stopped. It was followed presently by another sound, a high, monotonous whimpering. He tore his mind away from his thoughts and he turned. Robbie was still standing in the door of the kitchenette. One hand supported him against its frame. The other was rubbing his head in a circular movement. Around and around it went through his hair. His face was contorted and from his throat emerged the insistent lament. He looked as if he had lost his mind.

Stuart went to a chair and snatched up a pair of trousers. Without allowing himself to look full at the form on the floor, he reached across it and pulled a blanket down over it. Then he took the trousers to Robbie.

"Here, put these on," he said roughly. He shook the boy by the arm. Robbie recoiled from him but Stuart kept his grip on his arm and half-led, half-dragged him across the room to the door. Around and around Robbie's hand went through his hair and his whimpering rose in intensity.

"For God's sake, pull yourself together," Stuart ordered him. "And put your pants on." His words had no effect and he shook the boy more forcefully. "I don't want to hurt you but, by God, I'll give you a beating if you don't stop this."

"Why don't you shoot me, too?" Robbie screamed.

Stuart released Robbie's arm and lifted his hand to strike the boy, but Robbie flung himself against him and clung to him. He lifted a tear-streaked face. He smelled of vomit. "Why can't you love me?" he pleaded. "I wanted it so much. You never have."

Stuart fought back the revulsion he felt at the sick smell of him. "You can't imagine how sad it makes me for you to say that. Until two years ago, you were one of the lights of my life. I was so proud of you. I'm still very proud of your work. I hear of you quite often. Robi—isn't that the way you sign yourself—like Toni?—Robi is getting to be quite well known. I'll soon be referred to as Robi's father." He watched Robbie's face dissolve with grief and a sob broke from him. He buried his face against Stuart's neck and kissed it.

"I wanted so much for you to love me when I needed you," he cried through his sobs.

Stuart again fought back revulsion, now mingled with disbelief, as he felt Robbie's erection lifting against him. He remembered the time he had seen him playing with himself, thinking that he was going to be quite a man. "For God's sake," he said in a voice that had become hoarse with distaste. He held the naked boy and soothed him and felt his erection subsiding. He waited until the sobs had become shuddering sighs and then disengaged himself gently from his embrace.

"Put your pants on," he said. "I want to talk to you." Robbie did as he was told. Stuart took his arm and supported

408

him out to the path that led down through the terraces. He sat the boy on the retaining wall and seated himself beside him. "I don't know whether we can talk to each other but there are things I have to know," he said. "Are you going to report me to the police? I can't stop you, of course, but you won't be able to do it until after I'm gone."

Robbie sat doubled over with his head in his hands. "Why do you say it like that?" he asked in a tearful voice. "Why do you always—everything I've ever felt—you always want to destroy everything."

"I don't understand you, Robbie. Maybe I never will." He looked at the boy's bowed head for a moment and then peered into the night. "I don't know whether I can reach you. But think, youngster, think. How can I know what to expect of you? Is anything important to you? Do you have any standards?"

"You've never made me feel that yours could apply to me." His words were blurred as if his lips were sticking together. He had lost Maurice in the blasts of the gun. Secrecy was no longer possible. He was at his father's mercy again. "You don't approve of anything I think is good."

"I could try," Stuart said. "Perhaps I was wrong from the start but you were very young. I thought I could save you from what still seems to me a terrible misfortune. Maybe it was too late. Instead of trying to get you over it, perhaps I should've tried to help you face it and make it part of a decent life. I don't understand it. Maybe it'd help to talk about somebody who wasn't unlike you in some ways, age and background and so forth. Do you know that Edward Cumberleigh is dead?"

Robbie lifted his head. "I heard something. Is it true?"

"Yes, he was killed while he was training for the RAF. I had a chance to talk with Anne about him not long ago. He was apparently very fond of you. In love with you, Anne said. The point is, he didn't believe that his—whatever you want to call it—his special tastes should be made an excuse for shirking his responsibility. He was killed doing his part. I find you engaging in obscene acts with a man I despise, a man—I don't think it's too fanciful to put it like this—a man who killed Edward. Can't you understand why your behavior shocks me?"

He saw the focus of Robbie's eyes shift so that he seemed to be looking through him and beyond him and then he dropped his head again into his hands. Stuart straightened and went on. "Talking to Anne about Edward helped me to understand that whatever you are, you can make something good of it. It will never be easy for you. You can do it only with self-discipline and dedication to principles, to decency, to love. You can't do it by defiling yourself. You must accept the world's standards in all the ways they can be of value to you. I think I would give my life to make you believe this." He stopped, feeling a great ache in his soul. My son, he thought, and his heart seemed to stop beating as he saw the boy shake his head.

"What can I do?" Robbie whispered. "What can I do?"

Hope started up in Stuart. He leaned forward and put his arm around the boy's bare shoulder. "I've presented you with a big decision. These are times for decisions. Something is being decided in the world. I don't think it will be decided by war but we can all decide for ourselves and we can make our decisions count by everything we do and say. It's not too late for you, Robbie. I'm sure of that. I want you to have a happy life, believe me. I don't know whether you have had up till now." He gave Robbie a little hug and stood up. "I have a few things to do. I haven't much time. I'll be right back."

Stuart walked slowly back to the big house. He went into the bedroom and brought his bag out to the terrace and closed the great sliding doors behind him. If Robbie wanted to stay here tonight, he could do so. Agnes would come out tomorrow and put things away and lock up for good.

He paused on the terrace and surveyed once more the meaningless beauty he had made and went on to the car and left his bag in it. He collected some odd lengths of rope from the garage and started back up to Robbie's house.

Hearing his father coming, Robbie straightened and braced himself to face him. Shock had passed. He could think sanely now. He didn't regret Carl's death. It was a deliverance; he was free at last from his romantic and impressionable boyhood. He knew that he was better than his father thought and was embarrassed at showing it for fear that it would lead to more falsity. He wasn't a hero any more than he was a giddy sex-mad faggot. He knew that his father must have felt his brief erection. In the frenzy of the moment he hadn't cared. If understanding were possible between them, it would be easy to explain that feeling his father's protective arms around him had given him for a moment the sense of being held once more by Maurice. He wished he knew how to give him a glimpse of who he really was.

"Feeling better, fellow?" Stuart said quietly, coming close to him and putting his foot on the wall.

Robbie nodded. "I want to warn you," he said, scarcely daring to speak for fear of losing what this moment could mean to him. "The people we saw today, Carl and I, we're supposed to see again tomorrow. If we don't turn up they'll know something's wrong. They know where Carl has been. You haven't much time."

Stuart took a deep breath and passed his hand over his eyes. So he had been granted at least this much; his son would not betray him. It was the beginning. It was perhaps everything. "Thank you," he said. "Are you in any danger?"

"About this? I don't think so. I just came to be with Carl. I have no connection with anything else."

"I see. Do you have any idea what you're going to do now?"

"You know, about—" Robbie began hesitantly. His heart had started to pound. "Mother has never taken it like you. She knows but I don't think she lets herself imagine exactly what it means, so for her it hasn't been a problem."

"That's what I've gathered," Stuart said quietly.

"You see, it's not just something you decide not to do, like smoking or drinking."

"I understand," Stuart said. He supposed he couldn't expect him to take a vow of chastity, although others had, or buried it so deeply that it amounted to the same thing.

"I think Maurice is in England. That's where you're going, isn't it?"

"I'm going to try."

"After tonight I'm not sure I have the right to go to him. I hoped he wouldn't find out about my being here with Carl, but now it can't be a secret. Maybe he'll forgive me. Can you understand that I want to be with a man I love?"

"I understand you very little, Robbie, but I'm deeply moved by the way you say it."

"Then—then even if I don't find Maurice, I want to go with you."

The breath caught in Stuart's chest and he almost cried out with it. The earth seemed to reel and he steadied himself against the wall. His throat was tight and he was grateful for the dark that hid his tears. "Good," he said. "Do you want to see your mother?"

For an instant Robbie was tempted to say no for fear of breaking the fragile bond that had been born between them,

411

but he couldn't lie about something so precious. "Yes, I may not see her again for a long time."

"Yes," Stuart said, glad of his answer. "We'll stop by on our way tomorrow. Now I wish you'd go to the house and wait for me. I have one more thing I have to do."

"Is there anything I can—?" Robbie faltered.

"No, you've been through enough for tonight. Go to the house and see if there's anything there you want. Some of your things may've been moved. I'm leaving almost all my clothes here." He waited while Robbie started down toward the main house and then he hitched the rope up onto his shoulder and went on up to Robbie's house.

He went in, squinting slightly as if that would prevent him from seeing clearly. The formless shape under the blanket made his stomach turn over. His first glance told him that there was a great deal of blood. Agnes would have to make of it what she would. He brought a handful of dishtowels from the kitchenette and threw them down onto the worst of it and pulled the body out of the way. Then he stumbled to the door and leaned against it, waiting for his stomach to settle.

When he had himself under control, he went back and gathered the dishtowels up into a ball and pushed them under a fold of the blanket. He knew the next step was going to be the most difficult thing he had ever had to do in his life but there was no avoiding it. Tugging at the blanket, trying not to see what it contained, he rolled the body and tied it into an untidy bundle.

Heaving and sweating, he dragged it out of the house. Again he was forced to wait while his stomach turned over and finally was quiet.

He stumbled with his load around the back of the house to the end of it. Even in the dark, he knew every inch of the way. He hadn't much farther to go. At the edge of the property, the land fell away in a short steep drop to a sort of hollow that was almost a cave. He dragged the bundle to the edge of the small cliff and with what strength was left him gave it a push. He heard it land with a thud. It was the best he could do. The body would be discovered. Perhaps soon, perhaps not for some time. In any case, he would be gone.

He mopped his face on the tail of his shirt as he made his way back to Robbie's house. He felt suddenly numb with exhaustion. He stopped long enough to go through the rooms and gather up Carl's papers and personal effects. He took Robbie's suitcase and snapped off the light and left. Robbie was waiting for him on the terrace when he returned to the big house.

"Come along," he said, avoiding the boy's eyes. Robbie started toward him and Stuart glanced over his shoulder for a final glimpse of the place where he had spent the most important years of his life. For an instant, as his eyes moved over the statue and the row of columns, ruin seemed to hang over it all. He gazed at a vision of the future—all of it gone, all swept away, nothing left standing but one pink column against the blue and eternally tranquil sea.

He turned back to Robbie and put his hand on his shoulder and said, "Come on. We're going to sleep at Boldoni's. We want to get away first thing in the morning."

They drove, speaking little, along the sea toward Toulon in the bright early morning. Stuart concentrated on precautions to be taken for the immediate future. It was most important that they should be at the frontier by evening.

"I hope we won't be getting your mother out of bed," he said, glancing at his watch as they drove through a still-shuttered seaside resort.

"She's usually up pretty early," Robbie said. He sat stiffly, looking straight ahead of him, suffering from delayed shock. He had awakened in the middle of the night drenched with sweat, the ghastly moment fixed in clear detail in his mind. It had kept repeating itself all through the rest of his fitful sleep—the shot, blood spurting as Carl's head seemed to explode, the crash of his body.

He scarcely knew the man at his side but was awed by him. He hadn't believed that there was steel and passion concealed in his father's faltering body. He made even the best in himself—his work—seem trivial. Did he have the strength to follow where his father led him?

Perhaps his mother wouldn't let him go. Perhaps losing him would be more than she could bear. He would make a show of holding out against her and let his father give in to her pleading.

"What are you going to say—I mean, are you going to tell her about Carl?" he ventured after they had driven another fifteen minutes in silence.

"Good God," Stuart exclaimed. He swerved the car over to the side of the road and stopped with a squeal of tires. "Wait here a minute. Something I forgot. I'll be right back." Robbie watched him with astonishment as he left the car and crossed the road.

413

He had forgotten to destroy Carl's papers. He had gone through them last night at Boldoni's before going to bed and found nothing of interest but there was a risk of leaving telltale traces if he destroyed the things in Boldoni's stove. He had kept them all together in his pocket, planning to get rid of them as soon as he was on the road.

A grove of pines descended from the highway to rocks and the sea. Stuart hurried down through it until he was out of sight of the road and then squatted and began to empty his pockets, his hand trembling slightly at the sight of the incriminating documents. There were road controls all over the place. If he were stopped for any reason, what conclusions might be drawn if an extra set of identity papers were discovered on him?

He set a match to the papers and crouched over them with a stick, prodding them as they caught fire one after the other, watching as the flame leaped up, flickered, and went out. He ground the ashes into the earth with his foot.

"About Carl," he said when they were once more on their way. "Will it be a blow for your mother? I mean, would it be kinder to tell her or should we let her find out later? Will she be worried if she doesn't hear from him soon?"

"I shouldn't think so," Robbie said, hesitating as he grasped the implications of his father's words. Was this what death was like, this indifference, this nothingness? Yesterday he had seemed so irresistible. Being freed of him by death forced him to face the weakness that had made it impossible to escape him while he was alive. Maybe his father would give him strength. Maybe he would finally be worthy of Maurice. He went on, "I told you, there wasn't much—well, you know, I don't think it will be a great loss for her. She—well, she changed in prison. She rather expected to see him before we went back to Paris but if he doesn't turn up I don't think she'll wonder about it. I can say his plans changed."

"I see. In that case, perhaps it'd be better not to go into it. You could write her later." Silence fell between them again as Stuart went over Robbie's words in his mind. "Letters of passion" a year ago and resignation now. Poor Helene. The lawyer had suggested that the prison regime had been hard on her. Now Robbie spoke of a "change." That she should have aged was understandable but had she been completely broken? The thought of seeing her again began to grate on his nerves. He felt he ought to prepare himself for a shock but he couldn't imagine her beauty being anything but dignified by age.

They reached a crossroad and, following Robbie's directions, turned off the Toulon highway onto a country lane. In a few minutes they were rolling through flat vineyards pierced by an occasional cypress. In the distance they caught glimpses of the sea.

"Here we are," Robbie said, and Stuart turned the car into a dirt drive that ran through vines. Ahead of them a clump of trees partially concealed a house. Stuart's heart began to beat faster. He stopped the car under the trees and they got out and walked around the corner to the front of the house.

They found themselves before a white façade bathed in morning light. The house had the severe lines of a Provençal farmhouse but there were touches that gave it a prosperous look, a carved-stone cornice above the central door, a balustrade running around a paved terrace, freshly painted blue-black shutters at the windows. A huge tree cast its shadow across part of the terrace where a table was set for one with a china bowl and a checked napkin.

Stuart's first thought was that it looked restful and sane; there was none of the stage-decor look about it that their place had always had, even at the beginning when its very primitiveness had been a bit too idyllic. The door opened as they approached and a small gray-haired woman emerged, carrying a tray with a silver pot that flashed in the sun. She glanced at them as she set the tray on the table.

"*Bonjour, monsieur,*" she called. "Your mother will be down in a moment."

"It's Angèle. She's been with us for some time," Robbie explained. And then, "*Bonjour,* Angèle. You better bring some more cups." They had reached the two wide steps that led up to the terrace when Helene's voice came to them from within.

"Is that you, darling?" Her voice was warm and welcoming. "Heavens, you *are* an early bird." Shutters were thrown open with a clatter and Helene appeared at a window in the upper floor. "I didn't expect you so—" Her eyes met Stuart's and his heart seemed to stop. "Why, Stuart, what a nice surprise. I'll be right down." She left the window and Stuart was able to breathe again.

He had caught a glimpse of two wings of gray hair brushed back softly over her ears, of the great eyes in a face that had strangely altered. How? He hadn't had time to take it in. He waited tensely on the edge of the terrace, his eyes on the door.

He was vaguely conscious of Robbie stirring about beside the table. Then the door opened and Helene swept out, crossing the terrace first to Robbie, whom she gathered into her arms in a quick embrace with a murmured, "Darling," and then advancing to Stuart with lifted hands which she placed on his shoulders as she kissed him lightly on both cheeks. Somehow she had managed it, somehow she had swept away the years of estrangement, somehow she had made it seem natural for him to be here.

"How nice of you to come," she said. "I was going to write you."

Stuart could see her now. She was thin. That was all. Why all the talk of "aging" and "change"? She was superb. Her ample body had been fined down, her face was pure beauty of line and coloring. Her gray hair was enormously becoming. And, oh, the unquestioning acceptance of her greeting, the blessed satisfaction of feeling no barrier between them. She turned back to Robbie, putting her hand on Stuart's arm, and started toward the table. She faltered suddenly as if she had tripped and lifted her hand to her eyes, steadying herself against Stuart.

"Oh, dear, here we are all together again." She uttered a tight strangled laugh that threatened to break into tears. She raised her head and shook it and took a deep breath and moved with strong easy strides to the door. She was wearing a long dressing gown of dark red silk that clung to her startlingly spare frame.

"Angèle," she called from the door. "Bring lots of bread and butter and another pot of milk and—and preserves." She turned back to them, looking from Robbie to Stuart, and lifted her arms as if to embrace them. "Come. We'll have an enormous breakfast. I'm still not quite used to having all I want to eat." They gathered around the table where Robbie had placed two more chairs. As they seated themselves, Helene made a quick, discreet appraisal of Stuart. He was looking much better than he had last winter. There was no longer the wounded look in his eyes. He moved as if he had a firm grip on himself. She could meet him now without resisting him, without fighting him. She remembered and understood her reaction to him when he had come to the prison offering help, without experiencing any of the same emotions now. She had met her supreme test with only her own resources. She had proved herself and was whole. There was nothing in him or in herself that she feared.

Angèle brought a big basket of grapes in addition to the things Helene had ordered and Helene occupied herself with serving them. Robbie was acutely embarrassed by this reunion and amazed at the easy understanding that seemed to exist immediately between his parents and he kept his face averted over his bowl of coffee, waiting for his father to get around to an explanation of why they were here.

"Actually, we have very little time," Stuart said, breaking the ice. They were the first words he had spoken. He dreaded telling her of Robbie's decision. No matter how superb she looked, she must have suffered terribly, mentally and physically. The loss of Robbie might be the one blow from which she couldn't recover. In that case, had he the right to take him from her? "You see, this isn't exactly a casual visit," he explained.

"Oh?" Helene said, offering him sugar. "Are you taking Robbie back to Paris? Have Carl's plans changed?" Stuart glanced at Robbie, who kept his head bowed over his coffee.

"We're not going to Paris," he said. "It's time I did something about the war. I've just been waiting—well, I wanted to be sure that you and Robbie would be all right." Helene looked up at him and their eyes met and she looked suddenly grave. She put out her hand and touched his sleeve briefly.

"I'm afraid I haven't thanked you for all you did," she said. "You've been very good. At first, it was hard for me to—to admit I needed help, I suppose. I've thought about it since."

"You know I didn't expect to be thanked," he said, dropping his eyes. How different from what he had feared. Thank God, he had come. Thank God, he could leave here with this picture of her in his mind, this feeling in his heart. He plodded on with his explanations. "Anyway, it's time I did something. I'm going over into Spain. From there, I'll go to England—to the States if it's easier but eventually to England. That's where the war is."

"And Robbie?" she asked.

Stuart could feel her eyes burning into him. He looked at the table. "Robbie," he said, "would you like to explain?"

"I've told him I'd go with him," Robbie blurted. If she was going to protest, he hoped she would do so effectively enough to override all opposition. He couldn't bear to leave her in

417

tears. There was a moment of silence. Helene rose slowly. Stuart watched her as she took a couple of paces around the table, with her hands clasped in front of her. She stopped in back of Robbie's chair and put her hands on his shoulders.

"Do you feel this is something you have to do?" she asked.

Robbie shrugged and said nothing. He didn't feel that heroic declarations would be appropriate. She saw his long fingers tighten around the bowl of coffee and she knew that she could keep him with her. It was a blessed knowledge and she exerted a loving pressure on his shoulders. Yes, she could keep him and because she could keep him she must let him go; she must make her own life just as he must make his.

And yet, dear God, it was hard. Let him go—to what? To danger, perhaps even to death? She felt his shoulders rising and falling under her hands. Oh, God, keep him safe. At least, he wouldn't be with the Germans. She had feared Carl's influence. She was grateful to Stuart. How odd that everything seemed to be falling back into place. She dropped her hands from Robbie's shoulders and resumed her seat. "I see," she said abstractedly.

"But will you be all right?" Robbie stammered. Was this all she had to say? He was aware of his father's eyes on him and he brushed his hand nervously through his hair.

"You mustn't worry about me," she said lightly. She buttered a piece of bread, deriving from the homely act a sense of normalcy, perhaps even a sort of courage. "In times like these, we've all got to be self-reliant."

Robbie could hardly believe his ears. Did she care so little about his leaving? He darted a quick glance at Stuart and then lifted his head and faced him squarely. He enlisted himself unequivocally at his side; he was ready to follow this man. Carl was really gone. He hoped his mother wouldn't make difficulties. They would find Maurice. His father would like him and begin to understand. He would find ways to redeem himself in his father's eyes.

Stuart acknowledged his level gaze. He was as surprised as Robbie by Helene's self-control. What did it mean? Was it indifference, a complete withdrawal from life? Had the months in prison so crushed her spirit that she was resigned to anything that might happen to her? "So you see," he said, "we've got to be on our way soon. We've got to cross the frontier tonight. Boldoni's given me the name of a friend in Perpignan. I imagine it'll all be quite simple."

"What would we do without Boldoni?" Helene said with an easy laugh. "Robbie, darling, there are several of your suitcases here along with the things that were brought from the other house. Maybe you ought to look through them before you go. They're in the room on the right at the head of the stairs. You'll see."

"All right." Robbie finished his coffee and rose. "There's M. Forrestier," he added, lifting his hand in a restrained greeting. Stuart turned and saw a lean figure in riding clothes crossing through the vines in front of the house.

"Did you want me, Jean?" Helene called. The man lifted his hand and shook his head and passed on out of sight around the house. Strange, Stuart thought, to feel so much a part of their lives and to be so completely outside it. She and Robbie called people he didn't know by their first names, had lived in houses he had never seen, were served by maids who didn't even know who he was. . . . *She's been with us for some time. Did you want me, Jean?* Words on which whole lives were erected, words standing implacably between them and the past.

"That's my landlord," Helene offered in explanation. "A very nice man. He testified for me at the trial. The main house is back over there."

"I'm glad you have friends nearby." Stuart glanced around him. Robbie was gone. He pushed his cup from him and leaned his elbows on the table. "I know Robbie's leaving can't be easy for you, but I think it's the right thing for him."

"I do too," she said simply. He felt in her a deep quiet authority that was totally unfamiliar to him. They sat close together, their eyes averted.

"That's good," he said. "But what about you? Have you thought about going back to the States?"

"Oh, no, I belong here. I'm used to it now. Perhaps you belong most to the country where you've been in prison." She finished with a laugh.

"It's been a terrible time for you." He looked up at her hesitantly. She was sitting with her arms crossed on the table. There was a faint smile on her lips. He continued, watching her, "You're looking marvelous in spite of everything. And there's something—I don't know. You seem very different. Are you all right? I mean, are you coming out of this all right?"

"One lives and learns, I think." Her smile broadened.

419

Stuart felt his heart beating fast again. This was his moment. He held his hand out open in front of him. If the truth he had grasped was worth anything it must be equally valid for her. It must be communicable. He closed his hand and placed it next to hers. He looked at their two hands as they lay side by side, almost touching.

"Tell me," he managed, scarcely above a whisper. "Tell me what you've learned."

"Why, Stuart," she said with a trace of friendly mockery, "you've always been the one to tell me." As she spoke, he knew that he had said all he had to say. He had communicated. The truth lay clear and simple between them. He felt as if he had been confessed.

"I think we can talk to each other now," he said.

"Then you feel it, too?" she asked. Their eyes met and he nodded briefly. The nod seemed to release her, for she put her hand over his and began speaking rapidly. "In prison—at first, when I was alone, it was more terrible than you can imagine. But afterward, after I was sentenced—the other women, the routine. It's odd how quickly one gets used to things. Life suddenly seems so simple and so good. One thinks of the walls and the locked doors and knows that if they could be removed, the rest is easy. Can you understand? People struggle against walls that don't exist. When they're really there, holding you in, you understand how good life is and how simple the things are that you really need and—and how much of the trouble is in the mind—the struggling against things that don't exist. And now I'm free and I think of those poor creatures who are still shut up and I want to be immersed in life—I want to eat and sleep and reach out to people and sit in the sun and breathe this air and look out at these fields and I'm very happy. It reminds me a little of when we first went to St. Tropez, only then I didn't know."

She lifted her face to the sun and closed her eyes and as she finished she pressed his hand in hers. He looked at their joined hands and then at her lovely face, paler than he was used to seeing it, and he wanted to put his arms around her, not passionately—too much had happened to them for that—but with tenderness and affection.

"No, neither of us knew then," he said. She lowered her head and opened her eyes and looked at him for a long moment. He looked like a very good man, she thought.

"Oh, my dear," she said softly, "there's nothing to regret. The trouble started so far back, back at the beginning—our

420

meeting just after René lost his mind and—and everything. But we had some wonderful years."

"Wonderful," he said with difficulty. "Better, I suppose, than we deserved."

"And nothing is lost. Carl had to happen. I used to be ashamed—I didn't want you to find out that he treated me rather shabbily. But, you see, I don't mind anymore. In fact, it was your right to know. He's rather a scoundrel, Carl, but he'll end by regretting it. People finally punish themselves. Most of us don't find that out until it's too late. Our ruined lives. Do you remember? You don't feel that now, do you?"

"No, I don't feel that. I think I'm just ready for life. I feel the same thing in you."

"It does take a long time, doesn't it?" She pressed his hand, then disengaged her own. She selected a bunch of grapes and handed it to him and took one herself. They ate for a moment in silence.

He felt peace in her presence but he knew that when the time came there would be no wrench of parting. He would be taking something of her with him. Strange . . . yesterday this meeting hadn't figured in his plans, yesterday she had still been for him the woman who had screamed at him in prison, the woman he had imagined broken by months of confinement, abandoned and done for. Yesterday he had been alone, free, free of hope, free of faith, free of feeling. . . .

"I wonder how long it'll be before we see each again," he said at last.

"I wonder . . . Do write. And come if you can."

"Thanks. I'd like to." He looked at his watch. "We've really got to go. What's Robbie up to?"

She reached her hand out to his with a new urgency. "Help him," she said. They looked into each other's eyes and he nodded reassuringly.

"I want to. I'm going to do my best to find Maurice for him. Amazingly enough, I see that now as helping him."

Her eyes softened with fond, slightly playful complicity before she glanced over her shoulder and called up to the house: "Robbie."

"I'm coming," he answered, and they heard him thumping down the stairs. He came out onto the terrace and dropped a small suitcase. "There wasn't much worth bothering about," he announced.

Helene laughed and went to him. "Don't look so tragic, darling," she said, lifting her hand to his cheek and giving it a

421

pat. "I wish I were going with you. You're going to look rather stunning in a uniform. Send me your picture some time."

Stuart had risen, too, and stood awkwardly beside them. "Well, off we go."

She turned to him and hesitated for an instant and then she put her arms around his neck. He gathered her close, feeling her body strangely frail in his arms, frail and yet known and comforting. "Take care of yourself," he muttered. "Fatten yourself up."

They broke apart and Helene gave his stomach a flustered pat. "You do the opposite." Her voice hit two broken notes of laughter. She stretched out her arm to Robbie and lifted her hand quickly and pressed her eyes with her fingers.

"Oh, dear, don't let me forget anything. Oh, yes," she dropped her hand and there was a strained smile on her lips. "There's that sweater I knitted for you in prison. I'd like you to have it with you. Just a minute." She turned and hurried back into the house.

"I'm going to the car," Stuart said without looking at Robbie. He crossed the terrace and stumbled down the steps and around the house. He hunched himself into the car and rested his hands on the wheel. Thank God, it had happened. It made up for so much. He turned the car around and backed it up to the corner of the house in sight of the door. He saw Helene return, he saw them talking, he saw them put their arms around each other and embrace for a long moment. Then Robbie bent down and picked up the suitcase and started toward the car.

Helene stood in the door, supporting herself against the frame with one hand, and watched his retreating back.

"Have they gone?" a man's voice asked softly behind her. Her expression altered, but she did not turn.

"Oh, Jean, why are you hiding? Why didn't you come and speak to them?"

"Is the boy leaving?"

"Yes, he's leaving," Helene said, watching Robbie throw his suitcase into the back seat of the car.

"Who was the man?"

"My husband," Helene said without thinking.

"I didn't know you had a husband."

"I didn't, either," she said.

The door of the car slammed. Stuart and Robbie turned and waved. A strong brown hand slipped forward and took hers where it lay on the doorjamb. She clutched at it with all her strength as she lifted her other hand to wave in response. She no longer saw the car or its occupants. The tears she had been holding back welled up in her eyes and spilled over. She heard the roar of the motor and the clash of gears and she gripped the strong hand hard as she waved a blind farewell.